GW00506977

American Women's Ghost Stories in the Gilded Age

The Palgrave Gothic Series

Series Editor: **Clive Bloom**

Editorial Advisory Board: **Dr Ian Conrich**, University of South Australia, **Barry Forshaw**, author/journalist, UK, **Professor Gregg Kucich**, University of Notre Dame, USA, **Professor Gina Wisker**, University of Brighton, UK, **Dr Catherine Wynne**, University of Hull, UK.

This series of gothic books is the first to treat the genre in its many inter-related, global and 'extended' cultural aspects to show how the taste for the medieval and the sublime gave rise to a perverse taste for terror and horror and how that taste became not only international (with a huge fan base in places such as South Korea and Japan) but also the sensibility of the modern age, changing our attitudes to such diverse areas as the nature of the artist, the meaning of drug abuse and the concept of the self. The series is accessible but scholarly, with referencing kept to a minimum and theory contextualised where possible. All the books are readable by an intelligent student or a knowledgeable general reader interested in the subject.

Titles Include:

Timothy C. Baker
CONTEMPORARY SCOTTISH GOTHIC
Mourning, Authenticity, and Tradition

Dara Downey
AMERICAN WOMEN'S GHOST STORIES IN THE GILDED AGE

Barry Forshaw
BRITISH GOTHIC CINEMA

Margarita Georgieva
THE GOTHIC CHILD

David J. Jones
SEXUALITY AND THE GOTHIC MAGIC LANTERN
Desire, Eroticism and Literary Visibilities from Byron to Bram Stoker

Lorna Piatti-Farnell and Maria Beville (*editors*)
THE GOTHIC AND THE EVERYDAY
Living Gothic

Aspasia Stephanou
READING VAMPIRE GOTHIC THROUGH BLOOD
Bloodlines

Catherine Wynne
BRAM STOKER, DRACULA AND THE VICTORIAN GOTHIC STAGE

The Palgrave Gothic Series
Series Standing Order ISBN 978–1–137–27637–7
(*outside North America only*)

You can receive future titles in this series as they are published by placing a standing order. Please contact your bookseller or, in case of difficulty, write to us at the address below with your name and address, the title of the series and the ISBN quoted above.

Customer Services Department, Macmillan Distribution Ltd, Houndmills, Basingstoke, Hampshire RG21 6XS, England

American Women's Ghost Stories in the Gilded Age

Dara Downey
University College Dublin, Ireland

© Dara Downey 2014

All rights reserved. No reproduction, copy or transmission of this publication may be made without written permission.

No portion of this publication may be reproduced, copied or transmitted save with written permission or in accordance with the provisions of the Copyright, Designs and Patents Act 1988, or under the terms of any licence permitting limited copying issued by the Copyright Licensing Agency, Saffron House, 6–10 Kirby Street, London EC1N 8TS.

Any person who does any unauthorized act in relation to this publication may be liable to criminal prosecution and civil claims for damages.

The author has asserted her right to be identified as the author of this work in accordance with the Copyright, Designs and Patents Act 1988.

First published 2014 by
PALGRAVE MACMILLAN

Palgrave Macmillan in the UK is an imprint of Macmillan Publishers Limited, registered in England, company number 785998, of Houndmills, Basingstoke, Hampshire RG21 6XS.

Palgrave Macmillan in the US is a division of St Martin's Press LLC, 175 Fifth Avenue, New York, NY 10010.

Palgrave Macmillan is the global academic imprint of the above companies and has companies and representatives throughout the world.

Palgrave® and Macmillan® are registered trademarks in the United States, the United Kingdom, Europe and other countries

ISBN: 978–1–137–32397–2

This book is printed on paper suitable for recycling and made from fully managed and sustained forest sources. Logging, pulping and manufacturing processes are expected to conform to the environmental regulations of the country of origin.

A catalogue record for this book is available from the British Library.

Library of Congress Cataloging-in-Publication Data

Downey, Dara.
    American women's ghost stories in the Gilded Age / Dara Downey, University College Dublin, Ireland.
        pages cm—(Palgrave gothic)
        ISBN 978–1–137–32397–2 (hardback)
        1. American literature – Women authors – History and criticism. 2. Ghost stories, American – History and criticism – Theory, etc. 3. Women and literature – United States – History – 19th century. 4. Gothic revival (Literature) – United States. 5. Women in literature. 6. Material culture in literature. I. Title.
PS151.D68 2014
813'.08733099287—dc23   2014024393

For my parents

I go to bed at ten, and get up at six. I dash out in the rain, because it feels good on my face. I don't care for my clothes, but I will be well; and after I am buried, I warn you, don't let any fresh air or sunlight down on my coffin, if you don't want me to get up.[1]

'They're pooty enough to look at, as picters! but to marry one on 'em, an' have her around all the time, huggin' and sich like, would be too much for human nater – turn me into a skeleton if it wouldn't.'[2]

[1] Fanny Fern, 'Fashionable Invalidism' (1867), in *Ruth Hall and Other Writings*, ed. Joyce W. Warren (New Brunswick, NJ: Rutgers University Press, 1986), p. 342.
[2] Prentiss Ingraham, *Lantern-Jawed Bob* (Cleveland: Arthur Westbrook Co., 1908).

Contents

Acknowledgements

This book could not have been written without the help of numerous people. I am especially indebted to Professors Darryl Jones and Stephen Matterson, both in the School of English, Trinity College Dublin, for their advice, encouragement, and editing over the years, and particularly to the latter's careful and attentive reading of earlier drafts of the manuscript. The project culminating in this book was made possible by a two-year postdoctoral fellowship from the Irish Research Council for the Humanities and Social Sciences (now the Irish Research Council), which began in the Trinity Long Room Hub and continued in the English Teaching Assistants' Office at Foster Place. This project was developed under the expert mentoring of Stephen Matterson, whose insightful comments on earlier drafts of the book have contributed greatly to the depth and polish of the finished product. The help and support of the staff and postgraduate community in Trinity proved invaluable throughout my time there, particularly that of Aoife Fennelly, Niall Gillespie, and Jenny McDonnell, whose friendship, patience, and wisdom I have relied upon again and again, and of Elizabeth McCarthy, Bernice Murphy, Maria Parsons, and Sorcha Ní Fhlainn who often direct me along new and exciting avenues. I must also thank Ruth Doherty, Philip Geheber, Rachel Glover, Triona Kirby, Kates Roddy and Harvey, Miles Link, Emily O'Brien, Brendan O'Connell, Ann Patten, Amy Prendergast, Alex Runchman, Jim Shanahan, Julie Sheridan, Alan Smyth, Pádraic Whyte, and all those who have listened to my rants about the perils of psychoanalytical readings.

Since completing the fellowship, I have been fortunate to secure a lectureship in the School of English, Drama and Film, University College Dublin, where the support of my colleagues in the final stages of writing cannot be emphasized enough, especially that of Ron Callan, Maria Stuart, Nerys Williams, Clare Hayes Brady, Jennifer Daly, Fionnúala Dillane, Jane Grogan, Anne Mulhall, Emilie Pine, Anne Cleary, Tony Roche, Pauline Slattery, and many others. The staff of the British Library, the TCD Library, and the Harry Ransom Centre in Austin Texas were instrumental in the early stages of the research, and were universally helpful and accommodating. Finally, I would like to thank my family, June and Liam Downey, Niall and Conor Downey, and Cliona Neal for their financial and personal support and encouragement, and for buying me books at a young age.

Introduction

[handwritten margin notes: "Morrison?", "slave narrative?", "Beloved"]

Received wisdom tells us that, in supernatural fiction, '"uncomfortable houses" [...] are troubled because of some injustice or social inequality that left past inhabitants seeking help from the current owners of the property', and uncovering that injustice tends to lay the ghost to rest and terminate the haunting, along with the discomfort it causes.[1] The trouble is that this formulation never quite works in the United States.[2] American gothic is essentially a 'historical mode operating in what appears to be a historical vacuum.'[3] Lacking a lengthy past where secret horrors could lurk, New-World gothic texts feature a startling paucity of ghosts as such, not least because the United States' self-defining rhetoric worked hard to dissociate the 'new' nation from a past that was situated as fundamentally European. John L. O'Sullivan, who coined the term 'manifest density' to describe what was seen as the spiritual mission to settle and cultivate the vast North American continent, wrote in 1839 that

> our national birth was the beginning of a new history, the formation and progress of an untried political system, which separates us from the past and connects us with the future only; and so far as regards the entire development of the natural rights of man, in moral, polit-ical, and national life, we may confidently assume that our country is destined to be the great nation of futurity.[4]

While very serviceable as a political ideal, the repeated assertions that the United States was unfettered by a dark and troubling past made matters rather tricky for writers of imaginative fiction. As Henry James commented, in a work on Nathaniel Hawthorne,

1

one might enumerate the items of high civilization, as it exists in other countries, which are absent from the texture of American life, until it should become a wonder to know what was left. No State, in the European sense of the word, and indeed barely a specific national name. No sovereign, no court, no personal loyalty, no aristocracy, no church, no clergy, no army, no diplomatic service, no country gentlemen, no palaces, no castles, nor manors, nor old country-houses, nor parsonages, nor thatched cottages nor ivied ruins; no cathedrals, nor abbeys, nor little Norman churches; no great Universities nor public schools – no Oxford, nor Eton, nor Harrow; no literature, no novels, no museums, no pictures, no political society, no sporting class – no Epsom nor Ascot! Some such list as that might be drawn up of the absent things in American life [...] the effect of which, upon an English or a French imagination, would probably as a general thing be appalling.[5]

As Hawthorne pointed out in the preface to *The Marble Faun* (1860), this newness, and the (ostensible) attendant lack of anything mysterious or obscure lurking in the nation's short history, meant that nineteenth-century America was a country where 'actualities' were 'so terribly insisted upon' as to render the job of the non-realist writer difficult:

> No author, without a trial, can conceive of the difficulty of writing a romance about a country where there is no shadow, no antiquity, no mystery, no picturesque and gloomy wrong, nor anything but a commonplace prosperity, in broad and simple daylight, as is happily the case with my dear native land. [...] Romance and poetry, ivy, lichens, and wallflowers, need ruin to make them grow.[6]

To be a writer of that most paradoxical of genres, the American ghost story, is therefore to do battle with the ghostly, or at least to negotiate the ways in which spectrality might materialize in such a country. As James put it, 'It is a complex fate, being an American, and one of the responsibilities it entails is fighting against a superstitious valuation of Europe.'[7] Its ghost stories therefore occupy a strange liminal zone, relying for their uncanny effects upon a recreation of the plenitude of Old-World haunting, while always asserting and celebrating the constitutional lack of historical or mnemonic residue that characterizes the New.[8] It has therefore become a critical commonplace to assert that the absence of an extended Anglo-European history means that the American gothic is a gothic of the mind, concerned only with the complexities of internal psychological processes and the perils of psychic disturbance. Following Sigmund Freud's assertion that 'A large part of the mythological view of the world *is nothing but psychology projected into the external world*', and seduced by the ease with which the supernatural can be transformed into the psychoanalytical, many critics now agree that since the nineteenth century, in America in particular, representations of the uncanny have abandoned the interior spaces of the home and settled instead in those of the mind.[9] While some inroads are being made in expanding the methodological range of approaches to gothic fiction, film, and television, for decades, the critical consensus has been that 'the inheritors of old Gothic' specifically portray haunted or frightening spaces as nothing more than '"objective correlatives" of the psyche.'[10]

Apart from producing radically ahistorical readings that reduce textual particularities to the abstract workings of 'the psyche', such readings ignore the extent to which the brevity of the American past and the drive toward newness and independence themselves become sources of gothic unease. In Charles Brockden Brown's *Wieland, or, The Transformation* (1798), a young, orphaned family group, living in rural Pennsylvania just after the Revolutionary War, adheres to a set of religious and philosophical beliefs largely of their own devising, to the point where each member of the family is free to form his or her own opinions regarding the afterlife, divine authority, the existence of the supernatural, and humanity's place in the universe. From here, the plot inexorably entangles them in an ever-tightening web of perceived sexual misconduct, mass murder, and insanity, all of which takes place within the grounds of their isolated family home. As this suggests, psychoanalytical readings also obscure the extent to which American gothic situates itself in the world of the everyday, rather than inhabiting a distant past or foreign locales, as in the work of Anglo-European gothic writers such as Ann Radcliffe. Declaring his independence from previous literary models, in the preface to *Edgar Huntly* (1799), Brown, often dubbed the Father of American Gothic, exhorted his fellow Americans not to look abroad for sources of inspiration, insisting that 'the field of investigation, opened to us by our own country, should differ essentially from those which exist in Europe.' He notes that 'Puerile superstition and exploded manners; Gothic castles and chimeras, are the materials usually employed for this end', and is adamant that 'The incidents of Indian hostility, and the perils of the western wilderness, are far more suitable; and, for a native of America to overlook these, would admit of no apology.'[11]

Distracted by Edgar Allan Poe's declaration that 'terror is not of Germany, but of the soul', critics are all too eager to see American gothic as rejecting the entire material, external world along with the 'Gothic castles and chimeras' of older, European works.[12] In other words, it is all too often assumed that, in rejecting Old-World sources of dread, *all* American gothic writers saw New-World horror as arising *only* from the haunted psyche, rather than from the stuff of here and now.[13] Consequently, and 'Since the full impact of Freudianism [...], ghosts have tended to seem metaphors rather than facts of experience – except in certain naïve works, in which they are evoked to thrill the kind of mind which otherwise finds satisfaction in shabby séances and table-tapping.'[14] It is my contention here, however, that 'shabby séances and table-tapping', and the rooms and furniture that facilitated such activities, played a major role in a large number of gothic or uncanny short stories by American women who were writing around the end of the nineteenth century and the beginning of the twentieth. Often setting themselves in direct opposition to Poe's elevation of 'the soul' over the spaces and objects of everyday, middle-class existence (as discussed in Chapters 2 and 3), women's short gothic fiction in America frequently turned outward, to the burgeoning fantasy realm of domestic practical and decorative commodities that flooded the marketplace and cluttered the middle-class home. Grounding themselves firmly in a very material world, the stories discussed in this book (many of which were initially published in women's and family magazines such as *Godey's Lady's Book*, *Atlantic Monthly*, *Harper's Weekly*, *Lippincott's*, and *Cosmopolitan*) conjure up closely observed domestic interiors and furnish them with a wealth of material objects, which themselves play key roles in the eerie events they narrate.

In particular, these stories comment on, and often critique, the role that such commodities played in the construction of 'home' as a sanctuary, idealized as undefiled by the rigors and perceived moral and spiritual bankruptcy of the 'world' outside, and over which the wife ruled benevolently and without apparent effort. Specifically, by employing the frightening supernatural elements of the gothic in familiar, meticulously realized domestic settings, such tales dramatize both the intimate bond and the vicious struggle between the overwhelming plethora of commodities that crowded the nineteenth-century home, and the woman enjoined by social structures to keep them in check. Unless lucky enough to be in possession of some independent inheritance or heirlooms, the average married, middle-class, American woman between the Civil War and the First World War (the period generally defined as the Gilded Age) rarely held any property of her own.[15] The possession of her husband as much as the objects of her home, she was both intrinsic to and alienated from the spaces in which most of her time was spent. Indeed, it was only on the level of objects, of upholstery, knickknacks, and the 'clutter' that characterized the nineteenth-century interior, and through the choosing, purchasing (with her husband's money), and arranging of such commodities, that a middle-class wife could really claim the spaces of the home as her own.[16]

In the words of English ghost-story writer Rhoda Broughton, these are the 'important little trivialities that make up the sum of a woman's life', and indeed, while such sentiments might only be expressed by a privileged few, on almost every level of the social hierarchy, domestic and personal commodities, whether decorative or practical, played a central role in American women's work – or at least, this was how a significant proportion of literature chose to depict that work.[17] From the odds and ends strewn around the slave woman Dinah's kitchen in Harriet Beecher Stowe's *Uncle Tom's Cabin* (1852); through the flowery notepaper into which pallid young girls transform old rags in Herman Melville's 'The Paradise of Bachelors and the Tartarus of Maids' (1855); right up to the beautiful 'things' that cause the central narrative tension between a wealthy widow and her son in Henry James' *The Spoils of Poynton* (1895), fictional American women are intimately associated with physical, man-made things.[18] Those who populate the stories discussed here tend to occupy a middle ground between prosperity and manual labor or servitude; they are well-off wives and mothers (Chapters 1, 2, and 6), unmarried boarding-house owners in precarious financial and social positions (Chapters 3 and 4), and the young wife of a homesteader hoping to make it rich out West (Chapter 5). The tales they inhabit employ supernatural tropes in order either to literalize the contemporary association of women with things, so that domestic objects act as substitutes for female spectres, or to problematize it, in depicting objects as tyrannizing over their owners rather than vice versa.

In doing so, they acknowledge but also critique the insistence in American culture that, while woman's power within the home might reside only on the level of objects commonly perceived (as later chapters illustrate) as superficial trumpery and vain frivolity, nevertheless, on this level it was supreme.[19] Indeed, since advertising campaigns and interior decoration manuals insisted that 'People could create status not through their character but through their accumulation of luxuries', women found they could avail themselves of greater self-fashioning opportunities by making use of the very things they were forced by domestic ideology to concern themselves with anyway.[20] Cultural pressure on women to foster a 'deeply felt psychic investment in proprietary power over, and control of, objects of love' in the home, objects with personal significance calculated to produce a home-like atmosphere for husband and children, effectively functioned to conceal and compensate home-bound middle-class women for a lack of wider social and political control.[21] While 'respectability' made it all but impossible for such women to earn money for themselves, except under exceptional circumstances, what they could – and must – do was shop, selecting and purchasing the things that would make the home a pleasant refuge for busy husbands and a safe and moral place in which to raise children.[22]

An especially idealized vision of the relationship between American women and domestic interiors is presented in Poe's 'Landor's Cottage' (1849).[23] Coming upon a small cottage while slightly lost on his way to a nearby village, the narrator is struck by the woman of the house, whose eyes contain 'So intense an expression of *romance*, perhaps I should call it, or of unworldliness, as that which gleamed from her deep-set eyes, had never so sunk into my heart of hearts before. [...] this peculiar expression of the eye [...] is the most powerful, if not absolutely the *sole* spell, which rivets my interest in woman.' She has eyes of '"spiritual grey"', a detail that prepares us for the tasteful, rational, yet 'spirited' decoration of her home.[24]

> Nothing could be more rigorously simple than the furniture of the parlor. On the floor was an ingrain carpet, of excellent texture – a white ground, spotted with small circular green figures. At the windows were curtains of snowy white jaconet muslin: they were tolerably full, and hung *decisively*, perhaps rather formally, in sharp, parallel plaits to the floor – *just* to the floor. The walls were papered with a French paper of great delicacy – a silver ground, with a faint green cord running zig-zag throughout. Its expanse was relieved merely by three of Julien's exquisite lithographs *à trois crayons*, fastened to the wall without frames. One of these drawings was a scene of Oriental luxury, or rather voluptuousness; another was a 'carnival piece,' spirited beyond compare; the third was a Greek female head – a face so divinely beautiful, and yet of an expression so provokingly indeterminate, never before arrested my attention.

The sofa is made of 'plain maple painted a creamy white, slightly interstriped with green', while numerous flowers 'of gorgeous colors and delicate odor, formed the sole mere *decoration* of the apartment'; everything matches, and he notes, 'it is impossible to conceive anything more graceful.'[25] The sketch implies that a suitably 'spiritual' woman automatically creates decorative domestic effects that are harmonious, unobtrusive, and yet conducive to reverie. Like her own body, Annie Landor's house inspires affection and contemplation with an 'unworldiness' that is, paradoxically, evoked through material objects.

Nevertheless, ideals are difficult things to maintain, and, as many of the stories discussed here suggest, the relationship between the middle-class American housewife and the domestic spaces ostensibly submitting docilely to her benign dictatorship was by no means always so straightforward. As Chapter 5 argues, financial restrictions and the practical limitations of largely unsettled rural areas often made women's role as domestic decorators very difficult indeed, while Chapters 2, 4, 5, and 6 focus on stories in which commodities actively resist women's efforts to 'tame' them by integrating them into congenial domestic spaces. Rather than containing and transmitting real cultural values, for Daniel Miller, objects frequently operate by means of 'oppressive mechanisms', 'referring only to themselves and appropriating all other aspects of social relations to themselves through consumption.'[26] Far from genuinely being attached to a family or individual, they are slippery receptacles of memory, signifying their own commodity status, their own alien otherness, rather than anything we might imagine we can invest them with. A commodity can be seen as harboring what Jacques Derrida refers to as 'a body without body', another, inaccessible self that is hidden by its 'trivial, too obvious' surface, deflecting scrutiny and capable of being penetrated only by 'seeing without seeing'.[27] Indeed, Karl Marx asserted that the tendency to see things or objects as natural, self-evident, and stable is naive and delusory.[28] Things are not simply 'inert and mute, set in motion and animated, indeed knowable, only by persons and their words', but actively shape our relationship with the world and with ourselves.[29] In turn, as many of the chapters to follow illustrate, the consumption of commodities functions as a mechanism for sending but also receiving social messages, messages that do not simply 'express' one's place in society, but actively insert us into that place, determining our behavior and responses through their sheer irreducible physicality.[30]

For a table to be used as a table does, of course, involve it in the world of human action, subjecting it to human whim and desire. But a table harboring lurking splinters is a monster with sharp teeth, not because it has some unimaginable form of inner life, nor because the man (or indeed woman) of the house is a tyrannical monster, but rather because it forces its owners to be careful every time they rest their elbows on it, to keep children away from it, and to spend time fruitlessly attempting to smooth and polish it. As the stories discussed here imply, while memories may become attached to objects and the spaces that they occupy, these memories are not intrinsic to the objects. Things can therefore become alienated from their owners, even to the point of antagonism or outright malevolence, such as the 'poisonous' yellow wallpaper in Charlotte Perkins Gilman's story of the same name (Chapter 2), or the animated nightcap that attacks a middle-aged woman in Mary E. Wilkins' 'The Southwest Chamber' (Chapter 4). Chapters 4 and 6 also suggest that meanings can become unstuck from one set of people and circumstances, and transfer to others who have nothing to do with them, meanings so embedded in objects that they impose a frightening or hostile past onto an unsuspecting and incompatible present, transforming what should be a completely unrelated present into a mirror image of that past, to the detriment of those caught up in it. In other words, these stories imply that, rather than sitting around and waiting for our meanings to be inscribed upon them, and becoming empty of significance or agency once we abandon them, objects do things to us, and determine our behavior in ways over which we have little control.

In the context of late nineteenth-century America, matters were made worse by the extent to which the relatively new commodity culture clashed with an entrenched Protestant discourse that, as 'Landor's Cottage' suggests, privileged depth over surface; the expression in the eyes over overly showy beauty; harmony and tranquility over displays of wealth. In women's magazines, mourning manuals, and religious sermons alike, contemporary commentators stressed that physical objects should be associated with the body, which should in turn be associated with death, decay, and a dangerous temptation away from higher, spiritual emotions, since

> the body is the tabernacle, or tent, in which the spirit takes up its abode while on its journey to the promised land; and when this mortal habitation is dissolved, when the *tent* is struck by Death, then the soul is clothed upon with the immortal, and enters into its heavenly *house*, the building of God, where, its pilgrimage ended, it will dwell rejoicingly forevermore![31]

While primarily associated with religious doctrine, such thinking continued to pervade an increasingly secularized culture, anxious about the implications of its own prosperity.[32] As discussed in the chapters that follow, as American culture became ever more commercialized and commodity driven, material, and particularly ornamental, objects came under fire for a superficiality that bordered on immorality. And, considering how much time and emotional energy women were urged to expend in purchasing, arranging, and caring for commodities (or at least supervising others in doing so), it was women who bore the brunt of this censure. Critics have written at length about this intimate relationship between women and material culture during the Gilded Age, and the American women's ghost story from around this time is garnering increasing critical attention.[33] Nonetheless, there has been little or no sustained focus on the interactions between the two, or on the ways in which this relationship mediates that between women and a third term – that of the body, which, in a genre so concerned with incorporeal specters, is inextricable from the gender dynamics these stories construct.[34]

This book argues, therefore, that a remarkably large number of ghost stories by American women writers, specifically but by no means exclusively Charlotte Perkins Gilman, Emma Frances Dawson, Mary E. Wilkins, Elia W. Peattie, and Madeline Yale Wynne, engaged directly with the material and visual culture that played a prominent, even constitutive, role in the social and cultural life of the United States. The final decades of the century were a time both of great prosperity and of economic turmoil and social strife.[35] By 1867, despite numerous World's Fairs, the country found itself

in the midst of the worst economic depression in its history, and of a crisis of cultural morale as well. The reality outside the fairgrounds put the Expositions' triumphant pageantry in a context that was corrosively ironic. The technological marvels enshrined in their pseudo-Gothic temples promised industrial progress; but they also represented new forms of human misery and social danger. If they spoke on the one hand of the growth of Big Business, on the other they implied the bankruptcy and ruin of many small businesses and new a kind of competition that seemed, at times, like a form of warfare. The machines had made possible new forms of production; but they had also created a new and burgeoning class of factory workers, a 'proletariat' whose conditions of life and work did not at all conform to the canonical expectations of the American dream – expectations formed long before the war, when small farmers and independent artisans had formed the majority of the 'producing classes.' This new class had neither independence nor property nor plausible hopes of becoming economically self-sufficient. They were subordinated in their work to the service of the mighty machines and socially subjected by a wage system that made them dependent.[36]

At the same time, 'the development of true *mass media* with a national market' can be traced back to 'the 1830s and 1840s; but it [was] not complete until the 1890s', a shift evident in the vast array of short fiction produced, first in magazines, and later in anthologies and collections.[37] At mid-century, the perceived opposition between 'high' and mass or popular culture was sharply polarized along gender lines. Hawthorne's famous comment about that 'd _ _ _ _ d mob of scribbling women' implies that 'women writers pander to the masses (the very mob with which Hawthorne conflated them), undermining men aesthetically and economically.'[38] Nevertheless, the nineteenth century in America was also characterized by a continuum between 'realist' fiction and the ghost stories found in popular magazines, and this was certainly the case as the century drew to a close – indeed, it is debatable whether such strict divisions existed at all beyond the incensed imaginations of those who perceived themselves as usurped by inferiors.[39] Many of America's most canonical writers, including Henry James, Edith Wharton, Sarah Orne Jewett, and Willa Cather, all of whom worked in the realist mode, dabbled to a greater or lesser extent in tales of the supernatural, as did Mark Twain, Louisa May Alcott, Harriet Prescott Spoffard, Kate Chopin, and Harriet Beecher Stowe, to name but a few, along with writers like Poe, Hawthorne, and Melville, who are conventionally associated with mid-nineteenth-century American gothic.[40]

What is notable about this body of writing is the prevalence of what we now think of as short stories – brief fictional 'tales' or sketches, appearing initially in literary magazines.[41] As Poe wrote in 1844, the form particularly suited the comparatively new nation, since

> the country from its very constitution, could not fail of affording in a few years, a larger proportionate amount of readers than any upon the earth. I perceived that the whole energetic, busy spirit of the age tended wholly to the Magazine literature, to the curt, the terse, the well-timed, and the readily diffused, in preference to the old forms of the verbose and ponderous and the inaccessible [...].[42]

Poe therefore situated the cheap, quickly devoured, short prose tale 'within the cultural marketplace as just another necessity competing for the time and money of a potential consumer, when it already possessed cultural capital as a luxury good.'[43] Indeed, the short fictional narrative was the ideal form for a country in which society was 'in a state of flux, indeterminate and shifting', and where 'writing sustained fiction' that sought to portray 'how the society under [the author's] notice is framed' was by no means an easy task.[44] Precisely due to their brevity, which necessitated the omission of large amounts of social detail, such tales (and later stories) appear to deal with romance rather than realism, the workings of the inner life rather than the concrete details of social existence.[45] More generally, emphasizing open-endedness and ambiguity over closure and clear moral messages, the short story is frequently read as conjuring up spaces and experiences 'beyond normal perception' to effect a 'departure from the reader's typical experience of reality.'[46] Frank O'Connor, who is cited even more frequently than Poe in relation to these matters, insists that the short story is an 'outlaw' form, populated with figures and events alienated and abstracted from the consensual social world.[47] However, rather than bringing the reader *out* of 'normal reality', Gilded-Age American short stories in the female gothic mode assert, through the medium of the supernatural, that the everyday is itself problematic, even dangerous – that it is more than possible to be oppressed, even deformed by social structures that have been naturalized by familiarity and ubiquity.[48] They gesture widely beyond themselves, to a system of domestic isolation and atomization that is nonetheless social and, in a country where the middle classes accounted for a substantial proportion of the population, endlessly repeated.

This book therefore focuses on the materialist qualities of a certain species of American ghost story by (white, middle-class) women writers. Rather than employing objects as mere symbols, giving access to higher psychological or numinous realities, the stories discussed here figure the day-lit, domestic, familiar world as haunted by these objects themselves. Bearing witness to the position of objects within a wider economy of bourgeois behavior and attitudes, they acknowledge the very real contribution these objects made to the life of the middle-class wife in particular, and the extent to which they either bullied her around or permitted her to subvert her strictly defined role in ways that patriarchal society refused to acknowledge. In order to do justice to what these stories do and say, it is therefore vital that, rather than dismissing the fear experienced by their characters as proof of insanity or buried psychic trauma, and abstracting them in the timeless realms of psychoanalytical criticism, we take objects just as seriously as the stories themselves do, situating them within their cultural context, and, vitally, in relation to one another.

Doing so brings to the fore the central role played by materiality and visuality in ghost stories by American women from the final decades of the nineteenth century and the opening decades of the twentieth. In a genre so concerned with eerie 'appearances' of the dead or disembodied, and with living characters unpleasantly prone to 'seeing things', it is perhaps unsurprising that stories by writers such as Gilman, Dawson, Wilkins, Peattie, and Wynne, around whom each of the following chapters revolves respectively, should abound in references to contemporary visual and material culture.[49] Of this era, Wharton wrote, 'we have passed from the golden age of architecture to the gilded age of decoration' – in other words, from one concerned with form and volume, to one in which the superficial, even the factitious prevails.[50] An emphasis on the social and the material also highlights just how embedded these stories were within a period also known as the 'Progressive Era', characterized by mass social and cultural movements pushing for clothing, currency, educational, and dietary reforms, voting rights, temperance, bans on gambling and prostitution, and numerous other concerns that bore directly (although in very different ways) on the lives of both middle- and working-class women.[51] These stories are written at a watershed between the perceived clutter of the Victorian and the determined spring cleaning advocated by modernist architects and feminist reformers alike. Indeed, two exponents of such clearing out, Wharton and Willa Cather, themselves wrote ghost stories.[52]

The tensions of the era – between a desire for liberation and the need for stricter moral standards, between a joyful celebration of ornamental commodities and a revulsion toward their gross physicality or their status as the apparatus of gendered oppression – are essentially those that structure the stories discussed in this book. Indeed, they struggle to articulate the vexed relationship between this culture and the living and dead women who crowd their pages. In particular, they attempt to negotiate the problematic discourses surrounding the female body, the literal and figurative violence committed upon that body by a culture that simultaneously idolized and reviled the feminine form. Set in opposition to these troubled and troubling bodies is a vast array of brightly patterned objects and decorative fabrics, which actively structure and determine the workings of the plots. For actual female ghosts (in Chapters 3 and 4), objects function as a media of return, through which their anger and spite transcend the boundaries of death itself. For 'living' female characters (in Chapters 1, 2, 5, and, 6), however, objects are far more ambiguous, often hostile, proving to be dangerously independent from their 'owners', and frighteningly unpredictable.

As this implies, the group of stories that focalize the following chapters are by no means homogenous or univocal – indeed, the contrasts and dissonances between their various approaches to the relationship between women, objects, and spectrality is central to this book as a whole. Beginning in Chapter 1 with a general discussion of the repeated motif of dangerous portraits in women's fiction from around this time, it establishes the turbulent relationship between Gilded-Age American women writers and prevalent attitudes toward feminine beauty and moral depth. Chapter 2 extends this discussion, embedding Gilman's 'The Yellow Wall-Paper' within contemporary discourses surrounding the female body and mind on the one hand, and domestic decoration on the other. Emphasizing the story's critique of Poe's most famous tales and the objectification of the female form that underpinned them, this chapter therefore leads naturally to Chapter 3, which centers around Dawson's 'An Itinerant House'. Also laboring beneath Poe's shadow, Dawson's story moves us to the burgeoning American metropolis, and the chapter therefore examines the cultural energy poured into containing an allegedly deviant femininity in this new urban milieu. The concern with objectification and with animated objects that informs Chapters 2 and 3 is carried forward into Chapter 4, which employs Wilkins' 'The Southwest Chamber' as a vehicle for exploring the relationship between the ghost story and mourning culture, Spiritualism, and the emerging photographic industry. Chapter 5, focusing on Peattie's 'The House That Was Not', extends the idea of memory that runs through previous chapters, transporting it to the insistently empty spaces of the Western prairies, where domestic objects become far rarer and more difficult to interpret. This theme is also central to Chapter 5, which uses Wynne's 'The Little Room' to examine the ways in which domestic commodities could become frighteningly beyond the control of those who ostensibly owned and loved them.

In many ways overlapping, and weaving in and out of multiple other stories and forms of writing, these narratives revolve obsessively around concerns with materiality, physicality, and visuality. Structured upon tensions between display and privacy, between the body and the inner self, between surface and depth, and between image and substance, these texts, in a variety of ways and often with divergent results, radically interrogate easy or moralizing assumptions regarding women's relationship with the contents and decorative surfaces of the home, alternately (and at times simultaneously) critiquing women's inscription within domestic space and reappropriating that space as a site of power. Figured as a gothic locus of dread equally because of its imprisoning qualities and because it houses women who refuse to comply with the patriarchal norm, the home in these stories is uniformly somewhere in which women, in Wharton's words, become 'domesticated with the Horror, accepting its perpetual presence as one of the fixed conditions of life.'[53]

1
'Fitted to a Frame': Picturing the Gothic Female Body

When the narrator of Edith Wharton's 'Miss Mary Pask' (1925) goes to visit the eponymous spinster, an old friend, at her cottage in France, he is horrified to find himself confronted with what appears to be her specter. As he gradually recalls having read of her death several months previously, he remarks that 'what had shocked me was that the change was so slight – that between being dead and alive there seemed after all to be so little difference'.[1] It transpires that the reports of her demise had been greatly exaggerated – although not before the narrator temporarily loses his sanity as a result of the encounter, during which she describes her 'death' (a cataleptic trance) and her grave to him, while wheedling him to join her there forever in her cold embrace. Nonetheless, the body of the story, and Miss Pask's own depiction of herself as a ghost, strongly implies that an attempted seduction by the living woman would not have been or any less disturbing than by the dead one. The story therefore echoes Emily Dickinson's poem 510 (c. 1862), which begins, 'It was not Death, for I stood up. / And all the Dead, lie down – '. Despite this initially confident assertion, the poetic voice nonetheless adds, 'The Figures I have seen / Set orderly, for Burial, / Reminded me, of mine – '. What prompts her to make this comparison is her awareness that her 'Marble feet / Could keep a Chancel, cool – ', in other words, that her body is no longer flesh and blood, but instead frozen, hard and unchanging. This implication is confirmed when the speaker observes that the situation feels 'As if my life were shaven, / And fitted to a frame', the poem as a whole asserting a disturbing contiguity between her supposedly living self and the appearance of a dead body.[2]

The common element between Wharton's and Dickinson's texts – the eerie proximity and resemblance between living and dead women – is taken up and dramatized by a startling number of ghost stories and gothic tales by American women writers in the intervening decades, and most noticeably around the very end of the nineteenth century in the period often known as the 'Gilded Age'. In particular, these stories literalize the idea of being 'fitted to a frame', revolving around portraits, statues and photographs of women which prove dangerous to living women. Drawing on an American evangelical tradition in which the body and the material world are depicted as inherently sinful, placing the soul in peril by distracting it from the higher spiritual planes with the temptations of the flesh and of pecuniary desire, these stories center obsessively around women who marry artists, whose dead, often cruel and heartless, first wives were themselves transformed into portraits or statues. These beautiful, seductive images are repeatedly structured as morally suspect; and, like Dickinson's poetic persona, who perceives that she has become one more of the 'Figures [...] / Set orderly for burial', are frightening precisely because they suggest that the living woman could become all too easily another copy of the evil, painted, dead women whose portraits loom over her.

Perhaps the most straightforward example of this trope is Edna Worthley Underwood's story 'The Painter of Dead Women' (1910), which begins as the narrator's new Italian husband remarks on the number of young, beautiful, wealthy women who have gone missing in Naples over the last twenty-five years, before urging her to '"look particularly lovely"' for his friends at a ball that evening. On the way to the ball, she is concerned that the driver has missed the way, and the mansion at which he drops her is deserted, horribly silent yet lit with a dazzling luminescence that leaves her cold with terror, a space that she feels is more like 'a white and shining sepulchre' than a place for a party.[3] As her apprehension grows and she turns to flee, however, the door disappears, and she finds herself trapped, exposed to the 'demoniac power of light', which 'sent from polished corners and cornice quivering arrows into my eyes.' She soon becomes aware that 'A powerful and dominant brain had touched my own. For one unconscious moment it had ruled it and set upon it the seal of its thought.'[4] Seeing an elderly but regal man approach, she realizes that he is attempting to subdue her mind with a force that 'crippled my will and dulled me as does that sweet-smelling death which surgeons call the anæsthetic.' His gaze is emotionless and 'impersonal', and she somehow understands that 'No mark of material beauty had escaped it. It was the trained glance of a connoisseur which measures accurately. I might have been a picture or a piece of furniture.' Feeling that he can see right through her very flesh, she continues, 'Somehow, then, I felt that the body of me belonged to him because of this masterly penetration which substance could not resist.'[5]

In other words, the very gaze of the artist (who blurs uncomfortably with her suspiciously absent, equally image-conscious husband) here transforms the living woman into a thing, an immobile and defenseless object of his will. Admiring the narrator immensely, he tells her that he wishes to add her to his 'collection', but assures her that she need fear no sexual impropriety from him, since '"I love only dead women. Life reaches its perfection only when death comes. *Life is never real until then*"'.[6] Calling it 'sacred', he tells her, in a distorted echo of Edgar Allan Poe, that Death '"is the thing to be most desired by beautiful women"', because it saves them from old age and decay, freezing them forever at the moment of perfection – begging her, therefore, to allow him to kill her, so that he can preserve her as a '"triumphant [...] object of admiration"'.[7] Chilling as his assertions are, he has a point: in an economy in which a woman's looks are her future, no woman can afford old age, as evidenced by the many abandoned and dead wives in these stories. As an antidote to the social death of aging, he has replicated an ancient poison that causes a pleasurable, apparently painless death, while permanently arresting all signs of physical decomposition. Once she is injected with it, he tells the narrator:

> 'your body will attain the hardness of a diamond and the whiteness of fine marble. But it is months, years, before the brain dies. I am not really sure it ever dies. In it, like the iridescent reflections upon a soap bubble, live the shadows of past pleasures. There is no other immortality that can equal this I offer. Every day that you live now lessens your beauty. In a way every day is a vulgar death. It coarsens and over-colors your skin, dulls the gold in your hair, makes this bodily line, or this, a bit too full [...].'[8]

Showing her the other women to whom he has done this, including some surrounded by frozen peacocks and tigers, 'dancing' or reclining in various attitudes, he enthuses that as models they are ideal, allowing him to paint them for hours, and he casually mentions that some of them can still hear everything going on around them. His explanations of the effects he has sought to create with particular colorings of hair and skin are especially unsettling, testifying as they do to the extent to which the aesthetic impulse has usurped his ability to see these women as living, thinking individuals. Gleefully, however, the narrator outwits him before things can go too far, locking herself into a room as he leaves to get the poison, jumping out the window, and swimming off across the lake below, to be rescued by fishermen and reunited with her husband.

The story is clearly influenced by Robert W. Chambers' 'The Mask' (1895), which centers around a sculptor named Boris who has discovered a poison with identical freezing qualities, and which he uses to preserve small flora and fauna, but into which Boris's model, Geneviève, eventually throws herself as a result of a love triangle with his best friend, Alec (the first-person narrator). The artist's model is therefore transformed into a statue herself, and, we are told, '"Geneviève lies before the Madonna in the marble room. The Madonna bends tenderly above her, and Geneviève smiles back into that calm face that never would have been except for her,"' the statue and what should be her living model mirroring one another perfectly.[9] As in Underwood's story, it ends happily, with Geneviève reviving, but it is in many ways the more optimistic of the two, since Underwood's villain lives to continue his diabolical art project with other, less resourceful women. And indeed, very few of the other fictional women who encounter male artists eager to produce precise copies of the female form are so fortunate.

The most famous instance of this attitude regarding women's bodies is of course Poe's assertion (alluded to above) that 'the death [...] of a beautiful woman is, unquestionably, the most poetical topic in the world'.[10] As he outlined in 'The Philosophy of Composition' (1846), the statement implies that a dead woman, removed from the world of human action and transience, is more available to the mind of a poet or artist for reinterpretation than a living one. The dead woman, reduced to an idealized memory, is little more than an object of contemplation, offering no obstruction to the artist's attempt to transform her into a decorative, stylized aesthetic construction. This operation is made especially explicit in his short story 'Berenice' (1835), in which the narrator feels rather indifferent to his cousin 'During the brightest days of her unparalleled beauty', but becomes increasingly obsessed by her as disease wastes her mortal frame to a mere shadow of its former blooming loveliness. As she disappears physically, she appears more and more to his mind's eye, 'not as a being of the earth – earthly – but as the abstraction of such a being – not as a thing to admire, but to analyse – not as an object of love, but as the theme of the most abstruse although desultory speculation.' Even as he 'shudder[s] in her presence, and [grows] pale at her approach', he finds himself proposing marriage, and it is only when she finally seems to die, just before the anticipated wedding, that he initiates physical contact.[11] Somewhat predictably, this encounter takes the form of violence rather than affection; in a cataleptic trance, he gouges the teeth (with which he has become morbidly fascinated) from her yet-breathing mouth, killing her at the very moment that she has become most artistically and intellectually interesting to him.

The more disembodied she becomes, the more the narrator succeeds in subordinating her to his own abstract notions, as death permits her mortal frame to function as a passive vehicle for his imagination. By no means unique to Poe, the male artist's reduction of a living woman to a frozen, depersonalized *objet d'art* is paralleled by the discourses pervading American visual and material culture in the second half of the nineteenth century, as the aestheticized female figure became the pressure point for tensions surrounding issues of superficiality, factitiousness, and moral depth.

Policing the feminine surface

As the century drew to a close, the spirit of reform in American culture, particularly in the arena of women's rights and women's suffrage, converged with a series of economic crises and a concomitant drive on the part of manufacturers and advertisers to bolster consumption. The new commodity culture, and the explosion of colorful, seductive imagery harnessed to drive it, 'celebrated metamorphosis, the violation of boundaries, and the blurring of lines between hitherto opposed categories – luxury and necessity, artificial and natural, night and day, male and female, the expression of desire and its repression, the primitive and the civilized.'[12] Exuberant as this culture was, it existed in tension with the long-standing association in American Protestant culture of worldly desires with self-indulgence and spiritual barrenness.[13] The result of this clash of ideas was 'a thinly veiled social hysteria, channeled into evangelical crusades and pulpit jeremiads against wealth, warning that the nation was recapitulating the familiar historical cycle'; America, many believed, was becoming infected with the material and sensual decadence that destroyed the Roman Empire.[14] Specifically, the exponential growth of commodity culture made what were once luxuries more readily and cheaply available to a broader swath of the population, to the point where clothing and domestic interior decoration ceased to function as reliable markers of class or 'respectability'. American culture therefore sought to control and order the visual and the imaginative, by assigning specific meanings to specific images, in an attempt to reduce the chaos of multiple semantic possibilities that could all too easily lead to a parallel social chaos.

Protestant squeamishness regarding the visual, the material and the physical gained added impetus with the rise of the bourgeoisie in the eighteenth century, an explosion in social mobility that resulted in profound societal upheaval.[15] The privileging of the moral over the physical, and of the internal over the external, is part of a nexus of long-standing, particularly religious, assumptions in Western culture about the transience of the flesh and the material trappings of this world, which the Christian individual must readily cast off in favor of the eternal pleasures of heaven. Taking the form of Puritan sumptuary laws, which regulated the form and decoration of individuals' clothing, in Anne Bradstreet's 'The Flesh and the Spirit' (1678), for example, the Soul resists the Flesh's offers of gold and jewels, asserting,

> Thy flatt'ring shews I'll trust no more.
> How oft thy slave hast thou me made
> When I believ'd what thou hast said
> And never had more cause of woe
> Than when I did what thou bad'st do.
> I'll stop mine ears at these thy charms
> And count them for my deadly harms.
> Thy sinful pleasures I do hate,
> Thy riches are to me no bait.
> Thine honours do, nor will I love,
> For my ambition lies above.[16]

This emotionally freighted language, in which a triumph over worldly and physical desire determines the fate of one's immortal soul, collapses the body and the external world together, relegating everything but the interior of one's soul to the pits of hell. This idea was extended in Edward Taylor's 'A Fig for Thee, O Death', in which the poetic voice tells Death that, while his soul will escape mortality's grasp,

> My Body, my vile harlot, it's thy Mess,
> Labouring to drown me into Sin's disguise
> By Eating and by drinking such evil joys

> Though Grace preserved me that I ne're have
> Surprisèd been nor tumbled in such grave.[17]

Taylor's poem here feminizes the body, which, as in Bradstreet's, is associated with satanic temptation, with the spiritual death that yielding to such temptation guarantees, and with the 'disguise' fabricated by Satan, the Father of Lies. The physical and the external are here reduced to illusions, false surfaces that are not merely deceitful but actively dangerous – and, vitally, associated with femininity. From the eighteenth century onward, however, the sheer number and range of commodities to which an ever-increasing proportion of the population had access both undermined and gave added impetus to the doctrine of unworldliness and incorporeality. Wealth, and the outward appearance of respectability that wealth could procure, were no longer stable indicators of social status, class or moral character; '[e]xtravagant dress and the presentation of self as spectacle had become the signifiers of both the lady and prostitute'.[18]

As this and Taylor's poem suggest, it was the female form, specifically in relation to dress and physical attractiveness, that bore the brunt of the resulting antimaterial bias. A 1791 funeral sermon for a notably upright woman dwells upon the kind of woman the clergyman assures his listeners she was not. He thundered:

> Methinks I behold the celebrated beauty, glistening like a Goddess in the midst of her train, conscious of charms sufficient to command the hearts of men; she expects to find her every glance observed, her every nod obeyed: The glass and the fashion her only study; utter stranger to thought; easy and gay, she glides down the stream of life, unaware of the ocean of eternity to which it sweeps.[19]

Nor was the criticism of middle-class American women's excessive concern with dress and personal adornment restricted to male commentators; it was actively taken up by those agitating for women's rights. Suffrage supporter Fanny Fern's 1870 call for a more rational form of dress for women directly echoes Taylor's depiction of his own body as his 'vile harlot' and Bradstreet's evocation of the flesh as ensnaring the soul in triviality and waste. Fern urged her readers not

> to appear on the street in a dress befitting the street; leaving to those poor wretched women whose business it is to advertise their persons, a

free field without competition. If I seem to speak harshly, it is because I feel earnestly on this subject. I *had* hoped that the women of 1868 would have been worthy of the day in which they live. I had hoped that *all* their time would not have been spent in keeping up with the chameleon changes of fashions too ugly, too absurd for toleration. It is because I want them to *be* something, to *do* something higher and nobler than a peacock might aim at, that I turn heart-sick away from these infinitesimal fripperies that narrow the soul and purse, and leave nothing in their wake but emptiness.[20]

Such thinking dovetailed neatly with the demands of an increasingly middle-class populace, as the earlier admiration for physically imposing, healthily rounded, richly attired girls whose beauty was there for all to see, gave way to a vogue for quieter, shorter, thinner, more somberly dressed and simply adorned young ladies, a vision far more attainable for those of modest income.[21] The emphasis fell, therefore, on inner beauty, goodness and propriety, to which every girl could aspire with some self-scrutiny and self-control, and which, more importantly, could not be counterfeited. This 'inner beauty' (which could ensure outward beauty through 'moral cosmetics', the soul producing a positive effect on the body) was rendered all the more important by the pressure that American culture placed on women to function as the nation's moral exemplars, spreading their softening and civilizing 'influence' among the men in their lives, who have been 'hardened' by their contact with the rough world of work, commerce and public life among other men.[22] In his 1855 essay 'Woman', Ralph Waldo Emerson remarked that 'There is much that tends to give them a religious height which men do not attain'. The essay depicts women as walking 'evermore' among 'waves upon waves of rosy light' that they 'emit from their pores'. This light beams outward from interior depths that Emerson called 'sublime'; he asserted that woman's 'starry crown' was 'the power of her affection and sentiment', which effected 'infinite enlargements' in the minds and hearts of those around her.[23] Indeed, women's devotion to family life was, for Emerson, spontaneous, natural and fundamental to their nature, a calling to which women willingly sacrificed even 'the highest beauty', since

> The life of the affections is primary to them, so that there is usually no employment or career which they will not with their own applause and that of society quit for a suitable marriage. And they give entirely to their affections, set their whole fortune on the die, lose themselves

eagerly in the glory of their husbands and children. Man stands astonished at a magnanimity he cannot pretend to.[24]

In other words, Emerson saw women as voluntarily subordinating their problematic yet alluring surface to their self-effacing depths, cheerfully relinquishing the physical loveliness that helped them marry in the first place, in order to secure their husbands' and children's happiness. As one anonymous piece of advice literature urged,

> When women, who are the ornament of society, unite a solid under-standing and an honest heart to a graceful person, the natural incli-nation we have toward them, excites a mutual display of our most excellent qualities, then open in man a suitable desire to improve in every virtue. The pains we take to engage their affection, polishes and softens the asperity of temper, which is natural to us; their gaiety serves as a kind of counterpoise to our gravity and severity; in a word, men would be less perfect without female society.[25]

The central point of this passage is that a 'graceful person' was both vital and insufficient in and of itself – indeed, elsewhere, it was frequently depicted as a kind of trap to the virtue of the feminine soul inhabiting it. In the sentimental fiction of the early American Republic, including William Hill Brown's *The Power of Sympathy* (1789), Susanna Rowson's *Charlotte: A Tale of Truth* (1791), and Hannah Webster Foster's *The Coquette* (1797), even when heroines are lucky enough to be pretty and well dressed, should their moral beauty fail to match up with their outward appearance, disappointment or loneliness at best, ruin, preg-nancy and death at worst, are without a doubt to be their inevitable and unenviable fates.

Nevertheless, an attractive face and figure remained valuable feminine assets in American bourgeois culture, as Emerson's essay acknowledged, quoting 'a clear-headed man of the world', who asserted, '"I like women, [...] they are so finished"'. Emerson corroborated this viewing, stating that women 'finish society, manners, language. Form and ceremony are their realm. They embellish trifles', because their 'genius delights in ceremonies, in forms, in decorating life with manners, with proprieties, with order and grace.'[26] In other words, women were trivial and decora-tive so that men need not be, and it was therefore the duty of men to provide their womenfolk with the means and the lifestyle to give full rein to their talents. As American economic theorist Thorstein Veblen commented in 1899, 'earning a livelihood' was not considered to be '"women's sphere"', asserting that it 'grates painfully on our nerves to contemplate the necessity of any well-bred' woman engaging in such work. Her sphere was the domestic one, which 'she should "beautify"', and of which she should be the "chief ornament." The male head of the household is not currently spoken of as its ornament,' he noted wryly. The wife's only work was 'to consume vicariously for the head of the household', so as to establish and maintain that household's 'good name', and to dress in a manner that announced her leisured position.[27]

However, this confluence of personal and domestic appearance with domestic respectability often, Veblen noted, drove families to deprive themselves deliberately of 'the comforts or necessities of life in order to afford what is considered a decent amount of wasteful consumption', to the point where 'it is by no means an uncommon occurrence, in an inclement climate, for people to go ill clad in order to appear well dressed.' Women's social function meant that this impracticality mani-fested most obviously in late-nineteenth-century women's fashions in the United States, particularly the skirt, to which American culture displayed a 'tenacious attachment', precisely because it 'hamper[ed] the wearer and incapacitate[d] her for all useful exertion.' Similarly, the corset was 'a mutilation' that lowered 'the subject's vitality and render[ed] her permanently and obviously unfit for work', impairing 'the personal attractions of the wearer' so as to heighten her 'reputability' as a result of her 'visibly increased expensiveness and infirmity.'[28] Nor was he alone in this assessment; Fern also lamented the frequency with which the 'poor little fashion-ridden body' was burdened down with 'big rosettes upon their sides and shoulders, and loops, and folds, and buttons, and tassels, and clasps, and bows upon their skirts, and striped satin petti-coats, [...] and more colors and shades of colors', presenting 'a spectacle which is too disheartening even to be comical.'[29] Weighed down with consumer goods and ideological markers of class and moral goodness, the respectable female body all but disappeared in its own right, serving only as a vehicle for social meaning and control.

Selling the female form

Harangues chastising girls and women for neglecting their souls and their intellects in order to cultivate fair complexions and to accumu-late lace and ribbons and sofa cushions were therefore grossly unfair. Then, as today, popular and high culture joined forces to impress upon women that their appearance, and that of their homes, was of tantamount importance to their personal happiness and social status. Moreover, a pleasing personal appearance was indispensible to success on the marriage market. The debutante ball was 'an universal exchange, a market in which wares are offered and accepted or passed by for whatever is more attractive to the seeker'.[30] Commodity culture itself capitalized upon the marketability of the female form, literalizing young women's status as marketable goods in the form of cheap, mass-produced household prints or 'Fancy Pictures', often featuring voyeuristic and idealized representations of young working-class women engaged in domestic chores, positioned as objects of male fantasy and desire. Other popular images partook of the quality of melodrama, centering on 'the common visual signifier of a prostrate woman, a motif that was [...] used to depict female distress responses to everything from death to abandonment, disappointment in love and recollections of heartbreak – instantly recognisable yet prosaic representations.'[31]

At the same time, contemporary art historians and critics worked hard to justify the presence of both ancient and modern representations of unclothed women in public art galleries open to visitors of every class, age and gender, and to provide a viewing apparatus that would allow squeamish patrons simultaneously to see and to look past the acres of sensually arrayed female flesh that could otherwise render the visual arts morally suspect in the extreme. Existing on the borderland between 'high' or ideal art and popular depictions of feminine beauty and availability was Hiram Powers' immensely well-received statue *The Greek Slave* (1844), described by Henry James as 'so undressed, yet so refined, even so pensive, in sugar-white alabaster, exposed under little glass covers in such American homes as could bring themselves to think such things right.'[32] The sculpture (according to the extensive accompanying explanatory notes) depicted a young Greek girl captured by Turks, naked and chained to a post, presumably to be sold as a concubine. What rendered the image both socially and aesthetically acceptable was its suggestions of 'inner depth', a moral purity and acceptance of a hard fate that made her nudity almost irrelevant, except in that it also occasioned her supreme virginal goodness to shine forth, validating the viewer's sympathetic identification with her plight, while simultaneously deflecting the prurient or horrified gaze.[33] As commentators noted, beauty alone was no excuse for public nudity – we had to be taught something in the process, and that lesson was fundamentally about female suffering and chaste fortitude.[34]

Indeed, this very victimhood was seen by contemporaries as the statue's subject's source of power, giving her moral and spiritual superiority over those who both enslaved and gazed upon her.[35] The Reverend Orville Dewey gushed, 'The Greek Slave is clothed all over with sentiment; sheltered, protected by it from every profane eye. Brocade, cloth of gold, could not be a more complete protection than the vesture of holiness in which she stands.' Dewey essentially made the statue's body all but disappear, rendered transparent by the light of the statue's soul, while other commentators insisted that her modesty actively repelled the gaze of the multitudes who crowded around her.[36] Responses to Edward Brackett's sculpture *Shipwrecked Mother and Child* (1850), in which a nude, drowned woman lies on a rock, clutching her dead infant, similarly insisted that it was clothed with maternal purity and mortal sanctity. An accompanying poem, 'The Wreck', described the sculpture as 'Not in the garb of fashion dressed, / But in the beauty God expressed / When he made all mankind / In the glory of his mind.'[37] The conventional privileging of depth over surface was therefore harnessed as a means of transforming conspicuously gendered, disturbingly physical images into heavenly media that forbade even as they invited the gaze of the crowd. As James Jackson Jarves wrote in his 1855 book on the visual arts,

Female loveliness is the most fascinating type of humanity. In it we have the highest development of form and color as united in beauty. The lines of the perfect human form are the most beautiful in their graceful curvatures that Nature produces. [...] No hue of the animal or vegetable kingdom rivals the tints with which the charms of woman glow. They were bestowed as the strongest appeal to the sensuous heart. United with virtue they robe the sex with irresistible attraction. The Art that can make us feel the smoothness and elasticity of the female skin, its clear, translucent surface, not lustrous but tender from its delicate mingling of white and pale warm red, subdued by the nicest gradations of the purest and most pearly greys into sense – captivating loveliness, is scarcely of earthly mould.[38]

He added that, 'If to the physical ideal be added the greater loveliness of mind, which radiates from the features as light from the sun, elevating and purifying all things on which its glances rest', and if Art continued to pay home at the 'divine fountain' of this inner and outer beauty, then it would itself be elevated to otherwise unattainable heights of both aesthetic perfection and moral rectitude.[39] As this passage illustrates, however, such assertions exist in uneasy tension with the lingering descriptions of curves and skin, of the colors and textures of flesh. This tension is effectively critiqued in Underwood's 'The Mirror of La Granja' (1909), in which a young violinist falls in love with Zarabanda, a woman born centuries previously, whom he sees trapped in a mirror that reflects ghosts and dreams rather than physical reality, and from which he frees her with his playing. The violinist is obsessed, having been formerly disgusted or bored by the physical and moral flaws of 'real' women, loving only statues and portraits, since 'Nothing in womankind had made me so dislike the race as this union of external beauty and prosaic predictability.' Untainted by modern life, he feels that Zarabanda is his 'in a very real sense because [he] had created her', describing her, in a phrase calculated to repulse the female reader (whether she were 'delicate' *or* progressive) in particular, as 'an exquisite toy of flesh fashioned for love.'[40] He wishes to show her off to the world, in order to illustrate by contrast how far femininity has fallen from true beauty, while simultaneously indulging in erotic, orientalized reveries about the abandoned sensuality and Moorish splendor from which he imagines her having sprung (and which, as detailed further in Chapter 6, was central to late-nineteenth-century American marketing strategies).

As works such as *The Greek Slave* became themselves endlessly reproduced, as miniature copies, engravings, lamp stands, and other household items, the meanings so carefully attributed to art of this kind were inexorably destabilized. Indeed, as the century wore on, commodity culture became less coy, veiling the female form, not in ineffable purity, but in the very trappings of materialism from which moralizing writers and art critics strove to separate it. Women were positioned ever more overtly as valuable and attractive commodities, a newly vivified advertising sector seizing upon images of femininity as aesthetically pleasing platforms for material goods. At one commercial 'Carnival' in South Dakota in 1890, the display of merchandise included '"live" female mannequins who "wore" the goods being sold, some women covered with strawberries, oranges, and nuts and crackers, others adorned with diamonds, silks, and satins.' Lifelike artificial mannequins were not widespread before the 1910s, but tableaux vivants featuring 'statues' that then 'came to life' were a relatively common feature of such commercial theatricals.[41] Displays that included 'golden temples and pillars, rose-red velvet and lavender metallic hangings, carved animals, green and blue drapes, plush cushions, mythic female artifacts, and huge goddess figures' suggested that the female form was just one more commodity, employed to connote luxury and mystery, but also available for purchase.[42]

The cultural desire to reduce women's bodies to works of art also surfaced in less exotic settings. As photographical technology evolved into cheaper and more accessible forms, those who would otherwise never have been able to afford to have an image of themselves produced were queuing up to be transformed into portraits. A trade initially dogged by superstition in the nineteenth century, the relationship between photographer and sitter was, from the beginning, a difficult one, particularly for those uncomfortable with being scrutinized or horrified at the results. Since the sitter had to be immobilized in order to prevent blurring, the transaction entailed 'a more than faintly erotic surrender to another's will', and specifically to the masculine will of the phallic lens.[43] The tendency toward voyeurism and the objectification implicit in the photographic act was rendered more or less explicit in Elia W. Peattie's 'The Story of an Obstinate Corpse' (1898), in which a photographer is depicted as frequently telling his smoking buddies that

The world [...] was created in six days to be photographed. Man – and particularly woman – was made for the same purpose. Clouds are not made to give moisture nor trees to cast shade. They have been created in order to give the camera obscura something to do.[44]

It is this idea – that the female body by its very nature attracts a highly acquisitive artistic (generally male) gaze – that underpins a large number of supernatural short stories by American women writers from around the end of the nineteenth century. Narrating again and again the story of a portrait that seems to steal the life of a flesh-and-blood woman, from the point of view of a female character striving desperately to evade the fate of her unlucky predecessors, these stories function as implicit critiques of the victimization encoded within contemporary visual depictions of helpless female bodies. Moreover, the dread of repetition that is central to Underwood's 'Painter' underpins much of the anxiety regarding images that pervades this subgenre as a whole. Radcliffean 'female gothic' narratives dramatize the heroine's triumph over such repetition, by bringing to light dark and terrible facts, facts that the villain is determined to keep hidden.[45] The concealment of these facts means that 'the domestic activities over which the women are beginning to "rule" cannot be carried on', and benevolent female power is usurped by patriarchal tyranny. As one woman after another falls victim to the violence that ensues, it is only 'The exposure of the secret' that can free 'the female protagonist to reassert the primacy of "home" and its values by marrying the man of her choice', exorcizing the past and ensuring the proper gender balance in future marriages.[46] Heroines such as Adeline in Ann Radcliffe's *The Romance of the Forest* (1791), Charlotte Brontë's *Jane Eyre* (1847), and Maud Ruthyn in J. Sheridan LeFanu's *Uncle Silas* (1864) therefore succeed in sweeping all haunting presences from the house, castle or abbey, releasing the past in order to liberate the future from the toils of endlessly reiterated victimization.

While some Gilded-Age uncanny tales by American women feature optimistic endings of this nature, numerous others allow the villainous artists to live, or permit the seductive portraits of 'Evil Other Women' to tyrannize the lives of living characters by inspiring and perpetuating domestic cruelty, betrayal, or violence.[47] Indeed, even the happy marriages that conclude conventional gothic narratives ring hollow, coming as they do at the end of lengthy depictions of the horrors of the gothic house, which are themselves an only slightly exaggerated version of the potential horrors of marriage – namely, confinement in the home and patriarchal abuse.[48] It is therefore unsurprising that so many of the female protagonists in American women's gothic tales are newly married to men they seem hardly to know at all. As Henry James' Governess puts it in *The Turn of the Screw* (1898), in a statement that could easily serve as a definition of the gothic genre as a whole, 'An unknown man in a lonely place is a permitted object of fear to a young woman privately bred.'[49] In these stories, the threat posed to respectable young ladies by unknown men takes the form of a reifying male gaze mediated through artistic productions. Precisely because of the moral complexities surrounding images of the female form, allowing one's portrait to be taken is depicted in these narratives as an extremely perilous enterprise, reducing female characters to nothing more than their exteriors. Working within contemporary discourses that subjected women to rigorous moral standards, these stories portray visual representation as a trap; portraits freeze women in space and time, in a manner closely associated with death.[50] In a culture where excessive concern with outward appearance exposed women to harsh censure, one of the most frequent gothic motifs therefore revolves around the fear of becoming nothing more than a beautiful surface, at once vulnerable and vain, immobilized and yet engaged in narcissistic self-display.

'A thing of paint': Viewing the vampiric portrait

In Wharton's short story 'Mr Jones' (1928), the protagonist Lady Jane inherits a somewhat grim old mansion named Bells, of which she knows almost nothing. The housekeeper, Mrs Clemm, dutifully conveys to her the orders of the faithful old caretaker, Mr Jones, whom our heroine is told she cannot meet due to his advanced age and infirmity. One of his most strictly imposed dictates is that the new owner should not sit or entertain in the cozy blue parlor, due to an allegedly smoky chimney. For as long as anyone can remember, Mr Jones (who we eventually learn has been dead for quite some time) has been in charge of everything, but even after several months in residence, Lady Jane has only ever caught brief glimpses of him, despite being constantly under the restraint of his relayed orders, shivering and running up huge heating bills in the vast, draughty salon. Significantly, it is also in the forbidden blue parlor that the portrait of the unfortunate former lady of the house hangs, which depicts 'Between clusters of beribboned curls a long fair oval look[ing] out dumbly, inexpressively, in a stare of frozen beauty.'[51] The word 'oval' brings to mind Poe's 'The Oval Portrait' (1842), in which a painter's obsession with creating a remarkably lifelike portrait of his wife results in her death, possibly of neglect, but also possibly because her life force has been absorbed by the painting.

It initially appears that Wharton's story will offer a more optimistic vision than Poe's when, attempting to discover the history of this unnervingly lifeless young woman (designated only by the words 'Also His Wife' on the conjugal tomb), Lady Jane disobeys Mr Jones, opening a locked chamber and poking around in a desk over which she glimpses his shadowy figure hovering vigilantly and jealously. The desk drawers yield up a bundle of papers, missing from the house's official records, from which it becomes clear that the lady in the portrait had been both deaf and incapable of speech. A former owner of Bells, a penniless Viscount, had married her for her money and beauty. Soon disgusted by her disabilities, which rendered her an unsuitable wife for a man of his standing, it emerges that he abandoned her in her isolated new home, in which she was a virtual prisoner, details that support Lady Jane's reaction to her portrait. While a more conventional story would end here, with the spectral presences that render the house unhomely disappearing once the mystery is solved, matters at Bells quickly take a turn for the worse. Immediately following this revelation, the housekeeper is apparently strangled by the vengeful, ghostly hands of her long-dead superior, and when Lady Jane and her friends find her corpse, we are told that

> Mrs Clemm's room, like herself, was neat, glossy and extremely cold. Only Mrs Clemm herself was no longer like Mrs Clemm. The red-apple glaze had barely faded from her cheeks, and not a lock was disarranged in the unnatural lustre of her false front; even her cap ribbons hung symmetrically along either cheek. But death had happened to her, and had made her into someone else.[52]

The story culminates in this evocation of the dead housekeeper's icy, inhuman tidiness, which forms a structural parallel to the empty-eyed, melancholy, 'frozen beauty' of the dead woman in the portrait, while simultaneously standing in opposition to the color, life, and vibrancy of the objects that occupy the blue parlor.[53] A certain luxury of qualifiers is lavished upon the 'citron-wood desk', the old wooden paneling, the blue 'petit point fire-screen', and '"Those charming curtains with the parrots!"' about which one of Lady Jane's friends gushes effusively. Concluding with yet more death and horror rather than with the reestablishment of normality, the story consequently leaves us all too aware of the stark contrast between this lively depiction of objects and the chilling image of Mrs Clemm's inanimate corpse, with its uncomfortably close resemblance to the portrait.[54] For a woman to be painted into a portrait, the story implies, in an echo of Underwood's 'The Painter of Dead Women', is to be even less animated than an item of furniture, and is indistinguishable from being dead.

The gendered nature of this association becomes clear when we bear in mind that death has placed no bars upon Mr Jones' mobility or agency – indeed, it grants him greater authority over the household than in life. 'Also His Wife', as Lady Jane calls her, only half in jest, is trapped within pictorial space, in a mimetic representation of the blue parlor and not in the room itself, as she might be were she a ghost. Essentially incarcerated in the home of her husband's ancestors in life, unable to effect any change upon her surroundings, in death, she is exiled from its most pleasant room, just as Lady Jane herself is. Depicted in the portrait within the very same room as that in which the picture hangs, the representational echoing of spaces, rather than giving her power over those spaces, gives them power over her. Spellbound by her portrait within a voiceless body, the Viscountess has no chance of coming back from the dead, particularly when Mr Jones stands so firmly in her way, and is therefore as mute, powerless and imprisoned in death as she was in life, trapped eternally in the body, in the beauty of her youth, and in the confines of a marriage 'won' by this beauty, as much as in representation.

A similar echoing of portrait and room occurs in Emma Frances Dawson's 'A Stray Reveler' (1896), in which a woman's artist friend includes an image of her in a picture that hangs in and mirrors her drawing room. It transpires that the woman, named Aura, had been inadvertently responsible for the artist's fiancée's suicide, and the painting is an elaborate supernatural mechanism for the wreaking of his revenge. Aura lives under the shadow of his curse upon her, fixed within the limits of a memory from which she cannot escape, to the point where she feels compelled to furnish her room to match the picture exactly. The story implies that when she, like the fiancée, hangs herself, the artist's curse has been transmitted through the painting, her own life and death duplicating the horrors of the past. By driving her first to transform her living space into a static picture, and then to reduce herself to motionless corpse, the painting arrests time at a single, fatal moment, one that Aura is doomed to repeat.[55]

This sense of echoing repetitions is extended in Lurana W. Sheldon's 'A Premonition' (1896), which focuses on a young wife's discovery that her new husband has been poisoning his wives in order to create powerful paintings of the moment between life and death. The murdered women remain in the house as spectral prisoners, tiny, wizened, fleshless beings who appear to be invisible to the artist, Armand, but who attempt to warn the protagonist, Evelyn, of her impending doom. However, Evelyn mistakes the source of danger, shrinking in terror from these benevolent apparitions that were once her husband's wives and victims. The mistake renders it difficult for her to avoid the same fate as the subject of her husband's most recent painting, before which she 'recoil[s] instinctively', but which forces her 'to admit the artist's skill in depicting the agony of death upon those beautiful features.' As she stands 'transfixed' in front of it, what finally convinces her of the danger she is in is her realization that the incredible detail in 'the agony of drawn muscles and pinched and ghastly features', the 'blue drawn lines', 'purple shadows', and 'signs of bloating' can only suggest that it was drawn from a dying model, one who 'resembled [Evelyn] in age, in contour, and in feature.'[56] Once again, repetition is the specter looming over the text, banishing linear time and replacing it with endless, identical cycles. The pattern is only broken when the phantoms of Armand's dead wives implore her to set them free from the deathly prison of their former conjugal abode. As she watches them disappear, she begins to follow them out of the oppressive mansion, but is prevented by a very corporeal hand, which turns out to be that of her husband waking her up tenderly and telling her (rather patronizingly) that she has had a bad dream after eating lobster. This 'happy' ending is, however, too abrupt fully to exorcize the gothic dread of objectifying portraits conjured up by the story. Like Underwood's troublingly absent husband figure, Evelyn's rescuer blurs uncomfortably with his nightmare double, and it is all too easy to imagine a sequel in which the action repeats itself, but in the waking world instead of a trivialized dream.

Mrs Wilson Woodrow's 1909 short story 'Secret Chambers' presents a more unambiguously optimistic treatment of the trope, featuring a new and nervous wife who, on arrival in the conjugal home, comes across the by now inevitable painting of her predecessor. Adele, the dead but not forgotten first love of the protagonist's artist husband, Arnold, at first glance appears in the portrait as far more attractive and obviously feminine than the meek and pale Sylvia. Struck initially by the picture's extraordinary vision of 'feminine loveliness', in a passage which resembles the moralizing tracts against female vanity outlined above, closer inspection reveals something

> in the face which all the glow and radiance of a most seductive beauty but thinly masked. It had been in the flesh a mutable face, and as Sylvia continued to gaze steadily at it she seemed to see it change before her eyes. There was something in those pictured eyes that mocked and refuted the appealing sweetness of that rose-leaf smile. He who ran might read that it was an emotional face passionate to weakness; but few would discern beneath that soft, peach-bloom flesh the iron of a powerful will and of a tenacious and unscrupulous purpose.[57]

This 'powerful will' continues to pervades the house, and Sylvia feels that 'the portrait appeared to surround her, for the several large mirrors which the room contained seemed to give back a thousand reflections of it.' Hemmed in by myriad, deceptively seductive female surfaces, Sylvia feels as if 'she, the living, breathing woman, was as the shadow, while the portrait, a thing of paint, conveyed infinitely more effectively the illusion of life, the pride of the flesh.'[58] Her increasing awareness of the continued presence of the dead Adele in her new home is paralleled by Arnold's increasing absorption in his art, to the point where Sylvia feels all but widowed, ejected from her home by the combined forces of the memory of Adele and his growing artistic obsession. Worse still, as Sylvia wonders desperately how to reestablish herself at the forefront of his affections, the spirit of Adele begins to possess her consciousness, and she becomes furiously demanding, culminating in her very nearly slashing his completed masterpiece in order to draw his attention back to her. It transpires that Adele had first slashed his picture of Love (for which she presumably modeled) and then turned the knife on herself, and Sylvia now repeats the very words spoken by her predecessor, her mind and her voice invaded by the spirit of the dead woman as much as her home is. However, gothic repetition is not permitted to triumph in this story, as Arnold tells her that Art has saved him from the undead specter of Adele's clinging domination, because his new wife has encouraged and allowed his talent to flourish once again. A self-effacing muse rather than a selfish model, her influence is pure and true, and, as the story comes to a close, Sylvia effectively promises to redecorate so that he can be free of the dead beauty's evil influence forever, regaining control of the house, her husband, and herself, all in one fell swoop.

This dichotomy between the wicked subjects of portraits and the good women who evade such objectification structures M.E.M. Davis' Southern gothic 'At La Glorieuse' (1891), in which a strange, lovely, fascinating ghost, who appears in a window as if 'framed in a portrait', seeds discord among the men of two wealthy families.[59] Once again, the apparent vibrancy and allure of a painted dead woman seems to drain all life from a living, less obviously attractive one; the morally fault-less Félice, initially the object of affection of a young man seduced by the magnetic specter, appears, sitting on a tombstone, 'wan and ghostly in the lonely dusk'. This figurative spectralization intensifies as the memory of the beautiful, framed woman distracts her visitor, Keith, who had been on the point of pressing his suit. He barely registers Félice's presence, and eventually she walks away from him, 'moving like a spirit' into the dusk until she disappears.[60] Instead, the voluptuous ghost, who appears more real to him, and who he is convinced is being held prisoner in the house, lures him into a bedroom, where her portrait hangs. Finding him there, after what seems to be a sexual encounter with the specter, Félice's grandmother, who had feared precisely this series of events, tells him how the woman, Hélène, was in fact Félice's neglectful and potentially violent mother, who had had an affair with Keith's own father, causing an irreconcilable rift between the two husbands, once close friends. She describes Hélène as

'a radiant soulless creature, whose only law was her own selfish enjoyment, and whose coming brought pain and bitterness to La Glorieuse.
These were her rooms. She chose them because of the rose garden, for
she had a sensuous and passionate love of nature. She used to lie for
hours on the grass there, with her arms flung over her head, gazing
dreamily at the fluttering leaves above her. The pearls – which she
always wore – some coral ornaments, and a handful of amber beads
were her only dower, but her caprices were the insolent and extravagant caprices of a queen [...].'[61]

The archetype of the extravagant vampire woman, who surfaces again
in later chapters, she is outwardly beautiful but lacking in proper motherly or wifely qualities, desired and desiring; and, in Davis's story, is
ultimately triumphant. Keith abandons the house and Félice, haunted
by the memory of her mother; he only comes to his senses when he
loses a ring, the carrier of bad memories and fateful lust, that Hélène
had given to his father and that the ghost leaves for him to find. Freed
from its influence, he thinks immediately of Félice, and rushes back to
La Glorieuse, only to find that his living beloved has taken the veil.
Instead of the objectification that would have resulted in her repetition
of her mother's actions, she buries herself alive in a convent, in a move
that seems to extend the spectrality with which the contrast with her
mother's lovely image invests her.

When this is juxtaposed with Woodrow's, in which Sylvia feels herself
a 'shadow' when faced with her peerless predecessor, and Sheldon's,
in which Evelyn runs the risk of becoming another shrunken, imprisoned ghost along with Armand's other dead wives, Davis' story seems to
imply that the status of ghost confers no more dominance or freedom
within domestic space and domestic relationships than that of immobilized portrait. While the two might appear to be set in mutual opposition in these stories, ghostliness is not therefore an escape from the
problems of objectification, but actually a symptom. Indeed, many of
the dead women who populate later chapters of this book do not take
on corporeal form, and are far more powerful as a consequence. Several
women writers from around this time therefore made use of the possibilities opened up by the supernatural in order to offer a potential solution to the dangers of pictorial representation or objectification – but,
vitally, while evading the trap of the spectral form, which is just another
version of visual representation. Less drastic than confining oneself to
a nunnery, but arguably just as self-effacing, the stories discussed in the
chapters that follow suggest that avoiding the female form altogether,

and disappearing into the decorative surfaces and objects that abounded in the Gilded-Age American middle-class home, ensures a far less restrictive version of postmortem existence. The dead female characters in these stories reject the hazardous visual realm by embracing the very material 'trifles' in which writers such as Emerson imagined women invested so much emotional energy.

The empowering possibilities opened up by remaining an invisible poltergeist rather than a visible ghost are gestured toward in Harriet Prescott Spofford's 'The Amber Gods' (1860), to which Davis' story appears to pay some homage (especially in the form of the string of eponymous amber beads). The majority of Spofford's long tale is devoted to describing the adolescence of its narrator, Giorgione Willoughby, affectionately known as Yone, and her orphan cousin, Louise. Yone unabashedly describes her own warm, golden beauty at length, contrasting her 'full, bounteous, overflowing' self to the more pallid, selfless, ethereal charms of Louise, from whom she ultimately steals the attentions of a young man named Vaughan Rose.[62] The final part of the story is set ten years after Yone's marriage to Rose, which has been marred by her increasing awareness of his undiminished devotion to her cousin, and his growing repugnance for Yone's too fleshly and obvious gorgeousness. Indeed, it becomes clear that the body is by no means something that Yone continues to treasure as she had in her youth; it has become as disturbing and alienating for her as it is for her physically and emotionally distant husband. On her deathbed, where an unnamed disease has prostrated her, the masses of blond hair, of which she had been particularly proud, now fill her with horror. She writes, 'That cap-string has loosened now, and all this golden cataract of hair has rushed out over the piled pillows. It oppresses and terrifies me.'[63] She has moved so far beyond the body already that to be reminded of it is to be terrified. At the same time, speech and interaction with the living are denied to her. She is powerless, trapped in a body that is no longer a valuable or pleasure-giving asset but a liability, even an enemy. It is here that Spofford's story all but explicitly alludes to the problematic status of the objectified female body in nineteenth-century American culture. As her relationship with her husband, Rose, deteriorates, he begins to act out his desire to 'kill' her into a timeless, motionless art object. Yone describes how

> He became artist, – ceased to be man, – was more indifferent than the cloud. He could paint me then, – and, revealed and bare, all our histories written in me, he hung me up beside my ancestors. There

I hang. Come from thy frame, thou substance, and let this troubled phantom go! Come! for he gave my life to thee. In thee he shut and sealed it all, and left me as the empty husk. [...] I, from the slave of bald form, enlarged him to the master of gorgeous color; his blaze is my ashes.[64]

Her illness spiritualizes her beauty, rendering her more like Louise (and the idealized, near-bodiless women discussed in later chapters) even as her husband transforms her on canvas into a motionless monument to herself. She writes:

I saw my face in the hand-glass this morning, more lovely than health fashioned it; transparent skin, bounding blood with its fire burning behind the eye, on cheek, on lip, a beauty that every pang has aggravated, heightened, sharpened, to a superb intensity, flushing, rapid, unearthly, a brilliancy to be dreamed of. Like a great autumn leaf I fall, for I am dying, dying! Yes, death finds me more beautiful than life made me; but have I lost nothing? Great Heaven, I have lost all![65]

In life, she is an 'empty husk', exposed and naked, on public display within her own home, the 'transparent', 'unearthly' beauty of morti-fied flesh reminiscent of an idealized nineteenth-century domestic angel, dying so that others may be happy. By contrast, released from the body in death, she becomes invisible and vital, regaining the power and movement that had characterized her lost youthful self. Importantly, while no-one can see her, the story's final lines are notable for carefully described domestic details. She recounts how she

passed out of the room, down the staircase. The servants below did not see me, but the hounds crouched and whined. I paused before the great ebony clock; again the fountain broke, and it chimed the half-hour; it was half past one; another quarter, and the next time its ponderous silver hammers woke the house, it would be two. Half past one? Why, then did not the hands move? Why cling fixed on a point five minutes before the first quarter struck? To and fro, soundless and purposeless, swung the long pendulum. And, ah! what was this thing I had become? I had done with time. Not for me the hands moved on their recurrent circle any more.

I must have died at ten minutes past one.[66]

Spofford's text stops abruptly here. The narrative therefore leaves Yone standing eternally next to the clock that signals her removal from temporal existence, even as it illustrates her continued interaction with the objects and spaces of the living. Her ability to continue narrating beyond the expiration of her physical form suggests that she has succeeded in evading Rose's violently reifying artistic gaze, escaping her loveless marriage by dying and gleefully haunting the house that is no longer hers, thus ending the gothic repetition that has doomed her ancestors to be cruel and miserable. While Wharton's 'Also His Wife' remains incarcerated as a lifeless portrait surrounded by beautiful objects, Yone here seems to have established a more intimate relationship with the things in her home than she has in life. This passage dwells on the stairs and the clock to an extent unmatched by the rest of the story, where such details exist only as lifeless backdrops to her vibrant sensuality.

Appearing in abstract or fanciful patterns, swirling foliage or soaring birds, or simply the sight of a baby's shoe among the charred ruins of a cabin, the spectral female presences on which this book focuses go one step further again, effacing themselves completely while asserting their presence through previously inanimate objects. The physical presence of these women may be swallowed up by the material objects and decorative elements of the home, the position into which domestic ideology inserts them, but (in Chapters 3 and 4 especially) this absorption is nevertheless coterminous with their unsettling power over those objects and the spaces that surround them. In doing so, these narratives offer fantastical opportunities for their female characters to evade reification by, paradoxically, embracing superficiality in the form of the ornate patterns that adorn the rooms they occupy. As the next chapter illustrates, while domesticity and home life are the agents of oppression, domestic furnishings, commodities and interior decoration function as vehicles for memory, bearing witness to the oppression in which they participate. Indeed, when objects refuse to allow memories to be attached to them, as is the case in the stories discussed in Chapter 6, the prominent role that they play in a large number of eerie stories by American women writers from around the end of the nineteenth century permits such stories to articulate the vexed relationship between women and domesticity while avoiding the pitfalls of objectification. Even in the more pessimistic tales that I discuss, in their encounters with decorative and practical objects, female characters are rarely reduced to the helpless, dead, or immobilized gothic victims that so many of their counterparts become when they make the mistake of marrying men who love them only insofar as they can transform them into art.

Insane, angry, demonic, murderous and aggressively secretive, the women, both living and dead, around whom the following chapters center are profoundly ambiguous avatars of feminine empowerment and protest, inspiring fear as often as they feel it, and challenging the readerly instinct toward identification and sympathy. What unites these female characters, however, is their acknowledgment of the importance of domestic objects to middle-class women in nineteenth-century America, and the status of such objects, not as inanimate and trivial *things*, but as active agents in realistically evoked fictional worlds.

2
'Handled with a Chain': Gilman's 'The Yellow Wall-Paper' and the Dangers of the Arabesque

In her 1903 polemic *The Home: Its Work and Influence*, Charlotte Perkins Gilman thundered, 'This power of home-influence we cannot fail to see, but we have bowed to it in blind idolatry as one of unmixed influence, instead of studying with jealous care that so large a force be wisely guarded and restrained.'[1] Her point, throughout *The Home*, as well as her phenomenally successful *Women and Economics* (1898) and her feminist utopian novel *Herland* (1915), was that the middle-class home in Gilded-Age America was by no means a benign institution, and that claiming otherwise was both erroneous and pernicious. Combining sexual companionship, child-rearing, and economic dependence, the nineteenth-century middle-class American home turned women into slavish drudges, and men into selfish tyrants, yet, rather than criticizing or seeking to alter the system itself, she argued, society at large repeatedly blamed individual wives, husbands, children, even specific houses, for the ills found within it. Gilman therefore urged that drunkenness, infidelity, domestic violence, infant and maternal mortality and illness, juvenile delinquency, and psychological disorders such as neurasthenia should not be seen as symptoms of the moral degeneracy of those who display such behavioral problems. Instead, the home itself needed to be totally reconceived and reformed, along socialist and collectivist, rather than individualist and capitalist, lines. In particular, *Women and Economics* insisted that women needed financially and personally rewarding work outside of the home, in order to free them from their restricting and damaging condition as unpaid, unskilled house servants, personal shoppers, and legally sanctioned prostitutes.

It is these ideas that underpin what is perhaps now her most famous work, the 1892 short story 'The Yellow Wall-Paper'. This quasi-autobiographical tale graphically portrays the deleterious effects on a wife and new mother of her failure to recognize that the difficulties she experiences in adjusting to these roles are not unique. Never quite grasping that she belongs to a vast community of women equally trapped by and struggling against the confines of the single-family home, she is further entangled in its snare, to the point of insanity. Positing the wallpaper in her sickroom as offering insight into while obscuring the truth about what happens to women in the home, the story depicts decorative objects not as proof of feminine frivolity, vanity, or superficiality, but as active and malevolent agents in a harmful domestic system, imprisoning women in a gilded cage.

The narrator's husband, John, does exactly what the tale cautions against, attributing the effects of a system to the psychological disturbance of an isolated individual psyche, focusing on the symptom and the victim rather than the root cause. The social and personal forces rallied against the narrator prove too strong, and the objectified image of the individual female body effectively obstructs the narrator's vision, making it impossible for her to understand what the wallpaper in her room suggests about the role played by material objects in female oppression. Indeed, critical responses to the tale tend to mirror this obstruction, ignoring the systemic in favor of the psychological.[2] Faced with the construction of America as an unsettling historical void, one that forecloses the possibility of the engagement with buried pasts so central to Old-World haunted houses, interpretations of American gothic texts often fall back upon the psychopathology of individuals living within the house, reducing the events and indeed the house itself to functions of the psyche of those individuals. Many critics turn to Sigmund Freud's 'The "Uncanny"' (1919), the opening section of which is devoted to the proximity of meaning between the German words *heimlich* and *unheimlich*, the former having two, not entirely contradictory, meanings. The first is 'Intimate, friendlily comfortable; [...] arousing a sense of agreeable restfulness and security as in one within the four walls of his house.' The other, however, is 'Concealed, kept from sight, so that others do not get to know about it, withheld from others.' This second meaning shades into that of *unheimlich*, roughly translated as '"*the name for everything that ought to have remained ... secret and hidden but has come to light.*"'[3] Consequently, '*heimlich* is a word the meaning of which develops in the direction of ambivalence, until it finally coincides with its opposite, *unheimlich*. *Unheimlich* is in some way or another a sub-species of *heimlich*.'[4] From this, Freud concluded that both words refer to psychic processes relating to fear and anxiety, and that therefore,

> this uncanny is in reality nothing new or alien, but something which is familiar and old-established in the mind and which has become alienated from it only through the process of repression [...] something which ought to have remained hidden but has come to light.[5]

Despite the fact that his terminology explicitly alludes to domesticity and domestic space, he transformed this literal meaning into a rigidly figurative one, reading *through* his source material to find a more universal, individualizing meaning in the form of personal psychological disturbance. Indeed, he actively dismissed the motif of the haunted house as irrelevant to his argument, declaring it not truly *unheimlich*, 'because the uncanny in it is too much intermixed with what is purely gruesome and is in part overlaid by it.'[6] In doing so, he veered away from the sociocultural implications of the proximity of *heimlich* and *unheimlich*, which suggests that the idea of 'home' carries within it a sense of fear, alienation and darkness. Since, as Gilman herself put it, 'We reverence [home] with the blind obeisance of those crouching centuries when its cult began', Freud evaded such scandalous assertions, settling instead upon a highly individualized and pathologizing interpretation that is less critical of so powerful an institution as the home.[7]

As outlined above, taking their cue from Freud, literary critics such as Leslie Fiedler, Irving Malin, Benjamin Franklin Fisher, and Allan Gardner Lloyd-Smith read through and past the haunted or malevolent house *as* a house. The prevailing critical tendency has been to see the gothic and horror genres, particularly in America, as having abandoned the obvious and somewhat tawdry locale of the haunted ancestral castle at some point around the middle of the nineteenth century. Since then, critics persistently argue, horror has 'come inside' and is now correctly located in the haunted psyche rather than the haunted house (which, many agree, was only ever a metaphor for the haunted psyche anyway), psychoanalytical criticism having created the tools to reveal the 'real' meaning of such productions.[8] However, 'the application of psychoanalytic formulae to texts, or merely the exclusive concern with a protagonist's psyche, subjectivity, or emotional state', has resulted in a critical 'tendency to negate or explain away [...] historical, geographical, and political "surface" details.'[9] Such readings obfuscate the home's status as an embodiment and agent of domestic ideology, which, in the absence of historical depth, comes to the fore in American uncanny fiction, and which ghost stories by American women writers frequently positioned as a central locus of gothic dread. This prominent role played by domestic spaces and things can be at least partially attributed to the extent to which, as the nineteenth century blurred into the twentieth, commodity culture 'collapsed the distinction between the self and the commodities surrounding it.'[10] Unsurprisingly, given the prevailing gendered division of labor whereby men earned money while women spent it, that 'self' was generally female. The result, for Gilman, was a woman clad

In garments whose main purpose is unmistakably to announce her sex; with a tendency to ornament which marks exuberance of sex-energy, with a body so modified to sex as to be grievously deprived of its natural activities; [...] with a field of action most rigidly confined to sex-relations; with her overcharged sensibility, her prominent modesty, her 'eternal femininity', – the female genus homo is undeniably over-sexed.[11]

Gilman was especially critical of a model of domesticity that enforced women's investment in interior decoration by leaving her with no other creative outlet, seeing it as 'the desperate efforts of a trapped creature deprived of air and exercise and full use of her powers to put her energies to some use.'[12] She lamented the ubiquity of the 'home-bound woman' who sat, 'plump and fair, in her padded cage, bedizening its walls with every decoration, covering her body in costly and beautiful things; feeding herself, her family; running from meal to meal as if eating were really the main business of a human being.'[13] Gilman particularly condemned the unsystematized nature of unpaid domestic labor as creating 'uneasy activity', as the wife 'pour[ed] out her soul in tidies and photograph holders.' Railing against 'the jar and shock of changing from trade to trade a dozen times a day', *The Home* depicted this frenetic activity as 'a distinct injury, a waste of nervous force', which was the cause of 'fret and friction and weariness'.[14]

Sharing these concerns, scientists and domestic reformers sought to reduce some of this Sisyphean drudgery by simplifying the decorative contents of the home. Drawing on the new science of germ theory, they deplored wallpaper, along with dusty curtains and fussy china figurines, and indeed all highly patterned, embossed, or intricately carved decoration, as profoundly unhealthy, harboring dirt, disease, parasites, and dangerous chemicals, while causing mental unrest and even psychic disturbance.[15] As one decorating manual put it, strongly prefiguring Gilman's story,

> The decoration of the bedrooms cannot be too simple: the principal thing being to select a paper that has an all-overish pattern that cannot be tortured into geometrical figures by the occupant of the chamber, who, especially in hours of sickness, is well-nigh driven to distraction by counting over and over again the dots and lines and diamonds which dance with endless repetition before his aching eyes. For the same reason it is well to avoid the use of light or bright colours, and especially to study harmony of effect, and to eschew contrast.[16]

In other words, objects had very real effects on the lives, health, and sanity of those who lived among and through them, and it is this that recent developments in 'Thing Theory' have emphasized. Interpretations that position something as a mere symbol for or index to a character's psychic state mean that an object ceases to 'be itself', and 'is allowed no history of its own' because its 'specific qualities' are subordinated to 'those that illuminate something about the predicate to which they must yield.'[17] The life attributed to objects through symbolism or metaphor is not *their* life – it is a personification that directs meaning elsewhere. In order to rescue objects from a figurative regime that treats them as empty signs into which external meanings can be inserted, domesticating them in the process, these objects can be read as signifying metonymically rather than metaphorically. This is particularly important when one is dealing with fiction that employs supernatural tropes, since, 'When it is "naturalized" as allegory or symbolism, fantasy loses its proper non-signifying nature. Part of its subversive power lies in this resistance to allegory or metaphor. For it takes metaphorical constructions literally.'[18] This idea becomes somewhat clearer when placed in the context of Tzvetan Todorov's definition of 'the fantastic', which he situated as a delicate midpoint between 'the uncanny' (not to be confused with Freud's use of the term) and 'the marvelous.' Todorov's marvelous occurs in texts that present events that seem impossible in the world as we know it, but that assert that they are in fact possible and that 'new laws of nature must be entertained to account for the phenomena.' In the uncanny, on the other hand, it is ultimately made clear that 'the laws of reality remain intact and permit an explanation of the phenomena described' as the products of hallucination, delusion or trickery.[19] Furthermore, the marvelous corresponds to the mode of metaphor, or more accurately to allegory, and the uncanny to that of psychological realism. In the marvelous, the figurative is so fully elaborated that it takes on a life of its own, and no reference is made within the text to the 'real' world of which the textual one is but an image and a distortion. The gothic, relying as it does on the disbelief and horror of characters confronted with nightmares comes to life, rarely strays into the marvelous, and familiar examples include what we now think of as 'fantasy', such as J.R.R. Tolkien's *The Lord of the Rings* (1954–1955), which is frequently read as an allegory for the great wars of the beginning of the twentieth century, and C.S. Lewis' *The Lion, the Witch and the Wardrobe* (1950), which is difficult *not* to read as imaging Christ's death and resurrection. The uncanny, on the other hand, figures the bending of the laws of reality as taking place within the mind of a character in the text, and nowhere else, as in Ann Radcliffe's 'explained' gothic novels. Here, initially, the heroine is confronted by events so strange that she seems to have no choice but to interpret them as supernatural, only to be safely disillusioned later as each mystery is carefully explained away and attributed to human agency, accident or misunderstanding.

Todorov's third category is the fantastic, which he defined as 'that hesitation experienced by a person who knows only the law of nature, confronting an apparently supernatural event', a hesitation that ultimately proves irreducible, as is the case at the end of Henry James' *The Turn of the Screw*, which has left critics arguing bitterly over whether the ghosts are real, or merely products of the narrator's sexually frustrated psyche.[20] The fantastic therefore corresponds to the mode of metonymy, in which both terms of a figure are present simultaneously (the apparently impossible event or being, *and* a potential interpretation that would reveal it to be either figurative or illusory). The metonymic character of the fantastic means that 'one object does not *stand for* another, but literally becomes that other, slides into it, metamorphosing from one shape to another in a permanent flux and instability.'[21] Metaphor and allegory implicitly distinguish what is real from what is unreal. If the sun is compared to a great orange ball, the sun is actually there and the ball is not. In metonymy, on the other hand, both objects are 'real': for example, a child's muddied toy lying in the middle of a road is a common device for indicating a fatal traffic accident. In this second example, the dead child 'exists' in the fictional world of the text in a way that the ball in the previous example does not.

The advantage of reading a supernatural story like 'The Yellow Wall-Paper' metonymically is that doing so allows the wallpaper so central to the text to be read not as a mere symbol of the narrator's psychic break-down, but as an active agent in that breakdown. In other words, it is not relegated to a purely symbolic role, but taken seriously as a very material part of the domestic system that the story critiques. In fact, the story itself depicts Gilman's narrator as driven to insanity precisely because those around her cannot accept that the wallpaper is something more than superficial decoration. Her failure to convince her husband that all is not right with the room she occupies leaves her first appearing to be 'mad', and finally becoming so. As Emily Dickinson put it,

'Tis the Majority
In this, as All, prevail –
Assent – and you are sane –
Demure – you're straightway dangerous –
And handled with a Chain – [22]

Gilman versus Poe

As Gilman herself claimed, 'The Yellow Wall-Paper' was inspired by her own experiences of being prescribed S. Weir Mitchell's 'rest cure' for postnatal depression, which involved staying in bed during the day, eating frequently and copiously with the express purpose of gaining weight, and eschewing all intellectual or creative activity.[23] Finding herself on the brink of real insanity, Gilman discontinued the treatment and subsequently left her husband. Married to an aggressively unim-aginative doctor who has every faith in the cure, the story's narrator is denied such choices. The couple hire an old house for her conva-lescence, and John installs her in a large upstairs room, ignoring her preference for 'one downstairs that opened on the piazza and had roses all over the window, and such pretty old-fashioned chintz hangings.'[24] Chintz, a highly patterned fabric, is generally floral in nature, occasion-ally incorporating animals and used both for upholstery and women's clothing. Often perceived as vulgar and sentimental (featuring, for example, in Josephine Daskam Bacon's 1913 tearjerker of a ghost story, 'The Children'[25]), chintz speaks loudly of the stereotypically busily decorated, decidedly 'feminine' nineteenth-century parlor, and is the diametric opposite of the geometric abstractions of the 'arabesque' patterns of the yellow wallpaper in the room that the narrator is forced to occupy. This opposition directly echoes that set up by Edgar Allan

Poe, in his essay on home decoration, 'The Philosophy of Furniture' (1840). In a tastefully decorated room,

> distinct grounds, and vivid circular or cycloid figures, *of no meaning*, are here Median laws. The abomination of flowers, or representations of well-known objects of any kind, should not be endured within the limits of Christendom. Indeed, whether on carpets, or curtains, or tapestry, or ottoman coverings, all upholstery of this nature should be rigidly Arabesque.[26]

Some explanation for this preference can be identified in 'The Philosophy of Composition' (1846), which posited 'Beauty' as 'the province of the poem', defined negatively against 'Truth, or the satisfaction of the intellect, and [...] Passion, or the excitement of the heart.' Truth 'demands a precision, and Passion, a *homeliness* [...] which are absolutely antagonistic to that Beauty which [...] is the excitement, or pleasurable elevation, of the soul.' Even when Passion and Truth form part of the subject matter of the work of art, 'the true artist will always contrive, first, to tone them into proper subservience to the predominant aim, and, secondly, to enveil them, as far as possible, in that Beauty which is the atmosphere and the essence of the poem.'[27] Opposing Beauty both to the bald specificity of detail embodied by Truth and to the '*homeliness*', the familiar mundanity, and by extension even the domesticity, of Passion, Poe professed a positive aversion to the unmediated stuff of realism, to the stark portrayal of the everyday for its own sake. In relation both to flatly realistic and to obviously symbolic forms of representation, he asserted that

> in subjects so handled, however skilfully, or with however vivid an array of incident, there is always a certain hardness or nakedness, which repels the artistical eye. Two things are invariably required – first, some amount of complexity, or more properly, adaptation: and, secondly, some amount of suggestiveness – some under current [*sic*], however indefinite of meaning. It is this latter, in especial, which imparts to a work of art so much of that *richness* [...] which we are too fond of confounding with *the ideal*. It is the *excess* of the suggested meaning – it is the rendering this the upper current instead of the under current of the theme – which turns into prose (and that of the very flattest kind) the so called [*sic*] poetry of the so called transcendentalists.[28]

Poe argued here that realism, which is too prosaic, must be tempered by some suggestion of a buried figurative meaning, but this must not be permitted to take over to the point of becoming allegory, which is too explicit. The literary work should not 'present the reader with a provisional arrangement of reality', but rather seek 'to disengage the reader's mind from reality and propel it toward the ideal.'[29] Nowhere is this attempt to find a middle ground between real and ideal made more evident than in 'The Philosophy of Furniture', where Poe described in loving detail his ideal private chamber, plush, dimly lit, and richly but not extravagantly decorated. After providing a short list of necessary objects, furnishings, and ornamental elements, he cautioned that if 'repose' and 'tranquillity' are to be nurtured there, 'Beyond these things, there is no furniture.'[30] Such a room 'would allow, and indeed foster, a retreat to the interior chambers of the mind, with little intrusion of ordinary daylight to chase away the shadows of dreams', and neither would its inhabitant be interrupted by looking upon the vulgarly commonplace contents of the cluttered nineteenth-century parlor.[31] Gertrude Atherton's 1905 'A Monarch of Small Survey' described a typical American upper-middle-class parlor as 'funereal':

> The carpet was threadbare. White crocheted tidies lent their emphasis to the hideous black furniture. A table with marble top, like a graveyard slab, stood in the middle of the room. On it was a bunch of wax flowers in a glass case. On the white plastered walls hung family photographs in narrow gilt frames. In a conspicuous place was the doctor's diploma. In another, Miss Webster's first sampler. 'The first piano ever brought to California' stood in a corner, looking like the ghost of an ancient spinet.[32]

Poe's conception of beauty demanded that domestic space be purged of such extraneous and (to his mind) tasteless accumulation. Instead, his preference was for objects that allowed him to impose his own meanings upon them, rejecting those that might direct his thoughts by presenting him with images of flowers, animals, or indeed his own face (he is vehement that mirrors are an abomination).

This helps shed some light on John's selection, in Gilman's story, of a room papered in an intricate arabesque pattern, and his implicit rejection of the representational femininity of chintz. The arabesque, generally geometric in design, incorporated 'plant-based – or, alternatively, completely abstract – motifs, the elements of which can be infinitely repeated', often forming complex, interweaving patterns that are decorative and stylized rather than natural. While human, animal, and floral figures did appear in arabesque designs, they were deliberately artificial, moving beyond mimesis into fantasy.[33] Conversely, the grotesque was comprised of decorative elements that are 'autosemantic and heterogeneous in themselves as well as in comparison with each other (mixed beings consisting of animated, plant-based, and artificial elements); therefore, they cannot be repeated.'[34] This is nicely illustrated by John Ruskin's description of St. Mark's cathedral in Venice, where he described seeing 'a continual succession of crowded imagery, one picture passing into another, as in a dream; forms beautiful and terrible mixed together; dragons and serpents, and ravening beasts of prey, and graceful birds that in the midst of them drink from running fountains and feed from vases of crystal.'[35] The grotesque maddened the eye with an attractive yet exhausting spectacle that never cohered into a single, identifiable meaning, resisting unified interpretations, while the arabesque actively encouraged it.[36] Poe's insistence that the patterns on all coverings should be 'rigidly Arabesque' was prompted by the fact that such patterns did 'so much to stimulate the imagination', and could 'produce different meanings precisely because they [were] polysemic signs.'[37] Beneath this apparent 'freeing' of the viewer to image anything he or she wishes lies a desire to control interpretation, to bend it away from the concrete and the particular, which resists the imposition of meaning upon it, and toward the abstract and the universal.

'The Yellow Wall-Paper' is structured around precisely this opposition between an aesthetic of lack of explicit meaning (the arabesque) and one of presence (chintz), an opposition sustained in the couple's respective attitudes toward the house itself. The narrator harbors almost desperate fantasies of renting 'A colonial mansion, a hereditary estate, I would say a haunted house and reach the heights of romantic felicity – but that would be asking too much of fate!'[38] In other words, she longs for a house that is forthright about the fact that bad things have happened there. Indeed, in the works of Gilman's contemporaries, ghost-seeing becomes a potential source of female solidarity and community. In 'Are the Dead Dead?' (1897), Emma Frances Dawson's narrator writes, pleadingly,

> I cannot think that I alone, of all the world, have had such glimpse of the mysterious outlying region usually veiled from mortals. Whoever you are, now about to read what comes, I implore you comfort me, if you can, by writing: 'I, too, have heard and seen!' Come forward and share my burden before I lose my mind.

Since that awful experience I feel lifted above the paltry secret-keeping of this world. I own our spiritual kinship.[39]

No such kinship is available to Gilman's narrator. Declaring 'proudly [...] that there is something queer about' the place, she adds bleakly, 'John laughs at me, of course, but one expects that in marriage.' When the narrator insists that 'there is something strange about the house', he is adamant that 'what [she] felt was a *draught*, and shut the window.'[40] Closing the window is a display of power, designed to illustrate his underlying argument that people can physically and conceptually affect houses, and that the converse is patently absurd and impossible. This attitude also offers a potential explanation for why John, who she says is 'very careful and loving, and hardly lets [her] stir without special direction', insists that the narrator occupy a room decorated with arabesque wallpaper that she finds 'repellent, almost revolting'.[41] An open-ended pattern with no inherent significance in the motifs it depicts, the arabesque suggests that human occupants determine the meanings of the objects around them. Chintz, however, like the grotesque, is autosemantic; its floral patterns suggest only themselves, rather than endless imaginative possibilities. Arabesque suits John's purposes better than chintz because it offers no resistance to his display of agency over it. To allow that a house might be impervious to the will of its occupants, that it might signify in ways that he cannot control or alter, would undermine his insistence that a room of his choosing will have the effect he anticipates upon his wife's physical and psychological health.

The work of Gilman's contemporaries is redolent with houses and furniture and decoration that have an overtly negative effect on the women who have to live in and among them. In Lurana W. Sheldon's 'A Premonition', Evelyn looks on, appalled, as

the gloomy, frowning outlines of her new home rose up in the darkness before her. She seemed to hesitate with her foot on the carriage-step, as though invisibly detained by a spirit hand, while she glanced up curiously at the dismal structure; it was so unlike the stately mansion that her artist husband had described to her, and resembled more a monstrous, shapeless pile of stones than a luxurious or even comfortable residence.[42]

This opening neatly encapsulates the era's gendered views of domestic space, the suggestion being that her artist husband's vision is a distorting one, that he values wealth and appearance over comfort and welcome. Inside, she is greeted only by a 'dim light', which shows her 'a dingy room where the furniture was heavy and repulsive, and where the profusion and thickness of the draperies suggested suspicions of a fearful silence.' We are told, ominously, 'One could shriek aloud and not be heard beyond the doors; one could beat upon the floor and walls without so much as raising an echo.' The story implies that, since furniture and decoration are the currency in which women must deal, they ought to be fitted for feminine purposes, creating a pleasant ambience while remaining easy to clean and maintain. Instead, Evelyn is faced with the grim prospect of 'unyielding cushion[s]', 'musty from lack of sun and heavy with some mysterious horror', uncomfortable, unhealthy furniture and threatening atmosphere merging seamlessly.[43] This is not a house where the piling up of commodities functions as a means of absorbing, retaining and communicating the traces of women's dwelling within it, but an aggressively patriarchal mansion. Indeed, simply residing in his ancestral home changes Armand's entire demeanor, rendering him uncharacteristically gruff and angry with his wife. Alienating and silencing, the furnishings and decorations serve his ends rather than Evelyn's needs, repelling the imposition of new memories on her part, while refusing to yield up the secrets of those it embraces and of which it whispers maddeningly but indecipherably.

Gilman's story is even more explicit regarding the negative impact of a room chosen by a husband for a wife. The narrator's illness, a symptom of the effects that domestic life can have upon women, is closely related to her belief that, while the house may not be haunted, this is not to say that houses are unable to haunt, a belief that extends to domestic objects in general and to the wallpaper in particular. She comments, 'The paper looks at me as if it *knew* what a vicious influence it had!', continuing, 'I never saw so much expression in an inanimate thing before, and we all know how much expression they have!' She comments, 'I used to lie awake as a child and get more entertainment and terror out of blank walls and plain furniture than most children could find in a toy-store!'[44] Written in the wake of the publication of Karl Marx's *Capital*, her exclamations are particularly resonant. Marx set out to decipher 'the uncanny power that certain objects had acquired over consumers in a capitalist economy', in order to demonstrate that 'the commodity's seeming autonomy is the effect of alienated labour.' While '[i]n the past, the relations between producers were relatively clear, and objects knew their places', in the nineteenth century, 'through the increasing dominance of commodity production, relations between people appear[ed] as relations between the objects they exchange, and objects seem[ed] to take on the characteristics of subjects.'[45] In a famous passage, Marx argued that

> The form of wood [...] is altered if a table is made out of it. Nevertheless, the table continues to be wood, an ordinary, sensuous thing. But as soon as it emerges as a commodity, it changes into a thing which transcends sensuousness. It not only stands with its feet on the ground, but, in relation to all other commodities, it stands on its head, and evolves out of its wooden brain grotesque ideas, far more wonderful than if it were to begin dancing of its own free will.[46]

Here, in seeking to subject the mysteries of physical objects to intellectual scrutiny, Marx instead succeeded in rendering commodities haunted by relations that make them appear utterly independent of human action or will. The above passage suggests that a table can be inscrutably alive, not because of the role that it plays in human lives, nor because it is perceived as embodying the psyche of its manufacturer or owner, but because it *is* a table.[47] However, according to Derrida, the uncanny animation of inanimate objects, which renders them 'blurred, tangled, paralysing, aporetic, perhaps undecidable', has met with considerable cultural resistance:

> The flaw, the error of first sight is to see, and not to notice the invisible. If one does not give oneself up to this invisibility, then the table-commodity, immediately perceived, remains what it is not, a simple thing deemed to be trivial and too obvious. This trivial thing seems to comprehend itself [...], a quite simple wooden table. So as to prepare us to see this invisibility, to see without seeing, thus to think the body without body of this invisible visibility – the ghost is already taking shape – Marx declares that the thing in question, namely, the commodity, *is not so simple* (a warning that will elicit snickers from all the imbeciles, until the end of time, who never believe anything, of course, because they are so sure that they see what is seen, everything that is seen, only what is seen).[48]

Many of Gilman's contemporaries, particularly women writers, were quick to acknowledge the mysterious independence of objects from their owners, and specifically their tendency to influence human behavior, rather than vice versa. One writer noted that

The popularity of comfortable furniture [...] goes a great deal toward civilizing the people generally. It seems to us impossible for the human race to be good-natured and good tempered if forced to sit in a 'bolt upright' position in the extreme corner of a horse-hair covered sofa, with arms and back built on the very straightest and most perpendicular principle. [...] It is not surprising that our forefathers were given to atrocities and cruelties when they were brought up to endure such tortures as could be inflicted by the furniture of even twenty years ago; it served to deaden the sensibilities.[49]

Similarly, in a piece about Mary E. Wilkins, a reviewer quotes Johann Wolfgang von Goethe as asserting that 'the objects that surround us have their influence upon us', making us 'the slaves of objects around us.'[50] In Gilman's story, the narrator tells us that 'John is practical in the extreme. He has no patience with faith, an intense horror of superstition, and he scoffs openly at any talk of things not to be felt and seen and put down in figures.'[51] Like Derrida's snickering imbeciles, John can imagine nothing beyond the evidence of the senses. Undeceived by the superficial simplicity of objects and ignoring John's urgent exhortations 'not to give way to fancy in the least' (as he believes that this would exacerbate her condition), the narrator proceeds to see and interpret the 'invisible visibility' that resides within the wallpaper. She begins to conceive of it as containing two patterns, one covering and hiding the other. As she comments, 'The outside pattern is a florid arabesque, reminding one of a fungus. If you can imagine a toadstool in joints, an interminable string of toadstools, budding and sprouting in endless convolution – why, this is something like it.' She likens the swirling abstractions of this external pattern to 'strangled heads and bulbous eyes and waddling fungus growths' – in other words, to the distorted, heterogeneous 'monstrosities' of the grotesque, which are by their very nature antithetical to the abstract.[52] The inside pattern, by contrast, is 'always the same shape, only very numerous', the shape of 'a strange, provoking, formless sort of figure, that seems to skulk about behind that silly and conspicuous front design.'[53] 'Provoking' precisely because it is 'formless' and 'strange', the wallpaper tortures the narrator's consciousness with its indeterminacy, goading her to give form to the formless. Her persistence soon causes these figures to resemble women, kept in place by but attempting to free themselves from the front pattern that, after nightfall, takes the form of prison bars.

This substitution can also be traced back to the plot trajectory of Poe's 1838 story 'Ligeia'. The plot revolves claustrophobically around the enigmatic, eponymous, raven-haired wife of the narrator, her physical appearance, her intellect, his idolatry, her death after a long illness, and his subsequent prostration from grief, but also around his failure to remember how they met or who she is. Removing himself from the site of his bereavement, the narrator moves to England, where (mourning notwithstanding) he marries the Lady Rowena, who is in every respect Ligeia's polar opposite. The latter half of the narrative dwells primarily upon the archaic, gothic excess of the decoration of the hymeneal chamber to which he leads his blond, sketchily drawn second wife, and specifically upon the fabric of the tapestries, wall- and bed-hangings that, from different angles, display either arabesque or grotesque patterns. When, in an eerie reiteration of Ligeia's death, Rowena falls prey to a nameless and debilitating illness, she complains repeatedly of seeing strange and frightening things in the draperies, complaints that the narrator summarily dismisses. She finally succumbs to her malady, and the narrator watches over her body through the night, increasingly horrified as life seems to return to and then depart from the corpse, again and again. However, when she finally arises from her deathbed and casts off the cerements of the grave, it is no longer Rowena who stands in front of the narrator, but Ligeia, who appears to have possessed and transfigured the body of her pale successor.

In the final pages of Poe's story, it is the animation of the draperies that particularly oppresses and unnerves the narrator. Having made light of Rowena's fears, he is now a prey himself to precisely the same terrors – the fear that the objects he has chosen to decorate his home have somehow escaped his control, taking on a malevolent life of their own. Significantly, these fears disappear once he begins to focus on the body on the bed, as the narratorial gaze shifts from domestic objects to a minutely visualized depiction of Rowena's dying body. In what is little more than a catalogue of body parts, we are shown in graphic detail how 'the color disappeared from both eyelid and cheek [...]; the lips became doubly shrivelled and pinched in the ghastly expression of death; a repulsive clamminess and coldness overspread rapidly the surface of the body.'[54] Finally, when the corpse stands up from the bed, the narrator lingers again upon mouth, cheeks, and chin, before the revelation of height, eyes, and hair make it horribly clear that Rowena has been replaced by her dead predecessor. The minutely evoked spectacle of the female body therefore banishes the descriptions of furniture and decorations with which the latter half of the story is concerned; at precisely the same moment, the narrative ends abruptly.

It is for this reason that, just as the upholstery is no longer mentioned once Ligeia herself appears in the flesh, so the grotesque 'simple monstrosities' that adorn the room are all but forgotten as the narrative unfolds and the tapestries' arabesque nature is brought to the fore. In line with his preference for the abstractions of the arabesque over the distracting exuberance of more 'feminine' forms of interior decorating, Poe's narrators and his texts push toward representing women and the domestic as semantic blanks, open to interpretation and therefore offering no resistance to the conferral of a definitive and authoritative meaning upon them. In 'Ligeia', this is effected by circumscribing female figures within a specular regime surrounding the body, working from the principle that to render visible and knowable an object of fear is essentially to reduce its power to disturb and, in turn, to gain power over that object. Nevertheless, this triumph over the feminine is only achieved as the direct consequence of orchestrating a plot in which domestic objects fade into the background as the female body is made increasingly visible. In doing so, these stories betray a profound fear of material things, and of women's relationship with them, a relationship which, by partaking of the semantic slipperiness of metonymy, forecloses the possibility of binding the feminine within a fixed metaphorical regime. Nineteenth-century domestic ideology forced women into so close an interaction with things that they began to connote one another metonymically – to see a profusion of furniture and decoration was to think of women, and vice versa, so that meaning was always shuttling from one to the other. Faced with this unnerving semantic mobility, Poe's narrative gradually replaces material objects with the far more malleable spectacle of the female body. Even as Ligeia appears to make her triumphant return, vanquishing death itself, the plot transforms her into a vehicle for male certainty and knowledge. Moreover, as the next chapter illustrates, at the very moment that visibility and physicality are achieved, Poe's stories come to an sudden halt, refusing to grant his fictional women any further narrative space or agency, and effectively trapping them in the houses, texts, and bodies that have caused them to become sources of terror to men.

Arabesque Readings

In 'The Yellow Wall-Paper', the way in which the arabesque encourages the imposition of a single meaning upon its multivalent motifs is represented as a dangerous temptation, inscribing women who engage in such reading practices within conventional images of female insanity and abjection. The more the narrator applies her imaginative faculties to figuring out what exactly the arabesque wallpaper depicts, the fewer, less varied, and more recognizable its motifs appear, and the more her 'nervous weakness' is aggravated rather than relieved. Her postnatal depression is a symptom of her inability to adjust to a role that culture insists is natural to women, as well as an externalization of her refusal to do so. She is ill not only because culture automatically inserts her into a pattern where she does not fit, but also because she resists the insertion. It is therefore unsurprising that the spectacle of multiple women struggling against their own controlling pattern should agitate her more than the toadstools and eyes and fungus she initially sees. As she writes,

> Sometimes I think there are a great many women behind, and some-times only one, and she crawls around fast, and her crawling shakes it all over.
> [...]
> And she is all the time trying to climb through. But nobody could climb through that pattern – it strangles so; I think that is why it has so many heads.
> They get through, and then the pattern strangles them off and turns them upside down, and makes their eyes white!
> If those heads were covered or taken off it would not be half so bad.[55]

It is not so much the supernatural appearance of women emerging from the patterns in ordinary wallpaper that frightens the narrator, or even the dread that they might succeed in doing so. Instead, she is profoundly disturbed by the fact that they cannot escape, that the pattern is stronger than they are. The implication is that countless women are simultaneously experiencing both the violence of gender ideology and the difficulties of refusing its demands, forming a vast sociocultural web of oppression. Nonetheless, the confusion of pronouns in the above passage – between 'she' and 'they' – suggests that the oppression is so universal as to render the women she sees indistinguishable from one another. The women therefore play an ambivalent role as *part* of the irritating, ugly pattern. The rented house in the story consequently qualifies as a gothic castle, a space 'literally littered with female corpses whose tragic, repressed histories are unearthed during the course of [the heroine's] explorations.' The wallpaper exhibits a stylized version of the 'dreaded Female Gothic image of the imprisoned woman', an image that is often most dreaded by the heroine herself.[56] In Louisa May Alcott's *A Whisper in the Dark* (1889), for example, the heroine's mother is incarcerated in a mental asylum in a room directly above that in which the heroine is falsely imprisoned, and the heroine only ceases to fear her once she knows who she is, a revelation which coincides with her mother's death, too late for a tearful reunion.[57] In Gilman's story, as in Sheldon's, the narrator's fear of the imprisoned women in the wallpaper, victims of domestic ideology who have been horribly disfigured by it, makes her avert her gaze rather than confronting what they imply about her own circumstances.

As a result, and because they appear merely to form elements of the arabesque pattern rather than provide the ultimate 'meaning' that she is convinced it must conceal, she keeps struggling to find that meaning, until pronominal uncertainty and multiple images increasingly give way before a single female figure. As she begins to see the women outside in the grounds of the house during daylight hours, her sense of their multiplicity becomes eroded, and she muses, 'I often wonder if I could see her out of all the windows at once. But, turn as fast as I can, I can only see out of one at one time. And though I always see her, she *may* be able to creep faster than I can turn!'[58] From here, she begins to identify closely with the woman in the wallpaper, stating,

> I don't like to *look* out of the windows even – there are so many of those creeping women, and they creep so fast.
>   I wonder if they all come out of that wall-paper as I did?
>   [...]
>   I suppose I shall have to get back behind the pattern when it comes night, and that is hard!
>   It is so pleasant to be out in this great room and creep around as I please!
>   [...] here I can creep smoothly on the floor, and my shoulder just fits in that long smooch around the wall, so I cannot lose my way.

When her husband bursts into the locked room, her assimilation to the other woman is complete, and she gleefully tells him, '"I've got out at last, [...] in spite of you and Jane! And I've pulled off most of the paper, so you can't put me back!"'[59] The insanity that has overwhelmed her therefore coincides with a failed recognition of her shared experience with the women in the wallpaper, as fear pushes her away from community and toward hyperprivacy and personal isolation. This is precisely the position into which Gilman saw domestic capitalism as forcing middle-class housewives. In *Women and Economics*, she asserted that 'They obtain their economic goods by securing a male through their individual exertions, all competing freely to this end. No combination is possible.' This is exacerbated by the fact that 'Men meet one another freely in their work, while women work alone.' Consequently, 'The women's movements' have sought to counteract this atomization by cultivating 'the wide, deep sympathy of women for one another.'[60]

It is this sympathy that the narrator of 'The Yellow Wall-Paper' is tricked into rejecting by the arabesque nature of the wallpaper. By defining herself against the women implicated in the pattern, the narrator fails or refuses to intercept the message it conveys – that the room she occupies is a perilous place to be. The wallpaper was torn before she arrived, the bedpost is severely gnawed, 'the windows are barred [...], and there are rings and things in the walls', multiple signposts pointing to a wider context of oppression and imprisonment within everyday domestic space.[61] In the absence of a ghost, the wallpaper and the room it decorates come close to providing her with evidence of the home's deleterious effects upon its female inhabitants. Nevertheless, instead of reading these signs as duplicating the warning conveyed by the women in the wallpaper, she interprets the room as a nursery and the torn paper and bite marks as the work of children. She is therefore blinded to the implications of the house *as* a house, a place where women conduct their conjugal duties, work, give birth, die, and are sometimes destroyed by the rigors of domestic life.

In essence, the problem here is that she has replaced the subversive, metonymic grotesque with the arabesque, which tends toward unity and clarity of meaning. During the nineteenth century, the grotesque was closely linked to the fear of the socially destabilizing effects of commodity capitalism. Indeed, 'Carlyle and Marx both used the concept of the grotesque to describe the perverse experience of objects constituted by advertising and commodification.' The result was a disruption of the 'orderly surface of social experience', producing 'a form of manic activity severed from proper thought or coherent meaning.'[62] It was, in essence, the triumph of base matter over transcendent signification. Floral and animal designs were therefore rejected by Owen Jones' *Grammar of Ornament* (1856) as 'an *illicit realism* without design, a form of bodily presence that transgressed the proper formal boundaries of an object.' Cutting into the surface of an object, rendering it less smooth, 'decoration involves adding forms which threaten to overwhelm the functional shape of the object, producing [the effect of] bursting erupting bodies [...] design ritually labelled monstrous by design reformers and Modernists.'[63] In particular, 'any ornamentation that disguised or ignored the main lines of a room was in the poorest taste.'[64] Beyond such aesthetic scruples, the processes of machine manufacture made the kinds of abstract, stylized designs preferred by Jones and Poe far more desirable and cost effective. However, in the popular taste, the desire for realistic and highly wrought decoration remained strong throughout the century, sharply dividing the theorists from many of the users of these objects.[65] Gilman's story was written on the cusp of the twentieth century, the point at which modernist sensibilities began to view what they saw as Victorian clutter and excess as repulsive and grotesque.[66] By the 1870s, 'The term "Victorian" was already beginning to signify a unique kind of tastelessness which partakes of the freakish and grotesque.'[67] David Stove coined the term '*horror victorianorum*' to describe this attitude: 'that horror that even nowadays is felt [...] by almost everyone who visits a display of Victorian stuffed birds under glass, for example, or of Victorian dolls and dolls' clothes.'[68] The result is a dearth of such objects in museum collections, connected as they were with the practical rather than the artistic, the feminine, the disruptive, and the vulgar.

The overtly physical nature of the grotesque played a large part in what rendered it so objectionable, since it 'ignore[d] the closed, smooth, and impenetrable surface of the body and retain[ed] only its excrescences (sprouts and buds) and orifices, only that which leads beyond the body's limited space or into the body's depths.'[69] This riotous display of abject bodies went hand in hand with the 'fear of uncontrolled and uncontainable productive energy, of commodities compounded of unreconcilable or garbled principles of design, thrown up against one another in jumbled "battles" of styles, or placed incongruously in bizarrely inappropriate spaces.'[70] The grotesque disturbed the apparently smooth surface of 'normal' middle-class living; in Gilman's story, it threatens to expose the dark heart of the domestic experience for the very people who ostensibly created that experience – women. The horrific nature of what this testimony depicts, however, leads the narrator to misrecognize it, and she begins to be convinced that the room can truly become her own private space. When the rent expires and John's sister Jennie goes to prepare the couple's own house, the narrator feels immense relief, writing, 'So now she is gone, and the servants are gone, and the things are gone, and there is nothing left but that great bedstead nailed down, with the canvas mattress we found on it.' She comments, 'I quite enjoy the room, now it is bare again' (implying that she has seen it this way before, which she cannot possibly have done), describing it as 'quiet and empty and clean', and soon afterward begins stripping the paper from the walls, in order to liberate her newfound companion and alter ego.[71]

Matters are not quite as straightforward as this, however, since the relationship between women and property remained a vexed one in 'Progressive Era' America. As a passing reference to the Fourth of July insinuates, 'The Yellow Wall-Paper' is haunted by the specter of freedom. The narrator is seduced by the dream of a room that she thinks has become hers and hers alone. However, domestic ideology essentially denied the American ideals of individual freedom and self-determination to a large proportion of women. To occupy closed-off, private space that one owns and controls is to be free, but to occupy closed-off private space that one does not own and that is under the sway of another is to be held captive. Relieved of decoration and furniture, the narrator's sickroom is transformed into a locked prison cell to which she no longer holds the key (having thrown it out the window), implying that, for the middle-class wife, this is what underlies every nineteenth-century home once the ornamental surface has been stripped away.

However, despite her initial resistance to her husband's common-sensical approach to the house, like so many critics of American fiction, Gilman's narrator ultimately fails truly to see the 'visible invisibility', the 'body without body' of domestic ideology that the house connotes metonymically in the form of the multiple women she first sees in the wallpaper – a vision of mass female oppression and incarceration at the hands of the very home that purports to shelter and even empower them. The pattern mutilates and disfigures these female figures to the point where the narrator cannot bear to see them. However, assimilating themselves with the very domestic space that binds and chokes them, they have formed an uneasy alliance with the wallpaper. They, like the 'home-bound woman', appear as an accepted, habitual and even necessary element of the domestic world while all the time warping it by means of the 'freakishness' that the frenzied, lurid swirls of the wallpaper externalize. In this way, the story's literalization of the collaborative relationship between women and commodities suggests that the narrator *can* attain the privacy that she so desperately seeks, but only, crucially, and pessimistically, by accepting the limits of nineteenth-century gender roles. Furnished and decorated, the room's grotesqueries offer the narrator a privileged insight into the difficult relationship between women and houses, one that is predicated upon accepting one's absorption into domestic space, quite literally disappearing into the wallpaper.

Nonetheless, she cannot benefit from this offered insight, since she has established an antagonistic rather than a negotiative relationship with the home – and it is the home that wins. Because of the nature of the arabesque, the narrator is maneuvered into trying to discover a single meaning or truth in the wallpaper, and in doing so drags from their hiding place the female figures who have taken refuge there, appearing in all their gothic hideousness, twisted out of shape by the tyranny of the domestic. Frightened and repulsed, the narrator averts her gaze and rejects the compromise with the strangling pattern that they have embraced, searching for another, more stable, meaning rather than joining them. In doing so, ironically, she comes to mirror them exactly, metamorphosing from 'respectable' wife and mother to an avatar of the *fin-de-siècle* demonic feminine. After writing of how she 'thought seriously of burning the house' (the archetypal action of the Victorian madwoman in the attic), she bites the bed in anger, and wishes to do 'something desperate', imagining that jumping out the window would be 'admirable exercise'. When John returns from a trip to town and bursts into the room, she is crawling around on all fours, and he faints at the sight.[72]

In a final act of narrative revenge, the story therefore feminizes him by inflicting upon him an experience that corsets, dieting and lack of air and exercise inflicted upon the nineteenth-century female body. As her doctor, who has prescribed the 'rest cure', John has attempted to reinsert his wife into her body, to render her almost entirely corporeal by sleeping and gaining weight while eschewing all intellectual and creative activity. Contemporary medical thinking shrilly voiced anxieties surrounding emancipated women at the time, insisting that they were neglecting and imperiling the body (and particularly the reproductive organs), and risking psychological disorder, by embracing intellectual development.[73] It was 'better that the future mothers of the state should be robust, hearty, healthy women than that, by over study, they entail upon their descendants the germs of disease.'[74] According to one commentator,

> The nervous force, so necessary at puberty for the establishment of the menstrual function, is wasted on what may be compared as trifles to perfect health, for what use are they without health? The poor

sufferer only adds another to the great army of neurasthenics and sexual incompetents, which furnish neurologists and gynaecologists with so much of their material [...]. Bright eyes have been dulled by the brain-fag and sweet temper transformed into irritability, cross-ness and hysteria, while the womanhood of the land is deteriorating physically.

She may be highly cultured and accomplished and shine in society, but her future husband will discover too late that he has married a large outfit of headaches, backaches and spine aches, instead of a woman fitted to take up the duties of life.[75]

Consequently, as an anonymous article in praise of the rest cure makes horribly clear, medical science devoted itself to triumphing over the female will in order to subordinate it to the fertile, docile female body. In a passage unnervingly reminiscent of the end of 'Ligeia', the author invites us to

Think of the shudders, the horror of this soul as it is forced back into the body, – made to sleep, to take a pleasure in growing fat, to [...] smack its intangible lips! But I leave the playwright to explain the terrors of the courtship by which the soul was remarried to its carnal flesh. The curious facts are that when the woman rose from the bed, fat and rosy, the saint and poet had vanished; she was a housekeeper, a zealous cook; she took an eager part in village politics; and finally, she is the mother of a stout boy, and, you may be sure, is wedded to this world and the things thereof as long as he is in it.[76]

One potential outcome of resisting reembodiment was hysteria, which manifested via a 'vast, unstable repertoire of emotional and physical symptoms – fits, fainting, vomiting, choking, sobbing, laughing, paralysis – and the rapid passage from one to another suggested the lability and capriciousness traditionally associated with the femi-nine nature.'[77] Hysteria was therefore essentially grotesque, resisting a single unifying meaning. For one expert from the 1850s, the very presence of a hysterical woman within a house could render that domestic space

awful by the presence of a deranged creature under the same roof: her voice; her sudden and violent efforts to destroy things or persons; her vehement rushings to fire and window; her very tread and stamp in her dark and disordered and remote chamber, have seemed to penetrate the whole house; and, assailed by her wild energy, the very walls and roof have appeared unsafe, and capable of partial demolition.[78]

In other words, a house containing a hysterical woman was seen as the very opposite of the orderly home cared for by a submissive, efficient wife, and it is for this reason that, for contemporary readers of 'The Yellow Wall-Paper', 'the connection between madness and the protagonist's gender role constituted a scandal.'[79] Indeed, the hysterical woman herself constituted a scandalous mixing of femininity and intransigence, one that aligned her with the grotesque. Over the course of the eighteenth and nineteenth centuries, 'the female ceased to represent the writer's muse and with the Romantics, became instead a function of imagination that provided figurative language with a psychological source of meaning.'[80] This idealized vision of femininity functioned in precisely the same manner as the arabesque, an empty sign onto which external meanings could be affixed. This, at any rate, is the effect produced by Poe's 'Ligeia', where the entire movement of the narrative is toward disclosure, a moment of horrific specular fulfillment, in which the female body is subjected to a reifying narratorial and narrative gaze. This book as a whole argues that the problem of the spectral in American literature and culture is a problem of seeing, of looking, of being seen, and of eluding the gaze – not merely that of patriarchy, but (by extension) of knowledge, of desire for ontological certainty, clarity, and definition. In particular, images of dead, raped, or assaulted women that invite figurative readings can be seen as dangerously disingenuous, since 'the use of allegory [...] insists that we read past or through bodies; the violence they exhibit can paradoxically appear so blatant that it can barely be seen.'[81] Such representational forms themselves constitute a form of 'rhetorical violence' over and above the literal brutality that they depict, an 'expropriation of the feminine body, a reduction of this body to an object externally coded', since '[t]he violent reduction of a person to a sign literally kills the messenger, stripping the body that remains of any meaning of its own.'[82]

   Hysteria can be read optimistically as a disruptive sign, which 'jams' the operations of such allegorical violence, actively resistant to semantic ordering and defying legibility. The crawling, biting, animalistic lunatic that the narrator of 'The Yellow Wall-Paper' becomes is the epitome of the nineteenth-century abject women, frighteningly corporeal, a facsimile of Charlotte Brontë's Bertha Rochester, a source of masculine horror and everything that the decorous, slim, asexual wifely paragon or self-effacing muse is not. Unlike Bertha Rochester and Poe's Madeline Usher (discussed in the next chapter), however, Gilman's narrator leaves the house in which she has been buried alive still standing, creating a space for others to occupy, and this is precisely what the other female writers discussed here do, repapering her borrowed room with patterns that eschew the fluid abstractions of the arabesque.

3

'Dancing Like a Bomb Abroad': Dawson's 'An Itinerant House' and the Haunting Cityscape

> Few women writers have so strong a hold upon the public as Emma Frances Dawson. She is known and not known. She is sought and cannot be found. Her name is spoken and all acknowledge her superiority, but the voice drops to a mysterious whisper as they enquire: 'Have you ever seen Miss Dawson?'[1]

Written just a few years before the publication of Emma Frances Dawson's *An Itinerant House and Other Stories* in 1897, this description of the elusiveness of the largely forgotten San Francisco-based writer (once a close friend of Ambrose Bierce) suggests as much about the public perceptions of female authors, the anonymity of city life, and the slippery nature of Dawson's own characters, as it does about the woman herself. The title story, 'An Itinerant House' (1896), recounts how, when Felipa, a young Mexican boarding-house owner, dies of grief following the discovery that her lover (Anson) is married, he and his friends succeed in bringing her back to life with the help of their combined medical knowledge, some frenzied violin playing and a rather hazy conception of the possibilities of magnetism. In direct contrast to Edgar Allan Poe's customary narrative structure (explored in the previous chapter and below), which leads up to and abruptly halts at the moment at which the beautiful dead woman returns to life, the story unfolds from here, centering around Felipa's outrage at having been forcibly returned to her body against her will.

The male first-person narrator recounts how Felipa's eyes snap open and 'her lips formed one word: "Idiots!"' after which she refuses to speak. The men attempt to leave, conscious that 'People began to stir about the house. The prosaic sounds jarred on our strained nerves', but 'Felipa's upraised hand' detains them. A 'ghastly vision', she curses them, demanding to know what right they had to bring her back from a death that she welcomed, ordering them never to enter the room again and proclaiming '"These very walls shall remember – here, where I have been so tortured no one shall have peace!"' Stunned, the men depart, and the narrator notes that 'We saw her but once more, when with a threatening nod toward us she left the house.'[2] During the years that follow, several members of the group die in mysterious accidents, and Wynne and Arne, two total strangers who befriend the survivors, happen to lodge in the very room in which the revivification has occurred. Both men rapidly fall prey to identical wasting illnesses while inhabiting the cursed boarding house, which seems to move around the city at random, and to which the main characters repeatedly and unexpectedly find themselves returning. On each unwitting return, the narrator and Volz, the only other living member of the original group, fail to realize where they are until they unintentionally repeat the exact words that they speak when Felipa dies, the patterned wallpaper moves uncannily, and yet another of their friends expires before their eyes.

The story therefore revolves around both an eerily unpredictable cityscape and a sexually active, victimized, elusive woman, motifs that are central to the depiction of the nineteenth-century American city as a gothic locale. Erotically charged, anonymous to the point of alienation, and disturbingly disorienting, in works like Poe's 'The Man of the Crowd' (1840) and George Lippard's *The Quaker City, or, The Monks of Monk Hall* (1844), the urban landscape increasingly took on a dark and threatening aspect in the second half of the nineteenth century. In a period marked by economic upheaval and considerable financial uncertainty for businesses and individuals alike, the exponential growth of the American city produced a profound ambivalence in the nation psyche.[3] Characterized by 'perpetual movement', it was 'experienced both as an explosive kind of liberation and as an annihilating state of disintegration and disorientation'; in Lippard's terms, mid-century New York was 'a voluptuous Queen sitting in her gorgeous palace, drunk with wine and blinded by the glare of the festival of lights.'[4] Dawson's story simultaneously works within and against this vision of a frighteningly sexual, feminized, materialistic, and disordered urban landscape, while employing the shifting, illicit world of commodities as a kind of smoke screen for the feminine subject, thereby sidestepping the pitfalls presented by the commodified, objectified female body. In essence, 'An Itinerant House' therefore exploits the associations with female malevolence conjured up by the

American city, while refusing to materialize a ghost as such, evading the perils to which, as the foregoing chapters illustrate, visibility exposed Gilded-Age fictional (dead) woman. Instead, if offers us the specter of the city itself.

As Lippard's comment figuratively implies, many of the fears inspired by the rapid expansion of urban spaces coalesced around the issue of female sexuality, not least because the city offered women greater opportunities for personal freedom, public exposure, and financial gain than ever before. Precisely because the ideal woman was both 'pure' to the point of disembodiment and effectively incarcerated in the home, the eroticized, peripatetic female body came to occupy a central position in depictions of the city as a perilous place both for women and because of women. Urban growth was accompanied by a sharp rise in prostitution, contributing to perceptions of the city as 'dark, dangerous, and inherently sexual', as opposed to the ostensibly asexual, moral haven of the home.[5] The anxious sense that the fluidity and superficiality of city life made it impossible ever really to know the people one meets – to be certain of their moral and social status – found a ready scapegoat in the figure of the socially and geographically mobile woman, with the deceptively well-dressed prostitute as the avatar of dangerous urban womanhood par excellence. In a culture where femininity's sole purpose was transforming the home into a site of calm stability for world-weary men, the itinerant, urban woman figuratively rendered the spaces she occupied fluid and uncertain. It is for this reason that images of the female corpse proliferated in nineteenth-century depictions of the American city, functioning simultaneously as a warning of the violence seen as inherent in city life and as its antidote, providing an immobile female form to ensure the conceptual stability usually safeguarded by domestic femininity.

Working girls

As industrialization transformed the still-youthful republic from a largely agrarian society to one increasingly concentrated in urban centers, traditional social ties loosened, and individuals found themselves possessing 'a kind and amount of personal freedom which has no analogy whatsoever under other conditions.'[6] For women in particular, city life offered unprecedented opportunities for upward social mobility, and personal and financial independence, although the range of employment open to women remained limited, confined largely to teaching, dress-making, domestic service, and positions in shops. While all working women ran the risk of being accused of loose morals, or worse, being taken advantage of by predatory male employers, a position behind a sales counter carried distinct connotations of sexual impropriety, primarily because it placed the female body on display, along with the other merchandise.[7] Perhaps the most familiar of these pioneering, self-sufficient, self-commodifying city women was Mary Cecilia Rogers, the 'Beautiful Cigar Girl' whose apparently violent death inspired Poe's 'The Mystery of Marie Rogêt' (1842) and numerous other fictional and nonfictional narratives. Tastefully dressed and with 'pleasing manners', Rogers exemplified the uncertainties inherent in employing clothing as an indicator of class and respectability.[8] Mary Rogers looked like a 'nice girl', but was impossible to pin down socially, her occupation placing both her class and her sexual status in doubt. Overtly alluring and yet outwardly modest, she was a sexually ambiguous sign in a manner that aligned her with the deceptive appearance of the contemporary prostitute, who had considerable disposable income and economic motivation to purchase clothing, personal adornments and cosmetics, turning herself into her own marketable commodity.[9]

The problem, in essence, was with the emerging commodity culture itself, which made such social blurring possible. Seductive, sensual, often orientalized, and encouraging earthly desires long suppressed by Protestant ideology, this new material world celebrated aesthetics for its own sake, rather than for utility or as an index to inner moral goodness. Clashing uncomfortably with centuries of self-restraint and self-denial, the new culture became rapidly associated with the burgeoning feminist movement and the troubling figure of the New Woman, perceived as connoting feminized self-indulgence, waste, idleness, and irresponsibility.[10] Middle-class femininity therefore found itself in a rather awkward position; women were enjoined to spend money first in adorning themselves to procure husbands and then in the cause of producing a homelike space, yet doing so exposed them to censure for abandoning themselves to the excesses of selfish material desire.[11] In particular, Lori Merish argues that, for middle-class women, consumerism was associated with a lack of proper self-restraint, a disregard for proper social and physical boundaries, as overspending was implicitly linked with sexual promiscuity and a tendency to stray beyond the bounds of the home – in other words, independence.[12] Nineteenth-century American sculpture and art are therefore teeming with images of Pandora, in which the infamous box is a small, decorative affair that she looks at with desire, poised to destroy the world by indulging her hunger for both knowledge and material objects.[13]

Nor was this entirely a matter of figurative associations. In a job market that closely circumscribed the opportunities available to women, prostitution offered perhaps the quickest, most reliable, and least (economically) exploitative option for many.[14] Duplicitous and illegible in her unnerving resemblance to 'respectable' young women, the prostitute was most problematic because she revealed the (supposedly) superficial and constructed nature of all femininity.[15] Consequently, 'prostitutes – and especially streetwalkers – served both as symbols and as scapegoats for the social uncertainty that accompanied the changing urban community in the mid-nineteenth century', indexes to but also agents of the perceived erosion of public morals.[16] Indeed, the prostitute was accorded almost preternatural powers, portrayed as a vampire debasing the morals and sucking the lifeblood of vast numbers of men. In the words of one commentator writing in 1836, 'a few courtesans corrupt whole cities.'[17] Later in the century, James D. McCabe Jr. depicted prostitutes as 'living corpses'. Disfigurement and death inevitably lay in wait for the prostitute, since 'Disease of the most loathsome kind fastens itself upon her, and she literally rots to death. [...] Foul, bloated with gin and disease, distorted with suffering and despair, the poor creatures do what they can to hasten their sure doom.'[18]

Parallel to these associations with artificiality, monstrosity, and abject physicality, the prostitute or fallen woman was often figured in terms of restless, unsettling mobility. In 1896, the year Dawson's story was published, Bradford K. Pierce wrote, 'Vice gives a woman's nature a more terrible wrench than a man's. It is harder for her to draw a veil over the past; it seems constantly to come back to her and rebuke her and overwhelm her with disgrace.' Such a woman invariably found 'nearly every honourable door closed' to her.[19] In other words, the fallen woman was both irrevocably defined by her past (which was so imprinted upon her person as to be visible to polite society at large) and automatically vagrant, outcast, one who 'walks' rather than remaining 'safely' at home, with no hope of returning, and 'selling herself' remained her only means of support.[20] The prostitute was therefore the polar opposite of the domestic woman, one who, instead of remaining properly incarcerated in the home, 'dances like a Bomb, abroad,/And swings upon the hours'.[21]

As institutional changes made commercialized sex less visible toward the end of the century, the hostility directed toward the prostitute was transferred to the figure of the New Woman, who became 'a sexually freighted metaphor for social disorder and protest' during the Progressive Era. The 'single, highly educated, economically autonomous New

Woman' eschewed marriage, 'fought for professional visibility, espoused innovative, often radical, economic and social reforms, and wielded real political power.'[22] That power manifested primarily in an increased public foregrounding of issues such as 'appropriate or "rational" dress for women, contraception, the social purity movement – which advocated policing men's sexuality rather than women's – occupations for women, women abstaining from marriage, and the extension of the franchise to women.'[23] Neatly sidestepping these broader social issues, the many controversies that rapidly sprang up in response to the New Woman instead centered on the body and sexuality of the rebelling, home-denying woman. The all-too visible target of male resentment at women's widening independence and mobility, the discourses positing the female body as inherently diseased gained added impetus, bolstered by scientific jargon.[24] Women were increasingly defined by their sexual organs, and therefore as essentially unhealthy and weak, as well as potentially dangerous to men and children, particularly those who endangered their fertility by attempting to break out of the rigidly confined domestic role.[25]

As early as 1836, *The Sun* announced that 'public occupations are dangerous. A woman who works outside the home commits a biological crime against herself and her community.'[26] By the end of the century, 'educators, legislators and physicians' had banded together to assert loudly that any woman who placed extra-domestic work or intellectual stimulation 'above her duty to the race' – procreation and childrearing – 'not only risked nervous exhaustion and wasting diseases; she might also develop dangerously masculine physiological characteristics. Her breasts might shrivel, her menses become irregular or cease altogether. Sterility could ensue, facial hair might develop.'[27] These fears were predicated upon the idea that 'women's virtue depended upon their domestic isolation', and that to move outside of the home would therefore compromise that virtue, but also that, without a woman ensconced in the home, 'no sphere would remain to both tame and reward male aggression.'[28] This was especially important in the city, where many men lived in boarding houses bereft of virtuous female influence. As Jacob Riis wrote in *How the Other Half Lives* (1890), one such establishment was only dragged out of the utter degradation into which he saw it as having sunk by the intervention of

the new house-keeper, a mild-mannered, but exceedingly strict little body, who had a natural faculty of drawing her depraved surroundings within the beneficent sphere of her strong sympathy, and withal of exacting respect or her orders. The worst elements had been banished from the house in short order under her management, and for the rest a new era of self-respect had dawned.[29]

Similarly, in Charles L. Sheldon's evangelical tale, *In His Steps* (1897), a pure young woman is depicted as 'taming' the inhabitants of an urban slum:

> Rachel had not sung the first line before the people in the tent were all turned towards her, hushed and reverent. Before she had finished the verse the Rectangle was subdued and tamed. It lay like some wild beast at her feet and she sang it into harmlessness. Ah! What were the flippant, perfumed, critical audiences in concert halls compared with this dirty, drunken, impure, degraded, besotted humanity that trembled and wept and grew strangely, sadly thoughtful, under the touch of the divine ministry of this beautiful young woman.[30]

In the face of an increasingly urban and chaotic society, where the powers of the home were on the wane, women's domestic powers were put to public use as a means of cleansing society of the ills of drunkenness, prostitution, and their attendant diseases.[31] Vitally, however, this women's power was essentially disembodied, channeled through the voice and passive influence rather than physical action on the street and on the barricades. Woman was, ideally, 'pure as the glistening snow-clad peaks in midst of the moral degradation which taints manhood.'[32] As society became progressively more complex and unpredictable, these idealizations became ever more entrenched, with white, middle-class femininity stridently defined as fundamentally sexless and bodiless, even as women's destiny was seen to be ruled by their sexual organs.[33]

Predictable and effectively immobilized, the domestic woman, all but imprisoned or entombed within and conflated with a feminized yet male-dominated domestic space, was American society's solution to cultural vertigo, as Charlotte Perkins Gilman imagines a narrow-minded reader of her theories crying, "'Home, with the woman out – there is no such thing!'"[34] A female journalist remarked severely in 1868, 'All men whose opinion is worth having, prefer the simple and genuine girl of the past, with her tender little ways and pretty bashful modesties, to this loud and rampant modernization.'[35] As this suggests, the insistence on sedentary, dependent womanhood was all but inextricable from the sense of profound geographical instability produced by urban expansion. The bourgeois wife was, ideally, a point of stability and moral rectitude

in a world where the rigors of capitalism and the competitive environment of the workplace left American men emotionally stunted and
ethically compromised. Much nineteenth-century domestic ideology
was grounded in the assumption that men were rendered threatening
and morally suspect by work, which by its very nature is performed
outside of the home. According to Catharine Beecher, the man who
'has been drawn from the social ties of home, and has spent his life in
the collisions of the world, seldom escapes without the most confirmed
habits of cold, and revolting selfishness.'[36] Against this emotional
deformity, woman was the 'keeper of sensibility in a heartless world',
charged with a sacred duty to turn the home into a 'retreat' that would
'rescue the American man' from the poisonous atmosphere to which
he was constantly exposed in the world outside.[37] It was, therefore,
the middle-class wife and mother's moral duty to bury herself alive in
the home, so as to remain a fixed and purifying presence in an otherwise chaotic modernity, while unmarried women were urged to hide
away at home for their own safety. Women stayed still so that men
could roam the streets and wilderness at will, and for this reason 'any
woman alone on New York City streets at night could be arrested as a
prostitute.'[38]

The consolations of the dead woman

Nevertheless, keeping women still in an urban context was far from
easy. One potential solution was offered by the spectacle of the female
corpse, which, evacuated of subjectivity and offering no obstructions
to a reifying male gaze, was (like arabesque patterns) both docile and
conveniently available for figurative reinterpretation, while remaining
highly sexualized and indeed commodified. In Walt Whitman's 'The
City Dead House' (1867), for example, the body of a prostitute is simultaneously celebrated and denigrated as a symbol of female carnality and
physical corruption. The corpse is described as

> that wondrous house – that delicate fair house – that ruin!
>   That immortal house, more than all the rows of dwellings ever
> built!
>   Or white-domed Capitol itself, with majestic figure surmounted –
> or all the old high- spired cathedrals;
>   That little house alone, more than them all – poor, desperate
> house!
>   [...]

Dead house of love! house of madness and sin, crumbled! crush'd
House of life – erewhile talking and laughing – but ah, poor house!
dead, even then;
Months, years, an echoing, garnish'd house – but dead, dead,
dead.[39]

Sliding from the image of a noble, marble, public monument connoting
political or religious power, to a ruined, crushed, empty 'house of
madness and sin', abandoned by the soul in death, the poem implicitly condemned the material and the corporeal, and is but one example
of the proliferation of highly sexualized images of dead female bodies
that pervaded nineteenth-century art and culture. Among these were
numerous folktales about live burial, many of which involve young,
frequently pregnant brides subjected to appalling physical torments when
they are mistakenly placed living in the grave.[40] These 'representations
of beautiful women safely dead remained the late-nineteenth-century
painter's favourite way of depicting the transcendent spiritual value
of passive feminine sacrifice', while simultaneously transforming that
femininity into objects of a gaze unencumbered by the social restrictions
surrounding living women.[41] Reduced to the physical and the external,
the female corpse was rendered defenseless and violated, both (as argued
in Chapter 1) by the act of representation itself, and by the manner in
which the image positions the viewer, interpolating a male scopophilic,
even necrophilic gaze, rather than one of identification or empathy.
Representations of femininity that focused exclusively upon the materiality of a fetishized female body rendered that body little more than the
object of a male gaze, pure surface, devoid of interiority, easily defined,
studied, and understood.

Indeed, such images were often employed as a means of visualizing
death itself. Death as a concept is characterized by an irreducible resistance to knowledge. Since it is always 'outside any speaking subject's
personal experience', death can never be directly rendered, but must
instead be designated by way of metaphor.[42] A proliferation of objects,
rituals and discourses surrounding death and dying therefore struggle
to give identifiable shape to that which cannot be pictured or even
comprehended. The function of funeral rituals in general is to 'convert
"homeless souls" [...] into comfortably enshrined or immortalized souls'
by effecting '*the symbolic transformation of a threatening, inert image (of
the corpse) into a vital image of eternal continuity (the soul).*'[43] Statues and
pictures of the deceased present the most obvious vehicles for this figurative regime, the mimetic image of the dead person serving to herald

the separation of the idea of the individual from the defunct physical body, and to provide 'an acceptable memory-image of the dead to cancel out the sight of them after death.'[44] Gravestones and funerary sculpture engender 'a stable relation between subjects and objects', counteracting the uncomfortable fact that the newly deceased continue eerily to resemble the living.[45] In the nineteenth century, portraits and photographs of the dead fulfilled this function, as did the cosmetic manipulation of the corpse, culminating, particularly after the Civil War, in the practice of embalming, thus ensuring that there was a clear and stable image that could be attached to the unnerving void left by death.[46]

Moreover, the 'transformation of what was a living person and then an inanimate but destabilised decaying corpse into a permanent and stable inanimate representation' places the deceased firmly and irrevocably outside of the realm of the living. Such representations enact a freezing into fixity and reification of death's unnerving processes and conceptual elusiveness, asserting that the dead are undeniably dead, the past is ineradicably past, and that it is better for all involved that this should continue indefinitely to be the case. In a sense, however, as Elisabeth Bronfen argues, *all* art effectively does this to its subjects, the visual representation of a living individual 'killing' that individual by portraying him or her as motionless and changeless – as a dead object rather than a living subject. This was the logic behind the Victorian obsession with paintings and literary descriptions of dead women, which literalized the violence of visual representation at the same time as transforming femininity into the signifier of which death is the signified.[47] Femininity is particularly amenable to such figurative transformation, since 'Like the decaying body, the feminine is unstable, liminal, disturbing'; possessing 'no fixed signified in the symbolic order', femininity is therefore open to being exploited figuratively.[48] Used to signify, not itself, but death, the female dead body is made over into an empty cipher that gestures only beyond itself, denied self-determination in order to remove all sense of mystery and uncertainty for the (male) observer.

The need to give visible, concrete forms to death in this manner can be traced back to the idea that 'If security and empowerment is connected with the gaze in that something is made present to sight, then what remains absent from sight perturbs and questions power.'[49] This is the central impetus behind the detective genre, in which the plot is driven by the need to determine the facts surrounding a death – frequently that of a desirable woman. Until these facts have been established, the dead woman effectively occupies a 'revenant position', as the mystery surrounding both her death and her unknowable femininity means that proper burial cannot take place and her 'corpse can[not] lie peacefully'.[50] In other words, when the unnerving unknowableness of both women and death cannot be reduced by means of hard facts and visible markers, that woman becomes one of the walking dead.[51]

The death of a beautiful woman: Mary Rogers

The new urban landscape of nineteenth-century America was the natural birthplace of the detective story, not least as a result of a number of high-profile murders of beautiful young women who also fit perfectly the profile of urban femininity. While the 1836 murder of Helen Jewett, an 'up-market' New-York prostitute, eventually resulted in the conviction of one of her customers or lovers, that of a young woman named Mary Rogers in 1841 never went to trial, and offered to the emerging mass reading public an enigma that remains impenetrable to this day. The discovery on the shores of the Hudson of a corpse believed to be that of Rogers, a girl whose job in a New-York cigar shop had won her considerable fame due to her remarkable personal beauty, caused a media frenzy, including Poe's pioneering true-crime piece, 'The Mystery of Marie Rogêt'. Every newspaper in New York vied for public attention, spawning a swarm of conflicting information and clashing moral attitudes. While many saw the 'Beautiful Cigar Girl' as the innocent victim of one of the many gangs of marauding thugs that roamed the city's outskirts, or of a jealous lover's intemperate passions, others took the opportunity to vilify a female population associated both with an ungodly concern for personal adornment and with improper sexual forwardness. In the relatively unregulated city, temptations (both material and sexual) were many, and easily procured. Only a few months prior to Rogers' disappearance, the trial had taken place in New York of one Madam Restell, a notorious and highly successful abortionist who had caused the death of one of her clients during a botched operation, and who is described as 'brash, vulgar, audacious, and duplicitous, a woman, "tricked out in gorgeous finery."'[52] Commenting on the case, the *Police Gazette* screamed,

> It is well known that females frequently die in ordinary childbirth. How many, then, who enter her halls of death may be supposed to expire under her execrable butchery? Females are daily, nay, hourly, missing from our midst who never return. Where do they go? What becomes of them? Does funeral bell ever peal a note for their passage? Does funeral train ever leave her door? Do friends ever gather round

the melancholy grave? No! An obscure hole in the earth; a consignment to the savage skill of the dissecting knife, or a splash in the cold wave, with the scream of the night blast for a requiem, is the only death service bestowed upon her victims. Witness this, ye shores of Hudson! Witness this, Hoboken beach![53]

What is notable about this article is the subordination of images of personal pain and suffering on the part of the alleged victims to the insistence that proper burial must take place. The problem here is not that women have been tortured and killed, dismembered and silenced, unable to bear witness to what has been done to them, but rather that society at large is denied the opportunity to mourn them and to fix them firmly in the grave by discovering what has happened to them and where their bodies are. What haunts this passage is the knowledge that they have somehow, scandalously, evaded the all-seeing eye of modernity, rendering them literally uncanny. This piece therefore calls for a more penetrating social gaze, rather than an end to the violence itself; equally, it offers no critique of the system of confining acceptable sexual encounters to within the sphere of monogamous marriage, or the lack of reliable contraception that rendered such terminations necessary in the first place. While it was never proven that Rogers had procured an abortion, the press seized eagerly on this often dangerous operation, and the unscrupulous individuals who profited from urban women's need for the service, as the cause of her death. Poe even rewrote 'Marie Rogêt' in order to incorporate new 'evidence' regarding her visit to an abortionist. Fictional and 'factual' accounts of her death insistently coded her both as chaste, innocent victim, and as promiscuous shop girl, illicitly procuring abortions and running away with strange men, a personification of the dangerous, sexualized city.[54] The possibility of a single cause, and therefore a single image of Rogers' character, put a satisfying end to this agony of public speculation. As a writer in *The Tribune* announced,

Thus has the fearful mystery, which has struck fear and terror to so many hearts, been at last explained by circumstances in which no one can fail to perceive a Providential agency. [...] We rejoice most deeply at this revelation, and that the unhappy victim's death is relieved of some of the horrors with which conjecture, apparently well founded, has surrounded it.[55]

In the absence of a definite suspect, however, Mary Rogers' body itself was dwelt upon in several accounts, which lingered on the appalling transformation of 'what was but a few days back, the image of its Creator, the loveliest of his work and the tenement of an immortal soul', into 'a blackened and decomposed mass of putrefaction, painfully disgusting to sight and smell.' After a minute catalogue of her clothing, the piece quoted above goes on to detail her sunken eyes and distended jaw, describing the body as 'one mass of putrefaction and corruption, on which the worms were revelling at their will', clothed in a dress 'already so discolored and half rotten, as to render it almost impossible to be identified, and [which] was so impregnated with the effluvia from her person, that scarcely any person would venture to touch or examine it.'[56] An article in the *New York Herald* described her face as having been 'battered and butchered, to a mummy', to the point where her 'features were scarcely visible'.[57] Similarly, *The Times and Commerical Intelligencer* carried an article that recounted the moment when her fiancé, Daniel Payne, first saw her corpse:

> Her whom but a few days back, he had seen 'exulting in her youth', filled with life, hope and animation, whom he so ardently wished to make his wedded wife, to fold to his bosom, to press to his 'heart of hearts', now lay before him an inanimate mass of matter, so hideous and offensive that the bare idea of coming into contact with it was almost sufficient to make the gorge rise.[58]

These descriptions rendered external and physical the moral and sexual corruption that less sympathetic accounts saw as lurking in Mary Rogers' soul. Where once she had functioned as an uncomfortable mixture of purity and availability, of respectability and wanton self-display, in these passages the very instruments of her potential deception – her attractive body and tasteful clothing – are no longer alluring and misleading, but rather to all too revealing and repulsive.

Indeed, not merely women's clothing but the sheer number of commodities that the new industrial centers produced were seen as a profoundly destabilizing force in nineteenth-century urban life, driving countless middle-class men to ruin in their efforts to obtain them for demanding wives and lovers, and permitting women to revel in an illicit world of material objects, personal adornment and eroticized display. Disturbed by the apparently meaningless superficiality of commodity culture, nineteenth-century American culture strove 'to organize the meanings attached to commodities – to domesticate and moralize them', a cause taken up primarily by 'fashion magazine editors and authors of advice literature.'[59] The common vein running through such tirades and jeremiads was that it was the duty of the middle-class wife to bind the home's disparate contents together into an organizing system and a single unified meaning – that is, HOME – converting them from morally suspect vehicles of greed and vanity to vital components of domestic and conjugal felicity. The furniture and decoration in a home, chosen, arranged and cared for by the wife, although paid for by the husband, therefore testified primarily to her taste and her virtues.

Vitally, however, despite urging middle-class women to spend in order to keep themselves and their homes attractive to men, who might otherwise avail of the ample opportunities in city life to find their pleasures elsewhere, the advice books of the time cautioned against excess. Such works insisted earnestly 'that the female had depths far more valuable than her surface. By implying that the essence of the woman lay inside or underneath her surface, the invention of depths in the self entailed making the material body of the woman appear superficial.'[60] In particular, Nancy Armstrong asserts, 'Advice books, fashion magazines, and etiquette manuals cautioned young women against emulating the arts of the painted woman, sometimes a prostitute but more often a woman of fashion, who poisoned polite society with deception and betrayal by dressing extravagantly and practicing the empty forms of false etiquette.'[61] An 1839 article in *Godey's Lady's Book* cried, 'Oh! It is grievous to see a being standing upon the threshold of an immortal existence, created for glorious purposes, and with faculties to fulfil them, discussing the merits of a ribbon, or the form of a bow, or the width of a frill, as earnestly as if the happiness of her race, or her soul's salvation depended upon her decision.'[62] Another asserted grimly, 'Beauty without virtue is like a painted sepulchre, fair without, but within full of corruption.'[63]

Gilman herself saw the domestic, commodified woman as trapping men (particularly those in white-collar jobs whose 'respectability' depended on their wives not 'needing' to work) within an endless round of work and stress, constantly struggling to keep up with the material demands of their wives. As she put it, 'He thinks it right and beautiful to maintain the dainty domestic vampire, and pours forth his life's service to meet her insatiate demands.'[64] The purpose of the housewife was therefore

> To consume food, to consume clothes, to consume houses and furniture and decorations and ornaments and amusements, to take and take and take forever, – from one man if they are virtuous, from many if they are vicious, but always to take and never to think of giving anything in return except their womanhood, – this is the enforced condition of the mothers of the race.[65]

Gilman's *The Home* therefore asserted that 'There is no pathos, but rather a repulsive horror in the mass of freakish ornament on walls, floors, chairs, tables, on specially contrived articles of furniture, on her own body and the helpless bodies of her little ones, which marks the unhealthy riot of expression of the overfed and underworked lady of the house.'[66] In Gilman's view, housewives externalized their frustrations through commodities to such an extent that they themselves became embodiments of 'freakishness' and 'horror', adopting forms of clothing and personal adornment that could barely be distinguished from the riotous patterns and unrestrained consumerism overwhelming the interior of their homes.

Gilman's scruples were by no means universal, however, and disappearing into the material objects and decorative elements of the home this was precisely what the role of middle-class wife demanded of women in the nineteenth century.[67] Since the epitome of the feminine domestic ideal was 'not a woman who attracts the gaze as she did in an earlier culture, but one who fulfills her role by disappearing into the woodwork to watch over the household', so as not to be *seen* as pure surface, the wife herself had to *become* pure surface, by allowing the house to absorb her and conceal her as a visual object.[68] The respectable nineteenth-century wife must all but vanish into the furniture, even to the point of wearing chintz patterns all but identical to those covering her sofas, armchairs, walls, and floors; contemporary fashion also worked hard to effect this absorption by confining and restricting the body. So-called 'spiritual' women went to great lengths to downplay their physicality:

> nineteenth-century white women were expected to be delicate, with narrow ribs and tiny waists, to emphasize both their differences from men and their ethereal nature. Women wore corsets both to achieve a fashionable waist size and because of doctors' insistence that women's muscles were so delicate that a corset was needed to hold them in place.[69]

Consequently, 'The corseted body was the social body, controlled and regulated; the uncorseted body was a social disgrace.'[70] Paradoxically, then, by transforming herself into a visual and aesthetic object, the lady of the house could exploit the language of domestic respectability and the ideology that demanded that she fade into the background of the spaces of the home. In the logic of the supernatural fiction I discuss here, it became possible for fictional women to remove their problematic bodies from the public sphere in which they were vilified and restricted, and to escape instead into the inorganic world of commodified display, by attending to the very duties indispensible to 'true' femininity. After all, it was the furniture and interior decoration of a house that most fittingly and transparently displayed the middle-class wife's moral worth to those around her, so that the staging of her domestic virtues becomes inextricably bound up with otherwise redundant ornament and consumerism. By eschewing the visible, highly problematic body, female characters in such tales succeeded in gaining subversive power over the spaces of the home, as is made clear in Harriet Prescott Spofford's 'The Amber Gods', when, having finally been released from her dying body, which has been endlessly objectified by her artist husband, the narrator exclaims,

> Why! I thought arms held me. How clear the space is! The wind from outdoors, rising again, must have rushed in. There is the quarter striking. How free I am! No one here? No swarm of souls about me? Oh, those two faces looked from a great mist, a moment since; I scarcely see them now. Drop, mask! I will not pick you up! Out, out into the gale! back to my elements![71]

By rejecting the body, and embracing the complexities both of commodities and of death-as-absence, the freedom offered by post-mortem existence allows Yone to escape her husband's representational violence. Precisely this utopian, supernatural means of escape from physical constraint was essentially what was offered, first by Spiritualism, and near the end of the century, by New Thought and Christian Science, two enormously popular quasi-religious movements in the United States.[72] Relying on the power of mind over matter, these movements sought to purge society of impure elements in the form of both material wealth and sensual lust, which they saw as producing moral and physical degradation.[73] They therefore urged their followers (frequently women suffering from poor health, unhappy marriages, and financial difficulties) to cultivate and harness the disembodied power of thought in order to allow others to transcend the base matter from which they are made and by which they are tormented, and achieve a new, healthier, more prosperous and independent existence. For Mary Baker Eddy, founder of Christian Science, 'matter' was 'implicitly a code word for the body, and particularly for the female body with all its connotations of sexual vulnerability and social subordination.' Transcending the body could allow the subject's voice to be more clearly heard on the astral plane, opening her up to greater sources of power and knowledge.[74] New Thought therefore made use, as Spiritualism had around mid-century, of the long-standing sense in American bourgeois culture in particular that women were essentially self-sacrificing, desire-less, bodiless angels – in both cases, within radical movements that sought financial, sexual, and political equality for women. The new era of mankind's salvation, these modes of thinking insisted, would be led by pure, incorporeal women who could nonetheless control and shape matter to their will, through their innate proximity to the higher spiritual planes of knowledge and existence. The vision espoused by both New Thought and Christian Science was of a triumphant transcendence of all that was base, physical, and mortal. As one adherent described it,

> Sometimes my dauntless divinity shines even through my bones and skin like glass, as if the sea [?] of glass mingled with fire were taking place in my body. The rags of environments, the rags of knowledge of thoughts, the tatters of weariness – doth the mighty me have reckoning with such garbage![75]

In other words, in a society that demanded that women conceal their physicality, and where the female body was the subject of extensive, highly judgmental medical and social discourse, a number of radical women's movements figured a rejection of that body as a source of freedom and empowerment. Unable to find more practical solutions to social powerlessness, chronic illnesses, and loveless marriages, New Thought lured women with a vision of a new, decorporealized, utopian world – but often only once the body itself had perished. In Ursula Newell Gestfeld's *The Woman Who Dares* (1892), the heroine cannot save her husband from the terrors of bodily lust except by dying and becoming a ghost herself, her disembodied spirit leading him along the path of righteousness.[76] This glorification of death led one anonymous 1878 *Atlantic* article to describe derisively the anorexic, Spiritualized nineteenth-century American middle-class woman as one

> in whom all healthy bodily functions have given way, and only the nerves are left, [...] her only tie to the world is through neuralgia, anæmia, or other intangible aliment; her almost freed soul is apt to revel in spiritualism, devout mysticism, or some other trade or profession belonging to the dim border land between us and the world beyond.
>
> [...] Her religious raptures were full and ecstatic; her spiritual insight abnormal; her stomach, liver, and all the rest of the viscera had given up working long ago, and lay torpid; she did not sleep; she did not drink [...].[77]

Describing ailing women as 'emancipated souls, caged but in the frailest possible cobweb of the flesh', the author was harshly critical of these 'gentle, selfish victims preying upon the life of many a poor New England household', draining 'its vitality and its purse in true vampire fashion', while torturing their own souls and those of their families.[78] Be that as it may, what should be noticed is the sharp contrast between this anti-domestic, quasi-demonic, supernaturally potent subversion of conventional femininity, and the scenes depicting Mary Rogers' body, which exploited her violated corpse as the sign of a triumphant victory over the uncanny invisibility she had represented as a missing person, and the challenge to the social gaze that her liminal social status and illegible living body presented. Her dead body functioned both as a visual depiction of the line between the living and the dead, and as a vehicle for securing and fixing meaning and knowledge more generally. Rogers as a decomposing corpse was far less disturbing than as a missing person, or as a living but ambiguous social actor, to the point where catching the killer(s) became superfluous. What the articles quoted earlier focused on instead was the incontrovertible indicators of death, which serve to demarcate 'us', the living, from 'them', the dead, the feminine, the sexually deviant, and the working urban precariat.

'The Fall of the House of Usher'

Indeed, it is precisely the (dead) female body's ability to remove uncertainty and conclude narrative tension that lies behind Poe's 'The Fall of the House of Usher' (1839). At the end of 'Ligeia', transfixed in terror by the sight of his dead wife returned from the grave, Poe's narrator quotes himself as crying, '"Here then, at least [...] can I never – can I never be mistaken – these are the full, and the black, and the wild eyes – of my lost love – of the Lady – of the LADY LIGEIA."'[79] His voice is what terminates the narration: his is quite literally the last word, and whoever the figure standing in front of him may be, she is not permitted to name herself. In a single efficient assertion of power, the disturbing uncertainties as to which woman inhabits the body, and whether it really is Ligeia who has been moving the tapestries, have been reduced to a single meaning, a single name and a single body, just as the narrative comes to a sudden halt. What 'The Fall of the House of Usher' renders more or less explicit is the extent to which this final appearance of a female figure serves to counteract the disturbing sense that the contents of the home may not be entirely under the control of the male protagonists. 'Usher' opens with the (again male) narrator's arrival, in response to an urgent summons, at the remote and crumbling house of his childhood friend, Roderick Usher. Roderick is in the grip of an obscure disorder that hovers somewhere between the psychological and the somatic, and his sister, Madeline, is on the brink of death. We are told that Roderick

> was enchained by certain superstitious impressions in regard to the dwelling which he tenanted, [...] in regard to an influence [...] which some peculiarities in the mere form and substance of his family mansion had, by dint of long sufferance, he said, obtained over his spirit – an effect which the *physique* of the gray walls and turrets, and of the dim tarn into which they all looked down, had, at length, brought about upon the *morale* of his existence.[80]

Just like John in 'The Yellow Wall-Paper', the narrator treats this 'fancy' of Roderick's – that the physical world has power over the psychical, rather than vice versa – with disbelief. Nonetheless, the opening passages of the story make it clear that he too finds the house more than a little unsettling:

> I looked upon the scene before me – upon the mere house, and the simple landscape features of the domain – upon the bleak walls – upon the vacant eye-like windows [...] with an utter depression of soul which I can compare to no earthly sensation more properly than to the after-dream of the reveller upon opium – the bitter lapse into every-day life – the hideous dropping off of the veil.[81]

Large and aristocratic as the house may be, it is the qualities of domestic mundanity pervading it that are most unnerving to the narrator, the sense that it creates of a 'bitter lapse into every-day life', its failure or refusal to be or contain anything other than those things germane to domesticity. What renders the House of Usher an object of dread is its very 'homeliness', the dreary ordinariness of the place, which, in Poe's aesthetic model, is so inimical to Beauty. Like Whitman, who imagines madness and spiritual death lurking 'Under the broadcloth and gloves, under the ribbons and artificial flowers' in well-to-do homes,[82] as a servant leads Poe's narrator through the house, he cannot help but feel that

> While the objects around me – while the carvings of the ceilings, the sombre tapestries of the walls, the ebon blackness of the floors, and the fantasmagoric armorial trophies which rattled as I strode, were

but matters to which [...] I had been accustomed from my infancy – while I hesitated not to acknowledge how familiar was all this – I still wondered to find how unfamiliar were the fancies which ordinary images were stirring up.[83]

While furniture and decoration therefore loom large in the narrator's visual field, for much of the story, Madeline, the lady of the house, is rarely seen directly; 'coming from darkness and returning to it with no distinct locus of entry or exit', only once does she pass soundlessly through 'a remote portion of the apartment' in which Roderick and the narrator sit, never acknowledging their presence, as if already a ghost.[84] Perhaps unsurprising then, when Madeline dies, her marginal status is cemented as the men hastily bury her in a room far below the occupied areas of the house, after which Roderick becomes increasingly agitated, an agitation that the narrator finds contagious. Matters come to a head a week after Madeline is buried, a night marked by a particularly fierce storm, leaving the narrator unable to sleep for nameless dread, and trying in vain 'to reason off the nervousness which had dominion over' him. He struggles to trivialize his terror, but in doing so, he acknowledges that it is 'due to the bewildering influence of the gloomy furniture of the room – of the dark and tattered draperies, which, tortured into motion by the breath of a rising tempest, swayed fitfully to and fro upon the walls, and rustled uneasily about the decorations of the bed.'[85] If the narrator finds the furniture and decoration of the house uncanny at the beginning of the story, Madeline's death, just like Rowena's, has only served to makes matters worse.

Death permits Madeline to take the spectralization of the ideal domestic woman to its logical extreme, animating the *physique* of the house with the invisible feminine force that was so vital to the nineteenth-century American home. Consequently, rather than allaying the narrator's initial fears, his gazing upon the 'tattered draperies' and 'gloomy furniture' has in fact called forth and exacerbated them. This unsatisfactory state of affairs, however, is rapidly terminated by the plot, which substitutes the incontrovertible image of Madeline herself, and the knowledge that the house has become a gothic nightmare because they have buried her alive (rather than through some preternatural agency of its own), for this pervasive uncertainty. At the peak of the storm, as the narrator is desperately trying to soothe Roderick's fears while still in the grip of his own, sounds of a violent struggle are heard from below the room in which the men huddle. The sounds intensify until the men can no longer deny that 'without those doors there *did* stand the lofty and enshrouded figure of the lady Madeline of Usher. There was blood on her white robes, and evidence of some bitter struggle upon every portion of her emaciated frame.'[86] In a reiteration of 'Ligeia', the vague and formless terror felt by both men is therefore replaced with something far more concrete – a female form that evokes repulsion and horror – at precisely the same moment that the draperies cease to command narrative attention.

As in 'The Yellow Wall-Paper', what this implies is that the relationship between female characters and interior decoration, while constricting and imprisoning, nonetheless grants them some modicum of power, particularly over men, if they integrate themselves with the home's superficialities in what is little more than an exaggerated, supernatural version of the position into which domestic ideology already inserts them. Poe's stories open up a gap into which female writers could, and did, insert subversive reinterpretations of his plots, reinterpretations in which furniture and domestic decoration are not so easily dismissed, and women's bodies less easily located. Dawson's story in particular subjects its male characters to the terrifying potential of this strange alliance between the feminine and the decorative/material, while refusing to provide the certainty of presence and visibility in the form of a dead body or ghost. By vacating the narrative space while leaving a trace of herself there, Felipa in 'An Itinerant House' counteracts the containment within the body that the men have foisted upon her by bringing her back to life, never permitting herself to serve as a stabilizing force exploited to reduce the uncanny fluidity of the Gilded-Age American city.

'An Itinerant House'

Mirroring the chaotic and unstable nature of this urban landscape, slippery and unreliable causal links between the revivification and the subsequent deaths of young men dominate the story summarized at the beginning of this chapter, in particular in relation to two friends of the unnamed narrator, Wynne (an actor) and Arne (an artist), neither of whom is present at Felipa's death. Entirely by chance, both men rent out the very room where the revivification takes place, and ultimately die there of unspecified illnesses. Each time, the narrator and Volz only realize that they are in the same boarding house at the moment that their friend expires, and, on both occasions, gripped by a vague terror, the narrator strips off the grey wall covering to reveal a distinctive paper decorated with parrots, which looms large in the initial description of Felipa's death chamber.[87] As the narrator comments, while the men attempt to bring her back to life, 'The room gained an uncanny look, the macaws on the gaudy, old-fashioned wall-paper seemed fluttering and changing places', and this eerie animation recurs when Wynne and Arne die.[88] As both men effectively relive on their death beds Felipa's torment as she is wrenched back into her body, the room in which she was brought back to life, like Gilman's sickroom, bears ambiguous witness to what has happened there. Nonetheless, the impulse toward revelation remains in constant equilibrium with the conflicting forces of concealment, never yielding up a conclusive explanatory image. Arne is haunted by '"a dragging sense of something else [he] ought to paint."' He feels '"as if something had happened somewhere which [he] *must* show."' When the narrator inquires as to the nature of this 'something', Arne replies, '"I wish I could tell you [...]. But only odd bits change places, like looking in a kaleidoscope; yet all cluster around one centre."' Frustrated, he cries, '"If all could have been recorded! If emotion had the property of photographing itself on the surfaces of the walls which had witnessed it!"'[89] Like the story itself, and the city at its heart, the messages from the recent past that the room is broadcasting never form a coherent whole or assert a verifiable truth – Arne and Wynne die without ever knowing what their friends have done to Felipa. The cursed room therefore withholds from the reader as much as from the characters the comforts of concrete certainty, while all the time straining toward synthesis.

Although we know the center of the kaleidoscope to be Felipa, she is not named here, and all but disappears from the narrative after the initial scene of death and resurrection. Indeed, the repeated emphasis upon the room and its interior decoration is concomitant with the almost total absence of Felipa as a corporeal or even visible presence. In the opening pages, we are told, 'It was a dreadful sight. The dead woman's breast rose and fell; smiles and frowns flitted across her face.'[90] From the moment of her awakening, however, she is no longer described in such physical terms. Once reclaimed from death, and after making her terrible pronouncement, she simply passes out of the room, is glimpsed once in Acapulco by Arne, is mentioned later by Volz, who has heard independently that she has returned to Mexico, and that is all. However, the room itself continues to hint at the violence that they have perpetrated against her. The narrator finds himself repeating the phrase '"Better dead than alive"' (which he says just before Felipa revives) at horribly consonant moments. Similarly, on his deathbed, Wynne groans,

Is this hell? [...] What blank darkness! Where am I? What is that infernal music haunting me through all space? If I could only escape it I need not go back to earth – to that room where I feel choked, where the very wall paper frets me with its flaunting birds flying to and fro, mocking my fettered state [...].[91]

Unaware that anything untoward has happened there, Wynne is nevertheless retransmitting Felipa's own, very personal experiences. However, this possession does not result in Wynne's or Arne's knowing or understanding what has happened to Felipa, nor does the narrative allude to her directly on either occasion. It is for this reason that the narrator mentions '"Draper's theory of shadows on walls always staying"' in '"spectral outline"', and asks Volz, '"But how can the mist of circumstance sweeping over us make our vacant places hold trace of us?"'[92] Here, he comes close to pointing out the way in which the house and its interior decoration are at once 'vacant' *and* traced over by the memories of those who have owned and used them, vaguely evoking the past, but lacking in a ghost or other spectral manifestations that might prove identifiable indexes to that past.

However dangerous to men it might be, the house is therefore not haunted in the strictest sense, since Felipa herself never appears there. Despite also revolving around the reanimation of the corpse of a lovely woman, the story consequently varies significantly from those by Poe, since, where he breaks off, Dawson begins. 'Usher' and 'Ligeia' each builds up inexorably to a climax in which the dead woman herself appears, literally in the flesh, replacing the previous focus upon furniture and ornament, while Felipa returns from death only to disappear (literally) into the wallpaper with a voice and with the power that speech confers. Moreover, by vacating the narrative space while leaving a residue of her history there, she counteracts the containment within the body that the men have foisted upon her by bringing her back to life. The space that she occupies for most of the narrative is not the literal space of the dead revivified body, but an impossible nonspace that allows her to possess the room where the men's crime was committed without being trapped there. Indeed, it could be asserted that it is only after the disappearance of the body that the feminine author or narrative voice can speak – or rather write – at all, the 'death space' acting as a source of power because it denies the spectacle of the female body to the patriarchal, masculine gaze that seeks to reify and codify it.[93]

Rather than containing her, then, the boarding house is the place from which her reanimated body departs, a fact that becomes significant in light of the fact that burial and the erection of a monument not only fix the dead geographically and epistemologically but create the very notion of fixed geographical place, specifically in the disturbing mobile nineteenth-century American city. The tendency of urban ghosts to remain elusive and unreliable is brought to the fore in Elia W. Peattie's 'A Child of the Rain' (1898), in which the protagonist John, a street car conductor, having been rejected by his lover, sees a small, bedraggled child at the back of his 'car'. Beset by overwhelming anomie, he is initially unsurprised, despite failing to see anyone so small get on, because 'all was so curious and wild to him that evening – he himself seemed to himself the most curious and the wildest of all things.' Reflecting on the unpredictable nature of life and the chaos of urban existence, and befuddled by the darkness and condensation inside the omnibus, he loses sight of the child and begins to worry, but when he goes to speak with her, 'something went wrong with the lights. There was a blue and green flickering, then darkness, a sudden halting of the car, and a great sweep of wind and rain in at the door.' By the time 'light and motion reasserted themselves [...] the car was empty', and John notes that there is 'not even moisture on the seat where she had been sitting', prompting him to observe that 'he seemed to be getting expert in finding nothing where there ought to be something.'[94] Here, urban alienation, technological failure and the repeated specter of absence and loss invade the world of the senses, leaving them inadequate guides in a chaotic universe in which presence is repeatedly eroded.

Many commentators found it difficult to reconcile the image of the ghost with urban modernity, primarily because, as Edith Wharton acknowledged, spectral presences required 'continuity and silence', without which they disappeared, succumbing 'to the impossibility of finding standing room in a roaring and discontinuous universe.'[95] This is not to suggest, however, that what she calls the Gilded Age was completely unable to accommodate ghosts. Indeed, in '"All Souls"' (1937), she commented, 'As between turreted castles patrolled by headless victims with clanking chains, and the comfortable suburban house with a refrigerator and central heating where you feel, as soon as you're in it, *that there's something wrong*, give me the latter for sending a chill down the spine!', asserting, in an echo of Charles Brockden Brown, that she 'can imagine [ghosts] more wistfully haunting a mean house in a dull street than the battlemented castle with its boring stage properties.'[96] Pervading the mundane and the modern, which seems to provide plenty of 'continuity and silence', Wharton's ghosts functioned as convenient signposts, giving shape to the formless supernatural unease produced by the alienated, anonymous spaces of modernity; admittedly frightening, they were also reassuringly stable, identifiable and pointing to a fixed past.[97]

Deprived of the tethering force provided by either a living or a dead woman, the house in Dawson's story has been 'undomesticated' to the point where, much like Felipa's revived body, it refuses to remain in the one place, and unsettles those who try to live there. Wynne comments before falling ill that San Francisco makes him feel '"as if the scene was not set right for the performance now going on. There is a hitch and drag somewhere – scene-shifters on a strike."'[98] In a striking echo, an *Atlantic* article from 1882 asserted that

> It is not the arrangement of the furniture or the choice of pictures and ornaments that we find fault with in some parlors; the chairs are delightfully comfortable, and yet one is possessed with a spirit of unrest. Something jars and frets us; there are false notes and wrong keys struck in the attempted tune [...].[99]

Predictably, the article blames instead the (implicitly female) owner of the house for failing to produce a sense of harmony through slowly adding to the room's content – that is, for failing to make it feel 'lived in' by devoting her time, energy, and intellect to its decoration. In Dawson's story, without Felipa's cheerful, harmonizing presence (whether as landlady or as ghost), the boarding house is similarly 'possessed with a spirit of unrest'; upon moving into it, the men learn that 'five families had moved in and out during the last year.'[100] The story goes so far as to attribute its unpredictability to a relatively humdrum quirk of San Francisco itself. In the late 1800s and early 1900s, the city was famous for what were referred to as 'roving houses', buildings that were quite literally uprooted and moved elsewhere as spaces were altered and streets reorganized, largely as a result of flooding. It is this peculiarity, and the sheer force of the instability of turn-of-the-century urban life, which brings the men back again and again to the site of their crime. Moreover, the fatal nature of the room recalls contemporary denunciations of the urban boarding house as 'death-trap', prone to 'appropriating to itself every foul thing that comes within its reach, and piling up and intensifying its corruption out of all proportion to the beginning.'[101] Indeed, boarding houses were as socially unreadable as Mary Rogers herself; the line between brothel and boarding house was a very fine and easily transgressed one, the two kinds of establishment operating along identical lines, and the former often posing successfully as the latter.[102] What is more, many of the more exclusive brothels and assignation houses were expensively, lavishly, and tastefully decorated, while the more down-market put on a show of tawdry extravagance of their own, simultaneously highlighting the suspect nature of decoration and its importance as a marker of class and respectability.[103]

Manifesting primarily through the uncanny movement of the brightly patterned wallpaper in a house that imperils the boundaries of domestic space, then, Felipa represents a decorporealized, commodified woman who is by no means innocuous or innocent. She is disruptive, out of place, and a scourge upon the living: a vampire draining men of their vital force. She embodies a transgressive femininity, and undermines from within the idea of the moral 'depths' of the good middle-class woman, seizing upon and subverting the convergence between the Angel in the House and an unsettling and destabilizing spectrality. The repeated motif of the animated, exotically decorated wallpaper implicitly couples Felipa's refusal to rest quietly in the grave with a defiant assertion of the materialistic desires and exuberant superficiality that conventional thinking and consolatory literature saw as irreconcilable with 'proper' femininity. At the same time, by failing to appear in corporeal or anthropomorphic form, she eludes the objectifying operations of the patriarchal gaze.

While she herself openly expressed Spiritualist beliefs, Dawson's writing never indulges in the consolatory assertions of ontological certainty that characterized that movement.[104] Instead, 'An Itinerant House' makes use of the subversive power of invisibility and bodilessness advocated by Spiritualists and Christian Scientists, without ever producing an identifiable specter or vision of an afterlife. Indeed, the murderous manifestations of Felipa's anger destabilize the spaces of San Francisco more than ever, so that the male characters never know where they are, or where they might be safe. On his deathbed, Wynne demands of the narrator and Volz, '"how can I go outside my door to step on dead bodies? Street and sidewalk are knee-deep with them. They rise and curse me for disturbing them."'[105] In a city that cannot be tied down to a visible spectacle of knowable femininity, nothing is certain, and nothing stays still, even the dead. The story ends as, following Arne's death, Volz grabs the narrator's arm and they rush from the house, into 'a dense fog which made the world seem a tale that was told, blotting out all but our two slanting forms.'[106] This fog is the defining image of a story that furnishes the reader neither with closure nor with any satisfactory explanation for the events that have occurred. Having fled a house that is terrifying precisely because it is *not* inhabited by a ghost, Volz and the narrator are not free – they are lost.

4
'Solemnest of Industries': Wilkins' 'The Southwest Chamber' and Memorial Culture

In Elia W. Peattie's 'The Story of an Obstinate Corpse' (discussed in Chapter 1), the photographer Virgil Hoyt is asked to produce a post-mortem portrait of an elderly woman. When he develops the plates, however, there is something wrong with the picture, and he and his thoroughly spooked boss are reluctant to show them to the woman's bereaved daughter. Despite the fact that both the daughter and Hoyt confirm that there was nothing covering or obscuring the women's face when the photograph was taken, in the pictures, 'Over face and flowers and the head of the coffin fell a thick veil, the edges of which touched the floor in some places. It covered the features so well that not a hint of them was visible.' After recovering from her initial fainting fit, the daughter explains to the puzzled and rather embarrassed photographer that her mother was rather fond of having her own way, and invariably successful in getting it, adding, '"she never would have her picture taken. She didn't admire her own appearance. She said no one should ever see a picture of her"', to which Hoyt responds 'meditatively', '"Well, she's kept her word, hasn't she?"'[1]

Exerting from beyond the grave the 'strength of character' and 'immovable' will that Hoyt reads and admires in her lifeless features, instead of allowing herself to be exposed to the gaze of a stranger – and potentially of many others – the dead woman has somehow interposed a heavy veil, a conventional item of mourning dress, between her otherwise vulnerable features and the pitiless eye of the camera. While the woman herself only features in the narrative as a corpse, or in the reported memories of her daughter, she therefore remains an active agent, ordering things according to her wishes, and unnerving several people in the process. In this way, she claims kinship with another determined old dead woman – the spiteful Aunt Harriet whose poltergeist activities dominate the action of Mary E. Wilkins' story 'The Southwest Chamber' (1903).[2] Wilkins' tale concerns two middle-aged sisters who inherit the family mansion from which their mother's marriage to a 'poor man', disapproved of by her own mother and sisters, has exiled them. When the only living aunt dies, the two daughters, Sophia and Amanda, convert the mansion into a boarding house.[3] The final room to be rented out, to a schoolteacher named Louisa Stark, is the room in which their formidable Aunt Harriet passed away, and, for many of the residents, a source of superstitious dread. Confronted by an escalating series of bizarre and inexplicable occurrences, in particular the movement of their own accord of clothing and household items, first Louisa Stark, and then a succession of other guests vacate the room hastily, events that culminate in the sisters' leaving the house altogether.

While this ending might seem to enact the victory of the bitter aunt over the sisters and their own adopted, orphaned niece, the sight of her spectral image actually precipitates their final decision to relinquish a piece of property that is a drain on their meager resources, and that perpetuates the snobbishness and harsh intolerance that they have inherited from their grandmother's family. In other words, surrounded by furniture, clothing, and other household items that they struggle to redefine as practical and economical, they find the bad blood that rejected their mother coursing through their own veins. Their own rejection of this malign inheritance can therefore be seen as the living women's triumph over the ghostly Aunt Harriet's nasty legacy, even if they never quite succeed in fully exorcizing her. Nonetheless, this triumph is only made possible when the old woman makes the mistake that Dawson's self-effacing specter scrupulously avoids – eschewing poltergeist activity in favor of appearing in recognizable form in a mirror. At first, like Felipa, Aunt Harriet exercises her domestic power by manifesting invisibly through the objects in the house, but finally succumbs to the lure of the visible and, in a reiteration of the situation dramatized in 'The Yellow Wall-Paper', replaces multiple, multivalent phenomena with a single, identifiable specter. And, as Chapter 1 demonstrates, in the logic of these stories, to be visible is to be powerless.

At the same time, Aunt Harriet's reign of terror constitutes a direct rebellion against contemporary depictions of departed relatives. The post-mortem photography around which Peattie's story revolves was part of an extensive array of mourning practices that sought both to bear witness to loss and to make possible a continued communication between the living and the dead. These customs sanitized and all but canonized the departed in a manner that strove to forestall superstitious fear while whitewashing over the less comfortable details of ordinary lives, subordinating the deceased individual to the respectable memories and emotions of the living. In a culture that worked hard to deny the place of the past in the shiny new republic, mourning culture and Spiritualism carefully extricated the dead from the living, while rigidly controlling the meanings attached to them. Considering the immense popularity of Spiritualism itself as a quasi-religious belief system throughout the nineteenth century in the United States, there seems to be a bizarre paucity of overtly supernatural stories revolving around mediums or séances from this period, apart from a small number that undermine Spiritualism's credibility, such as Edith Wharton's 'The Looking Glass' (1935), which casts a spurious medium as preying upon a vulnerable aging wealthy woman. Much the same can be said of the trappings of mourning, the products of a vast industry of material goods and literary output, which nonetheless serve at most a peripheral function in uncanny supernatural tales by American women from around the end of the century. These glaring omissions can be accounted for by the fact that both mourning culture and Spiritualism were essentially committed to reducing any mystery and fear surrounding the dead, to fixing them firmly in their place beyond the day-lit world, and rendering them safe, benevolent, and lovable in the process. Arguably, Spiritualism's most radical move was its 'abolition of death', and this was equally the central purpose of sentimental mourning discourse, which focused on death as the 'last sleep' from which the soul rises perfected and eternally happy.[4] As such, then, both mourning and Spiritualism were the polar opposites of the gothic, where death continues to pervade life, and the horrors of the past repeat themselves endlessly in the present.

Wilkins' 'The Southwest Chamber' therefore situates itself firmly in the gothic mode by staging a resistance to the construction of the dead as universally benevolent, ethereal beings. At the same time, it follows the pattern set by Dawson in illustrating that angry dead women can maintain their hold over the land of the living only so long as they refuse to take the form of identifiable ghosts. The result is a story that dramatizes a (rather unlikeable) female specter's struggle to maintain control over her property from beyond the grave, juxtaposed with a group of (considerably more sympathetic) living women's struggle to wrest that power back from a tyrannical past that oppresses and stifles the present.

Where Felipa, for all the atrocities she commits on the bodies of innocent men, is undeniably a wronged and justifiably aggrieved phantom, Aunt Harriet is motivated largely by greed and begrudgery. The dead may not be sweet and benign in Wilkins' story, but this does not automatically transform them into avatars of female empowerment. 'The Southwest Chamber' can be read as encouraging the reader to applaud the ultimate thwarting of her mean-spirited plans, and consequently, also to applaud Sophia and Amanda's ultimate rejection of her house and all that it stands for, even as it is vital to acknowledge that Aunt Harriet has lost the power over domestic space for which, elsewhere, other female characters strive in vain. Overall, then, 'The Southwest Chamber' underlines the point made in Chapter 1 – that visual representations of the female form and past events that continue to haunt present circumstances are equally hazardous for female characters, living or dead.

Death and mourning

In his piece on 'Rural Funerals' (1820), Washington Irving wrote that 'The natural effect of sorrow over the dead is to refine and elevate the mind', because the ability to retain affection for an individual after death was indisputable evidence of the soul's 'superiority to the instinctive impulse of mere animal attachment.' Kept alive, not by 'the presence of its object', but rather by 'long remembrance', affection for the dead was both purer and more permanent than love of a living, present, corporeal person. The latter, Irving insisted, could not survive the ravages of time and bodily ageing, since 'The mere inclinations of sense languish and decline with the charms which excited them', while death only made matters worse, since base physical desire instinctively turned 'with shuddering disgust from the dismal precincts of the tomb.' A love that survives these changes because the survivor cherishes memories of the beloved dead was, by contrast, 'truly spiritual affection', 'a holy flame' that was 'purified from every sensual desire'.[5] Thomas Baldwin Thayer expressed identical sentiments, asserting that

> the memory of the dead often has for us a sanctifying power which the presence of the living, however sweet their communion, never had; and in our frequent thought of them, we find that our hearts and hopes are slowly disentangling themselves from the earthly, and steadily drifting heavenward.[6]

He continued, 'Death seems to sanctify all our thoughts of the departed; we willingly forget the evil, and remember only the good there was in them.'[7] As Irving put it, the grave 'buries every error – covers every defect – extinguishes every resentment! From its peaceful bosom spring none but fond regrets and tender recollections.'[8] In other words, the messy business of life is tidied up by death; the departed are automatically cleansed of all earthly, bodily associations in the same movement that the emotions of the living are purified and spiritualized. As Frederick Saunders, writing in 1853, put it, 'The earthly taint of our affections is buried with that which was corruptible, and the divine flame, in its purity, illumines our breast.'[9] In Irving's words, 'Who can look down upon the grave even of an enemy, and not feel a compunctious throb, that he should ever have warred with the poor handful of earth that lies mouldering before him.'[10] Free both of corrupting lust and embittering resentment, the living can move safely forward with their lives, secure in the knowledge that they have put such ignoble feelings behind them, and that the dead, if they choose to do so, will only come back in a spirit of good will and otherworldly love.[11] Depicting the love of the 'immortal dead' for the living as 'unchanging', Saunders exclaimed, 'How tenderly they look down on us, and how closely they surround our being! How earnestly they rebuke the evils of our lives.' As this suggests, the dead's benevolence was inextricable from their 'unchanging' nature – their existence beyond the vicissitudes of everyday life. He continued, 'The blessed dead [...] are fixed for us eternally in the mansions prepared for our re-union.'[12] The dead, in Thayer's words, were 'those who pursue no longer the fleeting, but have grasped and secured the real', having left the 'transient, changing, temporary' world in favor of heaven, 'where everything is permanent, fixed and final.'[13]

Within this context, excessive grief was frowned upon, as it implied that the mourner doubted the promises of eternal life and that loved ones would be reunited after death. In order to curb violent emotion, but also to ensure a proper solemnity, mourning dress both 'expressed grief' and 'enforced a social manner of grief that was to be maintained at all times', primarily 'by placing certain well-defined restrictions upon the mourner's social activity.'[14] In theory, 'To wear flattering or bright clothes after a death would have been regarded as callous or even immoral (especially where widows were concerned).'[15] Nonetheless, in practice, this situation entailed considerable hypocrisy. The greater the privacy the bereaved could command, the more the mourner could do as he or she wished, while maintaining a respectably grave façade.

Excessive, or indeed inadequate, grief could therefore be indulged in, as long as it remained carefully concealed from the world at large by a seamless surface of the deepest woe. In theory, 'the feeling of grief itself was all that mattered, and the privacy of its expression was the test of its sincerity and depth.' However, 'bourgeois demands for its public performance' compelled the mourner to wear 'her heart on her sleeve' by expressing 'her grief not privately but publicly.'[16] The result was a proliferation of consumer goods, as

> The sentimental image of the handkerchief drenched in tears by night became a black-edged handkerchief carried by day; the poetic image of the private keepsake of the lost loved one became a lock of hair displayed under the glass front of a jeweled broach backed in gold.[17]

Mourning was therefore inherently external and material, even as it defined itself as private and spiritual. In response to the growing demand for such consumables, 'In the 1840s and 1850s, [...] *maisons de deuil* such as Besson and Son of Philadelphia began to spring up in the largest American cities, and mourning departments appeared in the new large department stores.'[18] By catering for the ever-expanding spectrum of bereavement, from deepest mourning to half-mourning, these emporia, Karen Halttunen writes, 'contributed to the extreme literalness of middle-class views concerning the relationship between inner sentiment and its outer social expression.'[19] Propriety demanded the overt display of a vast array of specially designed (or hastily dyed) somber clothing, restrained personal ornaments, suitable domestic decoration, flowers, coffins, mementoes for funeral guests, and the funeral itself, in order to ensure that the family were treated with due circumspection.[20] The culture of mourning therefore provided an opportunity for middle-class self-definition through 'proper' displays of grief and solemnity. Items surviving in twentieth-century collections (only the tip of the iceberg) testify to the sheer variety of the 'ephemera' surrounding nineteenth-century mourning culture on both sides of the Atlantic, including

> black-edge mourning-envelopes and stationery; *immortelles* or artificial flowers protected by glass domes; embossed patterns around verses of a lugubrious nature; and dried, colourless leaves from wreathes long collapsed to dust [...] a paper-weight decorated with a view of a funerary urn beneath a weeping willow; a fire-screen embellished with a memorial text; a drawing of a family Mausoleum; a book

of exquisite water-colours and hand-written original verses recalling all the places associated with a women who died young (the last water-colour in the book being a view of her grave); memorial-cards, embossed with weeping willows, sorrowing figures, and hovering angels; memorial-card mounts to which memorial-cards could be fixed and the whole framed; linen handkerchiefs embroidered with black borders and tear-drops; a 'Vulcanite' ear-trumpet decorated with lace and ribbons, on a silk cord; mourning-fans of black silk with ebonised sticks; and items of mourning-dress.[21]

Other items listed by researcher James Stevens Curl included an extensive range of personal apparel and funeral accessories (including black gloves for every mourner in attendance), bookmarks, coverings for furniture, the intriguing 'padded chest protectors for widows (worn beneath mourning-dress)', and brooches containing portraits or mourning scenes fashioned from the hair of the deceased. The social pressure to maintain an appearance of genteel sorrow by spending lavishly on the accoutrements of the funeral often drove the less well-off into massive debt, as families struggled to meet the expenses incurred by the all-too-frequent deaths that marked the period.[22]

Much of this paraphernalia was pared back in the latter decades of the century, but still remained vital to the theatrics of 'respectability' and 'right feeling'. A sign of the mourner's sentimental propriety, the paraphernalia helped keep 'the work of grief in consciousness' by continually reminding the mourner of his or her loss.[23] Because mourning was situated with the 'feminine sphere' of the domestic and the affective, many middle-class women (or at least those who could afford it) found themselves in a semipermanent state of 'remembering', outwardly corralled within the boundaries of sentimental respectability and sincerity. The mourner therefore engaged in self-display and conspicuous consumption while simultaneously ostentatiously hiding away in the privacy of grief and the (ostensibly) gaze-diverting aesthetics of mourning.[24] Nonetheless, nineteenth-century society in the United States was by no means entirely comfortable with the commodification of grief that its sentimentalized view of death paradoxically insisted upon. The Reverend Orville Dewey castigated the 'trappings of grief' as 'indifferent and childish where there *is* real grief; and where there is not, they are a mockery.'[25] Even articles and stories published in the consumer-oriented *Godey's Lady's Book* actively condemned as factitious and unbecoming any form of mourning that replaced sentiment with ornament.[26] Hammering the message home, Timothy S. Arthur's 1841 cautionary tale 'Going into Mourning' is explicitly disapproving of the superficiality of mourning attire. So caught up are a family in the need to provide themselves with suitably gloomy yet becoming dresses that they insist that their seamstress, Ellen, sit up late to finish them, thus preventing her from tending to her ailing sister, who subsequently dies. Through the sacrifice of the two working-class girls, the middle-class Mary Condy realizes that her insistence upon wearing deep mourning has been motivated less by a desire 'to commemorate the death of her brother, [...] than to *appear before others* to be deeply affected with grief.'[27] In case the reader still has not grasped the meaning of the tale, Ellen refuses Mrs. Condy's offer of a black dress in the end, declaring that it would be of no use in restoring her lost sister, Margaret, to her.

In essence, the problem with mourning clothing was that, while it aimed to bear witness to the wearer's emotional depth and sincerity, its emphasis on form and appearance over feeling and interiority brought the mourner out of the realm of the private and the domestic, and into the dangerous world of commerce and materialism. Ideally, it functioned as an extreme version of the role of the middle-class wife and mother more generally, enjoined by domestic ideology to spend her husband's money in order to create a homelike environment in which respectability and the cultivation of sincere but restrained emotions could be nurtured. In other words, mourning attire was a particularly visible and emotionally freighted example of the precarious position of the middle-class wife, who (as mentioned in the previous chapter), it was insisted, must go shopping enough to fashion a pleasing domestic interior, but not so much as to be accused of extravagance or indulgence in sensual, material, selfish pleasures. In order to avoid this uncomfortable state of affairs, mourning dress and other objects had to be abstracted from the current of daily life, transformed from worldly commodities into meaning-laden mementoes, with no purpose or significance other than as reminders of the deceased person. As Thayer put it, 'In every home there is an enshrined memory, a sacred relic, a ring, a lock of shining hair, a broken plaything, a book, a picture, something sacredly kept and guarded, which speaks of death, which tells as plainly as words, of some one long since gone.'[28] Similarly, Josephine Daskam Bacon's 'The Children' asserted that 'What [the beloved dead] leave behind is worse than what they take with them; their curls and their fat legs and the kisses they gave you are all shut into the grave, but what they used to play with stays there and mourns them with you.'[29] Such senti-mental objects have been abstracted from the normal run of household management and order, no longer in use and signifying but one thing – loss. They are therefore both part of and external to daily domestic life, helping shore up the home's position as a separate sphere, undefiled by the ravages of capitalism.

This abstraction from the spaces of finance and production was even more securely effected by means of handcrafted mourning objects, which spoke of a purely private, personal grief, untainted by association with the marketplace. In the description of the Grangerford's house in Mark Twain's *Adventures of Huckleberry Finn* (1884), the interior is described as covered with pictures, some of which

> they called crayons, which one of the daughters which was dead made her own self when she was only fifteen years old. They was different from any pictures I ever see before – blacker, mostly, than is common. One was a woman in a slim black dress, belted small under the armpits, with bulges like a cabbage in the middle of the sleeves, and a large black scoop-shovel bonnet with a black veil, and white slim ankles crossed about with black tape, and very wee black slippers, like a chisel, and she was leaning pensive on a tombstone on her right elbow, under a weeping willow, and her other hand hanging down her side holding a white handkerchief and a reticule, and underneath the picture it said 'Shall I Never See Thee More Alas'. [...] Everybody was sorry [that the daughter had] died, because she had laid out a lot more of these pictures to do, and a body could see by what she had done what they had lost. But I reckoned that with her disposition she was having a better time in the graveyard.[30]

What Huck here attributes to peculiar individual predilections was in fact a national (female) pastime – the choosing, combining, and often personalizing of material objects to produce private meanings and to express private emotions.[31] Mourning portraits and other picto-rial depictions of the deceased or of grief 'were either made at home as drawings, paintings, or samplers, or were mass produced, usually as lithographs [which] simply omitted the name of the deceased on the featured tomb, and could be personalized after purchase.'[32] As the century wore on, post-mortem photographs such as that at the center of Peattie's 'Story of an Obstinate Corpse' became increasingly popular, their comparatively reasonable price rendering them more economi-cally available to the population at large than painted portraits, which there was not always time to sit for before death intervened.[33] The purpose of such images was 'to depict the dead as if they were alive' or just sleeping – although the success depended on the skill of the photographer.[34] In order to produce this effect, photographs of the dead entailed considerable handling of the corpse; an astonishing manual written by an experienced nineteenth-century post-mortem photographer details the multiple ways in which he was permitted to do almost anything he liked with dead bodies.[35] As the old woman in Peattie's story seems to fear, the practice also allowed the photographer a considerable license in gazing upon the face and figure of the deceased, a particularly problematic situation (as Chapter 1 argues) when the body was female. One photographer recalled a commission in the home of an attractive, impoverished woman whose daughter had just died:

> Gently we moved the death couch to the window in order to get the best light, though but a ray. What a face! What a picture did it reveal. Though the hand of God is most skilful, yet I thought, had the sculptor been there to chisel out that round forehead, to form that exquisite shoulder, to mark the playful smile about those thin lips, and to give the graceful curves to those full arms that lay across her now motionless heart, what a beautiful creation would come from his hands.[36]

Just as the disturbing material indulgence of mourning clothing and objects was confined within a regime of emotional depth, so was the improper sexuality of the photographer's leering gaze contained by the meaning attributed to such pictures. In H.T. Rogers' memoirs of his professional life, he took pains to emphasize the elevating feelings that should be associated with the pictures of the dead from which he made a considerable profit. He wrote, 'What emotions of gladness spring up from our hearts as we gaze upon the life-like presentations of the familiar faces, in life's journey no longer with us', and insisted that 'our domestic and social affections, and sentiments, are perpetuated and purified as we solitarily look upon the shadows of our departed friends.'[37] Open to interpretation as morbid, prurient, or simply vulgar displays of disposable income (or means of procuring it for those involved in the industry), mourning paraphernalia and pictures were therefore tightly constrained within a system of sentimental, respectable, controlled grief that portrayed the mourner, the mourned, and the mourning market, as equally angelic, respectable, and benign.

Spiritualism

In this context, the movement that arguably worked hardest to improve the public relations between living and dead was Spiritualism. Spiritualism in America began, arguably, with the publicity surrounding the Fox sisters in Hydesville, New York, who claimed to be communicating with spirits via a system of knocks, around 1848. Their activities rapidly formed the basis for a phenomenally popular religious movement centered around the desire to ascertain whether the individual personality survives physical death and can communicate with the living. Spiritualism was especially appealing during and after the Civil War, in what was essentially a period of national mourning, offering solace in the form of an apparent confirmation of the existence of the afterlife. Striving to undo what it saw as the ill effects of two centuries of Calvinistic thinking among the American Protestant middle classes, Spiritualism railed against the lingering superstitious dread of the returning dead as malign, and the lingering pious belief in the afterlife as a Puritan pit of despair and torment, where even the elect faced the prospect of eternal separation from loved ones who had not been saved.[38] Part of the attraction of Spiritualism, which still had ardent followers in the Gilded Age, was that it allowed for continued communication with the dead even if the corpse was unavailable (precluding the possibility of an actual grave site) or simply too horrible to contemplate.[39] It can therefore be seen as the epitome of the sentimental dematerialization of the dead discussed above, while simultaneously exploiting the cultural construction of women as pure, selfless angels, capable of positively influencing men and society at large by the extension of sympathy and gentle emotions. Emphasizing precisely these qualities in the hundreds of mediums 'discovered' in the United States throughout the century, Spiritualism equally figured the communicative dead as almost universally benevolent, spreading endless love to the living just as women supposedly did to those around them.[40]

Bodiless, ethereal, and sensitive to every vibration, such ghosts were in many ways the mirror of the feminine ideal. While men were seen both as 'slaves to passion' and to the evils of the marketplace, the ideal middle-class woman was above the base emotions that inspire indulgence and excess, and contact with the refined spirits of the dead, it was asserted, could actively prevent such sensual degeneracy. Spiritualism therefore 'made the delicate constitution and nervous excitability commonly attributed to women a virtue' rather than seeing it as a disqualification from the public life that mediumship demanded. In other words, it elevated the 'weak' feminine body to a position of superiority and authority, and justified the medium's public speaking role by insisting that the words she uttered were not her own, but merely transmitted through her extra-sensitive consciousness.[41] Indeed, it was seen as a specifically domestic and feminine form of belief. As one commentator noted in 1860, 'Not in the church, not in the capitol, but in the family, came the first demonstrable recognition of immortal life and immortal love – the holiest truth to the holiest place.'[42] Many saw the craze for small, private, parlor séances as an extension of the moral functions of the family, keeping husbands and offspring safely indoors and away from the temptations of 'the world'. In the words of the *Plain Guide to Spiritualism* (1863), 'During the long evenings, as friends and families gather around the social board, no enjoyment can become more genial and benign than that of seeking communion with those who have passed on to the land of eternal spring and perennial sunshine.'[43]

As the 1850s progressed, spirits went from moving tables and ringing bells to moving mediums' hands and even manipulating their voices, generally those of young, physically appealing girls and women, who gave the greatest impression of sincerity and passivity – in other words, of having little ability to think up the messages for themselves.[44] At the same time, however, Spiritualism foregrounded a form of interaction between a generally female medium and the contents of a normal middle-class home that threatened to undermine domestic stability and privacy. The spirits that were channeled during séances often manifested by flinging crockery around, shaking tables and drapery, and materializing sudden showers of fruit, flowers, and all manner of trinkets, apparently out of thin air. The séance effectively transformed the home into a theater, a space of public consumption, opening it up, not merely to living (and often paying) clients but to the otherworld itself, rendering the home, and its heart – the parlor, where séances traditionally took place – a porous and unpredictable medium, a passage to elsewhere, to the unknown, to death.

The figure of the medium served to crystallize and foreground hopes and anxieties surrounding women's role in the public sphere and their cultural visibility in the burgeoning capitalist marketplace.[45] Spiritualism necessitated, indeed condoned the public, highly theatrical display of women's bodies, often in ways that violated strict codes of decorum and respectability. Mediumship was a profoundly physical phenomenon, effectively contravening nineteenth-century restrictions on what constituted 'proper' behavior for ladies. The medium would 'become drowsy as if mesmerised', before falling 'into a trance or a series of strange contortions and movements.'[46] This troublesome physicality became increasing evident toward the *fin de siècle*, as the tenor of interest in life beyond the grave shifted slightly, and the emotive drive toward Spiritualism mingled with a more scientific interest in the preternatural. In England, the Society for Psychical Research (SPR) was founded in 1882, the American branch (the ASPR) in 1885, and both prospered until the mid-1920s. Euspasia Palladino, a medium investigated by the SPR around 1894 and 1895,

> presented an extraordinary spectacle – uninhibited, tempestuous, erotic – a vision far removed from the sedate ways of the academic corridor, the neatly controlled setting of the laboratory.
>
> Not only did Euspasia come out of trances charges with sexual energy, she sometimes seemed to shudder with pleasure while entranced. She claimed that, on occasion, the spirits brought her an invisible lover. A shy smile played across her face as she described, rather graphically, their encounters. She seemed to make the very air sparkle – and not just with figurative erotic energy.[47]

Few of the mediums investigated by the two Societies displayed either Palladino's volatile temper or her unsettling sensuous appeal. Nonetheless, a discomfort around the self-objectification that the trance state and the séance seemed to necessitate pervaded the professional and personal correspondence left by SPR and ASPR members. Even such apparently chaste and demure married women as the highly talented Leonora Piper (over whom the Societies shed much ink and sweat, so convincing were the phenomena she manifested) apparently apparently exercised an unnerving magnetic attraction over the hyper-rational men who sought to understand and quantify the effects they appeared to produce. Described by Deborah Blum as sober, sedate, and little, prominent members of the Society, including William and Henry James, found themselves drawn to Piper, as much because of her pleasing appearance and evident femininity as for her apparently remarkable skills.[48]

Flattering as such attention may have been, many mediums found, through such experiences, that 'mediumship, like prostitution', or indeed a loveless marriage, 'could involve relinquishing the use of one's body for pay.' For men, going to see a trance speaker presented 'a rare opportunity to look unrestrained at an unknown woman', while speakers were often criticized for wearing revealing or overly decorative or colorful clothing.[49] This was made particularly clear as, in the latter half of the century, increasingly spectacular manifestations were called for. While 'spirit portraits' of a loved one produced by a painter who had never seen the deceased made the dead more visible, mediums themselves began to be hidden inside cabinets, bound hand and foot, and often placed within sacks, in order to emphasize both the veracity of the materializations they produced and their own passivity and voicelessness, a position that was far from empowering.[50] The rise of the Societies for Psychical Research only exacerbated this situation, as mediums were poked and prodded in the name of science. One investigator, Richard Hodgson, was so determined to determine the truth or otherwise of the phenomena produced by Leonora Piper that he subjected her 'to every test he could reasonably conduct. He'd put ammonia-soaked cloth under her nose, dumped spoonfuls of salt, perfume, and laundry detergent into her mouth, pinched her until she bruised, all without provoking a flinch.'[51]

Whether concealed, bound and gagged in a cabinet, or wired up to electrodes in the laboratory of a group of psychic investigators, the body of the medium became the battleground over which was fought the struggle to ascertain whether or not spirits were real. Doing so effectively moved the focus away from the relationship that had initially been central to the Spiritualist movement – that between a woman and the objects in the home. By seizing upon domestic space and commodities as the conduit through which the otherworldly could manifest, séances and Spiritualism essentially invested houses and their contents with preternatural significance, albeit in the potentially comforting guise of contact with the beyond and proof of life after death. Indeed, it is not so much that séances *created* this quality within the relationship between women and domestic items as that they dramatized a broadly identifiable motif in contemporary discourse – the mysterious yet fundamental bond between a woman and the domestic objects with which she interacted on a daily basis. In precisely the same way that the final appearance of Ligeia and Madeline serves to reduce the terror that domestic objects arouse in Poe's narrators, the objectification, constraint and effective torture of the mediumistic subject disentangled her from the domestic surroundings in which she had most power and control.

The perils of domestic decoration

The exponential growth in the availability of luxury goods at the end of the nineteenth and the beginning of the twentieth century meant that accumulation and display were at once celebrated and deplored.[52] This was a time when

> The evolution of display and decorative strategies [...] helped forge a new commercial aesthetic that [...] carved out a wide terrain of desire and longing and contained the elements of a new secular carnivalesque, one that played at the margins of unacceptable thought and behaviour.[53]

Efforts to redraw these boundaries became something of a theme throughout the century, with Lydia Maria Child asserting in *The American Frugal Housewife* in 1832, 'The prevailing evil of the present day is extravagance', and that 'our present expensive habits are productive of much domestic unhappiness, and injurious to public prosperity.' Indeed, she sees excessive spending as inimical to the nation itself, warning, 'A luxurious and idle REPUBLIC! Look at the phrase! – The words were never made to be married together; everybody sees it would be death to one of them.'[54] As this implies, while interior decoration in many ways gave middle-class women the perfect platform from which to spread their moralizing influence to the wider world, it nonetheless remained a dangerously unstable realm, through which luxury, commerce and superficiality could invade the sanctity of the home, in literature as much as in life. The sheer numbers of commodities with which fictional homes, particularly toward the middle of the nineteenth century, were furnished meant that these objects were 'to a great extent [...] symbolically unencumbered' because, piled willy-nilly into the narrative frame, 'they could not be adequately (realistically) represented *and* assigned to reliable symbolic places.'[55] Crammed full of objects that 'threaten to burst out of its covers' and lacking 'a tight symbolic system', nineteenth-century fiction was, arguably, a kind of disorderly house, where stage props employed purely in the service of accuracy and realism resisted being kept in their places or assigned appropriate patriarchal symbolic meaning.[56]

The effective domestic incarceration of the middle-class housewife became the solution to the unsettling autonomy of *things*, in precisely the same way that she was seen as providing a stable center around which urban and rural spaces could be organized. Through the figure of the saintly, selfless woman, fashion and ornament were invested with moral and sentimental significance, transforming them from multi-valent agents of social chaos into apparently infallible indicators of one's gentility and sincerity. The woman bound these objects together, taming their disruptive potential; without her, they were frighteningly independent. However, just as proper mourning and Spiritualist transparency could slide all too easily into vain display, the line between good housekeeping and an illicit indulgence in consumer goods was a tricky one to walk, particularly since women are traditionally associated both with the materiality of the body and with the superficial facticity of man-made objects.[57] In order to ensure that her housekeeping efforts were not mistaken for a scandalous indulgence in the pleasures of the material world, as I have been arguing, the respectable nineteenth-century wife effectively had to disappear into the furniture.[58] A poem printed in *American Kitchen Magazine* in 1899 asked

> How can I tell her?
> By her cellar, –
> Cleanly shelves and whitened walls.
> I can guess her
> By her dresser,
> By the back staircase and halls,
> And with pleasure
> Take her measure
> By the way she keeps her brooms;
> Or the peeping
> At the keeping
> Of her back and unseen rooms.
> By her kitchen's air of neatness,
> And its general completeness.
> Where in cleanliness and sweetness
> The rose of order blooms.[59]

This near-symbiotic relationship between woman and house was perhaps most explicitly exemplified by the figure of Phoebe Pyncheon in Nathaniel Hawthorne's *The House of the Seven Gables* (1851), who encapsulates both the bodilessness of the domestic angel and a dedication to a form of housework that is all but invisible and requires no physical or even emotional effort:

There was a spiritual quality in Phoebe's activity. The life of the long and busy day – spent in occupations that might so easily have taken a squalid and ugly aspect – had been made pleasant, and even lovely, by the spontaneous grace with which these homely duties seemed to bloom out of her character; so that labour, while she dealt with it, had the easy and flexible charm of play. Angels do not toil, but let their good works grow out of them; and so did Phoebe.[60]

Phoebe therefore embodies the ideal of feminine domestic 'influence', rigidly opposed to the masculine world of work and of action, while still creating the *effect* of having literally and morally purified the home.[61] As Ralph Waldo Emerson put it, women 'inspire by a look, and pass with us not so much by what they say or do, as by their presence.'[62] Phoebe works, but without seeming to do so, avoiding all that is 'squalid and ugly' – that is, abject or physical – about house-work, seeming instead to perform her purification of domestic space simply by inhabiting it. Her housework therefore positions her as a sort of extension of domestic space itself, her spiritual nature ensuring that the house becomes somehow spontaneously clean in her presence. In much the same way, in Olivia Howard Dunbar's 'The Shell of Sense' (1908), in reference to her husband's attitude to her sister, the (dead) narrator remarks that 'Theresa had been there so long, she so defi-nitely, to his mind, belonged there. And she was, as I also had jealously known, so lovely there, the small, dark, dainty creature, in the old hall, on the wide staircases, in the garden ... '[63] This ideal spectralizes the domestic woman, subordinating her to and conflating her with the objects that surround her and the spaces they inhabit. Problematic as this absorption is, the stories I have been discussing reconfigure the domestic woman's putative invisibility and passivity as an equivocal realm of feminine power. The expanded possibilities offered by the supernatural allow, in the stories I examine throughout this book, the figurative spectrality of Phoebe Pyncheon to become a literalized display of poltergeist activity.

The adoption of Spiritualism came unsettlingly close to vain and seductive bodily display, while leaving the medium exposed and vulner-able (both to censure and to the gaze). By contrast, fictional women in ghost stories evade the dangers inherent in objectification altogether by disappearing into domestic objects and spaces, while reveling in the forbidden world of commodities and rejecting the sentimental domes-tication of the dead. These indecorous dead women in Gilded-Age supernatural fiction by American women therefore violate a number of injunctions simultaneously. As with Felipa, central to the depiction of

Aunt Harriet in Wilkins' story is her malevolence, which consists primarily in her continued assertion of a traumatic past that would be best forgotten. Vitally, however, she can only do so as long as she remains hidden in and by the objects she manipulates.

Material remembering and forgetting

Discussing the events that drive a series of guests out of the large and well-lit room in Wilkins' story, a young clergyman is shocked at the suggestion that '"a disembodied spirit – who we trust is in her heavenly home"' might be permitted by the Almighty to harm the living. In response, a woman who has not yet stayed in the southwest chamber asserts, rather smugly,

> '[...] I don't suppose a professing Christian would come back and scare folks if she could. I wouldn't be a mite afraid to sleep in that room; I'd rather have it than the one I've got. If I was afraid to sleep in a room where a good woman died, I wouldn't tell of it. If I saw things or heard things I'd think the fault must be with my own guilty conscience.'[64]

In other words, no respectable woman ought to have any reason to become one of the 'restless' dead. Aunt Harriet, who is not resting decorously in the grave, but shockingly, insists upon remaining in her former bedroom and upon ensuring that her possessions remain exactly as they were when she was alive, is evidently far from 'good'. The reformer Alice Blackwell Stone recalled that when asked if she intended coming back to communicate with them from beyond the grave on her death in 1893, her mother, the Suffragist Lucy Stone, replied primly, '"I expect to be too busy to come back."'[65] Similarly, in Mary Austin's ghost story 'The Readjustment' (1908), we are told that 'Emma Jossyln had been dead and buried three days. The sister who had come to the funeral had taken Emma's child away with her, and the house was swept and aired; then, when it seemed there was least occasion for it, Emma came back.'[66] In other words, short of needing to tidy the house further, no reason presented itself for a 'proper' woman to trouble herself to return from death. Moreover, cleaning and ordering the contents of a home were inextricable from putting the dead securely in their place. As Wharton writes in 'Miss Mary Pask', 'as a rule, after people die, things are tidied up, furniture is sold, remembrances are dispatched to the family.'[67] Packing away the objects associated with them therefore ensures that the dead remain within a very narrow signifying chain, confined within the family, the grave, and a carefully demarcated and completed past that cannot become entangled with the present. Emily Dickinson's poem 1078 amply illustrated the prevalence of this association, describing how

> The Bustle in a House
> The Morning after Death
> Is solemnest of industries
> Enacted upon Earth –
>
> The Sweeping up the Heart
> And putting Love away
> We shall not want to use again
> Until Eternity.[68]

In line with the denial of memory discussed in the next chapter, the drive here was toward drawing a firm line demarcating present and future from a past symbolized by a deceased individual. The need to separate the dead from the living, and America's relentlessly forward-looking mindset, were often difficult to reconcile with domestic and sentimental ideals, which advocated both thriftiness and a continued emotional bond with the dear departed, mediated specifically through household items such as Beth's chair in Louisa May Alcott's *Little Women* (1868/69), which remains in the house as a poignant reminder of the March family's irreparable loss. In less harrowing circumstances, countering the desire for purchasing more and more new things and throwing out the old was an increasing yearning for heirlooms, concrete symbols of the past that celebrated preservation rather than fashion. As an anonymous writer lamented in 1882, 'The old furniture and china is carried away piece by piece to decorate city houses; it would be much better if most of it could stay where it belongs.'[69] Auctioned or second-hand household items spoke too loudly of the vanished presence of the housewife, who had formerly (it is presumed) given them meaning and purpose. Abstracted from the organizing system that was 'home', Philippa Tristram asserts that 'those objects [...], when seen as discrete items, lose the qualities they possessed in combination.'[70] Wilkins' own house, which was described by a contemporary as 'full of her own quaint personality', is depicted as strewn with 'Old decanters, candlesticks, pewter plates and other memorabilia of "ye olden time", nearly all of which have come down to Miss Wilkins by inheritance [...] all the furniture is antique, having belonged to the owner's grandmother.'[71] The writer continues,

> 'I suppose', wrote Miss Wilkins to a friend when she was just settled in her new home, 'that my blue room is one of the queerest-looking places that you ever saw. You should see the people when they come to call. They look doubtful in the front room, but say it is "pretty"; when they get out here they say the rooms look "just like me", and I don't know when I shall ever find out if that is a compliment.'[72]

As this implies, despite functioning as markers of economy, social status, and a proper sentimental attachment to one's ancestors, inherited furniture also caused some social discomfort. The heirloom occupied a rather queasy, liminal status, functioning both as a direct link to a past made acceptable through respectable emotions, and as a haunted object, uncannily bodying forth a past that should be long dead and buried. In 'The Southwest Chamber', Louisa Stark, the first guest to stay in the room, is rendered distinctly uneasy when she catches sight 'On the stand beside the bed', of 'a little *old-fashioned* work-box with a picture of a little boy in a pinafore on the top. Beside this work-box lay, as if just laid down by the user, a spool of black silk, a pair of scissors, and a large steel thimble with a hole in the top, *after an old style*.'[73] Ordinary enough by themselves, the fact that she has not previously noticed these items is given added significance by their antiquity, which disturbs the smooth surface of the modernity she sees herself as inhabiting.

The uncanny possibilities of old or inherited objects is thrown into sharp relief in Peattie's 'A Grammatical Ghost' (1898), which opens, 'There was only one possible objection to the drawing-room, and that was the occasional presence of Miss Carew; and only one possible objection to Miss Carew. And that was, that she was dead.'[74] Miss Carew, who, we are told, 'had been dead twenty years', and who 'to the last of her life sacredly preserved the treasures and traditions' of her eminently respectable New-England family, begins haunting the drawing room of her former home, following the arrival of a family of distant cousins from 'out West', the brother of whom has inherited the Carew home. The contents had initially been packed off to '"Iowa or somewhere else on the frontier"', a state of affairs that the neighbors pronounce as '"dreadful"', but when the Misses Boggs, described as 'two maiden sisters, ladies of excellent taste and manners', take up residence, they set about restoring 'the Carew china to its ancient cabinets, and replac[ing] the Carew pictures upon the walls, with additions not out of keeping with the elegance of these heirlooms.'[75] As becomes clear, Miss Lydia Carew's spectral presence in the drawing room is only a partial vindication of the success of their decorative efforts, as she minutely inspects their china, their taste in paintings and reading material, and even their conversation for any signs of vulgarity, 'bad breeding', or poor taste. Harsh judgments cut both ways, however, and, appalled to witness a phenomenon that could never have happened in Iowa, not to mention rather scandalized that they should harbor anything so untoward as a ghost in their venerable mansion, the sisters find that

> The sofa pillows had been rearranged so that the effect of their grouping was less bizarre than that favored by the Western women; a horrid little Buddhist idol with its eyes fixed on its abdomen, had been chastely hidden behind a Dresden shepherdess, as unfit for the scrutiny of polite eyes; and on the table where Miss Prudence did work in water colors, after the fashion of the impressionists, lay a prim and impossible composition representing a moss-rose and a number of heartsease, colored with that caution which modest spinster artists instinctively exercise.[76]

During one of her curatorial appearances, 'suddenly, with a sharp crash, one of the old Carew tea-cups fell from the tea-table to the floor and was broken. The disaster was followed by what sounded like a sigh of pain and dismay.' Determined to preserve the past at all costs, Miss Carew therefore continues in death her proprietorial dominion over these objects, and is horrified at even the smallest loss. Consequently, what finally exorcizes her is her realization that she can no longer control either the objects or the manners displayed in her former home, upon the arrival of a gentleman, also from 'out West', whose grammar is so appalling that Miss Carew disappears with a 'flash' of 'mortal haste, as when life goes out at a pistol shot!' never to return.[77] What this story illustrates is not only the extent to which the normal role of lady of the house exists on a continuum with the role of ghost but also that what is eminently respectable and comforting in life becomes shameful and sinister when it reaches out from the past to grasp and control the present.

Precisely the same sense of the presence of a (dead) woman pervading the spaces of the living underpins Woodrow's 'Secret Chambers.' The protagonist's new mother-in-law advises her to redecorate the conjugal home, where her son Arnold had lived with his previous, now-dead wife. Stating that she is '"not impressionable or superstitious, but –"' Mrs Hartzfield tells Sylvia that '"The whole place is full of [Adele]"', continuing,

> '[...] She was a feminine Narcissus, and every person she met must be a pool and reflect her. She would tolerate no backgrounds, nor vistas, nor any relieving scenery; she wanted to fill the whole picture from frame to frame, and she could not even have conceived the idea of being one of a group. When she entered the room, she filled it. She filled a house. She took complete possession of your imagination, your will, or she know the reason why [...].'[78]

This dense passage neatly encapsulates many of the concerns at the heart of 'The Southwest Chamber' – a woman's domination of a house and its contents after death; the related possession of another individual through this post-mortem tyranny; and the desire to be seen. As Chapter 1 outlines, Arnold's first wife, Adele, the polar opposite of Phoebe Pyncheon, draws the gaze to herself, while one of Sylvia's 'good' points is that she knows 'when to efface herself' for the sake of her husband. By doing so, she manages in turn to efface Adele's memory, replacing the visually pleasing past with a more outwardly ordinary but morally superior present.[79] It is precisely this ill-advised attachment to self-display that allows her living relatives ultimately to triumph over Aunt Harriet in Wilkins' story.

'The Southwest Chamber'

What permits her reign of terror to remain unchallenged for much of the story is the family pride that ties Sophia Gill, the more rigid, harsher sister, to a house that is more of a liability and a drain on their meager resources than an asset. Despite being the very home from which their grandmother and aunt had mercilessly ejected Sophia and Amanda's mother, following her scandalous marriage to a poor man, Sophia in particular 'had always held her head high when she had walked past that fine old mansion, the cradle of her race, which she was forbidden to enter.' She insists that they keep the house, which is only possible after she and Amanda sell their own home and open up the ancestral abode to boarders, because their aunt, 'Harriet Ackley had used every cent of the Ackley money', leaving 'not a cent with which to pay for repairs and taxes and insurance', rendering the place a 'doubtful blessing'.

The house, in other words, is far from being a gift, and Aunt Harriet is determined to ruin their prospects even further by scaring away their lodgers. In her pride, Sophia inadvertently colludes with her malevolent relative, being perfectly willing to believe that her niece, sister, and boarders are suddenly and communally hysterical, disobedient, or forgetful, but entirely unwilling to believe that the strange occurrences that gain increasing momentum in the place could in any way be attributed to 'that southwest chamber in the dearly beloved old house of her fathers.'[80]

Her incredulity is aided by the fact that the trepidation inspired by the room is depicted repeatedly as radically disengaged from the mere mundane fact of someone's having died there. When Amanda goes to prepare it for Miss Stark, 'she could not have told why she had the dread. She had entered and occupied rooms which had been once tenanted by persons now dead. [...] There had never been any fear. But this was different.' The descriptive passage that follows lingers, not upon the possibility of any haunting presence, but upon the room itself, in which 'The furniture loomed out vaguely', and for much of the story it seems as if the room is haunted, not by a ghost, but by objects.[81] Water disappears from a pitcher, and clothes that Amanda and Sophia remove from the closet return as if by their own volition. The phenomena escalate, as things begin to be transformed into similar items of noticeably dissimilar appearance. When Miss Stark pins the lace at her throat together with a brooch, she feels 'a thrill of horror' when, in the mirror in front of her, '[i]nstead of the familiar bunch of pearl grapes on the black onyx, she saw a knot of blonde and black hair under glass surrounded by a border of twisted gold.' Later, she discovers that the sleeves of her good black dress have been sewn together, and when she goes to the wardrobe to hang up the dress she has been wearing, 'All the pegs were filled with garments not her own, mostly of somber black, but there were some strange-patterned silk things and satins.'[82] Much to her dismay, when she returns to the room with Sophia, the dresses have disappeared, replaced again by her own; so unsettling to her sense of normality is this series of small but exceptional events that she precipitously returns to her original room.

Despite the other boarders' dire warnings, Mrs Simmons, a stubbornly sensible widow, moves in, only to be almost strangled in her sleep by 'a queer, old-fashioned frilled nightcap', which again returns to the room whenever it is removed, and which persists in its murderous purpose even after Mrs Simmons has first thrown it out of the window and then cut it to shreds with a scissors.[83] The most significant moment comes when Mrs Simmons notices that the material (chintz, of course) covering a chair and the hangings on the bedstead, which is decorated with peacocks (in an unusual change from the parrots that dominate previous chapters) on a blue ground, has changed to red roses on a yellow ground, a phenomenon also noted by the librarian, Miss Lippincott some days earlier:

> Mrs Simmons was struck in her most venerable [*sic*] point. This apparent contradiction of the reasonable as manifested in such a commonplace thing as chintz of a bed-hanging, affected this ordinarily unimaginative woman as no ghostly appearance could have done. Those red roses on the yellow ground were to her much more ghostly than any strange figure clad in white robes of the grave entering the room.[84]

In conjuring up the image of a ghost while simultaneously asserting its absence from the spaces created by the narration, this passage crystallizes the story's implication in and subversion of turn-of-the-century associations of femininity and death, particularly the nexus of associations around whiteness, purity, and spirituality. The eponymous specter in Wilkins' 'The Lost Ghost' (1903) is a young girl who had been starved and frozen to death by her beautiful but promiscuous mother, whose skin and clothing are described as being 'white' four times in the space of a few lines. Appearing inexplicably in the female protagonist's house one day, 'She did not seem to run or walk like other children. She flitted, like one of those little filmy white butterflies, that don't seem like real ones they are so light, and move as if they had no weight.'[85] Like Hawthorne's heroine, this ethereal, colorless creature carries out household tasks invisibly, still caring for the home in which her mother's neglect has killed her.

Clad in flowing white and purged of all bodily associations, the conventional ghost that Mrs Simmons is sure would be less frightening than the eerily mutable chintz therefore recalls the Angel in the House, a spiritual being whose unswerving selflessness converged with her lack of earthly appetites, an almost spectral incorporeality symbolized by the spotlessness of her *habillements*.[86] Nineteenth-century bourgeois domestic ideology on both sides of the Atlantic enshrined an image of the ideal woman as one whose 'value resided chiefly in her femaleness rather than in traditional signs of status, a woman who possessed psychological depth rather than an attractive surface.' The middle-class domestic angel stood in sharp contrast to the privileged, beautiful, well-dressed, aristocratic woman who, Armstrong argues, 'embodied material instead of moral value, and displayed sensuality instead of constant vigilance and tireless concern for the well-being of others. Such a woman was not truly female.'[87] Castigating women who give themselves up to the study of 'outward beauty' and the 'tinsel glare' of fashionable dress, an American deacon named Amos Chase admonished in 1791 that overly showy beauty 'is frequently the fatal means of seduction and ruin', and worse, that the woman concerned with her appearance might 'invite in vanity and pride, disgraceful and disgusting, to fill her vacant mind.'[88]

'The Southwest Chamber' is rather more equivocal regarding superficial ornament and color. Its richly woven narrative fabric is studded with objects decorated with vivid hues and intricate patterns that it implicitly celebrates. The pitcher from which water mysteriously vanishes is described as covered with a blue and white pattern; the dresser in Aunt Harriet's room is meticulously drawn; and the sewing box that lies next to Louisa Stark's altered gown is evoked in minute detail. When Miss Stark, who wears 'a black India silk dress with purple flowers' embellished with lace, settles herself into the room, we are told, in more detail than is necessary for the plot, how she 'removed her bonnet, and its tuft of red geraniums lightened the obscurity of the mahogany dresser. She had placed her little beaded cape carefully on the bed.'[89] Similarly, the sisters' orphaned niece, Flora, is described as clad in an inherited wardrobe that came with the house, and that includes 'an obsolete turban-shaped hat of black straw which had belonged to the dead aunt', and a dress made from 'an ancient purple-and-white print.'[90] As all of this amply illustrates, lavishly ornamented material objects are here (as elsewhere) depicted as inextricable from respectable middle-class life. Wilkins' 'The Shadows on the Wall' (1903) also features intricate descriptions of domestic interiors, most notably when one female character enters a room carrying

> a lamp – a large one with a white porcelain shade. She set it on a table, an old-fashioned card-table which was placed against the opposite wall from the window. That wall was clear of bookcases and books, which were only on three sides of the room. That opposite wall was taken up with three doors, the one small space being occupied by the table. Above the table on the old fashioned paper, of a white satin gloss, traversed by an indeterminate green scroll, hung quite high a small gilt and black-framed ivory miniature taken in her girlhood of the mother of the family. When the lamp was set on the table

beneath it, the tiny pretty face painted on the ivory seemed to gleam out with a look of intelligence.[91]

The lamp reveals that, among all this decorative richness, these very surfaces – specifically the walls surrounding them – have recorded the shadowy image of one of the men of the family killing his brother. The lamp, the walls, and the room itself aid in the revelation of evil deeds, allowing the women to understand what has happened there. The disgruntled Aunt Harriet's chosen method of materialization, via 'strange-patterned silks' and gaudy chintz, is therefore part of a discourse situating such objects as instrumental in the maintenance of domestic peace, and almost identical to the home habits (in every sense) of the story's living characters.[92] Indeed, objects in general are directly associated with the financial and personal independence of the story's central characters. While Sophia has managed to buy their original, modest abode by teaching in a primary school, her sister 'crocheted lace, and embroidered flannel, and made tidies and pincushions, and had earned enough for her clothes' and those of their orphaned niece, Flora. Having come into their inheritance, however, they no longer need to purchase clothing for her, since her 'wardrobe was supplied for years to come from that of the deceased aunt. There were stored away in the garret of the Ackley house enough voluminous black silks and satins and bombazines to keep her clad in somber richness' indefinitely.[93] The lavish nature of this costume borders on the transgressive, strongly calling to mind Hester Prynne's illegitimate daughter, Pearl, in Hawthorne's *The Scarlet Letter* (1850).

What renders such objects problematic in Wilkins' story is not their associations with material indulgence, however, but their links to a traumatic and oppressive past. This is initially made clear when, staring at the impossibilities occurring in her room 'with eyes at once angry and terrified', Louisa Stark 'straightway began to wonder if there could be anything wrong with her mind. She remembered that an aunt of her mother's had been insane. A sort of fury with herself possessed her.'[94] This gothic fear of inherited insanity or 'badness', central to Alcott's *A Whisper in the Dark*, surfaces repeatedly in contemporary ghost stories. In Mary Heaton Vorse's 'The Second Wife' (1912), the protagonist, Beata, feels compelled to make small changes to the decoration and furniture of the conjugal home, apparently urged to do so by the presence of her husband's first wife, who had died of a nervous disease while Beata nursed her. She finds herself repeatedly 'shoving around the ornaments, rearranging them with a sort of bitter satisfaction, an inward glow quite out of keeping with her trivial occupation', and then suddenly not being sure where she is or why she is doing this.[95] She is horrified to realize that her very selfhood is under threat, that her body but also her mind and her emotions are being used by her predecessor in order to continue her domestic dominion into the present. Nevertheless, despite this strong psychological slant to the tale, the material world is inextricable from the fabric of the story, and decorative items are the medium through which this possession is effected.

A similar fear of the quasi-supernatural transmission of negative familial personality traits though inherited domestic things and spaces forms the crisis of 'The Southwest Chamber'. When Sophia spends the night in the room, in an effort to end the hysteria that has gripped her sister, her niece, and her lodgers, its contents remain demurely immobile. Instead, she finds herself filled with hostile thoughts and feelings, 'remembering what she could not have remembered' about her mother's exile from the family home, and is overwhelmed by 'bitter resentment' and 'malignant' feelings directed toward her mother, her sisters, her niece, and indeed herself. While 'Evil suggestions surged in her brain – suggestions which turned her heart to stone', nonetheless, 'by a sort of double consciousness she knew that what she thought was strange and not due to her own volition. She knew that she was thinking the thoughts of some other person, and she knew who. She felt herself possessed.' Sophia manages to overcome even this most intimate of invasions by exerting a 'strength for good and righteous self-assertion' that she has inherited, but in altered form, 'from the evil strength of her ancestors', turning 'their own weapons against themselves.'[96] However, it appears that Aunt Harriet's poisonous presence is less easily banished from the spaces and objects of the house than from her mind. When Sophia sits down at the dressing table, she is confronted with the fact that the possession extends to her personal appearance:

> She looked in the glass and saw, instead of her softly parted waves of hair, harsh lines of iron-gray under the black borders of an old-fashioned head-dress. She saw instead of her smooth, broad forehead, a high one wrinkled with the intensest concentration of selfish reflections of a long life; she saw instead of her steady blue eyes, black ones with depths of malignant reserve, behind a broad meaning of ill will; she saw instead of her firm benevolent mouth one with a hard, thin

line, a network of melancholic wrinkles. She saw instead of her own face, middle-aged and good to see, the expression of a life of honesty and good will to others and patience under trials, the face of a very old woman scowling forever with unceasing hatred and misery at herself and all others, at life, and death, at that which had been and that which was to come. She saw instead of her own face in the glass, the face of her dead Aunt Harriet, topping her own shoulders in her own well-known dress![97]

So appalled is Sophia (who flees the room) that she tells Amanda at once that they must sell the place, and insists that her sister never ask her about what has happened. Aunt Harriet has gone too far, and by emerging from out behind the objects in her death chamber and appearing as herself, she has unwittingly provided the final impetus needed for the Gill sisters to cut their losses and break free from the strictures of the past. As in *The House of the Seven Gables*, leaving the family mansion is here a triumph of the progressive present over the dead weight of the past, which must never be spoken of again, snapping the chain of 'ill will' that has, until now, passed down unbroken through their female relatives.

Abandoning the birds and flowers figured on the chintz upholstery in favor of her own face, Aunt Harriet has, like Ligeia, Madeleine Usher, and the women in Gilman's wallpaper, finally adopted the appearance of a traditional apparition, thereby clearing up any lingering mystery as to why the room and its contents are so eerily animated. As Amanda and Mrs Simmons' experiences indicate, Aunt Harriet's earlier manifestations through the room's material objects resist being interpreted as relating to Sophia and Amanda's mother, to the events of the past, or even directly to Harriet herself. It is not the sense that someone has died there or might reappear that is so unnerving, but merely the room itself. The mirror incident replaces the disturbingly multifarious phenomena of which the story is constructed, and which appear to be worryingly independent of human will or agency, with a single meaning – the wrongs of the past and the malice of an identifiable, visible woman. It would seem that Aunt Harriet too has been seduced by what is in effect an arabesque reading practice since, as with the Ligeia–Rowena relationship, one woman (Sophia) is here exploited as an empty vessel for the thoughts and features of another, and, as in Poe's stories, her appearance brings an abrupt close to the narrative. Although the sisters' departure indicates that their aunt has succeeded in driving them out of their home a second time, the ending of the story also terminates the spiteful old woman's post-mortem domestic tyranny, and they determine to abandon the place rather than allowing her spite to survive from beyond the grave.

A similar exorcism of a stubbornly persistent past occurs in Dunbar's 'The Shell of Sense'. Realizing that her husband and her sister have fallen in love during her long illness and particularly since her death, the spectral narrator is determined to prevent any consummation of this love, and strains her 'fluttering, uncertain forces' with a 'terrible effort', and suddenly, with 'a bright, terrible flash', she *attain[s] visibility*. Standing before the hesitant lovers, 'luminously apparent', her visibility allows her, much like Aunt Harriet, to look 'straight into Theresa's soul'.[98] Doing so, however, only scares the pair, who had been on the point of parting for fear of the dead woman's disapproval, into one another's arms. At the moment of her triumph over invisibility, then, she is thwarted by her own attempt both to materialize and to see where she has no right to see. Moreover, this effort finally severs her remaining ties to 'mortality', and all her 'gross and tenacious' emotions are transformed into unearthly benevolence, as she realizes that 'There will be no further semblance of me in my old home, [...] no dimmest echo of my earthly self.'[99] As with Aunt Harriet, here, becoming visible is precisely the movement that puts a halt to Dunbar's narrator's ability to manipulate the material world, although in her case, she simultaneously becomes a bodiless, selfless angel, the polar opposite of Aunt Harriet's malign presence.

The problematic nature of visibility in these ghost stories can, to some degree, be traced back to contemporary discourses surrounding photography, which was often figured as a means of arresting time in a chaotic modernity into which mortality too frequently intruded. As one commentator noted in 1863, 'with these literal transcriptions of features and forms, once dear to us, ever at hand, we are scarcely more likely to forget, or grow cold to their originals, than we should in their corporeal presence.'[100] Unlike the daguerreotype, a one-of-a-kind artifact, often housed in an elaborate casing, the image of which flickered in and out depending on the angle at which it was viewed, later photographic technologies were mass-produced, cheaper, easily copied, and with stable, flat images.[101] Indeed, the daguerreotype itself was associated with both obsolescence and spectrality, as evidenced by the fact that, in a comparison made repeatedly throughout the story, Miss Carew's phantom in Peattie's 'A Grammatical Ghost' bears a marked 'resemblance [...] to a faded daguerrotype [*sic*]. If looked at one way, she was perfectly discernible; if looked at another, she went out in a sort of blur.'[102] A visit to an early photo gallery in New York in 1846 prompted Walt Whitman to exclaim that the place contained 'a great legion of human faces – human eyes gazing silently but fixedly upon you, and creating the impression of an immense Phantom concourse – speechless and motionless, but yet realities', together forming a 'new world – a peopled world, though mute as the grave.'[103] Earlier still, an 1839 article prefigures Wilkins' and Dunbar's stories; the author, upon seeing a daguerreotype for the first time, stated tremulously, 'What would you say to looking in a mirror and having the image fastened! As one looks sometimes, it is really quite frightful to think of it; but such a thing is possible – nay, it is probable – no, it is certain.'[104] Unsurprisingly, the idea of having one's 'image fastened' was equally employed as a means of admonishing perceived female vanity and concern with outward appearance. As an 1851 article announced,

> Years spent in coquetry and caprice, in folly and frivolity, the entire abandonment to self-worship, and the entire neglect of mental culture, cannot pass without leaving an unlovely record on the face, and a background of embittered feeling, which no artistic power can render attractive. Stereotyped then, are the motives of the past.[105]

What this passage makes abundantly clear is that the moral 'depth' of the ideal nineteenth-century woman intimately involved her with surfaces – both those of her own body, which supposedly displayed her inner goodness or otherwise, and those of the home, which, in her role as glorified, unpaid housekeeper, she supervised and ordered. Aunt Harriet and Felipa simultaneously reclaim the spaces of the home for themselves, through those very surfaces. Not only do they remain within their houses, refusing to be relegated to the grave, but they also refuse to be housed in their own bodies on any level, instead appearing via a riotous explosion of ornament. As repetitive patterns of birds and flowers take the place of the image of the reified female body, these specters evade the gaze that sought to render unearthly phenomena easily defined, studied, and understood. They also constitute a powerful riposte to the cultural depiction of the dead as universally benign to their surviving 'loved ones', safely tucked away in eternal heavenly mansions. Paradoxically, by continuing to inhabit a woman's 'place' – the home – but also the blatantly worldly possessions that it contains, the murderous old woman's equivocal manifestations position her as radically *out* of place, and it is only when she allows herself to be objectified that she is returned to it. As the next chapter illustrates, had she remained invisible, and thus resistant to exorcism, her reign of terror could have continued among new generations of Ackley women indefinitely.

5

'Space Stares All Around': Peattie's 'The House That Was Not' and the (Un)Haunted Landscape

Elia W. Peattie's story 'The House That Was Not' (1898) opens as Flora, the newly married protagonist, joins her settler husband, Burt, on his ranch on the Western plains. Looking around at the landscape, she feels 'as if a new world had been made for her', but her tranquility is broken when she notices a little house off to the west that Burt has never mentioned. Wondering why he has omitted it from conversation, worrying that he seems not to wish her to meet their only neighbors, she quizzes him repeatedly, until, reluctantly, he gives in, telling her in no uncertain terms that '"There ain't no house there"', that he himself had gone to investigate it and found nothing. He recounts how, confounded, he asked a neighbor for information, and is told that

> '[...] a man an' his wife come out here t' live an' put up that there little place. An' she was young, you know, an' kind o' skeery, and she got lonesome. It worked on her an' worked on her, an' one day she up an' killed the baby an' her husband an' herself. Th' folks found 'em and buried 'em right there on their own ground. Well, about two weeks after that, th' house was burned down. Don't know how. Tramps, maybe. Anyhow, it burned. At least, I guess it burned!'
> 'You guess it burned!'
> 'Well, it ain't there, you know.'
> 'But if it burned the ashes are there.'
> 'All right, girlie, they're there then. Now let's have tea.'[1]

Of course, being a feisty little thing of seventeen, Flora is far from satisfied with this partial, paradoxical answer, so soon afterwards, we are told,

She got on Ginger's back – Ginger being her own yellow broncho – and set off at a hard pace for the house. It didn't appear to come any nearer, but the objects which had seemed to be beside it came closer into view, and Flora pressed on, with her mind steeled for anything. But as she approached the poplar windbreak which stood to the north of the house, the little shack waned like a shadow before her. It faded and dimmed before her eyes.

She slapped Ginger's flanks and kept him going, and she at last got him up to the spot. But there was nothing there. The bunch grass grew tall and rank and in the midst of it lay a baby's shoe. Flora thought of picking it up, but something cold in her veins withheld her. Then she grew angry, and set Ginger's head toward the place and tried to drive him over it. But the yellow broncho gave one snort of fear, gathered himself in a bunch, and then, all tense, leaping muscles, made for home as only a broncho can.[2]

The story comes to an abrupt halt here, offering nothing else in the way of explanation or development, leaving us as much in the dark as Flora is herself about what exactly she has experienced. It therefore succeeds in asserting that this version of the Great Plains is simultaneously marked and unmarked by the haunting memory of a troubled past, employing the supernatural as a means of juxtaposing two irreconcilable states. In doing so, 'The House That Was Not' rejects the consolatory and explanatory function of much gothic fiction, in which plucky heroines (like Sybil in Alcott's *A Whisper in the Dark*) reveal hidden pasts, thereby disentangling them from haunted presents.[3] Peattie's story therefore both acknowledges and resists the conventional insistence that America, and particularly the West, was fundamentally ahistorical. In narrating a past that conceals itself while refusing to remain concealed, Peattie's story is situated on the fault line between memory and amnesia that underpinned the nation's self-defining narratives, highlighting the problematic nature of haunting in a country so resistant to being marked by past events.

The slightness of Peattie's story renders it somewhat opaque to interpretation; however, juxtaposing it with contemporary discourses surrounding the 'empty' rural spaces of the United States, and women's role within these spaces, allows it to be read as an assertion of the failure of gothic plot trajectories in such a cultural landscape. By examining in turn the role of women in the great move Westward; the mnemonic characteristics of the land itself; and the part played by domestic objects in their lives and in the cultural construction of landscape, it becomes clear that, in the nineteenth-century American imagination, that land-scape was in fact *twice* haunted. On the one hand, the less inhabited regions of the American continent were often depicted as frightening simply because they testified to Nature's utter indifference to human struggles or memories. On the other hand, the efforts made to insist on the lack of human landmarks, even in the face of mass settlement and cultivation, which was often traumatic for those involved, left it haunted by half-remembered, fragmentary ghosts that could not be exorcized precisely because the memories attached to them could not be brought to light. The role of the gothic heroine therefore became at once imperative and impossible. Enjoined to uncover and release the haunting past, and yet coming up short against an insistence that this landscape could only ever be depicted as a source of plenty and prosperity, the Western gothic heroine found herself entangled in a double bind from which she lacked the tools to free herself or those around her. The repeated assertions of physical and temporal emptiness left her without the resources to identify past patriarchal abuses – or indeed to defeat them in the future. Unable to exorcize the past, she was equally unable to save herself from repeating it. The result was tales like Peattie's – truncated, lacking satisfactory explanations or conclu-sions, and ultimately pessimistic.

Reluctant pioneers

It is not in women that the pioneer spirit stirs; the horizon does not beckon them; hills and rivers are to them a barrier, not an invita-tion to explore. It was the men only who pressed on across the great plains; the women had little more to say than the horses who drew the wagons in which they sat. Where women had the deciding word no move was made.[4]

This passage, from John Beames' 1937 novel *An Army Without Banners*, illustrates nicely the stubborn insistence in United-States literature and thought that the largely unsettled land in the western areas of the continent was not women's sphere of action, that women were fundamentally unsuited to the Western experience. Frederick Jackson Turner, in his famous formulation, described the nineteenth-century American Frontier, the point at which the inexorable westward move-ment of exploration and civilization met the uncharted wastes of the virgin forest, trackless wilderness, or boundless prairie, as 'a military training school, keeping alive the power of resistance to aggression, and developing the stalwart and rugged qualities of the frontiersman.'[5] First and foremost, then, if the West was the defining American experience, then the ideal American subject was male.[6] In *The Great Plains* (1931), Walter Prescott Webb asserted that men who went westward to settle the vast and recently 'discovered' prairies enjoyed a considerable 'zest to the life, adventure in the air, freedom from restraint; men developed a hardihood that made them insensible to the hardships and lack of refinement.'[7] The American vision of femininity, by contrast, was not merely tied to the home but actively opposed to exploration and migration. The women who followed these men westward were perceived as overcome by 'fear and distrust of the land; they were lonely and missed the comforts of former homes and the cultural activities of former communities', as commentators agreed that women never actually wished to go West, and were miserable when they got there.[8] Francis Parkman similarly depicted women as 'divided between regrets for the homes they had left and fear of the deserts and savages before them', while Hamlin Garland's *A Son of the Middle Border* (1917) saw life on the frontier for a woman as characterized by 'deprivation, suffering, loneliness, heartache.'[9]

While such depictions were often unfairly exaggerated, serving to cement the image of the West as a fundamentally masculine milieu, the experience of moving there was certainly sharply polarized along gendered lines. Many American families had few choices but to pack up and leave during the nineteenth century, when population and economic pressures meant that many eastern regions could no longer support all those settled in them. These practical considerations often went hand in hand with rather more ideological lures, including the idea that the journey itself somehow constituted a feat of manhood that guaranteed greater personal freedom. The gender dynamics of this move, and women's dearth of career choices outside of marriage, meant that they were often dragged along on journeys for which they had little relish and over which they had little or no control. While John Mack Farragher notes that both men and women's diaries recorded a sense that the landscape of the West was 'one of the most beautiful and desolate sights they had ever seen', in every other way, he asserts, men and women's accounts of the journey itself, and of the social relations and duties attached to it, were very different:

Women were concerned with family and relational values – the happiness and health of children, home and hearth, getting along with the travelling group, and friendship, especially with women.

Men were concerned with violence and aggression – fights, conflicts, and competition, and most of all hunting.[10]

Engaged in 'the mission to bring light, law, liberty, Christianity, and commerce to the savage places of the earth', the language in which men were encouraged to move West and in which they were depicted as struggling to live there was essentially martial.[11] 'Unredeemed' Nature, not yet exploited by European settlement, was seen as cut off from God and hence essentially immoral and hellish; if 'wilderness was the villain', then 'the pioneer, as hero, relished its destruction' – a figuration that served neatly to motivate and justify the American desire to transform and tame it.[12] According to one mid-century guidebook for would-be settlers, 'you look around and whisper, "I vanquished this wilderness and made the chaos pregnant with order and civilisation, alone I did it."'[13] Similarly, as Bess Streeter Aldrich put it in her 1935 novel *Spring Came on Forever*, 'the wilderness was a giant with which to wrestle. It must be fought, – more, it must be overcome or it in turn would conquer them.'[14]

As Willa Cather's *O Pioneers!* (1913) made clear, however, men's efforts were to no avail without feminine aid. Of the protagonist's father, Cather wrote that 'in eleven long years John Bergson had made but little impression upon the wild land he had come to tame. It was still a wild thing that had its ugly moods; and no one knew when they were likely to come, or why. Mischance hung over it. Its Genius was unfriendly to man.'[15] It is only after his death, when his daughter Alexandra takes over the farm, that the family begins to prosper, and the land to lose its terrifying, hostile aspect – despite the best efforts of her ne'er-do-well brothers to send everything further into ruination. Increasingly relied upon to hold society together in a democratic state, the bourgeois woman therefore functioned as a kind of pressure point. Ralph Waldo Emerson saw feminine influence as civilizing mankind, asking rhetorically, 'What is civilization? I answer, the power of good women.'[16] Recruited to keep the States united, the ideal bourgeois woman was valued for what she did rather than for who she was.

Beneath the exciting surfaces of their action-packed, largely homosocial plots, novels such as Owen Wister's *The Virginian* (1902) and Zane Grey's *Riders of the Purple Sage* (1912) implicitly dramatize a family-oriented ideology which stressed that the need for women's alleged civilizing powers was particularly urgent in the comparatively lawless regions of the Great Plains and beyond, where the presence of (middle-class) women should ideally ensure that moral standards were kept.[17] The Western woman was a valuable commodity in a system that might appear to value male isolation and freedom, but that, for its economic success, required a replication of the nuclear family and an intensification of individual women's work. With the ratio of men to women standing at approximately ten to one, a guide for settlers from 1858 urged, 'We want families, because their homes and hearth stones everywhere, are the only true and reliable basis of any nation.'[18] As Dora Aydelotte wrote in her novel *Trumpets Calling* (1938), 'Men were needed to tame the wilderness, but it took women like Martha Prawl to make its waste places blossom like the rose' – in other words, to render these spaces beautiful, stable, and homelike.[19] The result was reams of cultural propaganda that claimed to 'show' (in direct contradiction to those who saw it as a bachelor's paradise) that the pioneer life was idyllic, one to which women 'adjusted' without difficulty or complaint – or rather, by suppressing the desire to complain. Depicting the wife as the 'queen' or 'mistress' of the house with which she was all but identified, and to which she ran joyfully, one mid-century commentator on Western life asserted that

> The wife knows what her duties are and resolutely goes about performing them. [...] She cooks his dinner, nurses his children, shares his hardships, and encourages his industry. She never complains of having too much work to do, she does not desert her home to make endless visits – she borrows no misfortunes, has no imaginary ailings. Milliners and mantua-makers she ignores – 'shopping' she never heard of – scandal she never invents or listens to. She never wishes for fine carriages, professes no inability to walk five hundred yards, and does not think it a 'vulgar accomplishment', to know how to make butter. She has no groundless anxieties [...]. She is, in short, a faithful, honest wife [...].[20]

This idealized portrait is all too transparently predicated upon the wife's suppression of any independent thought or desires, voluntarily burying herself in the house, in the midst of vast natural splendor. While their husbands worked hard but relatively unstructured days out in the open air, women rapidly found that the West was 'not their domain of action' – that they effectively facilitated but could not participate in the male freedom and enjoyment of fresh air, open spaces, and natural beauty central to prosettlement writing.[21]

The emphasis on feminine self-sacrifice meant that nineteenth-century, middle-class American women 'were socialized to adjust to almost every situation and relationship they encountered', and 'able to accommodate themselves to a landscape that insists on being accepted on its own terms', rather than seeking to conquer and subdue it. Arguably, then, they occupied 'a very different space from that which men occupy', one that positioned them within rather than against their environment, allowing them 'despite loneliness and isolation', to 'establish a kind of compatibility with it.'[22] While early novels depict (male) heroism as a struggle *against* the land and an antagonistic relationship with it, Carol Fairbanks argues that later works by women writers 'generally insist on women's heroism arising out of their ability to work *with* the land.'[23] What this often transformed into, however, was a simplistic conflation of woman and land, rather than a symbiotic interaction – a unity into which (in a familiar motif) the woman was all but absorbed. Mary Hartwell Catherwood's *The Spirit of an Illinois Town* (1897), for example, describes a central female character as

> Sprung out of hardship, buoyant and full of resources, big-hearted, patient, great, – how mightily did she express the soul of the West! [...]
> 'The Spirit of this town, – that's what she was; just as a beautiful ideal woman expresses the Goddess of Liberty. Pluck and genius and humility, boundless energy and vision, and personal power that carried everything before it, – all these covered with the soft flesh of a child just turning woman, – that was Kate.'[24]

In other words, the reconciliation to frontier life was filtered through the objectified body of a woman, which was itself inextricable from commodified land, in the process obscuring the conditions of exchange and manufacture that underpin the relationship between woman and land. Tellingly, the 'Spirit of the Town' is later killed in a tornado, implying that the relationship is by no means as benign as this imagery might seek to suggest. As Chapter 1 illustrates, representational violence slid all too easily into actual violence perpetrated against female characters – in this case, by the land itself. So how to escape this – how to avoid becoming subsumed into a landscape that is indifferent to humanity at best, and antagonistic at worst, and to which woman must be sacrificed in order to assure male profit and the forward march of the nation? The specific form taken by much American female gothic fiction offers one possible solution, exploiting the uncanny potential of this symbiotic relationship, and foregrounding its dark side in the form, not of conquest *or* sublimation, but of open and ongoing hostility between woman and land.

One reason for this hostility is that the superimposition of Eastern standards of homemaking onto the Western landscape, climate, and marketplaces was by no means a seamless one, exacerbating women's sense of displacement. The amount of work necessary in order to make life on the Frontier homelike entailed an endless, repetitive round of cooking, cleaning, sewing, and caring for the sick.[25] D.H. Lawrence evocatively described the frontier wife as a 'Poor haggard drudge, like a ghost wailing in the wilderness, nine times out of ten.'[26] Charlotte Perkins Gilman asserted that the country's asylums were largely inhabited by farmer's wives; and a report commissioned in 1862 warned that excessive emphasis on work, and a lack of awareness of women's needs for social outlets, material comforts, and a 'respectable' personal appearance, could lead to psychic breakdown and insanity.[27] Considerably earlier again, Alexis de Tocqueville had depicted the frontier wife as a noble sufferer, having sacrificed her own present for the future of her children and, by extension, her country. He described entering the cabin of a settler family, which was occupied by a woman 'in the prime of life', watching her children 'with mingled melancholy and joy: to look at their strength and her languor, one might imagine that the life she has given them has exhausted her own, and regrets not what they have cost her.'[28] The flow of energy went outward from the woman, and all that she received in return was a future that she may not live to see. De Tocqueville's brief description focuses in on her physical appearance, which, he remarked,

> seems superior to her condition, and her apparel even betrays a lingering taste for dress; her delicate limbs appear shrunken, her features are drawn in, her eye is mild and melancholy; her whole physiognomy bears marks of a degree of religious resignation, a deep quiet of all passions, and some sort of natural and tranquil firmness, ready to meet all the ills of life, without fearing and without braving them.[29]

While here, her own 'lingering' desire for material adornment is quickly subsumed into her 'religious resignation' that suppresses and overcomes the 'passions', the cabin itself bears the marks of her tastes. The impression is of a home cobbled together under difficult circumstances, dominated by 'a rude table, with legs of green wood, and with the bark still on them, looking as if they grew out of the ground on which they stood; but on this table a teapot of British china, silver spoons, cracked teacups, and some newspapers.'[30] The juxtaposition of a rugged, barely man-made surface and decaying but once-fine objects, brought from another life, foregrounds the wife's role in fashioning a homelike space out of the materials left to her by the rigors of the journey and the wear and tear of a life in which such objects could not be replaced. What this passage articulates most clearly is the relief with which the narrative gaze moves from the (ungodly) female desire to decorate herself to the (patriotic) impulse to decorate and furnish her home for the sake of her productive husband and promising, healthy children – at whatever cost to herself. It is here, however, that the possibility of resistance is opened up, within the uncertain cultural space of the commodity. In particular, even on the prairies, domestic objects were depicted in the Gilded Age as repositories of memory, and hence as a means whereby female characters could engage meaningfully with and leave their mark on the landscape.

Beloved battered objects

When she moves out West to Texas for the sake of her man, the main character of Loula Grace Erdman's *The Edge of Time* (1950) is shocked at the sheer emptiness of the prospect before her, a place where, in Emily Dickinson's words 'Space stares all around – '.[31] We are told,

> The first thing Bethany saw was nothing. Nothing at all. She pitched her mind in nothingness, found herself drowning in it as a swimmer drowns in water too deep for him.
> Here was more sky than she had ever seen before. That was all there was – sky. No houses, no trees, no roads. Nothing to break the landscape. She shrank from it, as one draws from sudden bright light.[32]

Even in the eastern part of the country, America 'suffer[ed] from poverty in the matter of ruins.' This was to be lamented, because

> a place where people have lived for a long time keeps many signs of their habitation, and nature grows into some likeness to humanity and a close association with the human lives that bloomed and faded and were covered with earth. Where there are grass-grown, crowded burying-grounds, with headstones from which the weather has had time to rub out the inscriptions, one likes to find as many relics as possible that the old inhabitants have left behind.[33]

Objects functioned as a means of providing an immediate past to the apparently pastless, unpopulated landscape, and venerable, stable, identifiable signs of an Anglo-European past were valuable in the United States more generally precisely because of their scarcity. Within this context, central to the role of pioneer wife was a cultural imperative urging women to attach personal memories to things in order to draw disparate individuals into the 'civilizing' sphere of the family. This is particularly evident in one of Peattie's more realist tales, 'The Three Johns' (1896), in which one of the eponymous male characters takes shelter in a cabin during a vicious dust storm, which turns out to house a woman and her three small children. When it is revealed that the woman, a recent widow, is alone out West, hoping to make a living for her young family all by herself, it rapidly becomes clear that objects and motherhood are inextricable. John Henderson watches the woman, Catherine, fold a 'blanket over the sleeping baby [...], and the action brought to her guest the recollection of a thousand tender moments of his dimly remembered youth.'[34] The redemptive powers of home life exert considerable influence:

> Henderson marvelled how she could in those few minutes have rescued the cabin from the desolation in which the storm had plunged it. Out of the window he could see the stricken grasses dripping cold moisture, and the sky still angrily plunging forward like a disturbed sea. Not a tree or a house broke the view. The desolation of it swept over him as it never had before. But within the little ones were chattering to themselves in odd baby dialect, and the mother was laughing with them.[35]

As well as providing a warm and welcoming home for children and men, however, objects also functioned as important markers of identity for the women who made use of them, and accrued even greater significance as the rigors of moving out West made them all the scarcer, and women found it difficult but often necessary to leave behind treasured possessions. One woman recalled her mother finally winning a battle with her husband to bring along her favorite rocking chair, and she then took to 'sitting in that chair in the midst of the endless plains when we stopped for the night.'[36] At the other end of the scale, wagon trains often came across what seemed to be cherished objects that had simply been abandoned in the middle of the trail.[37] Small acts of decoration and ornamentation, such as 'Coverlets, counterpanes, crocheted samplers, and most especially the elaborate patchwork or appliqué front pieces for quilts' therefore took on considerable emotional and psychological weight. As '[o]ne farm woman testified [...]: "I would have lost my mind if I had not had my quilts to do."'[38]

Highlighting Western women's deep-seated but often frustrated need to fulfill their cultural role by making their homes pleasing, another of Peattie's non-supernatural tales, 'Jim Lancy's Waterloo', which reuses the motif of a couple moving into an isolated cabin on the prairies, is far less confident than 'The Three Johns' about the ability of women and children to tame both the landscape and the men who inhabit it. 'Jim Lancy's Waterloo' effectively tells what could be the backstory of the woman in the little cabin that Flora can see but not find. From its very opening, marital strife is the dominant note, as the eponymous Jim insists that his wife Annie come out West to marry him earlier than originally planned, simply so that he can '"get the crops in on time."'[39] As they travel westward toward his embryonic farm on their wedding day, the divergence in their views of the prairie landscape is highlighted, as Annie cannot see the beauty that Jim claims to find there. In particular, he admires the vistas and the sense of freedom they engender, as opposed to what he sees as the more cluttered landscape back East. To Annie, however, 'The farm-houses seemed very low and mean', and she is appalled to note that 'There were no fences, excepting now and then the inhospitable barbed wire. The door-yards were bleak to her eyes, without the ornamental shrubbery which every farmer in her part of the country was used to tending.'[40] Here, the lack of *things* in the Western landscape foreshadows her inability, despite having made '"up [her] mind not to be lonesome"', to transform what is essentially her husband's workspace into a comfortable or even a functioning home.

Indeed, Jim's attitude toward the land, which mingles idealism and pecuniary desire, renders her job extremely difficult. In the episode on the train, while Annie gazes at the emptiness in horror, Jim views the land through what could be interpreted as Transcendentalist lenses. We see him looking for 'a long time'

at the gentle undulations of the brown Iowa prairie. His eyes seemed to pierce beneath the sod, to the swelling buds of the yet invisible grass. He noticed how disdainfully the rains of the new year beat down the grasses of the year that was gone. It opened to his mind a vision of the season's possibilities. For a moment, even amid the smoke of the car, he seemed to scent clover, and hear the stiff swishing of the corn and the dull burring of the bees.[41]

While the imagery here is romanticized, the gaze itself values beauty only insofar as it indicates commercial potential – his appreciation of the freshness of the prairie is never far away from a sense of what may be earned from it. In essence, then, we return here to the difference between the metaphorical and the metonymic – between reading through something and actually paying attention to its visible surfaces.

It is perhaps for this reason that Jim fails to perceive the warning implicit in the face of a woman they pass outside the train station, Mrs Dundy, whose greeting is friendly, but who is so wizened-looking (despite Jim's assurance that she is barely thirty years old) that the sight of her causes 'A tightening around her heart' that saps Annie's 'vivacity'. The movement from woman to house is seamless; looking bleakly from Mrs Dundy, whose eyes contain a spark of madness, to 'little famished-looking houses, unacquainted with paint, disorderly yards, and endless reaches of furrowed ground, where in summer the corn had waved', Annie comes upon her own house. It strikes her as 'a square little house, in uncorniced simplicity, with blank, uncurtained windows staring out at Annie, and for a moment her eyes, blurred with the cold, seemed to see in one of them the despairing face of the woman with the wisps of faded hair blowing about her face.'[42] The implication here is that ornament served an important social and personal function, one that was vital to women's ability to survive in spaces that were valued for economic output alone. Without it, as Lawrence acknowledges, they were little more than ghostly drudges, trapped in tiny, dismal homes, unable to indulge even in the 'freakish' riot of decoration condemned by Gilman. While de Tocqueville carefully distinguished personal beauty and ornamentation from domestic material charm, here, one becomes dependent upon the other, as is even more evident inside the conjugal abode, which is less grim, but also animated in a manner that is ominous rather than homely:

> Annie saw the big burner, erected in all its black hideousness in the middle of the front room, like a sort of household hoodoo, to be constantly propitiated, like the gods of Greece; and in the kitchen, the new range, with a distracted tea-kettle leaping on it, as if it would like to loose its fetters and race away over the prairie after its cousin, the locomotive.[43]

These primitive, supernatural, personified objects violently resist her efforts to keep them safely under control; it is therefore unsurprising that Annie's exertions in homemaking are thwarted at every turn. In the early months of their marriage, the couple 'amused themselves by decorating the house with the bright curtainings that Annie had brought, and putting up shelves for a few pieces of china. She had two or three pictures, also, which had come from her room in her old home, and some of those useless dainty things with which some women like to litter the room.' Nevertheless, as the weather turns, and money runs short, Annie's 'pretty wedding garments' become increasingly worn, while the endless round of work and sacrifice makes life considerably harder for both of them. Vitally, though, natural and human moods cannot be mapped directly on to one another here. Just as the kettle that predates Annie's arrival in the house defies her will, so the natural world blithely ignores the couple's plight, even as it fails to deliver its promised dividends. As autumn 'set[s] in', 'the brilliant cold sky hung over the prairies as young and fresh as if the world were not old and tired.' Nature, it seems, is cruelest in its total indifference to human suffering and toil, its idyllic appearance mocking their thankless struggles to avail of its riches. As the railroad tolls fleece Jim of all his profits, and their second crop is ruined, social realism blends with an inescapable sense of gothic repetition, and he tells Annie that they '"can't get out! And we're bound to stay and raise grain. And they're bound to cart it. And that's all there is to it."'[44] Having once given himself over to the prairie sublime, he has now given himself over to naturalist doom, to a sense of life as predetermined by vast, inhuman systems from which there is no escape or relief.

This sense of repetition is reinforced when Annie gives birth to a little girl who hardly sleeps, wailing continuously and sadly, and Mrs Dundy comes over to help her recuperate and keep up the housework. One day Annie asks for a mirror, and sees all too clearly that 'The color was gone from her cheeks, and about her mouth there was an ugly tightening. But her eyes flashed and shone with that same – no, no, it could not be that in her face also was coming the look of half-madness!' She realizes that, during their growing friendship, Mrs Dundy has been warning her gently that she too would become withered and half mad out on the prairies. When she mentions this to the older woman, Mrs Dundy responds '"How could I help knowing?"' Before long, she learns that Mrs Dundy has '"been sent to th' insane asylum at Lincoln. She's gone stark mad"'. The gossiping townsfolk who relay this news then laugh 'a little – a strange laugh; and Annie thought of a drinking-song she had once heard, "Here's to the next who dies."' Annie, all too aware that she herself might be 'next', must soon return to work, with the baby on her back. In what seems to be a version of Stockholm Syndrome, she too becomes caught up, as Jim is, in the glamour of the land; she has come to love the corn with something approaching mysticism, and brings the baby into it at night so that its rustling might send her off to sleep. The baby dies, however, and Annie leaves Jim, later telling him in a letter, '"it is not you I leave, but the soil, Jim! I will not be its slave any longer. If you care to come for me here, and live another life – but no, there would be no use. Our love, like our toil, has been eaten up by those rapacious acres"'.[45]

It is the suggestion of worship in both Jim and Annie's attitude to the land that proves most dangerous. It is not a welcoming or nurturing environment, but rather indifferent to humanity at best, and the more it demands of them, the less it gives back. The result is that (like so many would-be farmers at the time) Jim declares bankruptcy and sells his furniture to the bank. His face appears to have ceased to register any emotion whatsoever as the contents of the cabin are hauled away, and the local gossips are convinced that 'after all he couldn't have been very ambitious', since 'He didn't seem to take his failure much to heart.' However, when no one is watching, he leans 'forward, quickly, over a little wicker work-stand':

> There was a bit of unfinished sewing there, and it fell out as he lifted the cover. It was a baby's linen shirt. Jim let it lie, and then lifted from its receptacle a silver thimble. He put it in his vest-pocket.
> [...]
> Two months later, a 'plain drunk' was registered at the station in Nebraska's metropolis. When they searched him they found nothing in his pockets but a silver thimble, and Joe Benson, the policeman who had brought in the 'drunk', gave it to the matron, with his compliments. But she, when no one noticed, went softly to where the man was sleeping, and slipped it back into his pocket, with a sigh. For she knew somehow – as women do know things – that he had not stolen that thimble.[46]

What is evident here is the lack of real community or mutual under-standing; even when neighbors live in close proximity, secrets and feel-ings are kept close and private, to the point where misinterpretations of situations are rampant – a dangerous situation for anyone who might be in distress but who, due to the unwritten social code, is unable to communicate the fact. In the logic of the story, therefore, it is objects that mediate between individuals and memories when the landscape and popular knowledge cannot (or refuse to). At the same time, however,

Peattie's stories display a conviction that women's efforts to populate the wilderness with *things* in order to make it more homelike for men could end all too easily in self-sacrifice on the women's part. 'Two Pioneers', for example, asserts that

> Mademoiselle Ninon [...] was the only thing in that wilderness to suggest home. Ninon had a genius for home-making. Her cabin, in which she cooked, slept, ate, lived, had become a boudoir.
>
> The walls were hung with rare and beautiful skins; the very floor made rich with huge bear robes, their permeating odors subdued by heavy perfumes brought, like the spices, from St. Louis. The bed, in daytime, was a couch of beaver-skins; the fireplace had branching antlers above it, on which were hung some of the evidences of the fair Ninon's coquetry, such as silken scarves, of the sort the voyageurs from the far north wore; and necklaces made by the Indians of the Pacific coast and brought to Ninon by – but it is not polite to inquire into these matters. There were little moccasins also, much decorated with porcupine-quills, one pair of which Father de Smet had brought from the Flathead nation, and presented to Ninon that time when she nursed him through a frightful run of fever.[47]

Having survived for many years with her objects to sustain her as she devotes her time and energy to sustaining others, Ninon gives her last strength to clean and decorate the church and its statue of the Virgin Mary, and is particularly concerned that two lilies given to her as a present (she will not say by whom) should ornament the altar. Having done so, 'The next morning she lay dead among those half barbaric relics of her coquetry, and two white lilies with hearts of gold shed perfume from an altar in a wilderness.'[48] This story succinctly highlights an undercurrent in Peattie's work as a whole, which depicts domestic objects as the pioneer woman's salvation but also her doom. They may have allowed her to maintain some sense of self against the overwhelming emptiness, but they equally demanded a total self-abnegation, while paradoxically connoting an improper indulgence in sensual self-display. Indeed, for Mademoiselle Ninon, one gives way ultimately to the other, and death is the inevitable result. Even when Annie eventually escapes the pattern, the objects she uses to make clothing for her baby continue to sustain her estranged husband in the wilderness, and she is thrust out of the narrative frame altogether. As the 'hoodoo' kettle implies, the things she uses to make herself and others feel at home drive her near to distraction in her efforts to maintain them, turning on her with the full force of their inhuman demonism, a pattern that surfaces in a number of Peattie's tales.

And it is precisely this pattern that rendered the Western landscape gothic and threatening for her female characters. These stories essentially critiqued what Richard Slotkin refers to as the 'myth' that figured the American Frontier – and American life itself – as characterized by a relentless forward movement, by progress, self-actualization, and limitless profit made possible by limitless 'free' space. This myth bulldozes over the specifics of actual history, since, as Slotkin puts it, 'The past is made metaphorically equivalent to the present; and the present appears simply as a repetition of persistently recurring structures identified with the past.' Consequently, 'Both past and present are reduced to instances displaying a single "law" or principle of nature, which is seen as timeless in its relevance, and as transcending all historical contingencies.' The main problem with such thinking, he argues, is that it creates a 'fatal environment of expectations and imperatives' in which someone whose actions resonate with this symbolic (indeed, often rigidly allegorical) language 'can be entrapped.'[49] Only by reengaging with the specifics of history can the individual hope to break free from the strangling coils of myth, which seek to shape behavior and dictate actions, reducing the lives and experiences of individuals to mere vehicles and exemplars for repeating patterns. In the case of the American West, the myth automatically situated all who inhabited it within an optimistic project of nation building, in which the occupation of 'empty' land supposedly offered endless opportunities for personal happiness, freedom, and financial gain.

Situating gothic darkness within an open-ended fragment of story, 'The House That Was Not' dramatizes the dangerous effects of this mythic structure. This is a landscape that imprisons those who enter it within an endlessly repeating traumatic memory, a space that has 'only this one story to tell', precisely because it is never permitted fully to tell that story, because doing so might undermine the West's positive public image.[50] All that the landscape offers Flora by way of a clue to the imperfectly concealed past is the baby's shoe, and the spectacle of a house that appears and disappears, and that may be nothing more than an optical illusion. The story therefore draws attention to American culture's insistence that a landscape that had seen its share of hardship and suffering was nonetheless without history, and thus unhaunted. As a general rule, fictional commodities tend to be 'much more thoroughly mediated into and domesticated within a specific historical context' than the baby's shoe is; '[t]hen we see [them] as familiar, ordinary, and settled.' Something that appears totally out of context in an otherwise uninhabited landscape bears unnerving witness to 'the covertly "illegible" otherness of the object', and of the landscape itself.[51] The appearance of a man-made object in the wilds of the forest, the vast vacuum of the prairie, or the uninhabitable wastes of the desert is not simply unusual or surprising – it is actively disorienting for the viewer precisely because he or she is unlikely ever to learn how it got there or to whom it belonged. And it is here that we come to the irreducibly paradoxical attitude toward the great outdoors in the United States – the longing for open, uninhabited spaces, and the fear of actually occupying them.

The howling wilderness

The natural Western landscape has long been portrayed as not merely symbolizing but also actively encouraging liberty, democracy, and independence. Henry David Thoreau asserted in his essay 'Walking' that humanity would 'grow to greater perfection intellectually as well as physically under' the influence of the unspoiled, ostensibly unpopulated expanses that the people of the United States inhabited, spaces empty of (Anglo-European) human history. As he put it, 'We go eastward to realize history, and study the works of art and literature, retracing the steps of the race, – we go westward as into the future, with a spirit of enterprise and adventure.' He continued, 'Above all, we cannot afford not to live in the present. He is blessed over all mortals who loses no moment of the passing life in remembering the past.'[52]

The repetition of such sentiments within the United States' overlapping self-defining discourses has rendered America, in the words of Yi-Fu Tuan, 'the country in the world least hospitable to ghosts', not least because it works very hard to convince itself that it is without history, a past, or a cultural memory.[53] Throughout the nineteenth century, the United States' sense of what rendered it unique, and indeed superior to the ancient civilizations of the Europe, was founded largely upon the idea that its land remained unsullied by the dust of previous generations. Thomas Jefferson wrote in 1824, 'Can one generation bind another and all others in succession forever? I think not. The Creator has made the earth for the living, not the dead. Rights and powers can only belong to persons, not to things, not to mere matter unendowed with will.'[54] Expressing almost identical views, in describing Concord, Massachusetts (which could hardly be referred to as the wilderness, despite his best efforts), Thoreau wrote in *Walden* (1854), with a rather endearing nervousness, 'I am not aware that any man has built on the spot which

I occupy. Deliver me from a city built on the site of a more ancient city, whose materials are ruins, whose gardens cemeteries. The soil is blanched and accursed there, and before that becomes necessary the earth itself will be destroyed.'[55]

Patently, this is a nonsensical way in which to represent a landscape that had once supported thriving native populations, and that was rapidly appropriated by nonnative settlers over a period of several hundred years. Somewhat less evident is why so much time and cultural energy should have been devoted to asserting that the landscape was empty and that, somehow, this would always be the case. For the United States, nationhood had been achieved, not simply through forgetting, but through a positive assertion that *nothing has happened there*. As Ernest Renan has written, 'Forgetting, I would even go so far as to say historical error is a crucial factor in the creation of a nation', and this is precisely what Thoreau's outburst conveys – not merely that America has no past, but that no history or memories would ever accumulate there.[56] While this might appear to be an ideal means of ensuring that America avoids gothic darkness, David Mogen argues that a rejection of the past potentially creates the very effect it seeks to evade. Such a denial or splintering of what he calls a 'logocentric past, the point of seemingly solid, objective, and true reference that exists as the sure foundation of the present civilisation', seriously undermined the creation of optimistic narratives characterized by closure and certainty. All that is left, when history is placed under erasure, is a vision of 'dark ruins and shadowy presences whose experience is queasy, uncertain, chaotic, and unknown.'[57] In other words, instead of a history, nineteenth-century America had little more than a scattering of imperfect memories that appeared as gothic narrative fragments.

Peattie's story, and others like it, asserted that it was the attempts to conceal this gothic chaos with ahistorical 'myth' that made the American West so hazardous a place to occupy, not least because it left those occupying it vulnerable to repeating unwittingly the mistakes of those who came before them. The West in these stories becomes an active and malevolent agent, trapping its unsuspecting inhabitants within a powerful pattern in which human effort is mocked and undone by an indifferent or even hostile natural environment. Denied a knowable and shared past to uncover, female characters who should function as gothic heroines are left at the mercy both of the landscape *and* of a set of discourses that refuses to admit that anything bad ever happens in the West, to the point where traumatic pasts are repeated endlessly, without hope of exorcism or prevention. Nor should this be surprising, considering the sustained efforts made by American cultural apparatuses to present the landscape as uninhabited and therefore ahistorical. For the relatively new nation, wilderness was a source of cultural uniqueness, one of the few ways in which America appeared superior to Europe.[58] In this vast and sprawling nation, the visual arts in particular offered 'the promise of a complete and unitary landscape in place of a discontinuous and fragmented body politic.'[59] The influence of Transcendentalism transformed this vast nature reserve into a source of moral purity, starkly opposed to the materialistic morass of emerging urban realities, and potentially preserving the United States from the decadence and decline that had beset so many great cultures in the past.[60]

In order to be so available as the linchpin of national unity or personal salvation, however, the environment needed to be rendered an unmarked canvas or blank slate, onto which new, carefully controlled cultural meanings could be imposed, which, arguably, is precisely how the most prominent landscape painters of the century depicted the entire continent.[61] According to artist Thomas Cole, for example, the sublimity of the American landscape was that of 'a shoreless ocean un-islanded by the recorded deeds of the past.'[62] Later in the century, American landscape painters in the school known as Luminism 'embraced a visual universe purged of time, progress, and history', and transformed nature 'into an expansive and inexhaustible realm', unsullied by the marks of human habitation, ironically to make way for future habitation (and exploitation).[63] Indeed, several commentators have identified a sense in such paintings, as well as in literature, that the landscape contained the ability to transcend its own despoliation – that it could 'maintain its absolute integrity against organic decay or man's desecration' – in other words, that it was effectively self-cleaning.[64] In a Civil War lament, Oliver Wendell Holmes celebrated just this sense that historical tragedy somehow would not root in American soil:

> Our union is river, lake, ocean, and sky,
> Man breaks not the medal, when God cuts the die!
> Though darkened with sulphur, though cloven with steel,
> The blue arch will brighten, the waters will heal![65]

Similarly, James Fenimore Cooper's novels repeatedly imagine a wilderness landscape that systematically wiped itself clean of all traces of bloodshed and death.[66] In *The Deerslayer* (1841), a mere fifteen years after the massacre of a Huron village, almost no trace of the event remains, and the village itself is almost obliterated. Only the remains of the castle were still visible, a picturesque ruin. The storms of winter had long since unroofed the house, and decay had eaten into the logs. All the fastenings were untouched, but the seasons rioted in the place, as if in mockery at the attempt to exclude them. The palisades were rotting, as were the piles, and it was evident that a few more recurrences of winter, a few more gales and tempests, would sweep all into the lake, and blot the building from the face of that magnificent solitude. The graves could not be found. Either the elements had obliterated their traces, or time had caused those who looked for them to forget their position.[67]

In Cooper's earlier novel, *The Prairie* (1827), another massacre, this time of a Sioux village, leaves so little trace that the very next day, the countryside is described as a 'broad expanse of quiet and solitude' and as 'soft, calm, and soothing.'[68] Nevertheless, despite its close ties to America's self-professed forward-looking optimism, this persistent natural emptiness frequently took on distinct gothic overtones. In his 1831 *A Fortnight in the Wilderness*, de Tocqueville described the uninhabited American landscape as pervaded by 'a silence so deep, a stillness so complete, that the soul is invaded by a kind of religious terror.'[69] In almost identical terms, in 'Ktaadn' (1864), the usually wilderness-loving Thoreau uncharacteristically depicted Nature as 'vast and dread and inhuman', 'made out of Chaos and Old Night.'[70] Having climbed a particularly forbidding mountain, he encountered a bleak, inhospitable vista that, he asserted, was 'no man's garden, but the unhandselled globe':

> Man was not to be associated with it. It was Matter, vast, terrific, – not his Mother Earth that we have heard of, not for him to tread on, or be buried in, – no, it were being too familiar even to let his bones lie there [...]. There was there felt the presence of a force not bound to be kind to man. It was a place for heathenism and superstitious rites [...].[71]

What this passage emphasizes is the sheer alien nature of the landscape, one so much older and larger than humanity that it borders on malevolence. Indeed, despite his comments about 'superstitious rites', Thoreau quickly added that 'Only daring and insolent men, perchance, go there. Simple races, as savages, do not climb mountains, – their tops are sacred and mysterious tracts never visited by them.'[72] Some places were so awe-ful that even pagan devil worshippers dared not trespass there.

As the nineteenth century progressed, various sections of the continent were explored, settled, and then abandoned by industry and population movements. Consequently, constructions of the American landscape as frightening and dangerous tended increasingly to dwell less on the idea that humanity had never strayed into these regions, and more on the extent to which traces of habitation and farming were gradually but inexorably obliterated – the near impossibility of humanity's making any impact whatsoever upon the landscape. For Thoreau, this was largely a matter of perception; he described how, walking in 'familiar fields' around Concord, Massachusetts, one could suddenly find that familiar, 'man-made' sights 'fade[d] from the surface of the glass, and the picture which the painter painted stand[ing] out dimly from beneath. The world with which we are commonly acquainted leaves no trace, and it will have no anniversary.'[73] In other words, Nature always wins out; Culture's power to shape and contain the environment is temporary at best. Indeed, as became apparent several decades later, economic decline and the fast pace of change in a capitalist society were quick to aid Nature in her work. Far from functioning as a tamed and civilized landscape, the woods of New England became scattered with abandoned farmhouses that appeared, in Sarah Orne Jewett's terms, to be 'going back to the original woodland from which they were won.'[74] Jewett's stories and lyrical essays were, by and large, realist evocations of the eastern landscape. Nonetheless, they are occasionally subject to the eruption of the primeval gothic forces that settlers saw as inherent to the empty spaces of the West, moments that break free of the cozy storytelling of her fictional locales, Deephaven and Dunnet Landing, and stray into less easily mapped spaces.

Thus, in 'A Winter Drive' (1893), Jewett's narrator asserts that 'The people who live in the region of the Agamenticus woods have a good deal of superstition about them; they say it is easy to get lost there, but they are very vague in what they say of the dangers that are to be feared.' She begins by likening it to 'an unreasoning fear of the dark', but then mentions hints about bears and wild cats, before stating, 'as for a supernatural population, I think that passes for an unquestioned fact.' Only in relation to supernatural dread is there any sense of certainty, and disorientation reigns supreme. As she comments, 'I have often heard people say that there are parts of the woods where they would not dare to go alone, and where nobody has ever been, but I could never succeed in locating them.'[75] This is an unmappable landscape, where natural and supernatural fears overlap and intertwine, undermining and reinforcing each other by turns; it is unpredictable in its effects, the associations attached to it and its very geography.

A possible explanation for this labyrinthine quality is offered by another Jewett tale, 'The Grey Man' (1886), in which 'a laughing fellow', out of curiosity, breaks into a house rumored to be haunted. The young man is initially fascinated, despite the fact that 'The place was clean and bare, the empty cupboard doors stood open', but before long 'an awful sense that some unseen inhabitant followed his footsteps made him hurry out again pale and breathless to the fresh air and sunshine.' Minor in itself, this incident sets off an explosion of local gossip and storytelling, patchily woven into a story that 'grew more fearful, and spread quickly like a mist of terror among the lowland farms', becoming 'slowly magnified' with time. It becomes the stuff of legend: 'The former owner was supposed to linger still about his old home [...]. His grave was concealed by the new growth of oaks and beeches, and many a lad and full-grown man beside has taken to his heels at the flicker of light from across a swamp or under a decaying tree in that neighborhood.' When it becomes impossible to locate the owner's grave marker, the farmers living nearby find it even more difficult to imagine him as properly dead and gone. This escalation of fear is therefore directly proportional to the erosion of local memory and information – and indeed to the decline in superstition itself. As the narrator notes, 'As the world in some respects grew wiser, the good people near the mountain understood less and less the causes of these simple effects, and as they became familiar with the visible world, grew more shy of the unseen and more sensitive to unexplained foreboding.'[76] A landscape explicitly haunted by the fabrications of superstitious fear is therefore, in some respects, *less* frightening than one haunted by the knowledge that that superstition is no longer accessible as a guide to or explanation for the dread that the environment produces. The national unity conjured up by landscape painting therefore struggled in the face of 'the weakening of secure local attachments grounded in continuous family history, in oral communication, and in knowledge and experience that was place-specific.[77] The erosion of communal memory left only a vague sense of evil, while the lore that might have elucidated or identified such dangers was lost; the result is an unsettling sense of haunting absence that undermined locational security.

The rapid pace of population change in nineteenth-century New England littered the landscape with the ruins of habitation, farming, and industry.[78] Eerily suggestive as these ruins might be, their absence could almost be more disconcerting; Perry D. Westbrook notes that 'it takes only thirty to forty years for an abandoned house, if uncared for, to disappear almost entirely,' as indeed the house in Peattie's story does.[79] Where evidence of human activity is invisible, orientation becomes difficult, if not impossible. The narrator in Jewett's 'The Queen's Twin' (1899) is told by Mrs Todd, a local apothecary, the narrator's constant companion and guide to the New-England woods, that '"The men-folks themselves never'd venture into 'em alone; if their cattle got strayed they'd collect whoever they could get, and start off all together. They said a person was liable to get bewildered in there alone, and in old times folks had been lost"'. She attributes this to lingering fears both of Indians and of witchcraft, and describes how a group of women once lost their way while picking berries, and were only found the next day, less than half a mile from home, but completely dazed and disoriented from their night spent in the forest. One woman, Mrs Todd claims, '"was so overset she never got over it, an' went off in a sort o' slow decline"'.[80] Here, the latent memory of indigenous peoples and superstition is only vaguely recalled rather than retained as local knowledge. It is therefore a disruption or failure of memory that produces this maze-like, haunting landscape, leaving only suggestive fragments that increase instead of allaying fear, and that produce disorientation instead of allowing for cognitive mapping of an area.

From the time of the very earliest explorers, unfamiliar to and uncharted by European cartographers, America resisted efforts at coherent verbal representation. Journals written by explorers of the New World were, Kathleen M. Kirby asserts, initially characterized by confidence and objectivity. However, when fog, darkness, moving ice, or simply unexpected occurrences rendered such objectivity redundant and inaccessible, a considerably less self-possessed narrative voice emerged.[81] As Ambrose Bierce put it, 'one does not stride far in darkness', and, inevitably, the contingencies of the New-World landscape itself prevented the exploration of its emptiness from being the confident march forward into the unknown that it is often represented as having been.[82] Puritan settlers William Bradford and Mary Rowlandson referred to the 'empty' landscape as a 'hideous and desolate wilderness' and a 'vast and howling wilderness' respectively.[83] The memory of 'the infinite, undifferentiated space made visible in the National Land Survey of 1785'[84] as a place frighteningly unequipped with maps or cultural markers lingered on in the American literary imagination, resulting in such gothic portrayals as Bierce's sketch 'The Difficulty of Crossing a Field' (1888), in which a man literally disappears while strolling in a leisurely manner through a field. His neighbors, watching him from across the eponymous field and discussing business matters which they need to arrange with him, look away for a moment, and when they glance back, there is no sign of him. Similarly, in Bierce's story 'The Damned Thing' (1893), a man is savagely mauled to death by an invisible animal-like presence while his friend watches in horror and confusion. The jury investigating his death read an extract from a journal in which the deceased described his first encounter with the entity, when he '"observed the wild oats [...] moving in the most inexplicable way"', and commented that he could '"hardly describe it."' The journal continues, '"Nothing that I had ever seen had affected me so strangely as this unfamiliar and unaccountable phenomenon [...]. We so rely upon the orderly operation of familiar natural laws that any seeming suspension of them is noted as a menace to our safety, a warning of unthinkable calamity"'.[85]

What rendered the nineteenth-century American landscape uncanny and dangerous (particularly but not exclusively prior to the 'closing' of the Frontier in 1890) was the paucity of familiar and stable landmarks and points of orientation. While such absence could be liberating, meaning that movement was neither impeded nor circumscribed, nevertheless, as Tuan points out, 'To be open and free is to be exposed and vulnerable.' Without 'trodden paths and signposts', open, empty, undifferentiated space 'has no fixed pattern of established human meaning; it is like a blank sheet on which meaning may be imposed.' To this can be opposed '[e]nclosed and humanized space', which Tuan has termed 'place', which functions as 'a calm center of established values.'[86] In an echo of Wharton's comments about 'continuity and silence,' Tuan saw haunting as a means of transforming chaotic space into familiar place, since the appearance of a ghost bestows 'a numinous cast' upon a place, causing it to be 'set aside from the ordinary world.'[87] Apparitions impose meaning and coherence upon space, effectively 'endow[ing] it with value'.[88] Where America is concerned, however, the drive toward the denial of historical residue left little room for the comforting presence of ghosts, resulting in a landscape unpleasantly bereft of landmarks, particularly out West. In his 1835 *A Tour of the Prairies*, Washington Irving noted that

To one unaccustomed to it, there is something inexpressibly lonely in the solitude of a prairie. The loneliness of a forest seems nothing to it. There the view is shut in by trees, and the imagination is left free to picture some livelier scene beyond. But here we have an immense extent of landscape without a sign of human existence. We have the consciousness of being far, far beyond the bounds of human habitation; we feel as if moving in the midst of a desert world.[89]

Similarly, the narrator of Cather's *O Pioneers!* announces that 'Of all the bewildering things about a new country, the absence of human landmarks is one of the most depressing and disheartening.'[90] '[D]efined by absence' and 'inimical to human beings', the West was, in the words of Cornelia A.P. Comer's 1912 'The Little Gray Ghost', 'an untainted place where restless spirits would not come'.[91] What is notable about Peattie's writing is its emphasis on precisely the restlessness of spirits in the less inhabited regions of the United States – their elusiveness and their impermanence. Her story 'On the Northern Ice' (1898) begins by evoking the isolation of newly settled northern areas of the continent. In a passage that recalls the chapter in Herman Melville's *Moby Dick* on 'The Whiteness of the Whale', we are told that

> The winter nights up at Sault Ste. Marie are as white and luminous as the Milky Way. The silence which rests upon the solitude appears to be white also. Even sound has been included in Nature's arrestment, for, indeed, save the still white frost, all things seem to be obliterated. [...]
> In such a place it is difficult to believe that the world is actually peopled. It seems as if it might be the dark of the day after Cain killed Abel, and as if all of humanity's remainder was huddled in affright away from the awful spaciousness of Creation.[92]

This is an image of a deceptively underpopulated America, a version of nature that actively conceals or removes the signs of humanity's presence within it, one that seems both to attract and erase apparitions. We are told that 'Up in those latitudes men see curious things when the hoar frost is on the earth', including strange women who show up out of nowhere and disappear just as mysteriously, leaving only wolf tracks behind them. Even these traces are ephemeral, however. As the anonymous narrator assures us, 'John Fontanelle, the half-breed, could tell you about it any day – if he were alive. (Alack, the snow where the wolf tracks were, is melted now!)'[93] The landscape goes out of its way to erase the marks of what occurs there, and individual memories are too impermanent to make reliable archives. As in Jewett's 'The Grey Man', the death of inhabitants joins forces with Nature to reduce these stories to imperfectly recalled rumors. This is a landscape haunted as much by the lack of an authoritative version of the past as by 'restless spirits'.

Moreover, the story is explicitly concerned with the dangers posed by this ambiguously haunted wilderness to women. The protagonist, Hagadorn, wishes to marry a girl who '"had been skating in the afternoon, and she came home chilled and wandering in her mind, as if the frost had got in it somehow."'[94] Unaware of her death, her would-be lover skates toward her home one evening, to be groomsman at his friend's wedding and, he hopes, to make plans for his own. He finds himself impulsively following a mysterious female figure, only realizing when dawn comes that she has led him away from a vast rift in the ice that would have been his death. With this realization comes news of his beloved's death from a chill contracted while skating, and it becomes clear that her ghost has been his savior – that she has given herself in death to protect him from the dangerous landscape. Nevertheless, she is not permitted to haunt the locale in the long term. Skating home some nights after her death, and insisting, despite his friends' wishes, on waiting until after dark, Hagadorn

> had hoped for the companionship of the white skater. But he did not have it. His only companion was the wind. The only voice he heard was the baying of a wolf on the north shore. The world was as empty and as white as if God had just created it, and the sun had not yet colored nor man defiled it.[95]

The frozen wastes have returned to the state of Edenic, unhaunted purity described at the beginning of the story, wiping themselves clean of every memory of what might have occurred there. In less abstract terms, a woman is first killed by the wilderness and then denied the possibility of remaining there as a ghost; a man is saved from the depredations of Nature, while the woman who saves him is swallowed up by it. And it is here that we return to 'The House That Was Not', which goes one step further, implying that, because the memory of terrible things that women do and experience fades into the landscape so as to leave it a pleasant and prosperous habitation for men, living women cannot see the ghosts that might help them avoid the perils of frontier existence.

'The House That Was Not'

'The House That Was Not' echoes and reemphasizes the motifs that underpin the work of Peattie and her contemporaries. Burt, in his explanation for why there is no point in Flora's going to visit what she thinks must be neighbors, focuses on the landscape's tendency to produce inexplicable phenomena. He tells her, 'with benevolent emphasis',

'you're a smart one, but you don't know all I know about this here country. I've lived here three mortal years, waitin' for you to git up out of your mother's arms and come out to keep me company, and I know what there is to know. Some things out here is queer – so queer folks wouldn't believe 'em unless they saw. An' some's so pig-headed they don't believe their own eyes. [...]'[96]

He never seeks to deny that there's something strange about it – merely that specific or verifiable information is impossible to obtain, and that any attempt to come up with a viable theory in relation to the mysterious house is futile. He tells her, with what seems to be a gleeful embracing of the paradox that the house constitutes,

'Now you look over at that there house. You see it, don't yeh? Well, it ain't there! No! I saw it the first week I was out here. I was jus' half dyin', thinkin' of you an' wonderin' why you didn't write. That was the time you was mad at me. So I rode over there one day – lookin' up company, so t' speak – and there wa'n't no house there. I spent all one Sunday lookin' for it. Then I spoke to Jim Geary about it. He laughed an' got a little white about th' gills, an' he said he guessed I'd have to look a good while before I found it. He said that there shack was an ole joke.'[97]

While Geary does tell Burt about the woman and what she has done to her family and herself, the uncertainty as to whether it burned down or simply disappeared mirrors the hazy local gossip and folklore central to Jewett's work, an effect heightened by the tendency of both Geary and Burt to acknowledge the existence of the place while trying to deny it. The silencing of the events that have occurred there takes on the air of a local conspiracy, of the kind that haunted-house fiction often evokes as surrounding shunned buildings.[98] No-one wants to talk about it because bad things happen there, but, as I have been arguing, bad things happen in these isolated regions precisely because no one wants to talk about it. Poor old Thoreau would be horrified to learn that the 'virgin' land on which Peattie's couple have settled is already the site of a multiple murder, a suicide and, presumably, a mass grave. The land itself is there-fore repeatedly depicted as complicit in this erasure, insistently denying that it remembers anything about the house – despite, quite clearly, remembering it all too well. As one of Jewett's narrators remarks,

> Heaven only knows the story of the lives that the gray old New England farmhouses have sheltered and hidden away from curious eyes as best they might. Stranger dramas than have ever been written belong to the dull-looking, quiet homes, that have seen generation after generation live and die.[99]

That these stories will remain untold and unheard is not simply a product of faulty local memory in areas left desolate by westward or cityward migration – the very myth of the single-family dwelling itself forbids prying into its secrets. In 'The White Rose Road', Jewett's narrator notes how 'In spite of the serene and placid look of the old houses, one who has always known them cannot help thinking of the sorrows of these farms and their almost undiverted toil.'[100] In other words, it is impossible to be unaware of the sad stories that may be connected with such houses, and yet equally impossible to gain any real sense of the content of such stories, not least because it is all too easy to be fooled by their 'serene and placid' outward appearance. As Peattie's story implies, any efforts to fill in these gaps are hampered by a deep-seated societal unwillingness to discuss events that might undermine the optimism of the Western enterprise. As the above discussion illustrates, a profoundly gothic sense of the unknown and unknowable then arises from this *lack* of local memory or knowledge, the beholder's inability to pinpoint the source of a house's uneasy atmosphere.

In Peattie's tale, the prairie itself colludes in this suppression. Flora's attempts to glean some information about the little house by peering out 'her' window are thwarted since 'She could not guess how far it might be, because distances are deceiving out there, where the altitude is high and the air is as clear as one of those mystic balls of glass in which the sallow mystics of India see the moving shadows of the future.'[101] Once again, therefore, the American landscape (or rather, its cultural construction) baffles the gaze, hinders navigation, and makes it impossible for Flora to act as a proper gothic heroine, redeeming the present by uncovering and therefore exorcizing the past. Nineteenth-century landscape artists in particular radically edited New-World Nature, striving 'to keep the painful and less beautiful aspects of existence at bay.'[102] Cole insisted that the artist must wait 'for time to draw a veil over the common details, the unessential parts, which shall leave the great features, whether the beautiful or the sublime, dominant in the mind.'[103] He declared that any spectacle,

> unless founded and built upon truth will pass away like the breeze that for the moment ruffles the surface of the lake. Those founded on truth are permanent and reflect the world in perfect beauty. [...] By true art I mean imitation of true nature and not the imitation of accidents nor merely the common imitation that takes nature indiscriminately. All nature is not true. The stunted pine, the withered fig-tree, the flowers whose petals are imperfect are not true.[104]

This aesthetic attitude entailed 'the suppression of specific details – spatial obstacles, sudden discontinuities, or troubling discrepancies of scale – that disturb the sense of "proportion" and "relation"'.[105] Applying this logic to Peattie's tale, the sight of a burned-out house that has witnessed a horrific murder-suicide is a blemish, ruining the picturesque view of the landscape. This cultural erasure of memorials to traumatic events had serious implications for the experience of that landscape. Memorialization (like Tuan's ghosts) abstracts place from the realm of daily life and affixes it in time as much as in space. Marking a site as the location of a past event distinguishes it from the surrounding landscape, and provides a valuable signpost in otherwise homogenous surroundings.[106] Somewhere that has been memorialized stands out from the landscape and carries a clear emotional heft. With the little house in Peattie's tale, I would argue, the locals' urgent need to forget about it and what it might imply about family life on the frontier results in a failed memorialization, one that, rather than organizing undifferentiated space around it, exacerbates the unfamiliar nature of the landscape. Moreover, while memorializations, like myth, 'are potentially dangerous, for they can falsify and destroy the real past', nonetheless, 'they are also potentially beneficial, for they help free us from conscious or unconscious dependence on a mythical past.'[107] That is, by objectifying and alerting us to the existence of that past, they allow those living in the present to identify past dangers and avoid them. It is precisely this sense of the mythic that Flora, bereft of monuments bearing direct witness to past tragedy, is unable to escape.

As the story is so brief and ends so abruptly, with no resolution or indication of what the rest of her life might be like, the possibility of repetition looms large – the potential for the individual to be subsumed within the wider pattern of cultural myth rather than of individual history.

That Flora might be doomed to repeat the pattern set by her ill-fated neighbor, as Annie repeats that set by Mrs Dundy, is initially gestured toward when we are told that 'nothing interested her so much as a low cottage, *something like her own*, which lay away in the distance.'[108] While Annie is ultimately able to heed the warning implicit in Mrs Dundy's eyes, her neighbor's suicide before she ever arrives out West, along with the socially imperative attempts to forbid enquiry into the tragic past, leaves Flora without an ally, unprepared for the future and potentially at the mercy of socio-cultural forces that destroy women for the sake of men's happiness, safety, and prosperity. Indeed, while Jim Lancy's thimble allows the reader to see him as something more than just a 'plain drunk', functioning as a medium through which he mourns the losses he and Annie have incurred, the baby's shoe that causes Flora's horse to bolt for home is a far less comforting symbol. Both vividly evoke the anguished despair of the failure of motherly love to keep men and children safe from harm, but the shoe, shorn of backstory, drives Flora away from any sense of sympathy with or understanding for her uncanny double, who, like Hagadorn's lover, has found no room in the landscape for her to exist there as a ghost. Equally, it is possible to suggest that, determined to transmit her anger and pain into the present, Flora's deceased neighbor deliberately and maliciously avoids appearing as a ghost, since doing so, as I have been arguing, makes revelation and certainty, and hence exorcism, possible. With her predecessor ejected from local memory, Flora (like Gilman's narrator) is left prey to exactly the same fears and dangers that destroyed the neighbor, and we, as readers, are denied the comfort of knowing anything at all about her future fate, as the text abandons us to imagine the worst.

The erasure of the past, along with Burt's gruff, unsympathetic reluctance to discuss the place and his evasive, jokey answers to her urgent pleas for information, therefore hint at a potentially grim future for Flora. The failure and refusal to talk leave Flora feeling cut off from other women in similar circumstances, with whom she might share experiences and sensations – possibly the very problem that drove the other wife to destroy her family and herself. The excessive cultural energy poured into preventing the American landscape's being marked by the memories of traumatic events and violent death is precisely the force, in Peattie's story, that causes the isolation of women in the single-family home, which in turn causes the very violence and trauma that the United States would rather imagine never occurs there at all. Encountering what remains of this traumatic past is so confusing and inconclusive that, rather than bringing about change and renewal, as the revelation of the past in a conventional gothic narrative would, Flora is dragged back to the conjugal home, back to her husband's collusion in the suppression of uncomfortable truths, and her own subordination.

In the uninhabited spaces of the prairies, domestic objects' mnemonic function helped women respond to the cultural pressure to function as the 'heart' of the frontier. Peattie and her contemporaries depicted a Western landscape that was haunted precisely because it was empty of such memory-laden things. 'The House That Was Not' in particular attempts to map out the fraught role played by the commodity in a landscape positioned as the antithesis of a furnished and populated civilization. What all these stories insist upon, therefore, is that memory is what makes a landscape a fit place in which both to live and work, extending Gilman's insistence that the presence of a haunting can function as a form of guide or reference point for a female character stumbling through a social world that punishes her failure to fit into it. A landscape that calls to mind past horrors is haunted by the ghosts of those who endured them, while situating those horrors firmly *in* the past. A landscape haunted by uncertainty, however, cannot definitively extricate itself from the past horrors that it has difficulty naming or visualizing, and is therefore far more dangerous to its inhabitants. The nineteenth-century (fictional) American West was a scarred landscape precisely because it refused to show its scars.

6
'My Labor and My Leisure Too': Wynne's 'The Little Room' and Commodity Culture

In 1911, author Edna Ferber described a Chicago shop window as 'a work of art [...], a breeder of anarchism, a destroyer of contentment, a second feast of Tantalus.'[1] Veering sharply from praise to alarmed censure, Ferber's observation highlighted the ambiguous status of Gilded-Age commodity culture. At once seductive and threatening, the hold that this culture had over the female imagination in particular was exemplified by two novels from 1900 in which the relationship between women and objects has disastrous effects for others. In one, a young girl kills an older woman with a bucket of water because the woman has stolen one of her 'pretty shoes'. In the other, a young woman's desire for 'dainty slippers and stockings, [...] delicately frilled skirts and petticoats, [...] laces, ribbons, hair-combs, purses' prompts her married lover to steal money from his employer with which to run away with her, an act that ultimately leads to his death, homeless, friendless and penniless.[2] These are, of course, L. Frank Baum's *The Wonderful Wizard of Oz* and Theodore Dreiser's *Sister Carrie*, respectively, two novels which, albeit in very different ways, starkly dramatize the central role played by decorative commodities in women's lives in the final decades of the nineteenth century and the opening decades of the twentieth.

In both texts, the anarchy and destruction that Ferber associated with material desire fall upon secondary characters, leaving the female protagonists untouched. Indeed, ownership is depicted in each as personally empowering. For Carrie Meeber, the items of personal adornment that men buy for her to enhance her considerable charms function as magical keys, unlocking doors into a giddy world of fame and glamour from which her paramour, Hurstwood, is inexorably excluded. For Baum's Dorothy, the Silver Slippers convert her into an honored celebrity as she journeys through Oz and the glittering Emerald City, protect her from the powerful Wicked Witch of the West, and finally whirl her home to Kansas simply because she wishes it. *Sister Carrie* and *The Wonderful Wizard of Oz* can therefore be read as presenting relatively straightforward critiques of consumption, in which one individual's gain is another's loss, metonymically connoting the problematic relationship between middle-class consumers and lower-class factory workers, who were often the victims of horrific fires, collapsed buildings, and violent labor riots through the second half of the nineteenth century.

The kinds of uncanny tales I have been discussing are positioned almost exactly midway between the otherworldly fantasy of Baum's American fairy tale and the Marxian realism of Dreiser's Chicago (in which 'the so-called inanimate' commodities in department stores speak 'tenderly [...] for themselves' to Carrie, reminding her how well they would look on her).[3] Set in convincingly constructed, generally histori-cally grounded social worlds, abounding in meticulously evoked physical details, the spectral elements of turn-of-the-century American women's ghost stories cannot be disentangled from these details, while the narra-tive focus remains firmly embedded in the everyday world of contempo-rary America. As Dreiser's talking commodities imply, an alternate world of witches, munchkins, and flying monkeys is simply a more extreme version of the material imaginary that held sway in Gilded-Age America, where the terrors inspired by commodity culture could not be dismissed as purely the stuff of fantasy. It is this that Madeline Yale Wynne (who moved from Boston to Chicago in the latter decades of the nineteenth century) portrays graphically in her once-famous short story, 'The Little Room' (1895). The eponymous room dominates the story, an enigma at the heart of an otherwise unremarkable house occupied by two elderly unmarried New-England ladies, Aunt Hannah and Aunt Maria, sisters of the main female protagonist's deceased mother. Depending on who opens the door and when, the room appears alternately as a tiny china closet or as an exuberantly decorated parlor. Nevertheless, whichever version of the room presents itself to the gaze of the visitors, Hannah and Maria, its formidably stony-faced, ferociously industrious guard-ians, insist placidly that it has always been there, that the house has never changed in any way, and that they have no recollection of ever having been asked about the room. This profound instability in an otherwise unruffled reality, and the inability of characters to be sure of what they will find when they visit the house, results in the death of Margaret's mother (who had fond childhood memories of the little parlor); a serious argument between the protagonist and her husband on their wedding day; and a similar quarrel between Margaret's cousin, Nan, and her close friend, Rita.

'The Little Room' therefore insists that what was most dangerous about commodities is that they tempted middle-class women to see them as intimately connected with self-fashioning and personal development. In a culture in which even bleak novels such as Dreiser's could not help but assert that commodities were essential to individual fulfillment and social and financial success, and where fairy tales like Baum's depicted them as actively empowering and worth killing for, Wynne's tale suggests that to invest too much in material objects is to risk one's personal relationships along with one's sanity. 'The Yellow Wall-Paper' and 'The House That Was Not' posit domestic commodities as dangerous components of but also valuable witnesses to a wider system of domestic imprisonment; 'An Itinerant House' and 'The Southwest Chamber' strongly imply that poltergeist activity and the psychic emanations of a cursed room offer dead women more successful avenues for post-mortem revenge than the traditional spectral form. 'The Little Room', by contrast, is far more pessimistic about the relationship between women and objects, hinting instead that any personal investment in domestic commodities was both futile and hazardous – that such objects were in no way safe or reliable receptacles for personal memories or emotions.

This chapter therefore begins by outlining briefly the rise of the culture of display and commodification created by big business during the final years of the nineteenth century, before examining the ways in which commodities function in Wynne's story and others by her contemporaries. As previously argued, and as the specifics of these stories make clear, psychoanalytical models, which are conventionally employed by critics who analyze texts featuring supernatural events in an otherwise realistic setting, not only ignore but actively undermine the importance of material objects to the work of Gilded-Age women writers. This chapter ends, therefore, with a discussion of the ways in which, rather than lending themselves passively to our use and will, objects actively shaped (and continue to shape) behavior and experience, particularly for hardworking housewives, whom they sought to convert into slavish, unthinking avatars of the wider domestic system.

The commodity spectacle

What is especially noteworthy about Wynne's story is the continual repetition of the details of the contents of the room at the center of the narrative. The objects are evoked again and again by various characters (except the aunts, of course) in a manner that borders on the ritualistic, and that is in keeping with the late nineteenth-century culture of commercial and material display in the United States, as a swelling tide of commodities flooded the American cityscape. The spoils of trade and the products of industry, fueled by developments in technology, transport, and the aesthetics of display, including the invention of plate glass, commodity culture transformed the urban milieu into a glittering spectacle of consumption and accumulation. A wealth of exotic goods decorated and supplied even humble rural middle-class homes in the world described in these tales, while actual middle-class American homes at the time were festooned with "Canton shawls, Smyrna silks, Turkish satins, green parrots, Java sparrows, and Russian kopecks.'[4]

The rise of this new consumer culture was heralded by the 1876 Centennial Exhibition in Philadelphia, the first World's Fair in the United States.[5] Driven by the exponential pace of technological development and the vast resources of the newly 'conquered' continent, massive overproduction in the 1880s and 1890s forced retailers and traders to seek new markets for their products, and new methods of convincing consumers to buy more than they thought they needed.[6] Advertisers therefore 'increased their volume ten-fold between 1870 and 1900', going 'beyond the sober description of a product's features' that had characterized advertising for decades, and striving 'instead to incite in customers a generalized, omnivorous desire' by conjuring up 'a textual world of color, light, and spectacle emanating from goods.'[7] A major influence on turn-of-the-century advertising was L. Frank Baum himself, equally famous for his work on shop-window display, on which he published several books, as for his children's fantasy fiction – indeed, the two were all but inextricable. '[R]eadily grasp[ing] the magical potential of a single, isolated commodity', Baum urged 'merchants to rid their windows of clutter and crowding, to treat their goods theatrically, to immerse them in light and color, to place them in the foreground and single them out, and to make them come "alive"', so as to invest 'them with an emotional power that set them off and above other things.'[8] The new cultural emphasis on consumption over production pushed advertisers to foster active desire in the population, in an uphill struggle against deeply entrenched Protestant morality and its warnings about the dire consequences of lapses in self-control.[9]

As large sheets of plate glass became cheaper and more easily available, the American shop window developed into ever-more elaborate and theatrical forms, designed to encourage the popular gaze.[10] Behind them, the vast, multipurpose department store flourished, a real-life fantasy land where, in Dreiser's words, 'Each separate counter was a show place of dazzling interest and attraction.'[11] Targeting the middle-class woman with enough money and leisure time to shop for the ever-growing range of 'necessities' for the respectable home, the respectable family, and the respectable body, the department store added yet another set of activities to the wife's duties, while providing her with new independent leisure opportunities outside of the home. Exploiting the 'magic of surfaces' through juxtaposition with lavish ornamentation and imagery, such commercial spaces hinted at a 'faraway transcendence'.[12] Looking back at his career in 1925, display expert Arthur Fraser described the ideal window as giving the viewer a sort of 'glimpse into the interior of the temple', of something slightly forbidden and fleeting, yet potentially accessible.[13] Indeed, Wynne herself was part of this consumer culture. An artist and art teacher, she was also a highly trained metallurgist, practicing 'silver-smithing and jewelry-setting', among other decorative work, including sewing and decorating her own clothing, and helped establish an "Arts and Craft" association in her local area in Massachusetts. Her story inspired 'The Little Room Club', 'a group of painters, sculptors, writers, musicians, architects, and other art workers', which continued to meet well into the twentieth century.[14] In a volume of tributes collected after her death, Chicago heiress Lydia Avery Coonley Ward described Wynne's metalwork as a gorgeous array of

> vanquished metals – copper, silver, gold – in graceful curves and novel lines. Stones were encircled, crystals suspended, amber enfolded in coils, rings, and chains that send us to the woods to find their lovely counterparts, since histories of art do not reveal them. [...] Her intense love of color, her joy in rich hues and unusual combinations, doubtless revealed depths and gradations hidden from our eyes though multiplied to hers.[15]

According to contributor Elizabeth Head Gates, Wynne brought to Chicago 'an atmosphere of color, of intimate artistic life, where Venetian beads, in hitherto unimagined quantities and richness, blended with strange bits of embroidery; and where copper trays, iridescent with bold experiments in decoration, bore odd bits of hand-wrought metal.'[16] Wynne is situated here as participating in the mystification of decorative objects that marked the American *fin-de-siècle*, set among the rich colors and complex shapes that proliferated as much in the strategies employed by merchants and advertising experts as in the unique products of handicraft that stood in staunch opposition to commodification and mass production. Indeed, the mass-market magazines that flourished around this time – often featuring the sort of fiction examined here – such as *Cosmopolitan* or *Ladies' Home Journal*, would not have been possible without visually attractive advertising, the revenue from which helped keep publications afloat in an increasingly competitive and diversified market.[17] This kind of symbiotic and mutually beneficial relationship between commodity culture and (female) creativity was, however, the exception rather than the norm. As Baum and Dreiser's novels imply, the commercialized public sphere fostered an 'upsurge in longing [which] would trouble Americans for many decades, especially middle-class Americans, who would struggle to subdue and rationalize it and to understand its meaning and significance.'[18] While the rise of mass production was accompanied by 'an increasing investment of emotion in the ephemeral', the result was a profound uncertainty as to 'what constituted the "real" in a society increasingly attuned to mass production.'[19] Wynne's story tapped into precisely this struggle and these anxieties, centering as it did upon a visible yet inaccessible wonderland of objects, repeatedly revealing itself to and concealing itself from the ever-more frustrated protagonists.

'The Little Room'

Much like 'The Southwest Chamber', 'The Little Room' is studded with closely detailed descriptions of ornate objects. Margaret, the main protagonist, recounts how her orphaned mother, who had gone to live with the aunts at a young age, was once very ill and had been established in the little room to recuperate, a period that she recalls as 'one of her pleasant memories of her childhood; it was the first time she had been of any importance to anybody, even herself.' Margaret's mother vividly remembers a seashell that was a central element of the casual decoration of the room, and that 'she was only allowed to play with [...] when she had been particularly good.'[20] She has therefore cherished her memory of the little room and its contents, and has instilled a similar love of the place in Margaret, though for many years, she never sees it for herself. Nothing else in the story is accorded this level of descriptive attention – even the aunts are defined more by their characters than by their appearance – and the narrative style is notably spare. Margaret, who remembers the little room equally vividly from its surprise reappearance later on in her childhood, travels as an adult to the house to visit the aunts with her new husband, Roger, and fails to find the little room, which, during the train journey there, she has meticulously evoked for him:

> 'The India cotton was the regular blue stamped chintz, with the peacock figure on it. The head and body of the bird were in profile, while the tail was full front view behind it. [...]
>
> 'At the foot of the lounge were some hanging shelves with some old books on them. All the books were leather-colored except one; that was bright red, and was called the *Ladies' Album*. It made a bright break between the other thicker books.
>
> 'On the lower shelf was a beautiful pink sea-shell, lying on a mat made of balls of red shaded worsted.
>
> [...]
>
> 'Right at the head of the lounge was a light-stand, as they called it, and on it was a very brightly polished brass candle-stick and a brass tray, with snuffers. That is all I remember of her describing, except that there was a braided rag rug on the floor, and on the wall was a beautiful flowered paper – roses and morning-glories in a wreath on a light blue ground. The same paper was in the front room.'[21]

As rapidly becomes clear, it is precisely the closely observed and fondly remembered material contents of the little room that render this pleasant space psychically hazardous. Set against these strong recollections is the evidence of the senses, which again and again contradicts beloved memories. Consequently, much of the dialogue of the story is driven by the 'rational', 'realistic' interpretations that various uncomprehending (generally male) characters fabricate when their distraught, bewildered companions fail to find the room or closet they had expected. These 'explanations', far from clearing up confusion or removing uncertainty, cause considerable psychic anguish to the women who *know* that they have previously seen something other than what is now displayed to their astonished eyes. When Margaret's mother herself returned to the aunts' house as a married woman, excited to show it to her husband, the room was no longer there – just the china closet. Initially confused, she and her husband '"talked it over, and finally they concluded that my mother had been a very imaginative sort of a child and had read in some book about such a little room, or perhaps even dreamed it, and then had 'made believe', as children do till she herself had really thought the room was there."'[22]

A far less jovial version of this scenario is repeated when Margaret and Roger arrive at the house and sit down to dinner. Despite the fact that the last time she had been there, Margaret had seen the little room, 'On the table was the *gilt-edged china*' from the china closet, which she does not notice 'immediately, till she saw her husband smiling at her over his teacup; then she felt fidgety and couldn't eat', overcome with nervous anticipation as to what they will find behind the door. With sickening inevitability, the couple find only a 'shallow' closet lined with 'shelves [...] neatly draped with scalloped paper; on them was the gilt-edged china' that had also confronted her mother when she returned to the house as an adult, also with her husband.[23] Roger reacts with a cold anger, automatically assuming that she has lied to him all along, that there has never been a little room, that she is being uncharacteristically 'morbid', and repeatedly insists that they put the whole sorry incident behind them and never speak of her deception again.

Precisely the same situation had induced a less violent reaction in Margaret's father, faced with the same spectacle of the china closet when his new wife had promised him a little room, many years before the main action of the story. Margaret's parents are later able to laugh about it together, even turning the little room into a synonym for any strange or inexplicable occurrence, calling such things 'little-roomy'. Nonetheless, both husbands are adamant that the little room was never there in the first place. The appearance of the china closet where the wife has fully expected the little room to be is therefore repeatedly explained away by men who assert that the little room had never existed, and that the two women have been naively imagining or maliciously inventing the idyllic chamber. Uncanny repetition that is passed through the women in a family once again dominates a story about eerily unreliable domestic objects, cementing the relationship established in such fiction between heirlooms and an inability to escape a problematic past. Trying to convince Roger that she has not been lying, Margaret even feels that 'somehow her voice sounded to her as her mother's voice had when she stood there and questioned her sisters about the little room.'[24] Indeed, this situation is replicated near the end of the story, when, several years later, Margaret's cousin, Nan, and her close friend, Rita, plan to visit the aunts' house together and report back to Margaret on what they see there. Separated by the vicissitudes of travel, Nan arrives first, and sends word that she has seen the little room, but when Rita gets there, she finds only a china closet. The ensuing row threatens their long friendship, as, like the two men, Rita demands that Nan confess that she has seen no little room, or admit that she has never visited the house at all.

Failed or thwarted communication is therefore central to the troubling effects of the room. Once Roger has seen the china closet, Margaret feels that 'A cloud had come between them; he was hurt; he was antago-nized', and he says to her 'kindly enough, but in a voice that cut her deeply, "I am glad this ridiculous thing is ended; don't let us speak of it again."' His wife responds, '"Ended! [...] How ended?"' but it is clear that, for her husband (a counterpart of the husbands in Gilman's and Peattie's stories), the evidence of his senses is more than enough to justify burying the episode forever. Significantly, total silence on the issue is also what Margaret, her mother, and Nan and Rita meet with from the aunts. This has particularly devastating consequences when Margaret's father dies in the war, and she and her mother go to live with the aunts. Her mother is horrified to find not the china closet, but the little room. It is here that the story begins to imply that this apparently nurturing space is by no means a safe repository for cherished memo-ries. When Margaret's mother asks the aunts about it, '"They both said the house was exactly as it had been built – that they had never made any changes."'[25] As Margaret tells Roger,

> 'And that was the strangest thing about it. We never could make them remember that there had ever been any question about it. You would think they could remember how surprised mother had been before, unless she had imagined the whole thing. Oh, it was so queer! they were always pleasant about it, didn't seem to feel any interest or curiosity. It was always this answer: "The house is just as it was built; there have never been any changes, so far as we know."'

His response, even before he sees the china closet, is to say, soothingly, but infuriatingly, '"Well, don't talk any more about it, Margaret, if it makes you feel so."'[26] Just like John in 'The Yellow Wall-Paper', Roger insists that material things are unimportant and unproblematically reli-able in their unchanging physicality, but here, his and Margaret's father's pragmatism exists in collusion with the aunts' stony silence regarding the room. In particular, Roger chides his wife harshly for mentioning her mother. She feels 'a chill sense of withering under his glance' as she real-izes that he does not believe there was ever a little room, and he snaps, '"I really wish, Margaret, you would let it drop. I don't like to hear you speak of your mother in connection with it. It – [...] It doesn't seem quite the thing, quite delicate, you know, to use her name in the matter."'[27] Here, the proprieties of contemporary mourning culture interfere with Margaret's desire to figure out the intricacies of the house that effectively caused her mother's death, social form working hard to prevent any disclosures that might put a stop to the cycle. Roger is complicit in an act of silencing that refuses to acknowledge that domestic space might be anything other than straightforward or predictable, and therefore perpetuates the uncertainties that leave female characters at its mercy. Once again, then, the refusal to admit that *things* might have power is as upsetting and damaging to the female protagonist as the room itself is.

Moreover, it is for this reason that any reading that strictly opposes the inviting little room to the forbidding china closet is fundamentally flawed. Since Roger and Margaret's father both assume their wives are overly imaginative or untruthful when the little room fails to appear, it might seem that we should conclude that the china closet is the source and symbol of conflict, and that the appearance of the little room itself produces positive results, restoring interpersonal harmony and happiness. Jeffrey Weinstock reads the gilt-edged china and the peacock-printed chintz as representing two visions of marriage, one based on carefully categorized items that require work to keep them clean and safe, and the other on exotic decoration and symbols of travel and adventure.[28] Such a reading would seem to be supported by the contrast between the visual and affective richness of the little room, and the uniformity and 'shallowness' of the china closet, which provides only more things for the already hardworking aunts to clean, tirelessly and drearily. By contrast, the couch in the little room suggests exciting romantic possibilities, being (predictably) '"covered with blue chintz – India chintz – some that had been brought over by an old Salem sea-captain as a 'venture'. He had given it to Hannah when she was a young girl,"' but then failed to return and marry her, as everyone had expected he would.[29]

This pleasingly neat binaristic interpretation is, however, undermined by these very associations with lost love and thwarted freedom, and by the fact that it is the sight of the little room that effectively kills Margaret's mother. The new widow and her daughter arrive at the house convinced that the little room is nothing more than a false memory, a fantasy concocted by her mother as a child, and while Margaret, then aged eight, is delighted to find that there *is* a little room, she remembers thinking that her '"mother would faint. She clung to me in terror. I can remember now how strained her eyes looked and how pale she was."' She questions both aunts in turn, '"in that queer slow voice that made me feel frightened"', a voice that '"sounded weak and far off."' Maria '"without the slightest emotion"' insists, in a familiar refrain, that '"the house has never been altered'"', and reminds the mother that she used to play there as a child, while Hannah, also speaking '"pleasantly but unemotionally"', is adamant that she does not '"think you ever asked me about any china-closet, and we haven't any gilt-edged china that

I know of.'"'[30] She then becomes morbidly obsessed by the room. As Margaret puts it,

> 'It just seemed to break my mother down, this queer thing. Many times that summer, in the middle of the night, I have seen her get up and take a candle and creep softly down stairs. I could hear the steps creak softly under her weight. Then she would go through the front room and peer into the darkness, holding her thin hand between the candle and her eyes. She seemed to think the little room might vanish. Then she would come back to bed and toss about all night, or lie still and shiver; it used to frighten me.
>
> 'She grew pale and thin, and she had a little cough; then she did not like to be left alone. Sometimes she would make errands in order to send me to the little room for something – a book, or her fan, or her handkerchief; but she would never sit there or let me stay in there long, and sometimes she wouldn't let me go in there for days together. Oh, it was pitiful!'[31]

Neither version of the room produces a positive effect in the viewer, then. Its unreliability, and that of the objects it contains, disqualifies the contents of either space from functioning as a repository of beloved memories. The reappearance of the little room instead of the china closet ought to be a moment of joy, recognition, and a triumphant sense of having been right, of reestablishing the comfort, freedom, and self-coherence that Margaret's mother recalls feeling there as a child. Instead, whatever the characters see, discord and pain are the inevitable results.

The psychoanalytic solution

It would be all too easy to read a story featuring repetition, silencing, and apparent hallucination (as so many of the stories I have examined do) as prefiguring Sigmund Freud's thesis that the most uncanny of objects are those that were once familiar, but have been defamiliarized through repression. The story's chain of events seems to fit perfectly into the psychoanalytical method developed in the 1960s by Nicholas Abraham and Maria Torok, which they termed 'cryptonomy', the naming of a buried thing. Aunt Hanna's abandonment by the sea captain and subsequent spinsterhood; Aunt Maria's collusion in and repetition of the silence around this failure to marry that results in a scandal; Margaret's mother's grief at her husband's death; Margaret's own uncomfortable wedding night; and the disruption of her cousin Nan's quasi-lesbian relationship with another woman, all strongly imply an inherited, matrilineal sequence of sexual discord and unacknowledged grief. This, at any rate, would chime in perfectly with common psychoanalytical reading of specters and other supernatural occurrences.[32] Specifically, Abraham and Torok define the phantom as 'an undisclosed family secret handed down to an unwitting descendent', which must be literally discovered through analysis.[33] They argue that individuals are haunted by 'a memory [...] buried *without legal burial place*. The memory is of an idyll, experienced with a valued object and yet for some reason unspeakable. It is a memory entombed in a fast and secure place, awaiting resurrection.' Precisely because 'both the fact that the idyll was real and that it was later lost must be disguised and denied', the individual psyche establishes 'a sealed-off psychic place, a crypt in the ego', which is then somehow handed down through generations of a family.[34] As Abrahams asserted, 'What comes back to haunt are the tombs of others' – in other words, the things that others refuse to admit within their own psyches – so that we become 'possessed not by [one's] own unconscious but by someone else's.'[35]

The disturbed and disturbing objects and spaces that form the backbone of the stories examined here seem to invite us to expose and analyze the traumas concealed in the psyches of their frightened and frightening female protagonists. To do so, however, is, just like John and Roger, to ignore their insistence that domestic objects actively refuse female characters' efforts to attach personal emotions and meanings to them. Such readings obscure the central source of fear in these stories – houses, and the profusion of objects and decorative elements within them. Indeed, as argued in Chapter 2, Freud's discussion in his essay 'The "Uncanny"' of the meanings of the German words *heimlich* and *unheimlich* can be read as inadvertently implying that domesticity itself is inherently 'uncanny', an element of his argument that he fails (or refuses) to pursue. The literary sources that Freud employed depicted the privacy associated with domestic space as rendering that space mysterious and even frightening. He quotes from 'Daniel Sanders's Wörterbuch der Deutschen Sprache (1860, 1, 729),' a passage attributed to German writer Ferdinand Gutzkow, which reads

'The Zecks [a family name] are all Heimlich.' [...] '"Heimlich"? ... What do you understand by "Heimlich"?' 'Well, ... they are like a buried spring or a dried-up pond. One cannot walk over it without always having the feeling that water might come up there again.' 'Oh, we call it "unheimlich"; you call it "heimlich." Well, what makes you think that there is something secret and untrustworthy about this family?'[36]

Here, the very essence of bourgeois family values and private property produced a shudder of disquiet in those who were on the outside looking in. However, a true product of the nineteenth century, Freud could not help but see material objects as firmly and successfully ruled over by the Angel in the House, who would transform that house into nothing less than paradise. In an 1882 letter to his fiancée, Martha Bernays, his 'sweet child', at the beginning of a four-year separation during which he ensconced himself in a laboratory in Vienna, leaving her to wait for him in his mother's home while he probed relentlessly at the roots of human consciousness, he wrote, gushingly,

> Tables and chairs, mirrors, a clock to remind the happy couple of the passage of time, an armchair for an hour's pleasant daydreaming, carpets to help the housewife keep the floors clean, linen tied with pretty ribbons in the cupboard and dresses of the latest fashion and hats with artificial flowers, pictures on the wall, glasses for everyday and others for wine and festive occasions, plates and dishes [...] and the sewing table and the cosy lamp, and everything must be kept in good order or else the housewife who has divided her heart into little bits, one for each piece of furniture, will begin to fret. And this object must bear witness to the serious work that holds the household together [...].
>
> I know, after all, how sweet you are, how you can turn a house into a paradise, how you will share in my interests, how gay yet painstaking you will be. I will let you rule the house as much as you wish, and you will reward me with your sweet love and by rising above all those weaknesses for which women are so often despised.[37]

Despite Freud's best efforts to establish domestic necessities and decoration as extensions of the housewife's care and personality, the very ease with which he rattles off this list highlights such objects' implication in domestic ideology. The home might seem to allow women to assign personal signification to the objects under their care. Nevertheless, this is only window dressing, a strategy for distracting attention away from the extent to which the home and its contents actively dictated the housewife's behavior and activities. As discussed in previous chapters, both the solution to the chaos of consumer culture in the United States and the symbol of its more deleterious effects was the middle-class wife.

As the nineteenth-century came to a close, and as the range of available commodities continued to broaden, 'the household ceased to display the value of the man's income and instead took on the innermost human qualities of the woman who regulated the domestic economy.'[38] This shift took place as, according to Halttunen, 'The living room replaced the parlor as the most important room in the middle-class home around the turn of the century, and *personality* replaced *character* as the dominant conceptualisation of the self.'[39] '[E]arly nineteenth-century writers had pointed to the whole house as an expression of the owner's' character, defined as 'an almost lapidary substance upon which life was supposed to have etched its facets and flaws.' Near the end of the century, the focus moved to individual rooms and the multiplicity of interior spaces, designated by 'the word *personality*, now conceived as a protean effect: a display in which the personal proprieties of the self mingled with the stage properties of its immediate surroundings.'[40]

Turn-of-the-century American culture therefore strove to harness interior decorating as a vehicle for fluid, playful self-fashioning, loosened from traditional notions of morality and self-discipline.[41] Purchasing items of domestic and personal adornment was an activity increasingly lauded as an expression of self and of personal freedom, not least by the New Thought and Christian Science movements, which 'believed that the mental or spiritual world was the true reality, while the material world of daily life, the world of "matter," was merely a secondary creation of the mind.'[42] These movements therefore emphasized the power of the mind over material reality, asserting that one could attain whatever one desired through a mere exercise of the will, including financial success and, perhaps paradoxically, material objects, urging individuals to feel empowered rather than guilty about expressing and indulging their desires.[43] Consequently, 'New Thought tracts' functioned as 'the paradigmatic success literature of modern consumer capitalism.'[44]

This new, highly positive attitude toward material possessions takes center stage in what is arguably Mary E. Wilkins' most famous story, the nonsupernatural 'A New-England Nun' (1891). The story's heroine, Louise Ellis, who has been waiting fourteen years for her fiancé to return from Australia, has developed a rigid but personally satisfying domestic routine, revolving around aprons and books, sugar bowls and teaspoons, bird cages and sewing baskets. We are told, 'these little feminine appurtenances [...] had become, from long use and constant association, a very part of her personality.'[45] Unlike her neighbors, she does not keep her 'best china' in a 'parlor closet' unused, but (shockingly) dines from it every day, and sewing by her window 'during long sweet afternoons, drawing her needle gently through the dainty fabric', makes her feel as if 'she was peace itself.'[46] We are told that

> Louisa had almost the enthusiasm of an artist over the mere order and cleanliness of her solitary home. She had throbs of genuine triumph at the sight of the windowpanes which she had polished until they shone like jewels. She gloated gently over her orderly bureau-drawers, with their exquisitely folded contents redolent with lavender and sweet clover and very purity.[47]

Consequently, when her one-time sweetheart, Joe Dagget, finally returns to America, although they both automatically assume that they will still marry, 'Every morning rising and going about among her neat maidenly possessions, she felt as one looking her last upon the faces of dear friends. It was true that in a measure she could take them with her, but, robbed of their old environments, they would appear in such new guises that they would almost cease to be themselves.'[48] Discovering that Joe is actually in love with another, more spontaneous. local girl, both saddened and relieved, Louisa lets him go, and returns to her things more or less joyfully.

As this illustrates, in stuggling to keep commodities in their places, American culture posited the links between owner and objects as inherent and unbreakable. Seen by commentators such as Thorstein Veblen as a kind of dark arts, a false, fantasy world of desire, seducing people away from proper productive practices and honest hard work, and into behavior they could scarcely afford and against which they had little power of resistance, the new consumer culture responded with renewed efforts to dispel the long-standing sense that *things* were morally and financially perilous.[49] Speaking in fond tones of 'a long-lived-in-house, filled with beloved traps and trifles', an anonymous contributor to the *Atlantic Monthly* (1883) allowed that 'Desires for certain objects of art lead some persons into careers of wretched extravagance', but continued, 'to a person who is sensible, and has a proper amount of self-control, there need be no such danger. Indeed, it is the things we saw and loved, and knew to belong to us, and yet did not take or buy, that cause us most sorrow.'[50] The writer celebrated

> people who have not outgrown the instinct for making to themselves idols, and who fill their homes with shrines, old and new. They build themselves a wall of happiness with their treasures, and if one brick has not been secured it always leaves a gap; its place cannot be filled

in with anything else. From the person who clings desperately to a few things that are dear from long association, to the person who has a mania for making collections and filling cabinets, is a very wide range, but it is the same instinct, – a love of things. The often-quoted depravity of inanimate objects seems a slur to them; they understand only the friendly and companionable side of nature and art; they unconsciously personify things, and attribute much sensitiveness to them.[51]

Describing 'the small ghost of a cigarette-case' that haunted the author, who failed to buy it once in Italy, he or she speculated that 'the influence of our surroundings' might play 'a greater part in the development of our characters than we have ever recognized', suggesting that individuals' intense feelings toward particular objects may have been given to them 'with a wise and secret purpose', one that mere reason cannot hope to explain or comprehend.[52] What this passage articulates is a conviction that the financial and psychic dangers of commodity culture are effectively exorcized through the creation of emotional bonds with objects – that things need not be frightening or treacherous if we love them enough.

A similar movement from discomfort with things to an intimate relationship with beloved possessions is depicted in Sarah Orne Jewett's 'Lady Ferry' (1879), in which the narrator, a young girl named Marcia, must go to stay with relatives while her parents are on a protracted sea voyage. When she realizes that she is homesick and begins to cry, her older cousin Agnes comforts her by asking if she would 'like some bread and milk with [her] supper, in the same blue china bowl, with the dragon on it, which [her] father used to have when he was a boy?' In a house evidently filled with meaningful objects from the past, Marcia almost immediately apprehends that there is some mystery about the house, from which the adults seem anxious to protect her. Writing many years later, she remarks that even 'when one came away, after cordiality, and days of sunshine and pleasant hospitality, it was still with a sense of this mystery, and of something unseen and unexplained.' She continues, 'Not that there was any thing covered and hidden necessarily; but it was the quiet undertone in the house which had grown to be so old.'[53]

This sense of mystery intensifies as Marcia forms a tentative friendship with an elderly woman known only as Lady Ferry, who lives in the vast old house and appears to have arrived there out of nowhere, so many years ago that nobody knows how old she is or where she came from. Marcia notes that 'It was strongly impressed upon my mind that I must ask no questions, and that Madam was not to be discussed. No one distinctly forbade this; but I felt that it would not do', and Cousin Agnes tells her explicitly 'that by daylight I should go everywhere, except to Madam's rooms: I must wait for an invitation there.'[54] When the little girl finally breaks the taboo and asks Martha, the maid, about the old lady, she is told how

> 'Folks tell all kinds of strange stories. She's fearful old, and there's many believes she never will die; and where she came from nobody knows. I've heard that her folks used to live here; but nobody can remember them, and she used to wander about; and once before she was here, – a good while ago; but this last time she come was nine years ago; one stormy night she came across the ferry, and scared them to death, looking in at the window like a ghost. She said she used to live here in Colonel Haverford's time. They saw she wasn't right in her head – the ferry-men did. But she came up to the house, and they let her in, and she went straight to the rooms in the north gable, and she never has gone away; it was in an awful storm she come, I've heard, and she looked just the same as she does now. There! I can't tell half the stories I've heard, [...] but I guess most everybody thinks there's something mysterious.'

While these local rumors whisper that she cannot die, Lady Ferry herself tells everyone that she is old enough to have met Queen Elizabeth I, but is also convinced that her own death is either imminent or has already happened, to the point of setting up her rooms for her own funeral on a regular basis. She summons Marcia to visit her on the day of one of these funerals, for which she has moved all the chairs to face an empty space at the center of the room, where she says her coffin is to be set. This episode is notable for the wealth of descriptive detail that suddenly invades the previously rather impressionistic tale:

> There were two tall chests of drawers in the room, with shining brass handles and ornaments; and at one side, near the door, was a heavy mahogany table, on which I saw a large leather-covered Bible, a decanter of wine and some glasses, beside some cakes in a queer old tray. And there was no other furniture but a great number of chairs which seemed to have been collected from different parts of the house.[55]

Lady Ferry hopes wistfully that Marcia will be able to attend her funeral, and tells her, earnestly, in a passage that emphasizes the material nature of contemporary mourning culture, '"I would have ordered you some gloves if I had known; but these are all too large for your little hands. You shall have a ring; I will leave a command for that"; and Madam seated herself near me in a curious, high-backed chair.' Marcia is initially frightened by these lugubrious proceedings, and 'The open space where Lady Ferry had left room for her coffin began to be a horror to me.' However, her dread is rapidly dissipated when Lady Ferry 'opened a drawer containing some old jewelry; there were also some queer Chinese carvings, yellow with age', prompting her to chatter 'to Lady Ferry of [her] own possessions, and some coveted treasures of [her] mother's, which were to be [Marcia's] when [she] grew older.' Here, the horror of impending old age and death is immediately allayed by the memories tied up in objects, and by Lady Ferry's assurance that these objects will be passed down from the dead to the living. As, I would argue, the passage from Gutzkow quoted by Freud suggests, mysterious private lives can seem uncanny when viewed from without, but once initiated into these mysteries, Marcia has now come inside, as it were, and is no longer scared.

Nonetheless, 'in spite of [...] being amused and tearless', she cannot help feeling 'as if her imagined funeral were there in reality, and as if [...] the solemn company of funeral guests already sat in the next room to us with bowed heads, and all the shadows in the world had assembled there materialized into the tangible form of crape.' Indeed, she remembers that on the previous evening, Lady Ferry had told her 'that all her friends were gone', and speculates, 'Perhaps she expected their ghosts: that would not be stranger than all the rest.' Mediated through beloved objects, however, the ghostly presences that may or may not crowd into the room are simultaneously eerie *and* comforting, as Lady Ferry herself is. Veiled in a cloud of fragrance that seems to permeate rooms where she is never seen, and wearing clothing that Martha pronounces 'unearthly looking' (and that she's heard once 'belonged to a Mistress Haverford who was hung for a witch', including one dress that Marcia fancies is covered in flowers resembling the 'wicked little faces' of 'faded little imps'), Marcia admits that it is only her sweet smile and musical voice that prevent Lady Ferry from being 'a terror to [her].' When the elderly woman opens the same drawer as before, 'It creaked, and the brass handles clacked in a startling way', but even this gently unnerving sound is forgotten when she took out a little case, and said I might keep it to remember her by. It held a little vinaigrette, – a tiny silver box with a gold one inside, in which I found a bit of fine sponge, dark brown with age, and still giving a faint, musty perfume and spiciness. The outside was rudely chased, and was worn as if it had been carried for years in somebody's pocket. It had a spring, the secret of which Lady Ferry showed me.[56]

Her fear abandoned, the little girl instinctively kisses her uncanny benefactress not once but twice, to the evident pleasure of Lady Ferry. Beautiful things are therefore portrayed in the story as transforming the terror of decay, loss, and the terrible anachronism of great old age into a continuous narrative linking the immemorial past to a stable future. As 'The Yellow Wall-Paper' and 'The House That Was Not' suggest, the presence of a ghostly past could provide vital anchors for the present, even while producing a sense of supernatural dread, and a domestic secret could in fact render a home even more homelike, for those in possession of it, for precisely the same reasons that it was frightening for outsiders.

The material problem

Be that as it may, attitudes toward objects, and women's interactions with them, were not always so positive, nor are these interactions necessarily always empowering for female characters. The rise in 'emerging expressions of obligatory kindness mediated by goods', including 'the giving of flowers as gifts, the leaving of cards, and the stuffing of Christmas stockings with presents', ultimately 'raised questions', Simon J. Bronner asserts, regarding 'the real meaning and feeling of façades in a consumer landscape of signs.'[57] Torn between the antimaterialist Protestant ethos of the still-powerful recent past, and a new, commercialized morality that insisted that to have and to be seen was to be good, American society labored to give meaning to the mass of goods crowding its shops and homes. Close association of individual objects with an individual human personality went some way toward reconciling these tensions. Property was therefore detached from the harsh economic sphere, and situated as the vehicle for affective bonds and personal interiority, moral depth displayed through material surfaces.[58] Ideally, then, domestic decoration permitted the middle-class housewife to imprint her personality upon the contents of her home. She may not have owned them, but they were hers to choose, to arrange, and, most importantly, to live with. However, the problem lay in the balance of power, and it was far too easy for the housewife to slip from being what Abba Goold Woolson called 'The Queen of Home', to being ruled by one's husband's possessions, which, like the kettle in Peattie's 'Jim Lancy's Waterloo', were often disturbingly independent, indifferent, or even antagonistic.[59]

This is precisely the premise of Peattie's short story 'The Room of the Evil Thought', which dramatizes the horrifying effects of a failure to eject the dead from the spaces of the living, discussed in Chapter 3. The story focuses on a room where the furniture belonging to a dead murderer is not sold or tidied away, but remains in a rector's house for the use of a new family who move in. It quickly becomes apparently that anyone who spends any time there is overcome with murderous impulses toward their loved ones, resulting in the grandmother's screaming to be taken out of it and refusing to enter it. Concerned for her health, the family

> laid her on the sofa, hemmed around with cushions, and before long she was her quiet self again, though exhausted, naturally, with the tumult of the previous night. Now and then, as the children played about her, a shadow crept over her face – a shadow as of cold remembrance – and then the perplexed tears followed.
>
> [...] though the fire glowed and the lamp burned, as soon as ever she was alone they heard her shrill cries ringing to them that the Evil Thought had come again.[60]

Domestic objects in this story function as agents of control and sanity, hemming the grandmother in and keeping her safe and harmless all at once. At the same time, light, warmth, and soft cushions are depicted as utterly ineffectual as agents of beneficence against the memories of evil deeds and notions that domestic space can contain. In other words, the superficially cozy arrangement of objects is here powerless against the accumulation of memories that (like in 'An Itinerant House') are irrelevant to those who move in unawares. This point is emphasized when the grandson Hal goes to smoke in the room. The next morning, his sister finds him pacing the room, in visible distress. When she asks what the matter is,

> for answer he threw his arms about the little table and clung to it, and looked at her with tortured eyes, in which she fancied she saw a gleam of hate. She ran, screaming, from the room, and her father came and went up to him and laid his hands on the boy's shoulders.

And then a fearful thing happened. All the family saw it. There could be no mistake.[61]

Hal attacks his father for no apparent reason and is punched firmly for it. In an effort to prevent himself from likewise attacking his sister, it is to the 'little table' that he clings, as if the simple object can act as his salvation. What the story illustrates, however, is that such faith in domestic commodities is sadly misguided, as these very objects and spaces have themselves become the medium through which evil is communicated. In other words, they continue to be meaningful for the previous owner (an idle and moody rector who had apparently cut a man's throat and then his own, on board a ship bound for Australia after leaving his parish). It is through the home and its contents that malevolent memories are perpetuated and renewed, endangering inhabitants who have no other connection to the emotions that continue, uncannily, to occupy the house. This is not a matter of the sins of the fathers, but of the furniture. As 'The Southwest Chamber' also asserts, objects that have belonged to more than one person are unnervingly capable of housing divergent and often violently conflicting meanings beneath their pleasing surfaces. In particular, these stories insist that such communication is unavoidable in the discontinuous world of emerging urbanized modernity, where new owners are not necessarily related to the former ones, and where the past lingers on as the terrifying traces of total strangers.

In Wynne's 'The Little Room', these very lines of communication from past memories to present users of furniture and decorative items seem even more tangled, indeed broken. It might be possible to situate Aunt Hannah as the center of the confusion – that her desire to forget about the objects given to her by the lamented sea captain results in blocked memories haunting the house. Nevertheless, this voluntary amnesia leaves the objects available for Margaret's mother to form her own bonds of affection with the shell and the couch. What is startling is that even these bonds are not enough to keep the objects still – indeed, it is their very ability to take on different significations for different people that renders them unstable and unreliable. Depicting commodities, and the spaces that house them, as refusing to conform with our profoundly held mental images of them, 'The Little Room' figures objects as slippery friends at best. Essentially arabesque in nature, and therefore not conceptually solid enough to provide a sense of chronological or even spatial continuity, things (*all* things, no matter what they looked like) were not safe places to keep one's memories, however much they might have appeared to invite such mnemonic attachment. Indeed, in Wynne's story, the more inviting they are, the more elusive and illusory they prove to be.

The very notion of private property, which 'suggests a close relationship between person and thing', in fact, Daniel Miller argues, 'works to produce precisely the opposite effect', producing instead 'abstract relationships between anonymous people and postulated objects.' Precisely because 'Private property as a notion conflates the direct relationship between the individual and those objects with which he or she is associated in self-construction with those over which he or she has legal rights', it is therefore possible for an individual 'to own an object with which he or she may have no personal relationship, thus preventing others from realizing their potential for achieving such a relationship.'[62] Hell-bent on selling off the vast surplus of goods piling up in storehouses across the United States, the burgeoning advertising industry, and the economists and commentators whose writings bolstered commercial enterprise, worked hard during these decades to conceal the abstract, emotionally chilly, and often socially abusive nature of ownership of material goods. As Karl Marx put it, 'If commodities could speak, they would say this: Our use value may interest men, but it does not belong to us as objects. What does belong to us as objects, however, is our value. Our own intercourse as commodities proves it. We relate to each other merely as exchange-values.'[63]

The problem with the objects in Wynne's little room is that they should not be exchangeable with the contents of the china closet, because, for Margaret Grant and her mother, those in the little room are far more emotionally valuable than those in the china closet. Nonetheless, the flickering back and forth between the two implies that market forces override such personal considerations, rendering *everything* potentially exchangeable. The aunts' house is haunted, not by memories, but by commodities' refusal to retain any – by absence, rather than presence. In this way, it prefigures Jacques Derrida's dissociation of spectrality from anthropomorphic phantoms or spirits. Indeed, conventional phantoms tend to be conspicuously absent from American gothic novels and stories, due to the insistence that the United States is a nation without a past.[64] Derrida's notion of 'hauntology' pivots around his conviction that solid explanations – whether in the form of recognizable ghostly presences or psychoanalytical debunking exercises – effectively function as a form of exorcism. In other words, haunting cannot be tied down to any specific origin or source without dissipating, since it cannot be disentangled from uncertainty and a lack of knowledge. The spectral, he argues, should therefore be seen as a state of being rather than an object:

> *Es spukt.* Difficult to translate [...]. It is a question of ghost and haunting, to be sure, but what else? The German idiom seems to name the ghostly return but it names it in a verbal form. The latter does not say that there is some *revenant,* spectre, or ghost; it does not say that there is some apparition, *der Spuk,* nor even that it appears, but that 'it ghosts', 'it apparitions'. *It is a matter* [Il s'agit], in the neutrality of this altogether impersonal verbal form, of something or someone, neither someone nor something, of a 'one' that does not act. *It is a matter* rather of the passive movement of an apprehension [...].[65]

Consequently, all traces of haunting 'obediently evaporate as soon as the trajectories of history, legacy and property are reinstated to their rightful places', in an intrusive 'imposition' that seeks to 'solve' rather than understand the nature and function of haunting itself.[66] Discussing the uncanny life that commodities seemed to take on in the nineteenth-century capitalist marketplace and that was carried through into the homes of those who purchase them, Marx acknowledged that, in the minds of the majority, 'A commodity appears at first sight an extremely obvious, trivial thing.' However, because the exchange value accorded to commodities was the product of an abstract conception of labor time rather than correlating with use value or even a specific production process, there was 'absolutely no connection with the physical nature of the commodity and the material [*dinglich*] relations arising out of this.' Indeed, once they moved from the factory to the marketplace, the process of exchange, even as it remained a 'definite social relation between men', took on instead 'the fantastic form of a relation between things', so that 'the products of the human brain appear as autonomous figures endowed with a life of their own.' The commodity is therefore 'a very strange thing, abounding in metaphysical subtleties and theo-logical niceties.'[67]

Marx's and Derrida's comments have effectively rendered the language and imagery of supernatural fantasy inextricable from the hard cold facts of economic reality. Precisely because, in the primarily middle-class United States, the capitalist marketplace pervaded every aspect of the normal world, the apparently fantastic attributes of the commodity were intrinsic to quotidian reality. Wynne's story depicts this as an extremely frightening state of affairs indeed for housewives, bound up as their daily lives were with the very material conditions of the home. This is initially signaled when Margaret warns Roger that he might not be prepared for what she calls '"the decorum of my aunts. They are simply workers. They make me think of the Maine woman who wanted her epitaph to be, 'She was a *hard* working woman.'"' The association between death and domestic labor is extended when she imagines that the elderly sisters '"will die standing; or, at least, on a Saturday night, after all the house-work is done up."' Like Emily Dickinson's poetic persona, they have no time to stop for Death, nor to 'put away' either their labor or their leisure for anything so improper as dying.[68] These assertions are borne out on the couple's first evening at the house, when, 'After supper [Margaret] offered to help about the dishes, but, mercy! she might as well have offered to help bring the seasons round; Maria and Hannah couldn't be helped.'[69]

On an even more sinister note, we are told that the aunts '"never would leave home for a day"', even to attend Margaret's mother's wedding – or, presumably, her funeral.[70] It is precisely this shut-off privacy, and the apparently murderous work ethic that cannot be extricated from it, that is at the center of the story's critique of domestic relations. When Margaret asks them about the little room, they use housework as a mechanism for deflecting unwanted questions, 'washing dishes and drying them on the spotless towels with methodical exactness; and as they worked they said that there had never been any little room, so far as they knew; the china-closet has always been there, and the gilt-edged china had belonged to their mother, it had always been in the house.' Repeating this mantra, they display 'not a sign of interest, curiosity, or annoyance, not a spark of memory.' Recalling an identical scene in her childhood, when her mother discovers the little room instead of the expected china closet, Margaret remarks, '"How cold their gray eyes looked to me! There was no reading anything in them."'[71] Both the hard work and the domestic privacy that the aunts practice so rigidly function as a shield, preventing all inquiry that might reveal that the spaces of the house exceed or warp those of physical 'reality'. In other words, the ideologies surrounding domesticity itself make it difficult, if not impossible, to query the accepted normality of the ways in which houses and their contents recruit women, transforming them into unquestioning avatars and extensions of a vast, impersonal system.

The power of this system is made depressingly clear through the effect that the house has on Nan and Rita, who are positioned outside of the system of heterosexual marriage. The disagreement that results from the irresolvable confusion regarding who has seen what makes Nan turn 'actually pale, and it was hard to say whether she was most angry or frightened. There was something of both in her look.' Unable to sleep, the previously inseparable pair

> talked and argued, and then kept still for a while, only to break out again, it was so absurd. They both maintained that they had been there, but both felt sure the other one was either crazy or obstinate beyond reason. They were wretched; it was perfectly ridiculous, two friends at odds over such a thing; but here it was – 'little room', 'china-closet', – 'china closet', 'little room.'

The real crisis comes the following morning, when 'Nan was tacking up some tarlatan at a window to keep the midges out.' When Rita offers 'to help her, as she had done for the past ten years', Nan replies with a '"No, thanks"', which 'cut her to the heart'.[72] The thing that repeats itself, over and over in the house, among previously happy couples, is therefore not merely silence and animosity but also a form of domestic labor that isolates the worker from those around her. Just as Margaret's mother's obsession with the room hastens her decline and death, so the house traps other women into an excessive, harshly independent devotion to cleaning and caring for objects, one that undermines rather than nurtures interpersonal bonds.

Furthermore, the story underscores the perilous nature of domestic space by refusing to reduce the uncanny effects of the mystery by positing a clear origin for the house's spatial instability. Although Wynne bowed to public pressure and produced 'A Sequel to the Little Room' for the collection published in the same year as the original story, far from clearing up the mystery, the sequel deepens it, conjuring up 'the mystical and the grotesque of the New England temperament' without ever pinning the blame on a single individual or event.[73] Discovering at the very end of the original story that the house has burned to the ground before Nan and Rita can visit it together, the sequel follows them through the New-England countryside, as they attempt to piece together the house's story and that of its occupants. While it does emerge that Hannah had brought a lamp to the little room in the middle of the night, potentially causing or even deliberately starting the fire, the gossip and half-told stories that the girls hear add up to little more than a further muddle of rumor, speculation, and a rural suspicion of enquiring strangers, leaving Nan, Rita, and the reader no wiser than before.

Wynne's story, and many of those discussed in this book, implies that what Bill Brown calls the 'otherness of things' – their irreducibility to extensions of ourselves – should be recognized and taken seriously.[74]

Whether seen as housing cherished memories or multiplying tiresome chores, commodities remained and remain fundamentally exchangeable with one another. Within this system of exchange, in an aggressively consumerist economy, there was little room for human emotion, and little pity for those who worked tirelessly to maintain them. Far from being simply transparent expressions of a housewife's care and personal labor, they remained foreign, indifferent objects. What 'The Little Room' dramatizes most devastatingly is the extent to which objects could trick those who used and loved them into thinking the exact opposite. Worse still, the sheer callous independence of things from their owners and users is made just as evident by the warm and cozy little room as by the rigid china closet, as the death of Margaret's mother makes horribly clear.

As Wilkins' story 'The Hall Bedroom' (1903) suggests, the glittering realm of *fin-de-siècle* commodity culture was as dangerous as it was enticing. The protagonist, and those who occupy his rented room before him, are transported through the room's ordinary contents into a fantasy world of strange and exotic sensory experience, perhaps becoming free and fulfilled there but also effectively dying to their loved ones or to life as we know it.[75] The implication is that objects are dangerous precisely because they are so seductive. 'The Little Room' further cautions that, unaware of who has made or previously owned them, a woman corralled within the hyperprivate domestic sphere should be wary of investing objects with affective significance. These objects functioned both as a means of distracting women from the lack of power they had, and of luring them into thinking that these objects themselves constituted the realm of women's power. The fierce autonomy of domestic objects and spaces, their constant shrugging off of the meanings apparently attached to them, their faithless ability to become meaningful for others and in contradictory ways, repeatedly belied this power in the stories examined here. Indeed, Wynne's genteel gothic supernaturalism transforms the battle over signification into one over physical and spatial predictability, as rooms shift and objects move, disappear, or become completely different objects apparently of their own accord, literalizing their unreliability.

The stories discussed here effectively insist that, behind the obvious façade of bricks and mortar, the middle-class home automatically connoted not only a wider system of middle-class morality but also of capitalist exchange and ownership. Domestic ideology automatically inserted the occupant into a range of behaviors including socially prescribed isolation, in order to maintain privacy, heterosexual relations, and women's unpaid labor. A house, however simply furnished, was therefore by its very nature a disorderly house, haunted by the commodities that fulfilled the practical functions that were carried out there – by the very things that rendered it homelike. There is always far more to a room, a house, and their decorative contents than meets the eye, and, Wynne's story cautions, what you do not know, or refuse to see, can most definitely hurt you. Things always elude our grasp, and this is why, where Gilman, Dawson and Wilkins left theirs empty for others to occupy (potentially more successfully), there was only one possible way for Wynne (like Flora's neighbor) to end her story – by burning the house to the ground.

Afterword

Why the ghost story declined in the years following the First World War has been amply rehearsed by critics.[1] Nevertheless, as this book illustrates, even until the late 1930s, American women were continuing to produce eerie tales in which material objects play a vital role. However, it was not until Shirley Jackson emerged in the late 1940s and 1950s that the relationship between women and domestic spaces and commodities would surface with such force in American supernatural fiction. Perhaps more importantly, Jackson remained largely unsupported by the kind of community of writers who shared concerns and a figurative language that, as I have been arguing, characterized the Gilded Age in the United States. Apart from some aspects of the work of Ira Levin, Robert Marasco, and Anne Rivers Siddons, women's interactions with the things that, to this day, even in an 'enlightened', 'postfeminist', twenty-first-century Ireland, continue to define life and work for so many, have ceased to be the stuff of well-known gothic fiction. Examining that relationship and identifying a body of texts that narrate it, are both urgently needed and well beyond the scope of the current volume. There is, in other words, far more to be done. Indeed, the (deliberately) constricted nature of this book's source material and focus is not merely a matter of chronology; what it also leaves out, rather glaringly, is the issue of race. Prominent as material culture is in American women's ghost stories from the end of the nineteenth century, their richness and variety move them far beyond the bounds of the relatively narrow motif outlined in the preceding chapters. Among others, the figure of the non-Anglo-Saxon domestic servant, and the issue of his or her relationship with supernatural forces unknown to the generally white protagonists of these stories, are important elements of such tales, and are ripe for reexamination and critique, not least through the medium of the kinds of materialist readings I advocate here.

I would therefore like to finish by emphasizing that it should not be taken on trust that the ghost story is an obsolete genre, unsuited to the dissection of modern anxieties, cultural tensions, and troubling social relationships. If *The Guardian's* 'Winter Fiction Special' is anything to go by, uncanny tales about objects have not fallen out of favor altogether.[2] The magazine featured stories by Lionel Shriver and Jeannette Winterson about minutely detailed haunted houses, and one by Ned Beauman about a mad artist whose work proves fatal to those who spend too much time near it. Ideally situated to give voice to the frictions and uncertainties of post-credit-crunch life, it is to be hoped that a revival of the form will result in a critical reappraisal of the genre, which is broader in scope and implication than psychoanalytical criticism might suggest. Specifically, the authors discussed in this book employed the supernatural in order to find impossible solutions to the problematic place occupied by the female body, 'feminine' clothing, and women's activities in a hostile, censorious, inflexible social world. Impractical and often unsatisfactory as total physical disappearance might be, it leaves us with the question of how contemporary writers might approach precisely these same issues. The problem of the material, which, in 2014, has seen both a resurgence in feminist thinking and a patriarchal backlash via issues as broad as rape culture, body shaming, religiously inflected clothing, and the contents of music videos, seems more pressing than ever.

Notes

Introduction

1. Melissa Edmundson, 'The "Uncomfortable Houses" of Charlotte Riddell and Margaret Oliphant', *Gothic Studies* 12:1 (2010), pp. 51–67, 51–52.
2. For the sake of brevity, 'America' is used throughout as synonymous with 'the United States', but it is acknowledged that they can be employed to mean quite distinct things.
3. Teresa A. Goddu, *Gothic America: Narrative, History and Nation* (New York: Columbia University Press, 1997), p. 9. The word 'gothic' is given a small 'g' throughout this book (outside of quotations), in order to distinguish it from the English Gothic novels of the late eighteenth century. The term 'gothic' here is employed as a general means of designating overtly gloomy, although not always overtly supernatural, texts, operating within a broad set of conventions defined as 'gothic'. For a discussion of generic issues, see Jarlath Killeen, 'Irish Gothic Revisited', *The Irish Journal of Gothic and Horror Studies* 12 (June 2011) (http://irishgothichorrorjournal.homestead.com/jarla-thresponse.html, accessed February 20, 2014).
4. John L. O'Sullivan, 'The Great Nation of Futurity', *The United States Democratic Review* 6:23 (November 1839), pp. 426–430, 426.
5. Henry James, *Hawthorne* (London: MacMillan and Co., 1879), p. 44.
6. Nathaniel Hawthorne, Preface to *The Marble Faun: or, The Romance of Monte Beni* (Boston: Ticknor and Fields, 1860), pp. vii–ix.
7. James, 'Letter to Charles Eliot Norton (1872)', quoted in Robert Weisbuch, *Atlantic Double-Cross: American Literature and British Influence in the Age of Emerson* (Chicago: University of Chicago Press, 1986), p. 279.
8. The word 'uncanny' is used throughout this book (outside of quotations) in the general sense of 'unknown, inexplicable, and eerie', rather than in the specific (and quite different) senses used by Freud and Tzvetan Todorov.
9. Sigmund Freud, *The Psychopathology of Everyday Life*, ed. James Strachey, trans. Alan Tyson (New York: Norton, 1960), pp. 258–59, italics in original. See, for example, Anthony Vidler, *The Architectural Uncanny: Essays in the Modern Unhomely* (London and Cambridge, Massachusetts: The MIT Press, 1992), p. 6.
10. Irving Malin, *New American Gothic* (Carbondale: Southern Illinois University Press, 1962), p. 79.
11. Charles Brockden Brown, Preface to *Edgar Huntly; or, Memoirs of a Sleep-Walker with Related Texts*, eds Philip Bernard and Stephen Shapiro (Indianapolis and Cambridge: Hackett, 2006), pp. 3–4.
12. Edgar Allan Poe, Preface to *Tales of the Grotesque and Arabesque* (Philadelphia: Lea and Blanchard, 1840), p. 5.
13. A significant number of the essays in Kevin J. Hayes (ed.), *The Cambridge Companion to Edgar Allan Poe* (Cambridge: Cambridge University Press,

2002) illustrate this particularly starkly. However, many of the essays collected in Charles L. Crow (ed.), *A Companion to American Gothic* (Oxford: Wiley Blackwell, 2013) demonstrate concerted efforts to move away from this critical orthodoxy.

14. Leslie Fiedler, *Love and Death in the American Novel* (Middlesex: Penguin, 1982), p. 496.

15. See Alan Trachtenberg, *The Incorporation of America: Culture and Society in the Gilded Age* (New York: Hill and Wang, 2007).

16. Daniel Miller, *Home Possessions: Material Culture Behind Closed Doors*, ed. D. Miller (Oxford and New York: Berg: 2001), p. 7.

17. Rhoda Broughton, 'The Truth, the Whole Truth, and Nothing but the Truth' (1868), in Michael Cox and R.A. Gilbert (eds), *The Oxford Book of Victorian Ghost Stories* (Oxford: Oxford University Press, 1991), p. 75.

18. Uncanny tales by women writers, including Edith Wharton's 'The Lady's Maid's Bell' (1902), Georgia Wood Pangborne's 'Broken Glass' (1911), and Josephine Daskam Bacon's 'The Unburied' (1913), figured the relationship between domestic servants and the objects they do not own but that structure their daily labours. The class and racial issues raised by these stories, and others like them, including Charles Chesnutt's 'Po' Sandy' (1899), while germane to my discussion, merit more detailed and complex analysis than would be possible here, nor would it be desirable to relegate these issues to a single chapter, deserving as they are of fuller treatment.

19. Lori Merish, *Sentimental Materialism: Gender, Commodity Culture, and Nineteenth-Century American Literature* (Durham and London: Duke University Press, 2000), p. 8.

20. Simon J. Bronner, 'Reading Consumer Culture', in Bronner (ed.), *Consuming Visions: Accumulation and Display in America, 1880–1920* (New York and London: Norton, 1989), p. 51.

21. Merish, pp. 4–5.

22. Louisa May Alcott, for example, was forced to 'go into service' as a result of her family's depressed circumstances. See Madeleine B. Sterne, *Louisa May Alcott: A Biography* (Lebanon: Northeastern University Press, 1999), p. 64f.

23. Poe's thoughts on interior decoration are dealt with in more detail in Chapter 2.

24. Poe, 'Landor's Cottage', *Flag of Our Union* 4 (Boston, June 9, 1849), p. 2, italics in original.

25. Poe, 'Landor's Cottage', p. 2, italics in original.

26. D. Miller, *Material Culture and Mass Consumption* (Oxford: Basil Blackwell, 1991), p. 48.

27. Jacques Derrida, *Specters of Marx: The State of the Debt, The Work of Mourning, and the New International*, trans. Peggy Kamuf (London: Routledge, 1994), pp. 149–150.

28. Karl Marx, *Capital: A Critique of Political Economy*, Vol. I, trans. B. Fowkes (London: Penguin, 1976), p. 163ff.

29. Arjun Appadurai, 'Introduction: Commodities and the Politics of Value', in Appadurai (ed.), *The Social Life of Things: Commodities in Cultural Perspective* (Cambridge: Cambridge University Press, 1988) pp. 3–63, 4.

30. Appadurai in Appadurai, p. 31.

31. Thomas Baldwin Thayer, *Over the River; or, Pleasant Walks into the Valley of Shadows, and Beyond...* (Boston: Thomkins and Co., 1864), pp. 91–92, italics in original.

32. See William Leach, *Land of Desire: Merchants, Power, and the Rise of a New American Culture* (New York: Vintage Books, 1994).

33. See Karen Halttunen, *Confidence Men and Painted Women: A Study of Middle-Class Culture in America, 1830–1870* (New Haven and London: Yale University Press, 1982); and Merish, op. cit. Jeffrey Andrew Weinstock, *Scare Tactics: Supernatural Fiction by American Women* (New York: Fordham, 2008), and Lynette Carpenter and Wendy Kolmar, *Haunting the House of Fiction: Feminist Perspectives on Ghost Stories by American Women* (Knoxville: University of Tennessee Press, 1991) cover similar ground to this book, but in broader terms.

34. Thomas H. Fick, 'Authentic Ghosts and Real Bodies: Negotiating Power in Nineteenth-Century Women's Ghost Stories', *South Atlantic Review*. 64:2 (Spring 1999), pp. 81–97, goes some way toward addressing issues of spectrality and embodiment, but is primarily focused on texts in which apparent 'ghosts' turn out in fact to be 'living' women.

35. Larzer Ziff, *American 1890s: Life and Times of a Lost Generation* (Lincoln and London: University of Nebraska Press, 1979), pp. 78–80.

36. Richard Slotkin, *The Fatal Environment: The Myth of the Frontier in the Age of Industrialisation, 1800–1890* (Norman: University of Oklahoma Press, 1994), p. 5.

37. Slotkin, *Fatal Environment*, p. 32; and Robert Eldridge, 'Introduction', in John Pinkney and Robert Eldridge (eds), *An Itinerant House and Other Ghost Stories* (Portland, Maine: Thomas Loring, 2007), p. xl.

38. Ellen Burton Harrington, 'Introduction', in Harrington (ed.), *Scribbling Women and the Short Story Form: Approaches by American and British Writers* (New York: Peter Lang, 2008), p. 2.

39. G.R. Thompson, 'Washington Irving and the American Ghost Story', in Howard Kerr, John Crowley, and Charles L. Crow (eds), *The Haunted Dusk: American Supernatural Fiction, 1820–1920* (Athens: University of Georgia Press, 1983), pp. 13–36, 33.

40. See Harry Levin, *The Power of Blackness: Hawthorne, Poe, Melville* (Chicago and London: Ohio University Press, 1980).

41. Andrew Levy, *The Culture and Commerce of the American Short Story* (Cambridge: Cambridge University Press, 1993), p. 1. For a discussion of the difference between a 'tale' and the more modern 'short story' during the nineteenth century in America, see Brander Matthews (ed.), *The Short-Story: Specimens Illustrating Its Development* (New York: American Book Company, 1907).

42. Poe, letter to Charles Anthon (October 1844), in John Ward Ostron (ed.), *The Letters of Edgar Allan Poe*, 2 vols., Vol. I (Cambridge: Harvard University Press, 1948), p. 268.

43. Levy, p. 24.

44. George P. Lathrop, review of Sarah Orne Jewett's collection, *The Mate of the Daylight*, *Atlantic Monthly* 53 (May 1884), pp. 712–713.

45. See, for example, Norman Friedman, 'Recent Short Story Theories', in Susan Lohafer and Jo Ellyn Clarey (eds), *Short Story Theory at a Crossroads* (Baton Rouge and London: Louisiana State University Press, 1989).

46. Harrington, p. 6.

47. Frank O'Connor, *The Lonely Voice: A Study of the Short Story* (1963) (New York: Melville House Publishing, 2004).
48. As the titles of several of the collections discussed in subsequent chapters illustrate, the writers examined here consciously saw themselves as writing 'short stories'.
49. *In Memory of Madeline Yale Wynne* (1918), Lawrence J Gutter Collection of Chicagoana, University of Illinois at Chicago (https://archive.org/stream/inmemoryofmadeli00lawr/inmemoryofmadeli00lawr_djvu.txt, accessed January 7, 2014), p. 5. As this volume makes clear, a number of the authors mentioned above knew one another personally and professionally.
50. Edith Wharton and Ogden Codman Jr., *The Decoration of Houses* (New York: Charles Scribners and Sons, 1914), p. 196.
51. Leach, p. 177.
52. Willa Cather, 'The Novel Démeublé', *The New Republic* 30 (April 12, 1922), pp. 5–6.
53. Wharton, 'Afterward', in *The Ghost Stories of Edith Wharton* (New York: Scribner, 1997), pp. 58–91, 84. See Ted Billy, '"Domesticated With the Horror": Matrimonial Mansions in Edith Wharton's Psychological Ghost Stories', *Journal of American and Comparative Cultures* 25:3–4 (March 2003), pp. 433–437.

1 'Fitted to a Frame': Picturing the Gothic Female Body

1. Wharton, 'Miss Mary Pask', in *Ghost Stories*, 147–62, p.161.
2. Emily Dickinson, 510, 'It was not Death, for I stood up', in Thomas H. Johnson (ed.), *Emily Dickinson: The Complete Poems* (London: Faber and Faber, 1975), pp. 248–249.
3. Edna Worthley Underwood, 'The Painter of Dead Women' (1910), in *A Book of Dear Dead Women* (Boston: Little, Brown and Company, 1911), 64–91, pp. 65–67.
4. Underwood, 'The Painter', pp.68–69.
5. Underwood, 'The Painter', pp.73–74.
6. Underwood, 'The Painter', pp.75–76, italics in original.
7. Underwood, 'The Painter', pp. 78–79.
8. Underwood, 'The Painter', pp. 81–82.
9. Robert W. Chambers, 'The Mask', in *The King in Yellow* (1895) (Middlesex: The Echo Library, 2007), p. 36.
10. Poe, 'The Philosophy of Composition', *Graham's Magazine* 28:4 (April 1846), 163–167, p. 164. A full elucidation of what precisely Poe means by this phrase is beyond the scope of the current study, and has been undertaken in Elisabeth Bronfen, *Over Her Dead Body: Death, Femininity and the Aesthetic* (Manchester: Manchester University Press, 1992).
11. Poe, 'Berenice', *Southern Literary Messenger* 1 (March 1835), 333–336, p.334.
12. William Leach, 'Strategists of Display and the Production of Desire', in Bronner, pp. 131–132.
13. See David E. Stannard, *The Puritan Way of Death: A Study in Religion, Culture, and Social Change* (New York: Oxford University Press, 1977), especially p. 72ff.

14. Angela Miller, *The Empire of the Eye: Landscape Representation and American Cultural Politics, 1825–1875* (Ithaca and London: Cornell University Press, 1993), p. 36.

15. See Halttunen. See also Nancy Armstrong, *Desire and Domestic Fiction* (New York and Oxford: Oxford University Press, 1987).

16. Anne Bradstreet, 'The Flesh and the Spirit' (1678), in Joseph R. McElrath, Jr., and Allan P. Robb (eds), *The Complete Works of Anne Bradstreet* (Boston: Twayne, 1981), pp.175–76.

17. Edward Taylor, 'A Fig for Thee, O Death!' (c. 1685), in Nina Baym (ed.), *The Norton Anthology of American Literature*, 5th ed. (New York and London: W.W. Norton and Co., 1998), Vol. I, 350–51, p. 350.

18. Margaret Beetham, *A Magazine of Her Own: Domesticity and Desire in the Women's Magazine, 1800–1914* (London: Taylor and Francis, 1996), p. 105.

19. John Murray, *A Welcome to the Grave. A Sermon Delivered at the Presbyterian Church at Newbury-Port: Occasioned by the Death of Mrs. Phebe Lane* [...] (Newbury-port, MA: J. Mycall, 1791), p. 32.

20. Fanny Fern, 'Rag-Tag and Bog-Tail Fashions', in *Ginger-Snaps* (New York: Carleton, 1870) (http://www.gutenberg.org/files/40504/40504-h/40504-h.htm#RAG-TAG_AND_BOB-TAIL_FASHIONS, accessed February 2, 2014), n.p.

21. See Armstrong; and Halttunen, p. 56ff.

22. Halttunen, p. 88f; and Nancy F. Cott, *The Bonds of Womanhood: 'Woman's Sphere' in New England, 1780–1835* (New Haven and London: Yale University Press, 1977), p. 64ff.

23. Ralph Waldo Emerson, 'Woman: Address to the Women's Rights Convention, 20 September 1855', in Ronald A. Bosco and Joel Myerson (eds), *The Later Lectures of Ralph Waldo Emerson, 1843–1871* (Athens: University of Georgia Press, 2010) Vol. II, 18–29, pp. 22–23.

24. Emerson, 'Woman', pp. 19–20.

25. Anon., *Advice to the Fair Sex, in a Series of Letters, Chiefly Concerning the Graceful Virtues* (Philadelphia, 1803), p. 17.

26. Emerson, 'Woman', p. 21.

27. Thorstein Veblen, *The Theory of the Leisure Class*, ed. Martha Banta (Oxford: Oxford University Press, 2007), pp. 118–119.

28. Veblen, p. 111 and pp. 113–114.

29. Fern, 'Rag-Tag and Bog-Tail Fashions', n.p.

30. Constance Cary Harrison, *The Well-Bred Girl in Society* (Philadelphia, 1898), p. 10.

31. Sonia Solicari, 'Selling Sentiment: The Commodification of Emotion in Victorian Visual Culture', *19: Interdisciplinary Studies in the Long Nineteenth Century* 4 (2007), 1–21, pp. 2–3 and p. 8 (www.19.bbk.ac.uk, accessed January 25, 2014).

32. James, *William Whetmore Story and His Friends*, Vol. I (Boston: Houghton Mifflin, 1903), pp. 114–115.

33. See Halttunen, p. 73f., for a discussion of scanty clothing as revealing a woman's 'sincerity'.

34. Joy S. Kasson, *Marble Queens and Captives: Women in Nineteenth-Century Art and Sculpture* (New Haven and London: Yale University Press, 1990), pp. 57–58.

35. Kasson, p. 69f.

36. Orville Dewey, 'Powers' Statues', *Union Magazine of Literature and Art* 1 (October 1847), 160–161, p. 160, quoted in Kasson, pp. 58–59; and Kasson, p. 61.
37. Edward A. Brackett, 'The Wreck', in *My House: Chips the Builder Threw Away* (Boston: Richard G. Badger, Gorham, 1904), pp. 71–73. See Kasson, p. 127f.
38. James Jackson Jarves, *Art-Hints: Architecture, Sculpture, and Painting* (New York: Harper and Brothers, 1855), p. 152.
39. Jarves, p. 152.
40. Underwood, 'The Mirror of La Granja' (1909), in *Dead Women*, 92–132, pp.126–127.
41. Leach, p. 58, p. 64f. and p. 176.
42. Leach in Bronner, p. 118.
43. Martha A. Sandweiss, 'Undecisive Moments: The Narrative Tradition in Western Photography', in Sandweiss (ed.), *Photography in Nineteenth-Century America* (New York: Harry N. Abrams Inc., 1991), 99–127; and Alan Trachtenberg, 'Photography: The Emergence of a Keyword', in Sandweiss (ed.), 17–47, p. 27.
44. Elia W. Peattie, 'Story of an Obstinate Corpse' (1898), in *The Shape of Fear and Other Ghostly Tales* (Middlesex: The Echo Library, 2008), p. 28.
45. Ellen Moers, *Literary Women* (New York: Doubleday, 1976), pp. 90–110.
46. Kate Ferguson Ellis, *The Contested Castle: Gothic Novels and the Subversion of Domestic Ideology* (Urbana and Chicago: University of Illinois Press, 1989), p. 37.
47. Eugenia C. DeLamotte, *Perils of the Night: A Feminist Study of Nineteenth-Century Gothic* (New York and Oxford: Oxford University Press, 1990), p. 153ff.
48. DeLamotte, pp. 185–186.
49. James, *The Turn of the Screw and The Aspern Papers*, Anthony Curtis (ed.) (London: Penguin, 1986), p. 164.
50. See Weinstock, p. 184.
51. Wharton, 'Mr. Jones', in *Ghost Stories*, 188–218, p. 205.
52. Wharton, 'Mr Jones', p. 216.
53. Wharton, 'Mr Jones', p. 212.
54. Wharton, 'Mr Jones', p. 206 and p. 200.
55. Emma Frances Dawson, 'A Stray Reveler' (1896), in *An Itinerant House and Other Stories* (San Francisco: William Doxey, 1897), 75–90.
56. Lurana W. Sheldon, 'A Premonition', *Godey's Lady's Magazine* (132: 789) March 1896, 273–276, p. 275.
57. Mrs. Wilson Woodrow, 'Secret Chambers', Harper's (1909), *Harper's* (1909) in Catherine A. Lundie (ed.), *Restless Sprits: Ghost Stories by American Women, 1872–1926* (Amherst: University of Massachusetts Press, 1996), 175–191, p. 180.
58. Woodrow in Lundie, p. 180.
59. M.E.M. Davis, 'At La Glorieuse', *Harper's Monthly Magazine* (December 1891), 77–94, p. 78.
60. Davis, pp. 86–87.
61. Davis, p. 90.
62. Harriet Prescott Spofford, 'The Amber Gods', in *The Amber Gods and Other Stories* (Boston: Ticknor and Fields, 1863), 1–66, p. 5.
63. Spofford, 'The Amber Gods', p. 60.
64. Spofford, 'The Amber Gods', p. 62.
65. Spofford, 'The Amber Gods', p. 60.

66. Spofford, 'The Amber Gods', pp.65–66.

2 'Handled with a Chain': Gilman's 'The Yellow Wall-Paper' and the Dangers of the Arabesque

1. Charlotte Perkins Gilman, *The Home: Its Work and Influence* (1903) (New York and Oxford: AltaMira Press, 2002), p. 5.
2. Several of the critical perspectives in Catherine J. Golden (ed.), *The Yellow Wallpaper: A Sourcebook and Critical Edition* (New York: Routledge, 2004) successfully situate the story culturally but nonetheless repeatedly return to psychological interpretations of the events narrated therein. The same can be said of Carol Margaret Davidson' otherwise subtle article, 'Haunted House/ Haunted Heroine: Female Gothic Closets in "The Yellow Wallpaper"', *Women's Studies* 33 (2004), pp. 47–75. See Mary Jacobus, 'An Unnecessary Maze of Sign Reading', in *Reading Women: Essays in Feminist Criticism* (New York: Columbia University Press, 1986), pp. 229–48 for a straightforward psychosexual reading of the story.
3. Sigmund Freud, 'The "Uncanny"', in *The Standard Edition of the Complete Works of Sigmund Freud: Volume XVII (1917–1919): An Infantile Neurosis and Other Works*, trans. James Strachey (London: Hogarth and Institute of Psychosis, 1955), pp. 223–224, italics and ellipsis in original.
4. Freud, 'The "Uncanny"', pp. 222–226.
5. Freud, 'The "Uncanny"', p. 241.
6. Freud, "The 'Uncanny'", p. 241.
7. Gilman, *Women and Economics: A Study of the Economic Relation Between Women and Men* (1898) (New York: Prometheus Books, 1994), p. 204.
8. Vidler, p. 12. See also Andrew Smith, 'Hauntings' in Catherine Spooner and Emma McEvoy (eds), *The Routledge Companion to Gothic* (London: Routledge, 2007), pp. 147–154; Benjamin Franklin Fisher, 'Poe and the Gothic Tradition', in Kevin J. Hayes (ed.), *The Cambridge Companion to Edgar Allan Poe* (Cambridge: Cambridge University Press, 2002); and Allan Gardner Lloyd-Smith, *Uncanny American Fiction: Medusa's Face* (Basingstoke and London: Macmillan, 1989).
9. Robert Mighall, *A Geography of Victorian Gothic Fiction: Mapping History's Nightmares* (Oxford: Oxford University Press, 1999), p. xiii.
10. Halttunen, 'From Parlor to Living Room: Domestic Space, Interior Decoration and the Culture of Personality', in Bronner, p. 189.
11. Gilman, *Women and Economics*, pp. 53–54.
12. Marilyn Chandler, *Dwelling in the Text* (Berkeley: University of California Press, 1991), p. 146.
13. Gilman, *The Home*, pp. 179–180.
14. Gilman, *Women and Economics*, p. 257 and pp. 155–156.
15. Marty Roth, 'Gilman's Arabesque Wallpaper', *Mosaic* 34:4 (2001), pp. 1145–1162; Eileen Cleere, 'Victorian Dust Traps', in William A. Cohen and Ryan Johnson (eds), *Filth: Dirt, Disgust, and Modern Life* (Minneapolis and London: University of Minnesota Press, 2005), pp. 133–154, 135–136; and Tom Lutz, *American Nervousness, 1903: An Anecdotal History* (Ithaca and London: Cornell University Press, 1991), p. 230.

16. Rhode and Agnes Garrett, *Suggestions for House Decoration in Painting, Woodwork, and Furniture*, 2nd ed. (London: Macmillan and Co, 1877), p. 69. See also Anon, 'A Color Cure', *The Atlantic* (March 1882), p. 425.

17. Elaine Freedgood, *The Ideas in Things: Fugitive Meaning in the Victorian Novel* (Chicago and London: University of Chicago Press, 2006), p. 10.

18. Rosemary Jackson, *Fantasy: The Literature of Subversion* (London and New York: Routledge, 1988), p. 41.

19. Tzvetan Todorov, *The Fantastic: A Structural Approach to a Literary Genre*, trans. Richard Howard (Ithaca, New York: Cornell University Press, 1975), p. 41.

20. Todorov, p. 25. See Deborah Esch and Jonathan Warren (eds), *The Turn of the Screw: Authoritative Text, Contexts, and Criticism* (New York and London: W.W. Norton, 1999).

21. R. Jackson, pp. 41–42.

22. Dickinson, 435, 'Much Madness is divinest Sense – ', in Johnson, p. 209.

23. Gilman, 'Why I Wrote "The Yellow Wall-Paper"' (1913) in Baym, Vol. II, pp. 699–670.

24. Gilman, 'The Yellow Wall-Paper', in Denise D. Knight (ed.), *The Yellow Wall-Paper, Herland, and Selected Writings* (London: Penguin, 2009), p. 167.

25. Bacon, 'The Children' (1913), in Lundie, 73–90.

26. Poe, 'The Philosophy of Furniture', in *The Complete Tales and Poems of Edgar Allan Poe* (London: Penguin, 1965), p. 463.

27. Poe, 'The Philosophy of Composition', p. 164.

28. Poe, 'The Philosophy of Composition', p. 167, italics in original.

29. Richard Wilbur, 'The House of Poe', in Robert Regan (ed.), *Poe: A Collection of Critical Essays* (New Jersey: Prentice-Hall, 1967), pp. 99–100.

30. Poe, 'The Philosophy of Furniture', p. 466.

31. Chandler, p. 49.

32. Gertrude Atherton, 'A Monarch of Small Survey' (1905), in *The Bell in the Fog and Other Stories* (London: Wordsworth, 2006), pp. 73–74.

33. Patricia L. Skarda and Nora Crow Jaffe, 'Introduction', in Skarda and Jaffe (eds), *The Evil Image: Two Centuries of Gothic Short Fiction and Poetry* (New York and Scarborough, Ontario: New American Library, 1983), p. xiv.

34. Gabrielle Rippl, 'Wild Semantics: Charlotte Perkins Gilman's Feminization of Edgar Allan Poe's Arabesque Aesthetics', in Karen L. Kilcup (ed.), *Soft Canons: American Women Writers and the Masculine Tradition* (Iowa City: University of Iowa Press, 1999), pp. 124–125.

35. John Ruskin, *The Stones of Venice*, 3 vols., Vol. II (Boston: Estes and Lauriat, 1894), p. 75.

36. See Colin Trodd, Paul Barlow and David Amigoni (eds), *Victorian Culture and the Idea of the Grotesque* (Aldershot and Brookfield: Ashgate, 1999).

37. Rippl, in Kilcup, pp. 124–125.

38. Gilman, 'The Yellow Wall-Paper', p. 166.

39. Dawson, 'Are the Dead Dead?', in *An Itinerant House*, p. 283.

40. Gilman, 'Yellow Wall-Paper', pp. 166–167, italics in original.

41. Gilman, 'Yellow Wall-Paper', pp. 167–168.

42. Sheldon, 'A Premonition', p. 273.

43. Sheldon, 'A Premonition', p. 274.

44. Gilman, 'Yellow Wall-Paper', p. 170.

45. Nicholas Daly, *Modernism, Romance and the Fin-de-Siècle: Popular Fiction and British Culture, 1880–1914* (Cambridge: Cambridge University Press, 1999), pp. 90–91.
46. Marx, p. 163.
47. Derrida, p. 155ff.
48. Derrida, p. 149–150, italics in original.
49. Unnamed commentator, quoted in Merish, pp. 122–123.
50. Kate Upson Clark, 'Literary Women in their Homes II – Mary E. Wilkins', *The Ladies' Home Journal* (August 1892) (http://public.wsu.edu/~campbelld/amlit/freemanhome.htm, accessed December 5, 2013), n.p.
51. Gilman, 'Yellow Wall-Paper', p. 166.
52. Gilman, 'Yellow Wall-Paper', p. 175 and p. 181.
53. Gilman, 'Yellow Wall-Paper', p. 171.
54. Poe, 'Ligeia', in *Complete Tales*, p. 664.
55. Gilman, 'Yellow Wall-Paper', pp. 178–179.
56. Davidson (2004) p. 52 and p. 62.
57. Alcott, 'A Whisper in the Dark (1863)', in Stern (ed.), *Plots and Counterplots: More Unknown Thrillers of Louisa May Alcott* (London: W.H. Allen, 1977), pp. 291–292.
58. Gilman, 'Yellow Wall-Paper', p. 179.
59. Gilman, 'Yellow Wall-Paper', pp. 181–182.
60. Gilman, *Women and Economics*, p. 109, p. 307, and p. 139.
61. Gilman, 'Yellow Wall-Paper', p. 168.
62. 'Introduction', in Trodd, Barlow and Amigoni, p. 13.
63. Shelagh Wilson, 'Monsters and Monstrosities: Grotesque Taste and Victorian Design', in Trodd, Barlow and Amigoni, pp. 143–171, 150–151, and 153, italics in original.
64. Halttunen in Bronner, pp. 172–173.
65. Wilson, in Trodd, Barlow and Amigoni, pp. 154–155; and Lucy Hartley, '"Griffinism, Grace and All": The Riddle of the Grotesque in John Ruskin's *Modern Painters*', in Trodd, Barlow and Amigoni, 81–95, 83.
66. 'Introduction', in Trodd, Barlow and Amigoni, p. 2.
67. Wilson, in Trodd, Barlow and Amigoni, p. 145.
68. David Stove, *The Plato Cult and Other Philosophical Follies* (Oxford: Basil Blackwell, 1991), p. 19; and Wilson, in Trodd, Barlow and Amigoni, p. 143.
69. Mikhail Bakhtin, *Rabelais and His World* (Bloomington: Indiana University Press, 1984), p. 317.
70. Wilson, in Trodd, Barlow and Amigoni, p. 147.
71. Gilman, 'Yellow Wall-Paper', p. 181.
72. Gilman, 'Yellow Wall-Paper', pp. 181–182.
73. Carroll Smith-Rosenberg, *Disorderly Conduct: Visions of Gender in Victorian American* (New York: Alfred A. Knopf, 1985), p. 258.
74. Board of Regents, University of Wisconsin, *Annual Report for the Year Ending September 30, 1877* (Madison, 1877), p. 45.
75. William Edgar Darnall, 'The Pubescent Schoolgirl', *American Gynecological and Obstetrical Journal* 18 (June 1901), p. 490.

76. Anon., 'A Cure for Vampire Women', *Atlantic Monthly* (April 1878), pp. 545–556 (http://www.public.coe.edu/~theller/soj/cca/y1878.html#April, accessed December 10, 2013), n.p.
77. Elaine Showalter, *The Female Malady: Women, Madness and English Culture, 1830–1980* (London: Virago, 1995), p. 129.
78. John Conolly, *Treatment of the Insane Without Mechanical Restraints* (1856) (London: Dawson's, 1973), pp. 149–150.
79. Rippl, in Kilcup, p. 127.
80. Armstrong, p. 14.
81. Bronfen, p. xi; and Shirley Samuels, *Romances of the Republic: Women, Family and Violence in the Literature of the Early American Nation* (New York and Oxford: Oxford University Press, 1996), pp. 11–12.
82. Bronfen, p. 50; and Diana Fuss, 'Corpse Poem', *Critical Inquiry* 30:1 (Fall 2003), (http://mendota.english.wisc.edu/~clc/fuss.pdf, accessed August 31, 2013), n.p.

3 'Dancing Like a Bomb Abroad': Dawson's 'An Itinerant House' and the Haunting Cityscape

1. Ella Sterling Cummins, *The Story of the Files: A Review of California Writers and Literature* (1893), p. 226, quoted in Eldridge, p. xxvii.
2. Dawson, 'An Itinerant House' (1896), in *An Itinerant House*, p. 8.
3. Beryl Satter, *Each Mind a Kingdom: American Women, Sexual Purity and the New Thought Movement, 1875–1920* (Berkeley: University of California Press, 2001), p. 114.
4. Elizabeth Wilson, *Adorned in Dreams: Fashion and Modernity* (London: I.B. Tauris, 1985), p. 60; and George Lippard, *The Empire City, or, New York by Night and Day. Its Aristocracy and Dollars* (1850) (Philadelphia: T.B. Peterson and Brothers, 1864), p. 42.
5. Amy Gilman Srebnick, *The Mysterious Death of Mary Rogers: Sex and Culture in Nineteenth-Century New York* (New York and Oxford: Oxford University Press, 1995), pp. 8–9.
6. Georg Simmel, 'The Metropolis and Mental Life', in *The Sociology of Georg Simmel*, trans. Kurt Wolff (New York: The Free Press, 1950), pp. 409–426, quoted in Srebnick, p. 35.
7. Srebnick, pp. 46–47 and p. 52.
8. Halttunen, p. 60ff.
9. Srebnick, p. 48; and Marilyn Wood Hill, *Their Sisters' Keepers: Prostitution in New York City, 1830–1870* (Berkeley: University of California Press, 1993), p. 34, p. 89 and p. 303.
10. Leach, pp. 104–107; and D. Miller, *Material Culture*, p. 148.
11. Merish, p. 45.
12. Merish, pp. 67–68.
13. Kasson, pp. 190–201.
14. Hill, p. 2 and p. 64.
15. Angelika Rauch, 'The *Trauerspiel* of the Prostituted Body', *Cultural Critique* (Fall 1988), pp. 77–88, 82–86.
16. Hill, p. 113, p. 171 and p. 213.

17. *The Sun* (June 21, 1836), quoted in Hill, p. 65.

18. James D. McCabe, Jr., *Lights and Shadows of New York Life: or, the Sights and Sensations of the Great City* (Philadelphia: National Publishing Company, 1872), quoted in Hill, p. 87.

19. Bradford K. Pierce, *Half Century With Juvenile Delinquents, or, New York House of Refuge and Its Times* (1896), p. 95, quoted in Hill, p. 75.

20. Hill, p. 285.

21. Dickinson, 512, 'The Soul has Bandaged moments –', in Johnson, p. 250.

22. Smith-Rosenberg, pp. 245–246.

23. Joseph W. Childers, 'Industrial Culture and the Victorian Novel', in Deirdre David (ed.), *The Cambridge Companion to the Victorian Novel* (Cambridge: Cambridge University Press, 2001), pp. 77–96, 94.

24. Hill, p. 255.

25. Satter, pp. 28–29.

26. *The Sun* (June 21, 1836), quoted in Hill, p. 67.

27. Smith-Rosenberg, p. 260.

28. Satter, p. 35.

29. Jacob Riis, 'What Has Been Done', in *How the Other Half Lives: Studies Among the Tenements of New York* (1890) (http://www.bartleby.com/208/, accessed February 2, 2014), n.p.

30. Charles M. Sheldon, *In His Steps: 'What Would Jesus Do?'* (Chicago: Advance Publishing, 1897), p. 78.

31. Satter, p. 52.

32. Benjamin Orange Flower, 'The Era of Woman', *The Arena* 4 (1891), p. 382.

33. Barker-Benfield, p. xxviii.

34. Gilman, *The Home*, p. 337.

35. Elizabeth L. Lynton, 'The Girl of the Period', *The Sunday Review* 25 (March 14, 1868), p. 340.

36. Catharine Beecher, *The Elements of Mental and Moral Philosophy, Founded upon Experience, Reason and the Bible* (Hartford: Peter B. Gleason and Co., 1831), p. 263.

37. Halttunen, p. 59.

38. Hill, p. 77.

39. Walt Whitman, 'The City Dead House', from *Leaves of Grass*, in *Complete Poetry and Selected Prose* (Boston: Houghton Mifflin, 1959), p. 260.

40. Jan Bondeson, *Buried Alive: The Terrifying History of Our Most Primal Fear* (New York and London: Norton, 2001), pp. 65–66. See also Rodney Davies, *Buried Alive: Horrors of the Undead* (New York: Barnes and Noble, 1998).

41. Bram Dijkstra, *Idols of Perversity: Fantasies of Feminine Evil in Fin-de-Siècle Culture* (New York and Oxford: Oxford University Press, 1986), p. 50; and Kasson, p. 110f.

42. Bronfen, p. 54. See also Philip A. Mellor, 'Death in High Modernity: The Contemporary Presence and Absence of Death', in David Clark (ed.), *The Sociology of Death: Theory, Culture, Practice* (Oxford: Blackwell/The Sociological Review, 1993), p. 26; and Tony Walter, 'British Sociology and Death', in Clark, p. 266.

43. Robert Jay Lifton, *The Broken Connection: On Death and the Continuity of Life* (New York: Simon and Schuster, 1979), p. 95, italics in original.

44. S.C. Humphreys, 'Death and Time', in S.C. Humphreys and Helen King (eds), *Mortality and Immortality: The Anthropology and Archaeology of Death* (New York and London: Academic Press, 1981), p. 273.

45. Bronfen, p. 6. See also Humphreys in Humphreys and King, p. 268; J.P. Vernant, 'Death with Two Faces', trans. J. Lloyd, in Humphreys and King, p. 285; and Sarah Webster Goodwin and Elisabeth Bronfen (eds), *Death and Representation* (Baltimore and London: John Hopkins University Press, 1993), p. 14.

46. See Dan Meinwald, 'Memento Mori: Death and Photography in Nineteenth-Century America', *CMP Bulletin* 9:4 (California Museum of Photography, University of California, 1990) (http://vv.arts.ucla.edu/terminals/meinwald/meinwald.html, accessed October 14, 2013), n.p.

47. Bronfen, p. 78.

48. Goodwin and Bronfen, 'Introduction', p. 14; and Bronfen, p. 55.

49. Bronfen, p. 123.

50. Bronfen, p. 294.

51. See Robert Pogue Harrison, *The Dominion of the Dead* (London and Chicago: University of Chicago Press, 2003), p. 39.

52. Quoted in Srebnick, p. 99.

53. *The National Police Gazette* (November 8, 1845), quoted in Daniel Stashower, *The Beautiful Cigar Girl: Mary Rogers, Edgar Allan Poe and the Invention of Murder* (New York: Berkeley Books, 2006), p. 252.

54. Srebnick, p. 80.

55. *The Tribune*, quoted in Srebnick, p. 31.

56. *The Post*, quoted in Srebnick, pp. 76–77.

57. Quoted in Srebnick, p. 76.

58. Quoted in Stashower, p. 106.

59. Jackson Lears, 'Beyond Veblen: Rethinking Consumer Culture in America', in Bronner, pp. 83–84.

60. Armstrong, p. 76.

61. Halttunen, p. xv. See also Bronfen, p. 69.

62. 'Fashion Principle', *Godey's Lady's Book* 18 (January 1839), p. 8.

63. 'The Gatherer', *Godey's Lady's Book* 7 (December 1833), p. 310.

64. Gilman, *The Home*, p. 297.

65. Gilman, *Women and Economics*, pp. 118–119.

66. Gilman, *The Home*, p. 220.

67. See Ralph J. Poole, 'Body/Rituals: The (Homo)Erotics of Death in Elizabeth Stuart Phelps, Rose Terry Cooke, and Edgar Allan Poe', in Kilcup, p. 244.

68. Armstrong, p.80; and Jean-Christophe Agnew, 'A House of Fiction: Domestic Interiors and the Commodity Aesthetic', in Bronner, pp. 133–156.

69. Satter, p. 32.

70. Beethan, p. 85.

71. Spofford, 'The Amber Gods', p. 65.

72. Satter, p. 79.

73. Satter, p. 60f.

74. Satter, p. 68, p. 71.

75. Emma Curtis Hopkins to Charles and Myrtle Fillmore, December 4, 1894, p. 2, quoted in Satter, p. 96.

76. Satter, p. 133.

77. Anon., 'A Cure for Vampire Women', n.p.
78. Anon., 'A Cure for Vampire Women', n.p.
79. Poe, 'Ligeia', in *Complete Tales*, p. 666.
80. Poe, 'House of Usher' (1839), in *Collected Tales*, p. 235.
81. Poe, 'Usher', in *Collected Tales*, p. 231.
82. Whitman, 'Song of the Open Road', in *Complete Poetry and Selected Prose*, p. 114.
83. Poe, 'Usher', in *Collected Tales*, p. 233.
84. Chandler, p. 58; and Poe, 'Usher', in *Collected Tales*, p. 236.
85. Poe, 'Usher', in *Collected Tales*, p. 241.
86. Poe, 'Usher', in *Collected Tales*, p. 245.
87. It is worth noting that Dawson herself kept parrots as pets, and the birds loomed large in the exaggerated reports of the dilapidated 'cabin' in which she died alone at the age of 75. See Eldridge, in Pinkney and Eldridge, p. xxxiiff.
88. Dawson, 'An Itinerant House', in *An Itinerant House*, p. 4.
89. Dawson, 'An Itinerant House', p. 22.
90. Dawson, 'An Itinerant House', p. 3.
91. Dawson, 'An Itinerant House', p. 18.
92. Dawson, 'An Itinerant House', pp. 23–24. This would appear to refer to John William Draper's *History of the Conflict Between Religion and Science* (1874) (London: Watts and Co., 1927).
93. Claire Raymond, *The Posthumous Voice in Women's Writing from Mary Shelley to Sylvia Plath* (Aldershot and Burlington: Ashgate, 2006), p. 16 and p. 12.
94. Peattie, 'A Child of the Rain' (1898), in *The Shape of Fear*, pp. 33–34.
95. Wharton, 'Preface', in *Ghost Stories*, p. 9.
96. Wharton, 'Preface' and '"All Souls"' (1937), in *Ghost Stories*, p. 9 and pp. 275–276, italics in original.
97. See Weinstock, p. 7.
98. Dawson, 'An Itinerant House', p. 11.
99. Anon, 'Pleasant Rooms', *The Atlantic* (April 1882), pp. 567–569.
100. Dawson, 'An Itinerant House', p. 14.
101. Riis, *Other Half*, n.p.
102. Srebnick, p. 57ff; and Hill, p. 197.
103. Hill, p. 195, p. 219ff and p. 322.
104. Eldridge, p. xxviii.
105. Dawson, 'An Itinerant House', p. 18.
106. Dawson, 'An Itinerant House', p. 30.

4 'Solemnest of Industries': Wilkins' 'The Southwest Chamber' and Memorial Culture

1. Peattie, 'The Story of an Obstinate Corpse', in *The Shape of Fear*, p. 30.
2. While she is often known as 'Mary Wilkins Freeman', I refer to her throughout as 'Wilkins' rather than 'Freeman', not only because the latter was her married name, but because many of her stories, including the collection *The Wind in the Rose-Bush and Other Stories*, were published under the name 'Mary E. Wilkins'.

3. For a discussion of the issues surrounding women's keeping boarding houses in nineteenth-century America, see Kleinberg, in Bryden and Floyd, p. 147 and p. 154.

4. Ann Braude, *Radical Spirits: Spiritualism and Women's Rights in Nineteenth-Century America*, 2nd ed. (Bloomington and Indianapolis: Indiana University Press, 2001), p. 201.

5. Washington Irving, 'Rural Funerals' (1820), in *The Sketchbook* (London: Bell and Daldy, 1873), 157–171, p.162 and p.166.

6. Thayer, p. 253.

7. Thayer, p. 250.

8. Irving, 'Rural Funerals', pp. 167–168.

9. Frederick Saunders, 'Citations from the Cemeteries', in *Salad for the Solitary and the Social* (New York: Lamport, Blakeman and Law, 1853), p. 77.

10. Irving, 'Rural Funerals', p. 168.

11. Merish, p. 129.

12. Saunders, p. 77, quoting from the *London Eclectic*.

13. Thayer, pp. 91–92.

14. Halttunen, pp. 137–138.

15. James Stevens Curl, *The Victorian Celebration of Death* (Gloucestershire: Sutton Publishing, 2004), p. 200.

16. Halttunen, pp. 138–139.

17. Halttunen, p. 139.

18. Meinwald, Part 4, 'The Funeral', n.p.

19. Halttunen, p. 143.

20. Meinwald, Part 4.

21. Curl, p. 195.

22. Curl, p. 201, 197.

23. Curl, p. 209; and Ruby, p. 110.

24. Ruby, p. 165.

25. Dewey, *On the Duties of Consolation, and the Rites and Customs Appropriate to Mourning* (New Bedford: B. Lindsey, 1825), p. 6.

26. Halttunen, pp. 141–142.

27. T.S. Arthur, 'Going into Mourning', *Godey's Lady's Book* 23 (October 1841), 170–174, p. 174, italics added.

28. Thayer, p. 249.

29. Bacon, 'The Children', in Lundie, p. 81.

30. Mark Twain, *The Adventures of Huckleberry Finn* (New York: Harper and Brothers, 1912), pp. 135–136.

31. See Elizabeth Seigel, *Playing With Pictures: The Victorian Art of Photocollage* (Chicago: Art Institute of Chicago/Yale University Press, 2009).

32. Meinwald, Part 5, 'The Cemetery'.

33. Jay Ruby, *Secure the Shadow: Death and Photography in America* (London and Cambridge, Mass.: The MIT Press, 1995), p. 28.

34. Meinwald, Part 2, 'The Body'. See also Gary Laderman, *The Sacred Remains: American Attitudes Towards Death, 1799–1883* (New Haven and London: Yale University Press, 1996), p. 3.

35. Ruby, p. 59 and pp. 54–55.

36. Gabriel Harrison, quoted in Ruby, p. 56.

37. H.J. Rogers, *Twenty-Three Years Under a Sky-Light, Or, Life and Experiences of a Photographer* (1872), pp. 42–43, quoted in Ruby, p. 175.
38. Braude, p. 36f.
39. Laderman, p. 170.
40. Braude, p. 38f.
41. Braude, p. 5, p. 61, p. 70, and p. 83f.
42. *Herald of Progress* 1 (1860), p. 3, quoted in Braude, p. 24.
43. Uriah Clarke, *Plain Guide to Spiritualism* (Boston: William White and Co., 1863), p. 182.
44. Braude, pp. 17–23 and p. 87.
45. See Alex Owen, *The Darkened Room: Women, Power, and Spiritualism in Late Victorian England* (Chicago and London: University of Chicago Press, 2004).
46. Ronald Pearsall, *The Table-Rappers: The Victorians and the Occult* (Gloucestershire: Sutton, 2004), p. 43, quoting from Sophia De Morgan, *From Matter to Spirit: The Result of Ten Years Experience in Spirit Manifestations* (1863), p. 4.
47. Deborah Blum, *Ghost Hunters: The Victorians and the Hunt for Proof of Life After Death* (London: Arrow Books, 2007), p. 238.
48. Blum, passim.
49. Braude, p. 123 and pp. 107–108.
50. Meinwald, Part 5; and Braude, p. 174f.
51. Blum, p. 181.
52. See Bronner in Bronner, pp. 13–53.
53. Leach in Bronner, pp. 131–132. See also Lears, pp. 83–84; and Agnew, p. 138f, both in Bronner.
54. Lydia Maria Child, *The American Frugal Housewife* (1832) (New York: Samuel S. and William Wood, 1838), p. 90 and p. 99.
55. Freedgood, p. 158 and pp. 4–5.
56. Freedgood, p. 10.
57. Bronfen, p. 69.
58. See Merish, p. 72.
59. Layout in original. *American Kitchen Magazine* (September, 1899), quoted in Margaret Horsfield, *Biting the Dust: The Joys of Housework* (London: Fourth Estate, 1997), p. 46.
60. Hawthorne, *The House of the Seven Gables: A Romance* (1851) (New York, Toronto and London: Signet, 1961), p. 7.
61. Ann Douglas, *The Feminization of American Culture* (London and Basingstoke, Papermac, 1996), p. 76.
62. Emerson, 'Woman', p. 19.
63. Olivia Howard Dunbar, 'The Shell of Sense', *Harper's* (December 1909), in Lundie, 52–61, p. 58.
64. Mary E. Wilkins, 'The Southwest Chamber', in *The Wind in the Rose-Bush and Other Stories of the Supernatural* (London: John Murray, 1903), p. 133.
65. Alice Stone Blackwell, *Lucy Stone: Pioneer of Women's Rights* (Boston: Little, Brown and Co., 1939), p. 278.
66. Mary Austin, 'The Readjustment' *Harper's* (1908), in Lundie, 46–51, pp. 46–47.
67. Wharton, 'Mary Pask', in *Ghost Stories*, p. 136.
68. Dickinson, 1078, 'The Bustle in a House', in Jackson, p. 489.

69. Anon, 'Deplorable Improvements', *The Atlantic* (June 1882), p. 856.
70. Philippa Tristram, *Living Space in Fact and Fiction* (London and New York: Routledge, 1989), p. 261.
71. Clark, 'Literary Women in Their Homes II', n.p.
72. Clark, n.p.
73. Wilkins, 'The Southwest Chamber', in *The Wind in the Rose-Bush*, p. 136, italics added.
74. Peattie, 'A Grammatical Ghost', in *The Shape of Fear*, p. 63.
75. Peattie, 'A Grammatical Ghost', p. 64.
76. Peattie, 'A Grammatical Ghost', p. 66.
77. Peatte, 'A Grammatical Ghost', pp. 67–68.
78. Woodrow, 'Secret Chambers', in Lundie, p. 177.
79. Woodrow, in Lundie, p. 181.
80. Wilkins, 'Southwest Chamber', pp. 116–17 and p. 159.
81. Wilkins, 'Southwest Chamber', pp. 109–110.
82. Wilkins, 'Southwest Chamber', p. 129 and p. 138.
83. Wilkins, 'Southwest Chamber', p. 143.
84. Wilkins, 'Southwest Chamber', pp. 148–149.
85. Wilkins, 'The Lost Ghost', in *The Wind in the Rose-Bush*, p. 215.
86. Sandra M. Gilbert and Susan Gubar, *The Madwoman in the Attic: The Woman Writer and the Nineteenth-Century Literary Imagination*, 2nd ed. (New Haven and London: Yale University Press, 2000), p. 615ff.
87. Armstrong, p. 20.
88. Amos Chase, *On Female Excellence. Or, A Discourse, in which Good Character in Women is Described; and the Worth and Importance of Such Character, Contemplated* (Litchfield: Collier and Buel, 1791), pp. 10–11.
89. Wilkins, 'Southwest Chamber', p. 128 and p. 124.
90. Wilkins, 'Southwest Chamber', p. 120.
91. Wilkins, 'The Shadows on the Wall', in *The Wind in the Rose-Bush*, p. 56.
92. Wilkins, 'Southwest Chamber', p. 138.
93. Wilkins, 'Southwest Chamber', p. 119.
94. Wilkins, 'Southwest Chamber', p. 130.
95. Mary Heaton Vorse, 'The Second Wife', *Harper's* (February 1912), in Lundie, 203–216, p. 210.
96. Wilkins, 'Southwest Chamber', p. 161.
97. Wilkins, 'Southwest Chamber', p. 162.
98. Dunbar, in Lundie, p. 59, italics in original.
99. Dunbar, in Lundie, pp. 60–61.
100. Marcus Aurelius Root, *The Camera and the Pencil, or, The Heliographic Art* (Philadelphia: J.P. Lippincott and Co., 1864), pp. 43–44.
101. Trachtenberg, in Sandweiss, p. 26.
102. Peattie, 'A Grammatical Ghost', pp. 64–65.
103. Whitman, 'Visit to Plumbe's Gallery', *Brooklyn Daily Eagle and Kings County Democrat* (Brooklyn, New York) 5:160 (July 2, 1846), p. 1. See also Trachtenberg, in Sandweiss, pp. 26–27 and p. 37 for a discussion of the fears and superstitions regarding the photographic process.
104. N.P. Willis, 'The Pencil of Nature', *Corsair* 1 (April 13, 1839), p. 71.
105. Y.T.S., 'Life in the Daguerreotype, No.II. The Operating Room', *Daguerreian Journal* 2 (November 1851), p. 374.

5 'Space Stares All Around': Peattie's 'The House That Was Not' and the (Un)Haunted Landscape

1. Peattie, 'The House that Was Not' (1898), in *The Shape of Fear*, pp. 26–27.
2. Peattie, 'The House That Was Not', p. 27.
3. See in particular Ellis and DeLamotte.
4. John Beames, *An Army Without Banners* (1937), quoted in Carol Fairbanks, *Prairie Women: Images in American and Canadian Fiction* (New Haven and London: Yale University Press, 1986), p. 6. See also Virginia Scharff, *Twenty Thousand Roads: Women, Movement, and the West* (Berkeley: University of California Press, 2003), p. 3.
5. Frederick Jackson Turner, 'The Significance of the Frontier in American History', in *The Frontier in American History* (New York: Henry Holt, 1920), p. 15.
6. See Susan J. Rosowski, *Birthing a Nation: Gender, Creativity, and the West in American Literature* (Lincoln and London: University of Nebraska Press, 1999).
7. Walter Prescott Webb, *The Great Plains* (Lincoln: University of Nebraska Press, 1959), p. 505.
8. Fairbanks, p. 7.
9. Francis Parkman, *The Oregon Trail* (New York: New American Library, 1950), p. 50; and Hamlin Garland, *A Son of the Middle Border* (New York: Grosset and Dunlap, 1917), p. 63.
10. John Mack Farragher, *Women and Men on the Overland Trail* (New Haven and London: Yale University Press, 1979), p. 14.
11. Slotkin, p. 8.
12. Roderick Frazier Nash, *Wilderness and the American Mind*, 4th ed. (1967) (New Haven and London: Yale University Press, 2001), pp. 24–25.
13. Sidney Smith, *The Settlers' New Home: or the Emigrant's Location* (London: 1849), p. 19.
14. Bess Streeter Aldrich, *Spring Came on Forever* (New York: D. Appleton-Century, 1935), p. 100.
15. Cather, *O Pioneers!* (1913) (New York: Dover, 1993), pp. 7–8.
16. Emerson, 'Woman', p. 20.
17. Farragher, p. 95.
18. Lackmann, p. 120; and William Wadsworth, *The National Wagon Road and Guide* (San Francisco: Whitton, Towne, 1858), pp. 140–141.
19. Dora Aydelotte, *Trumpets Calling* (New York: D. Appleton-Century Co., 1938), pp. 58–59.
20. John Ludlum McConnel, *Western Characters, or Types of Border Life in the Western States* (New York: Redfield, 1858), pp. 131–132.
21. Annette Kolodney, *The Land Before Her: Fantasy and Experience of the American Frontiers, 1630–1860* (Chapel Hill: University of North Carolina Press, 1984), p. 129.
22. Fairbanks, p. 74 and p. 170.
23. Fairbanks, p. 170
24. Mary Hartwell Catherwood, *The Spirit of an Illinois Town, and, The Little Renault: Two Stories of Illinois at Different Periods* (Boston: Houghton, Mifflin and Co., 1897), p. 490.

25. Satter, p. 153ff; and Merish, p. 21.
26. D.H. Lawrence, *Studies in Classic American Literature* (1923), in Ezra Greenspan, Lindeth Vasey and John Worthen (eds), *The Cambridge Edition of the Letters and Works of D.H. Lawrence* (Cambridge: Cambridge University Press, 2003), p. 34.
27. Gilman, *Women and Economics*, p. 267; and Dr. W.W. Hall, 'Health of Farmer's Families', in *Report of the Commissioner of Agriculture for the Year 1862* (Washington D.C.: Government Printing Office, 1863), pp. 462–470.
28. Alexis de Tocqueville, Appendix S, *Democracy in America*, trans. Henry Reeve (http://www2.hn.psu.edu/faculty/jmanis/toqueville/dem-in-america1.pdf, accessed January 31 2014), p. 812.
29. De Tocqueville, p. 812.
30. De Tocqueville, p. 811.
31. Dickinson, 510, 'It was not Death, for I stood up', in Johnson, p. 248.
32. Loula Grace Erdman, *The Edge of Time* (New York: Dodd, Mead and Company, 1950), p. 53.
33. Anon, 'Deplorable Improvements', *The Atlantic* (June 1882), p. 856.
34. Peattie, 'The Three Johns' (1896), in *A Mountain Woman* (New York: Doubleday and McClure, 1900), p. 84.
35. Peattie, 'The Three Johns', pp. 85–86.
36. Farragher, pp. 70–71, quoting from Frances C. Peabody, 'Across the Plains DeLuxe in 1865', *Colorado Magazine* 18 (1941), 71–76, p. 72.
37. Farragher, p. 170.
38. Farragher, p. 56, quoting from Nancy A. Hunt, 'By Ox-Team to California', *Overland Monthly* 67 (April 1916). See also Fairbanks, p. 114, p. 116 and p. 174.
39. Peattie, 'Jim Lancy's Waterloo', in *A Mountain Woman*, p. 37.
40. Peattie, 'Jim Lancy's Waterloo', p. 41.
41. Peattie, 'Jim Lancy's Waterloo', pp. 38–39.
42. Peattie, 'Jim Lancy's Waterloo', pp. 44–45.
43. Peattie, 'Jim Lancy's Waterloo', p. 46.
44. Peattie, 'Jim Lancy's Waterloo', p. 46, p. 48, and pp. 54–55.
45. Peattie, 'Jim Lancy's Waterloo', p. 58 and pp. 65–66.
46. Peattie, 'Jim Lancy's Waterloo', pp. 67–68.
47. Peattie, 'Two Pioneers', in *A Mountain Woman*, p. 155.
48. Peattie, 'Two Pioneers', p. 169.
49. Slotkin, p. 24 and p. 20.
50. Paul Fisher, *Hard Facts: Setting and Form in the American Novel* (New York and Oxford: Oxford University Press, 1987), p. 109.
51. Robert E. Abrams, *Landscape and Ideology in American Renaissance Literature* (Cambridge: Cambridge University Press, 2004), pp. 49–50.
52. Henry David Thoreau, 'Walking', *The Atlantic* (June 1862) (http://www.theatlantic.com/magazine/archive/1862/06/walking/304674/, accessed February 1, 2014), n.p.
53. Yi-Fu Tuan, *Landscapes of Fear* (Oxford: Basil Blackwell, 1979), p. 127.
54. Thomas Jefferson to John Cartwright (1824), in Andrew A. Lipscomb and Albert Bergh (eds), *The Writings of Thomas Jefferson*, Memorial Edition, Vol. XVI (Washington, DC: Thomas Jefferson Memorial Association of the United States, 1903–1904), p. 48. Jefferson is here closely paraphrasing Thomas

Paine, 'The Rights of Man' (1791–1792), in Michael Foot and Isaac Kramnick (eds), *Thomas Paine Reader* (London: Penguin, 1987), p. 204.

55. Thoreau, *Walden, or Life in the Woods* (1854) (Boston: Houghton Mifflin, 1909), p. 291.

56. Ernest Renan, 'What is a Nation?' (1882), in Homi Bhabha (ed.), *Nation and Narration* (London: Routledge, 1990), p. 11.

57. David Mogen, Introduction to *Frontier Gothic: Terror and Wonder at the Frontier in American Literature*, eds David Mogen, Scott P. Sanders and Joanne B. Karpinski (London and Toronto: Associated University Presses, 1993), pp. 16–17.

58. See A. Miller. See also John F. Sears, *Sacred Places: American Tourist Attractions in the Nineteenth Century* (New York and Oxford: Oxford University Press, 1989), p. 4; Barbara Novak, *Nature and Culture: American Landscape and Painting, 1825–1875* (New York and Oxford: Oxford University Press, 1995), p. 59; and Nash, p. 67.

59. A. Miller, p. 210.

60. Novak (1995), p. 10ff and p. 67; and Nash, p. 86 and p. 88.

61. A. Miller, p. 137.

62. Thomas Cole, 'Essay on American Scenery', in John McCourbey (ed.), *American Art, 1700–1960* (Englewood Cliffs, N.J.: Prentice-Hall, 1965), p. 108. See also Abrams, p. 8.

63. A. Miller, p. 288.

64. Novak (1995), p. 152 and Nash, p. 85.

65. Oliver Wendell Holmes, 'Brother Jonathan's Lament for Sister Caroline' (1861), in *The Works of Oliver Wendell Holmes*, 13 vols., Vol. 12 (Boston: Houghton Mifflin, 1892), pp. 284–286.

66. Davd C. Lipscomb, 'Water Leaves No Trail: Mapping Away the Vanishing American in Cooper's Leatherstocking Tales', in Helena Michie and Ronald R. Thomas (eds), *Nineteenth-Century Geographies: The Transformation of Space from the Victorian Age to the American Century* (New Brunswick, N.J. and London: Rutgers University Press, 2003), 55–71, p. 64ff.

67. James Fenimore Cooper, *The Deerslayer*, ed. James Franklin Beard (Albany: State University of New York Press, 1987), p. 546.

68. Cooper, *The Prairie: A Tale* (1827) (London: Richard Bentley, 1836), p. 389.

69. De Tocqueville, 'A Fortnight in the Wilderness', in George Wilson Pierson (ed.), *Tocqueville in America* (Garden City, New York: Anchor Books, 1959), pp. 178–179.

70. Anon, 'Woodland Mysteries', *The Atlantic* (July 1882), pp. 137–138.

71. Thoreau, 'Ktaadn', in *The Maine Woods* (1864) (http://thoreau.eserver.org/ktaadn06.html, accessed February 1, 2014), n.p.

72. Thoreau, 'Ktaadn', n.p.

73. Thoreau, 'Walking,' n.p.

74. Sarah Orne Jewett, 'The White Rose Road', *Atlantic Monthly* 64 (September 1889), pp. 353–360 (http://www.public.coe.edu/~theller/soj/saw/wrose-at.htm, accessed February 1, 2014), n.p. All subsequent references to Jewett texts will refer to unpaginated texts available on this website, *The Sarah Orne Jewett Text Project*, ed. Terry Heller (1998–2003).

75. Jewett, 'A Winter Drive', in *Country By-Ways* (1893).

76. Jewett, 'The Gray Man', in *A White Heron and Other Stories* (1886).

77. A. Miller, pp. 213–214.
78. Perry D. Westbrook, *Sarah Orne Jewett and Her Contemporaries* (Metuchen, N.J., and London: The Scarecrow Press, 1981), p. 4. See also Charles C. Nott, 'A Good Farm for Nothing', *The Nation* 49 (November 21, 1889), 406.
79. Westbrook, p. 5. See A. Miller, p. 188f., for a further discussion of the effects of migration on the New-England human landscape.
80. Jewett, 'The Queen's Twin', *Atlantic Monthly* 83 (February 1899), pp. 235–246, n.p. It seems likely that this story is the inspiration behind Stephen King's 'Mrs. Todd's Shortcut' (*Redbook*, May 1984), in which a woman shows preternatural command of the New-England woods.
81. See Kathleen M. Kirby, *Indifferent Boundaries: Spatial Concepts of Human Subjectivity* (New York: The Guilford Press, 1996), p. 46ff.
82. Ambrose Bierce, 'A Watcher By the Dead' (1891), in E.F. Bleiler (ed.), *Ghost and Horror Stories of Ambrose Bierce*, (New York: Dover, 1964), p. 44.
83. See Bernice M. Murphy, *The Rural Gothic in American Popular Culture: Backwoods Horror and Terror in the Wilderness* (Basingstoke, Palgrave Macmillan, 2013), p. 48ff.
84. J.B. Jackson, 'The Order of a Landscape: Reason and Religion in Newtonian America', in D.W. Meinig (ed.), *The Interpretation of Ordinary Landscapes* (New York and Oxford: Oxford University Press, 1979), p. 155.
85. Bierce, 'The Damned Thing' (1896), in *Stories*, p. 35.
86. Tuan, *Space and Place: The Perspective of Experience* (Minneapolis and London: University of Minnesota Press, 1977), p. 54.
87. Tuan, *Landscapes of Fear*, p. 128.
88. Tuan, *Space and Place*, p. 6.
89. Irving, *A Tour of the Prairies* (Paris: Baudry's European Library, 1835), p. 49.
90. Cather, *O Pioneers!*, p. 7.
91. Jane Tompkins, *West of Everything: The Inner Life of Westerns* (New York and Oxford: Oxford University Press, 1992), p. 71; and Cornelia A.P. Comer, 'The Little Gray Ghost', *Atlantic* (1912), in Lundie, p. 102.
92. Peattie, 'On the Northern Ice' (1898), in *The Shape of Fear*, p. 10.
93. Peattie, 'On the Northern Ice', p. 12.
94. Peattie, 'On the Northern Ice', p. 12.
95. Peattie, 'On the Northern Ice', p. 13.
96. Peattie, 'The House That Was Not', in *The Shape of Fear*, p. 24.
97. Peattie, 'The House That Was Not', p. 26.
98. See, for example, Brown's *Wieland*, and more recently, Stephen King's *'salem's Lot* (1975).
99. Jewett, 'The Landless Farmer', *Atlantic Monthly* 51 (May 1883), pp. 627–637.
100. Jewett, 'The White Rose Road'.
101. Peattie, 'The House That Was Not', pp. 24–25.
102. Novak (2007b), p. 67.
103. Cole to Asher B. Durand (Januray 4, 1838), in Rev. Louis Legrand Noble, *The Life and Works of Thomas Cole* (1853) (Hensonville, NY: Black Dome Press, 1997), p. 248.
104. Cole, 'Lecture on Art', quoted in Barbara Novak O'Doherty, 'Some American Words: Basic Aesthetic Guidelines, 1825–1870', *American Art Journal* 1:1 (Spring 1969), pp. 78–91, 85.
105. A. Miller, p. 150.

106. David Lowenthal, 'Age and Artifact: Dilemmas of Appreciation', in Meinig, p. 109.
107. Lowenthal in Meinig, p. 125.
108. Peattie, 'The House That Was Not', p. 25, italics added.

6   'My Labor and My Leisure Too': Wynne's 'The Little Room' and Commodity Culture

1. Edna Ferber, 'Maymeys from Cuba', *The American Magazine* 72 (September 1911), pp. 705–711.
2. L. Frank Baum, *The Annotated Wizard of Oz*, ed. Michael Patrick Hearn (New York and London: Norton, 2000), p. 224; and Theodore Dreiser, *Sister Carrie* (1900) (New York: The Modern Library, 1917), p. 24.
3. Dreiser, p.109.
4. Westbrook, pp. 6–7.
5. Leach, p. 32.
6. Merish, p. 89; and Leach, p. 16 and p. 36.
7. Satter, p. 33; and Bronner in Bronner, p. 51
8. Leach in Bronner, p. 107, p. 110 and p. 116.
9. Satter, p. 219. See also Merish, p. 2.
10. Leach, p. 39ff. and p. 61.
11. Dreiser, p. 24; and Satter, p. 220.
12. Leach, p. 45 and pp. 53–54.
13. Quoted in Leach, p. 70.
14. *In Memory of Madeline Yale Wynne*, pp. 7–9. See also Weinstock, p. 24 and p. 59.
15. *In Memory of Madeline Yale Wynne*, pp. 12–13.
16. *In Memory of Madeline Yale Wynne*, p. 18.
17. Leach, p. 43.
18. Leach in Bronner, p. 102.
19. Solicari, p. 1.
20. Madeline Yale Wynne, 'The Little Room', in *The Little Room and Other Stories* (Chicago: Way and Williams, 1895), pp. 7–39, pp. 1–17.
21. Wynne, 'The Little Room', pp. 15–17.
22. Wynne, 'The Little Room', pp. 11–12.
23. Wynne, 'The Little Room', p. 26, italics in original.
24. Wynne, 'The Little Room', p. 27.
25. Wynne, 'The Little Room', pp. 11–12.
26. Wynne, 'The Little Room', pp. 22–23.
27. Wynne, 'The Little Room', pp. 27–28.
28. Weinstock, pp. 61–64.
29. Wynne, 'The Little Room', p. 14.
30. Wynne, 'The Little Room', pp. 20–21.
31. Wynne, 'The Little Room', pp. 22–23.
32. See Peter Buse and Andrew Stott, 'Introduction: A Future for Haunting', in Buse and Stott (eds), *Ghosts: Deconstruction, Psychoanalysis, History* (Basingstoke and London: Macmillan, 1999), p. 13.
33. Nicholas T. Rand, 'Introduction', in Rand (ed.), Nicolas Abraham and Maria Torok, *The Shell and the Kernel: Renewals of Psychoanalysis*, Vol. I (Chicago and London: University of Chicago Press, 1994), p. 16.

34. Abraham and Torok, '"The Lost Object – Me": Notes on Endocryptic Identification', in Rand, p. 141, italics in original.
35. Abraham, 'Notes on the Phantom', in Rand, pp. 172–173. See also Athena Vrettos, 'Displaced Memories in Victorian Fiction and Psychology', *Victorian Studies* 49:2 (Winter 2007), pp. 199–207.
36. Freud, 'The "Uncanny"', in Strachey, p. 223, italics in original.
37. Freud, letter to Martha Bernays (August 18, 1882), in E.L. Freud (ed.), *Letters of Sigmund Freud 1873–1939* (London: Hogarth Press, 1961), pp. 25–28.
38. Armstrong, p. 83 and pp. 86–87.
39. Halttunen in Bronner, p. 158. See also Merish, p. 3.
40. Agnew in Bronner, p. 142. See also Halttunen in Bronner, p. 172, p. 177 and pp. 185–186, italics in original.
41. See D. Miller, 'Introduction', in *Home Possessions*, p. 7.
42. Satter, p. 3.
43. Leach, p. 129; and Satter, p. 167 and p. 176.
44. Satter, p. 7. See also Leach, p. 227.
45. Wilkins, 'A New England Nun' (1891), in *A New England Nun and Other Stories* (New York: Harper and Brothers, 1891), p. 1.
46. Wilkins, 'New England Nun', p. 2 and p. 9.
47. Wilkins, 'New England Nun', pp. 9–10.
48. Wilkins, 'New England Nun', p. 8.
49. Leach, p. 232f.
50. Anon., 'Ungathered Flowers', *The Atlantic* (June 1883) (http://www.public. coe.edu/~theller/soj/cca/y1883.html#Flowers, accessed February 1, 2014), pp. 854–856, n.p.
51. Anon., "Ungathered Flowers," n.p.
52. Anon., 'Ungathered Flowers', n.p.
53. Jewett, 'Lady Ferry', in *Old Friends and New* (1879) (http://www.public.coe. edu/~theller/soj/ofn/ferry.htm, accessed February 1, 2014), n.p.
54. Jewett, 'Lady Ferry', n.p.
55. Jewett, 'Lady Ferry', n.p.
56. Jewett, 'Lady Ferry', n.p.
57. Bronner, in Bronner, p. 52.
58. Merish, p. 16.
59. Abba Goold Woolson, *Woman in American Society* (Boston: Roberts Brothers, 1873), p. 258ff.
60. Peattie, 'The Room of the Evil Thought', in *The Shape of Fear*, p. 39.
61. Peattie, 'The Room of the Evil Thought', p. 39.
62. D. Miller, *Material Culture*, pp. 120–121.
63. Marx, pp. 176–177.
64. Brown's *Wieland*, James' *The Turn of the Screw*, Shirley Jackson's *The Haunting of Hill House* (1963), and Mark Z. Danielewski's *House of Leaves* (2000) are cases in point here.
65. Derrida, p.172, italics and translation in orginal.
66. Buse and Stott, p.12.
67. Marx, pp. 163–165.
68. Dickinson, 712, 'Because I could not stop for Death – ', in Johnson, p. 350.
69. Wynne, 'The Little Room', pp. 9–10 and pp. 25–26.
70. Wynne, 'The Little Room', p.10.

71. Wynne, 'The Little Room', p. 22 and pp. 29–30.
72. Wynne, 'The Little Room', pp. 36–37.
73. *In Memory of Madeline Yale Wynne*, pp. 37–38.
74. Bill Brown, 'Thing Theory', *Critical Enquiry* 28:1 (Autumn 2001), pp. 1–22, 12.
75. Wilkins, 'The Hall Bedroom' (1903), in William Patten (ed.), *Short Story Classics (American)*, Vol. 4 (New York: P.F. Collier and Son, 1905), pp. 1275–1299.

Afterword

1. See Weinstock; Julia Briggs, *Night Visitors: The Rise and Fall of the English Ghost Story* (London: Faber, 1977); Vanessa Dickerson, *Victorian Ghosts in the Noontide: Women Writers and the Supernatural* (Columbia: University of Missouri Press, 1996); and Andrew Smith, *The Ghost Story, 1840–1920* (Manchester: Manchester University Press, 2012).
2. 'Winter Fiction Special', *The Guardian* (December 21, 2013).

Index

<u>Intro</u> - ok but focus is going to be narrow
& there is some repetition here. And the
depth int materialism — or what whatever calls
'the gilded age of decoration' needs itself to
be rooted in American history & ideas ab 'the
conspicuous consumption of wealth' (not just
middle-class mores). (Ok - dealt with in chap 1)

<u>Chap 1</u> Opens with poor & limited reading of
arthur May Park? / Not nuanced —
Premise of chapter ok and range of material
is good but critical readings are a little
pedestrian sometimes.

<u>Chap 2</u> - quite an interesting 'take' on 76 yrs —
That material objects (including the wallpaper)
are part of the domestic system but the story
critiques? — & connect w the 'archetype' (p69) are
interesting. — Objects being influence on people
instead of vice versa (Marx, Bourdieu). Some
good insights but <u>Economics</u>. Good use of <u>human ref</u>
Economics. Unusual & sophisticated reading.

<u>Chap 3</u> Switch to the city scape & death?
prostitution — Ok & if preamble here ab Mary Rogers.
(71 →) Bronfen etc. A lot on Mary Rogers.
Dis seems rather gratuitous? Weak link on p.76 'An
Fall of the House of Usher' / Liguin / Dawson's /
Haunted House' / Peattie, 'A Child of the Rain' /
A rather disjointed chap? Not
particularly coherent?

Chap 4 Memorial culture — funeral culture,
mourning paraphernalia; the commodification of grief;
Spiritualism/ the female body of the medium.
— but also 'Domestic decoration' — Disjointed

110-115,   photography/
Again, the historical/cultural content of this
chapter do not always cohere with the stories.

Chap 5 — Interesting — but some overlap
with Bernice M's book in the section on
'murderer'. Interesting on the A. landscape as
'self-cleansing'. — but all this wd have been
better coming before to stories No analysis is
no merging of the chapter. Material not v.
   well organised?   Beattie — Jewett —
   Bierce

Chap 6 — OK but one's out for theory of
things? but uses Abram — Torok theory of
cryptonomy, & then Derrida — but the objects
related to capitalist exchange & ownership.

This book is not sure what its focus is?
women & the Gothic? bondage? American history?
Materialism?   — a bit piecemeal
            shifting focus

Printed and bound by CPI Group (UK) Ltd, Croydon, CR0 4YY